Seven
Gothic
Tales

Seven Gothic Tales

by

Isak Dinesen

Vintage Books

**A Division of Random House
New York**

Library of Congress Cataloging in Publication Data

Blixen, Karen, 1885-1962.
    Seven Gothic tales.

    Reprint of the 1939 ed., issued in series: The Modern library of the world's best books.
    CONTENTS: The deluge at Norderney.—The old chevalier.—The monkey. [etc.]
    I. Title.
PZ3.B62026Se 9 [PR6003.L545]   823   72-662
ISBN 0-394-74291-5

Manufactured in the United States of America

89

Vintage Books Edition, September 1972

Contents

The Deluge at Norderney

URING the first quarter of the last century, seaside resorts became the fashion, even in those countries of Northern Europe within the minds of whose people the sea had hitherto held the rôle of the devil, the cold and voracious hereditary foe of humanity. The romantic spirit of the age, which delighted in ruins, ghosts, and lunatics, and counted a stormy night on the heath and a deep conflict of the passions a finer treat for the connoisseur than the ease of the salon and the harmony of a philosophic system, reconciled even the most refined individuals to the eternal wildness of the coast scenery and of the open seas. Ladies and gentlemen of fashion abandoned the shade of their parks to come and walk upon the bleak shores and watch the untameable waves. The neighborhood of a shipwreck, where, in low tide, the wreck was still in sight, like a hardened, black, and salted skeleton, became a favorite picnic place, where fair artists put up their easels.

On the west coast of Holstein the bath of Norderney thus sprang up and flowered for a period of twenty years. Along the sandy roads of the downs fine carriages and coaches came, to unload trunks and cartons, and ladies on small feet, whose veils and chenilles blew about them in the fresh breeze, in front of neat little hotels and cottages. The Duke of Augustenburg, with his beautiful wife and his sister, who was a fine wit, and the Prince of Noer honored the place with their presence. The landed nobility of Schleswig-Holstein, with pins and needles in their legs from the new political stir, and the representatives of old Hamburg and Lübeck merchant houses, worth their weight in gold, together undertook the pilgrimage into the heart of nature. The peasants and fishermen of Norderney themselves learned to look upon the terrible and faithless gray monster westward of them as upon some kind *maître de plaisir*.

Here was a promenade, a club, and a pavilion, the rendezvous in the long summer evenings of many sweet colors and sounds. Ladies with marriageable daughters, over whose heads barren seasons of the courts and towns had washed, now watched fruitful courtships ripen on the sunny beach. Young dandies managed their mounts on the long sands in front of clear eyes. Old gentlemen dug themselves down into political and dynastic discussions in the club, their glasses of fine rum at their sides; and their young wives walked, their cashmeres on their arms, to a lonely hollow in the downs, still sun-baked from the long summer day, to become one with nature, with the lyme grass and the little wind-blown pansies, and to gaze straight up at the full moon, high in the pale summer sky. The very air had here in its embrace a scornful vigor which incited and renewed the heart. Heinrich Heine, who visited the bath, held that the persevering smell of fish which clung to them would in itself be enough to protect the virtue of the young fishermaidens of Norderney. But there were other nostrils and hearts to which the rank briny smell was intoxicating, even as the smell of gunpowder over the battle field. There was even a small casino, where the coquetry with the dangerous powers of existence could be carried on in a different measure. At times there were great balls, and on fine summer evenings the orchestra played upon the terrace.

"You do not know," said the Princess of Augustenburg to Herr Gottingen, "what a place this is for making you clean. That sea breeze has blown straight through my bonnet and my clothes, and through the very flesh and the bones of me, until my heart and spirit are swept, sun-dried, and salted."

"With Attic salt, I have noticed," said Herr Gottingen, and, looking at her, he added in his heart: "God, yes. Precisely like a split cod."

In the late summer of 1835 a terrible disaster took place at the bath of Norderney. After a three days' storm from the southwest, the wind sprang around to the north. This is a thing that happens only once in a hundred years. The tremendous mass of water driven up by the storm was turned and pressed down in the corner, upon the Westerlands. The sea broke the dikes in two places and washed through them. Cattle and sheep were drowned by the hundred. Farmhouses and barns came down like card castles before the advancing waters, and many human lives were lost even as far as Wilsum and Wredon.

It began with an evening of more than ordinarily heavenly calm, but of stifling air and a strange, luminous, sulphurous dimness. There was no distinguishable line of division between the sky and the sea. The sun went down in a confusion of light, itself a dull red like the target upon the promenade. The waves seemed of a curious substance, like jellyfish washing up on the shore. It was a highly inspiring evening; many things happened at Norderney. That night the people who were not kept awake by the beating of their own hearts woke up, terrified, by a new, swiftly approaching roar. Could their sea sing now in this voice?

In the morning the world was changed, but none knew into what. In this noise nobody could talk, or even think. What the sea was doing you could not tell. Your clothes were already whipped off you before you got in sight of the sand, and the salt foam whirled sky high. Long and towering waves came in behind it, each more powerful than the last. The air was cold and bitter.

The rumor of a ship run aground four miles to the north reached the bath, but nobody ventured out to see it. Old General von Brackel, who had seen the occupation of East Prussia by Napoleon's armies in 1806, and old Professor Schmiegelow, the physician to the princely house of Coburg, who had been in Naples at the time of the cholera, walked out a little together, and from a small hill watched the scenery, both quite silent. It was not till Thursday that the flood came. By then the storm was over.

By this time, also, there were not many people left at Norderney. The season had been drawing to a close, and many of the most illustrious guests had gone before the time of the storm. Now most of the remaining visitors made haste to depart. The young women pressed their faces to the window panes of their coaches, wild to catch a last glimpse of the wild scenery. It seemed to them that they were driving away from the one real place and hour of their lives. But when the grand coach of Baron Goldstein, of Hamburg, was blown straight off the road on the dike, it was realized that the time for quick action had come. Everybody went off as speedily as possible.

It was during these hours, the last of the storm and the first of the following night, that the sea broke the dikes. The dikes, made to resist a heavy pressure from seaward, could not hold when sapped from the east. They gave way along a stretch of half a mile, and through the opening the sea came in.

The farmers were awakened by the plaintive bellowing of their animals. Swinging their feet out of bed, in the dark, they put them down in a foot of cold, muddy water. It was salt. It was the same water which rolled, out to the west, a hundred fathoms deep, and washed the white feet of the cliffs of Dover. The North Sea had come to visit them. It was rising quickly. In an hour the movables of the low farmhouses were floating on the water, knocking against the walls. As the dawn came, the people, from the roofs of their houses, watched the land around them change. Trees and bushes were growing in a moving gray ground, and thick yellow foam was washing over the stretches of their ripening corn, the harvest of which they had been discussing on the last days before the storm.

There had been such floods before. A few old people could still recount to the young how they had once been snatched from their beds and hurled upon rafts by their pale mothers, and had seen, from the collapsing houses, the cattle struggle and go under in dark water; and how breadwinners had perished and households had been ruined and lost. The sea did such things from time to time. Still, this flood lived long in the memory of the coast. By coming on in summer time, the deluge assumed the character of a terrible, grim joke. In the annals of the province, where it kept a place and a name of its own, it was called the flood of the Cardinal.

This was because in the midst of their misery the terror-stricken people got support from one already half-mythical figure, and felt at their side the presence of a guardian angel. Many years after, in the minds of the peasants, it seemed that his company in their dark despair had shed a great white light over the black waves.

The Cardinal Hamilcar von Sehestedt had, during the summer, been living in a small fisherman's house at some distance from the bath, to collect his writings of many years in a book upon the Holy Ghost. With Joachim de Flora, who was born in 1202, the Cardinal held that while the book of the Father is given in the Old Testament, and that of the Son, in the New, the testament of the Third Person of the Trinity still remained to be written. This he had made the task of his life. He had grown up in the Westerlands, and had preserved, during a long life of travels and spiritual work, his love for the coast scenery and the sea. In his leisure hours he would go, after the example of St. Peter himself, a long way out on the sea with the fishermen in their boats, to watch their work. He had with him in his cottage only a sort of valet or secretary, a man by the name of Kasparson. This man was a former actor and adventurer, a brilliant fellow in his way, who spoke many languages and had been given to all sorts of studies. He was devoted to the Cardinal, but he seemed a curious Sancho Panza for the noble knight of the church.

The name of Hamilcar von Sehestedt was at that time famous all over Europe. He had been made a Cardinal three years before, when he was only seventy. He was a strange flower upon the old solid wood of the Sehestedt family tree. An old noble race of the province had lived for many hundred years for nothing but wars and their land, to produce him. The one remarkable thing about them was that they had stuck, through many trials, to the ancient Roman Catholic faith of the land. They had no mobility of spirit to change what they had once got into their heads. The Cardinal had nine brothers and sisters, none of whom had shown any evidences of a spiritual life. It was as if some slowly gathered and quite unused store of intellectuality in the tribe had come out in this one child of it. Perhaps a woman, imported from outside, had dropped a thought into the blood of it before becoming altogether a Sehestedt, or some idea in a book had impressed itself upon a young boy before he had been taught that books and ideas mean nothing, and all this had mounted up.

The extraordinary talents of young Hamilcar had been recognized, not by his own people, but by his tutor, who had been tutor to the Crown Prince of Denmark himself. He succeeded in taking the boy off to Paris and Rome. Here this new light of genius suddenly flared up in a clear blaze, impossible to ignore. There existed a tale of how the Pope himself, after the young priest had been presented to him, had seen in a dream how this youth had been set apart by providence to bring back the great Protestant countries under the Holy See. Still, the church had tried the young man severely, distrustful of many of the ideas and powers in him, of his visionary gift, and of the most striking feature of his nature: an immense capacity for pity which embraced not only the sinful and miserable but seemed to turn even toward the high and holy of the world. Their severity did not hurt him; obedience was in his nature. To his great power of imagination he joined a deep love of law and order. Perhaps in the end these two sides of his nature came to the same thing: to him everything seemed possible, and equally likely to fall in with the beautiful and harmonious scheme of things.

The Pope himself, later, said of him: "If, after the destruction of our present world, I were to charge one human being with the construction of a new world, the only person whom I would trust with this work would be my young Hamilcar." Whereupon, however, he quickly crossed himself two or three times.

The young Cardinal, after the church had handled him, came out a man of the world in the old sense of the word, but in a new and greater proportion. He moved with the same ease and grace amongst kings and outcasts. He had been sent to the missionary monasteries of Mexico, and had had great influence with the Indian and half-caste tribes there. One thing about him impressed the world everywhere: wherever he went, it was believed of him that he could work miracles. At the time of his stay in Norderney the hardened and heavy coast people took to thinking strange things of him. After the flood it was said by many that he had been seen to walk upon the waves.

He may have felt handicapped in this feat, for he was nearly killed at the very start of events. When the fishermen from the hamlet, as the flood came on, ran to his assistance, they found his cottage already half a ruin. In the fall of it the man Kasparson had been killed. The Cardinal himself was badly wounded, and wore, all during his rescue work, a long, blood-stained bandage wound about his head.

In spite of this the old man worked all day with undaunted courage with the ruined people. The money that he had had with him he gave over to them. It was the first contribution to the funds which were afterward collected for the sufferers from all over Europe. Much greater still was the effect of his presence amongst them. He showed good knowledge of steering a boat. They did not believe that any vessel holding him could go down. On his command they rowed straight in amongst fallen buildings, and the women jumped into the boats from the house roofs, their children in their arms. From time to time he spoke to them in a strong and clear voice, quoting to them the book of Job. Once or twice, when the boat, hit by heavy floating timbers, came near to capsizing, he rose and held out his hand, and as if he had a magic power of balance, the boat steadied itself. Near a farmhouse a chained dog, on the top of its kennel, over which the sea was washing, pulled at its chain and howled, and seemed to have gone mad with fear. As one of the men tried to take hold of it, it bit him. The old Cardinal, turning the boat a little, spoke to the dog and loosened its chain. The dog sprang into the boat. Whining, it squeezed itself against the old man's legs, and would not leave him.

Many peasant households had been saved before anybody

thought of the bath. This was strange, as the rich and gay life out there had played a big part in the minds of the population. But in the hour of danger old ties of blood and life were stronger than the new fascination. At the baths they would have light boats for pleasure trips, but few people who knew how to maneuver them. It was not till noon that the heavier boats were sent out, advancing fathom-high over the promenade.

The place where the boats unloaded, on their return landward, was a windmill which, built on a low slope and a half-circular bastion of big stones, gave them access to lay to. From the other side of it you could somehow move on by road. Here, at a distance, horses and carts had been brought up. The mill itself made a good landmark, her tall wings standing up, hard and grim, a tumbledown big black cross against a tawny sky. A crowd of people was collected here waiting for the boats. As they came in from the baths for the first time there were no tears of welcome and reunion, for these people they carried, luxuriously dressed even in their panic, with heavy caskets on their knees, were strangers. The last boat brought news that there were still, out at Norderney, four or five persons for whom no place had been found in the boat.

The tired boatmen looked at one another. They knew the tide and high sea out there, and they thought: We will not go. Cardinal Hamilcar was standing in a group of women and children, with his back to the men, but as if he could read their hardening faces and hearts he became silent. He turned and looked at the newly arrived party. Even he seemed to tarry. Below the white bandages his eyes rested on them with a singular, a mysterious expression. He had not eaten all day; now he asked for something to drink, and they brought him a jug of the spirits of the province. Turning once more toward the water he said quietly, *Eh bien. Allons, allons.* The words were strange to the peasants, for they were terms used by the coachmen of the nobility, trained abroad, for their teams of four horses. As he walked down to the boat, and the people from the bath dispersed before him, some of the ladies suddenly and wildly clapped their hands. They meant no harm. Knowing heroism only from the stage, they gave it the stage's applause. But the old man whom they applauded stopped under it for a moment. He bowed his head a little, with an exquisite irony, in the manner of a hero upon the stage. His limbs were so stiff that he had to be supported and lifted into the boat.

It was not till late on Thursday afternoon that the boat was again on its way back. A dead darkness had all day been lying upon the wide landscape. As far as the eye reached, what had been an undulating range of land was now nothing but an immense gray plane, alarmingly alive. Nothing seemed to be firm. To the crushed hearts of the men rowing over their cornfields and meadows, this movableness of what had been their foundation and foothold was unbearable, and they turned their eyes away from it. The clouds hung low upon the water. The small boat, moving heavily, seemed to be advancing upon a narrow horizontal course, squeezed in between the mass of weight below and what appeared to be a mass of weight above it. The four people lately rescued from the ruins of Norderney sat, white as corpses, in the stern.

The first of them was old Miss Nat-og-Dag, a maiden lady of great wealth, the last of the old illustrious race which carried arms two-parted in black and white, and whose name meant "Night and Day." She was close to sixty years, and her mind had for some years been confused, for she, who was a lady of the strictest virtue, believed herself to be one of the great female sinners of her time. She had with her a girl of sixteen, the Countess Calypso von Platen Hallermund, the niece of the scholar and poet of that name. These two ladies, although they behaved in the midst of danger with great self-control, gave nevertheless that impression of wildness which, within a peaceful age and society, only the vanishing and decaying aristocracy can afford to maintain. To the rescuing party it was as if they had taken into the boat two tigresses, one old and one young, the cub quite wild, the old one only the more dangerous for having the appearance of being tamed. Neither of them was in the least afraid. While we are young the idea of death or failure is intolerable to us; even the possibility of ridicule we cannot bear. But we have also an unconquerable faith in our own stars, and in the impossibility of anything venturing to go against us. As we grow old we slowly come to believe that everything will turn out badly for us, and that failure is in the nature of things; but then we do not much mind what happens to us one way or the other. In this way a balance is obtained. Miss Malin Nat-og-Dag, while perfectly indifferent to what should become of her, was also, because of the derangement of her mind, joining, to this advantage of her age, the privilege of youth, that simple and arrogant optimism which takes for granted that nothing can go wrong with it. It is even doubtful whether she believed that she could die. The girl of sixteen, pressed close to her, her dusky tresses loosened and blown about her, was taking in everything around her with ecstasy: the faces of her companions, the movements of the boat, the terrible, dull-brownish hue of the water below her, and was imagining herself to be a great divinity of the sea.

The third person of the rescued party was a young Dane, Jonathan Mærsk, who had been sent to Norderney by his doctor to recover from a severe attack of melancholia. The fourth was Miss Malin's maid, who lay in the bottom of the boat, too terrified to lift her face from the knees of her mistress.

These four people, so lately snatched out of the jaws of death, had not yet escaped his hold. As their boat, on its way landward, passed at a little distance the scattered buildings of a farm, of which only the roofs and upper parts of the walls appeared above the water, they caught sight of human beings making signs to them from the loft of one of these buildings. The peasant boatmen were surprised, for they were certain that a barge had been sent to this place earlier in the day. Under the commanding glances of young Calypso, who had caught sight of children amongst the castaways, they changed their direction, and with difficulty approached the house. As they were drawing near, a small granary, of which only the roof was visible, suddenly gave in, fell, and disappeared noiselessly before their eyes. At this sight Jonathan Mærsk rose up in the boat. For a moment he tried to follow the dispersing bits of wreckage with his eyes. Then he sat down again, very pale. The boat grated along the wall of the farmhouse and at last found a holdfast in a projecting beam, which made it possible for them to communicate with the people in the hayloft. They found there two women, one old and one young, a boy of sixteen, and two small children, and learned that they had been visited by the rescuing barge about three hours before. But they had profited by it only to send off their cow and calf, and a small collection of poor farm goods, heroically remaining themselves with the rising waters around them. The old woman had even been offered a place in the barge, with the animals, but she had refused to leave her daughter and grandchildren.

The boat could not possibly hold an additional load of five persons, and it had to be decided quickly who of the passengers should change places with the family of the farmhouse. Those who were left in the loft would have to remain there till the boat could return. Since it was already growing dark, and there was no chance of bringing a boat along until dawn, this would mean a wait of six or seven hours. The question was whether the house would hold out for so long.

The Cardinal, rising up in his fluttering dark cloak, said that he would stay in the loft. At these words the people in the boat were thrown into dark despair. They were afraid to come back without him. The boatmen let go their hold on the oars, laid their hands on him, and implored him to stay with them. But he would hear nothing, and explained to them that he would be as much in the hand of God here as anywhere else, even though perhaps under a different finger, and that it might have been for this that he had been sent out on this last journey. They saw that they could do nothing with him, and resigned themselves to their fate. Miss Malin then quickly pronounced herself determined to keep him company in the hayloft, and the girl would not leave her old friend. Young Jonathan Mærsk seemed to wake from a dream, and told them that he would come with them. At the last moment·Miss Malin's maid cried out that she would not leave her mistress, and the men were already lifting her from the bottom of the boat when her mistress cast upon her the sort of glance by which you judge whether a person is likely to make a satisfactory fourth at a game of cards. "My pussy," she said, "nobody wants you here. Besides, you are probably in the family way, and so must hold onto futurity, my poor girl. Good night, Mariechen."

It was not easy for the women to get from the boat into the loft. Miss Malin, though, was thin and strong, and the men lifted her and placed her in the doorway as one would plant a scarecrow in a field. The small and light girl followed her as lithely as a cat. The black dog, on seeing the Cardinal leave the boat, whined loudly and suddenly jumped from the rail to the loft, and the young girl hauled it in. It was now high time for the peasant family to get into the boat, but they would not go before they had, loudly weeping, kissed the hands of their relievers and piled blessings upon them. The old woman insisted on handing over to them a small stable lantern with a couple of spare tallow candles, a jug of water, and a keg of gin, together with a loaf of the hard black bread which the peasants of the Westerlands make.

The men in the boat shoved off, and in a moment a belt of brown water lay between the house and the boat.

From the door of the hayloft the derelicts watched the boat withdraw, very slowly, for it was heavily laden, across the heaving plane. The branches of tall poplars near the house floated upon the surface of the water and were washed about violently with it. The dark sky, which all day had lain like a leaden lid upon the world, suddenly colored deep down in the west, as if the lid had been lifted a little there, to a flaming red that was reflected in the sea below. All faces in the boat were turned toward the loft, and when they were nearly out of sight they lifted their arms in a farewell greeting. The Cardinal, standing in the doorway of the loft, solemnly raised his arms to them in a blessing. Miss Malin waved a little handkerchief. Soon the boat, fading from their sight, became one with the sea and the air.

As if they had been four marionettes, pulled by the same wire, the four people turned their faces to one another.

"How will he do to dance with?" a young girl asks herself, when, at the ball, the *Chapeau* is presented to her. She may even add: "How will he do as a beau, an *Épouseur,* the Intended of my life?"

"How will these people do to die with?" the castaways of the hayloft, scrutinizing each other's faces, asked themselves. Miss Malin, always inclined toward a bright view of things, found herself satisfied with her partners.

The Cardinal gave expression to these thoughts. The old man stood for a little while in deep silence, as if it took him time to get used again to the steadiness of a house, after a day spent in boats upon the restless seas, and to an atmosphere of comparative quiet after long hours of incessant danger—for nothing was likely to happen here at the moment—to get used, also, after his work with the broken-hearted peasants and fishermen around him, to the company of his equals. Slowly his manner changed from that of a commander to that of a convive. He smiled at his companions.

"My sisters and my brother," he said, "I congratulate myself upon being amongst brave people. I am looking forward to what hours I shall, under the favor of God, spend with you here. Madame," he said to Miss Malin, "I am not surprised at your gallantry, for I know about your race. It was a Nat-og-Dag who, at Warberg, when the King's horse was shot under him, jumped from his own horse and handed it to the King, with the words: 'To the King, my horse; to the enemy, my life; to the Lord, my soul.' It was a Svinhoved,[1] if I am not wrong—your great-great-grandfather—who, at the sea battle of Koege, rather than expose

[1] The name means "hog's head."

the rest of the Danish fleet to the danger of fire from his burning ship, chose to go on fighting with his last breath, until the fire reached the powder room, and he was blown up with his crew. Here," he said, looking around him at the loft, "I may say it: Blessed are the pure in blood, for they shall see——" He paused, reflecting upon his theme. "Death," he concluded. "They shall see, verily, the face of death. For this moment here, for us, our fathers were brought up, through the centuries, in skill of arms and loyalty to their king; and our mothers, in virtue."

He could have said nothing which would better have strengthened and inspired the hearts of the women, who were both fierce devils in racial pride. But young Jonathan Mærsk, the bourgeois amongst them, made a gesture as if of protest. Nevertheless he said nothing.

They closed the door of the loft, but as it was hanging loose, and kept knocking about, the Cardinal asked the women if they could not find something with which to tie it fast. The girl felt for the ribbon which had tied her hair, but it had blown away. Miss Malin then gracefully lifted her petticoat and took off a long garter, embroidered with rosebuds. "The zenith in the career of a garter, My Lord," she said, "is generally in the loosening, not in the fastening, of it. On that account the sister of this ribbon, which is now being sanctified by your holy hand, lies in the vault of the Royal Mausoleum of Stuttgart."

"Madame," said the Cardinal, "you speak frivolously. Pray do not talk or think in that way. Nothing sanctifies, nothing, indeed, is sanctified, except by the play of the Lord, which is alone divine. You speak like a person who would pronounce half of the notes of the scale—say, *do, re* and *mi*—to be sacred, but *fa, sol, la,* and *si* to be only profane, while, Madame, no one of the notes is sacred in itself, and it is the music, which can be made out of them, which is alone divine. If your garter be sanctified by my feeble old hand, so is my hand by your fine silk garter. The lion lies in wait for the antelope at the ford, and the antelope is sanctified by the lion, as is the lion by the antelope, for the play of the Lord is divine. Not the bishop, or the knight, or the powerful castle is sacred in itself, but the game of chess is a noble game, and therein the knight is sanctified by the bishop, as the bishop by the queen. Neither would it be an advantage if the bishop were ambitious to acquire the higher virtues of the queen, or the castle, those of the bishop. So are we sanctified when the hand of the Lord moves us to where he wants us to be. Here he may be about to play a fine game with us, and in that game I shall be sanctified by you, as you by any of us."

When the door of the loft was closed, the place became dark, but the little lantern on the floor shed a gentle light. The loft looked like a home to the hearts of the derelicts. It was as if they had lived here a long time. The farmers had lately harvested their hay, and half the loft was stacked with it. It smelled very sweet and made a clean and soft seat. The Cardinal, who was very tired, soon sank down into it, his long cloak spread around him on the floor. Miss Malin faced him from the opposite side of the lantern. The young girl sat next to her, her legs crossed, like a small oriental idol. The boy, when at last he sat down with them, took a seat upon a ladder which lay on the floor, and which raised him a little above the others. The dog kept close to the Cardinal. Sitting up, its ears back, from time to time it seemed, in a deep movement, to swallow its fear and loneliness. In these positions the party remained for most of the night. Indeed, the Cardinal and Miss Malin kept theirs, as will be heard, until the first light of dawn. All their shadows, thrown away in a circle from the center of the stable lamp, reached up to the rafters under the roof. In the course of the night it often seemed as if it were these long shadows which were really alive, and which kept up the spirit and the talk of the gathering, behind the exhausted people.

"Madame," said the Cardinal to Miss Malin, "I have been told of your salon, in which you make everybody feel at ease and at the same time keen to be at his best. As we want to feel like this tonight, I pray that you will be our hostess, and transfer your talents to this loft."

Miss Malin at once fell in with his suggestion and took command of the place. During the night she performed her rôle, regaling her guests upon the rare luxuries of loneliness, darkness, and danger, while up her sleeve she had death itself, like some lion of the season, some fine Italian tenor, out of the reach of rival hostesses, waiting outside the door to appear and create the sensation of the night. Some people manage to loll upon a throne; Miss Malin, on the contrary, sat in the hay as upon one of those tabourets which are amongst the privileges of duchesses. She made Jonathan cut up the bread and hand it around, and to her companions, who had had no food all day, the hard black crusts held the fragrance of the cornfields. In the course of the night she and the Cardinal, who were old and faint, drank between them most of the gin in the keg. The two young people did not touch it.

She had, straight away, more than she had asked for in the task of making her companions comfortable, for hardly had the Cardinal spoken when he fell down in a dead faint. The women, who dared not loosen the bandages around his head, sprinkled them with water out of the jar. When he first recovered he stared wildly at them, and put his hands to his head, but as he regained consciousness he gently apologized for the trouble he had given them, adding that he had had a fatiguing day. He seemed, however, somehow changed after his recovery, as if weaker than before, and, as if handing some of his leadership and responsibility to Miss Malin, he kept close to her.

It may be well at this point to give a brief account of Miss Malin Nat-og-Dag:

It has been said that she was a little off her head. Still, to the people who knew her well, it sometimes seemed open to doubt whether she was not mad by her own choice, or from some caprice of hers, for she was a capricious woman. Neither had she always been mad. She had even been a woman of great sense, who studied philosophy, and held human passions in scorn. If Miss Malin had now been given the choice of returning to her former reasonable state, and had been capable of realizing the meaning of the offer, she might have declined it on the ground that you have in reality more fun out of life when a little off your head.

Miss Malin was now a rich woman, but she had not always been that, either. She had grown up an orphan girl in the house of rich relations. Her proud old name she had always had, also her very proud big nose.

She had been brought up by a pious governess, of the sect of the Hernhuten, who thought much of female virtue. In those days a woman's being had one center of gravity, and life was simpler to her on this account than it has been later on. She might poison her relations and cheat at cards with a high hand, and yet be an *honnête femme* as long as she tolerated no heresy in the sphere of her specialty. Ladies of her day might themselves fix the price of their hearts and minds and of their souls, should they choose to deal with the devil; but as to their bodies, those were the women's stock in trade, and the lowering of the sacred standard price for them was thought of as disloyal competition to the guild of the *honnêtes femmes,* and was a deadly sin. Indeed, the higher a young woman could drive up the price individually, the greater was her state of holiness, and it was far better that it should be said of her that for her sake many men had been made unhappy, than that she should have made many men happy.

Miss Malin, urged on by her disposition as well as her education, ran amuck a little in her relation to the doctrine. She took the line, not only of defense, but of a most audacious offensive. Fantastical by nature, she saw no reason for temperance, and drove up her price fantastically high. In fact, in regard to the high valuation of her own body she became the victim of a kind of megalomania. Sigrid the Haughty, the ancient Queen of Norway, summoned to her all her suitors amongst the minor kings of the country, and

then put fire to the house and burned them all up, declaring that
in this way she would teach the petty kings of Norway to come
and woo her. Malin might have done the same with an equally
good conscience. She had taken to heart what her governess had
read her out of the Bible, that "whoever looketh on a woman to
lust after her hath already committed adultery with her in his
heart," and she had made herself the female counterpart of the
conscientious young male of the Gospel. A man's desire for her
was to her, as probably to Queen Sigrid, a deadly impertinence,
and as grave an offense as an attempted rape. She showed but little
feminine *esprit de corps,* and appeared not to consider in the
least that it would have been hard on the honest young women in
general if the principle had been carried through, since their whole
field of action lay between the two ideas, and, by amalgamating
them, you would put as quick an end to their activity as you
would to that of a concertina player by folding up the concertina
and hooking its two end pieces together. She cut a slightly pathetic
figure, as do all people who, in this world, take the words of
Scripture *au pied de la lettre.* But she did not at all mind what
sort of figure she cut.

In her youth, however, this fanatical virgin cut no mean figure
in society, for she was highly talented and brilliant. Though not
beautiful, she had the higher gift of seeming so, and in society she
played the part of a belle when far lovelier women were left un-
attended. The homage that she received she took as the natural
tribute to a Nat-og-Dag, and she was not insensitive to flatteries
which concerned her spirit and courage, or her rare gifts for music
and dancing. She even chose her friends mostly amongst men, and
thought women a little stupid. But she was at the same time ever
on the outlook, like a fighting bull for a red cloth, or a crusader for
the sign of the half-moon, for any sign of the eye of lust, in order
to annihilate the owner without pity.

Yet Miss Malin had not escaped the common fate of human beings. She had her romance. When she was twenty-seven, already

an old maid, she decided to marry after all. In this position she felt like a very tall bitch surrounded by small yapping lap dogs. She was still prepared to burn up the petty kings who might come to woo her, but she picked out her choice. So did Queen Sigrid, who swooped down on the Christian hero, Olav Trygveson, and in the saga can be read the tragic outcome of the meeting of these two proud hearts.

Malin, for her part, picked out Prince Ernest Theodore of Anhalt. This young man was the idol of his time. Of the highest birth and enormously rich, since his mother had been a grand duchess of Russia, he was also handsome as an angel, a *bel-esprit*, and a lion of Judah as a soldier. He had even a noble heart, and no frivolity in his nature, so that when, to the right and left of him, fair women died from love of him, he grieved. With all this he was an observer; he saw things. One day he saw Miss Malin, and for some time saw little else.

This young man had obtained everything in life—and women in particular—too cheaply. Beauty, talents, charm, virtue had been his for the lifting of his little finger. About Miss Malin there was nothing striking but the price. That this thin, big-nosed, penniless girl, two years older than he, would demand not only his princely name and a full share in his brilliant future, but also his prostrate adoration, his life-long fidelity, and subjection in life and death and could be had for nothing less,—this impressed the young Prince.

Some people have an unconquerable love of riddles. They may have the chance of listening to plain sense, or to such wisdom as explains life; but no, they must go and work their brains over a riddle, just because they do not understand what it means. That the solution is most likely silly in itself makes no difference to those possessed by this particular passion. Prince Ernest had this mentality, and, even from his childhood, would sit for days lost in riddles and puzzles—a pastime which, in his case, was taken as a proof of high intellectuality. When, therefore, he found this hard nut to crack, the more easily solved beauties faded before his eyes.

So nervous was Prince Ernest about this first risk of refusal which he had taken in his life—and God knows whether he most dreaded or coveted it—that he did not propose to Malin Nat-og-Dag until the very last evening before he was to depart for the war. A fortnight later he was killed upon the battle field of Jena, and he was clasping in his hand a small gold locket with a curl of fair hair in it. Many lovely blondes found comfort in the thought of this locket. None knew that amongst all the riches of silken tresses that had weighed him down, only this lock from an old maid's head had been to him a wing feather of a Walkyrie, lifting him from the ground.

If Malin had been a Roman Catholic she would have gone into a nunnery after the battle of Jena, to save, if not her soul, at least her self-respect, for, say what you will, no maiden makes such a brilliant match as she who becomes the bride of the Lord. But being a good Protestant, with a leaning toward the teachings of the Hernhuten, she just took up her cross and carried it gallantly. That nobody in the world knew of her tragedy fell in well with her opinion of other people, namely, that they never did know anything of any importance. She gave up all thought of marriage.

At the age of fifty she came unexpectedly into a very great fortune. There were people who understood her so little as to believe that it was this that went to her head and caused there the confounding of fact and fantasy. It was not so. She would not have been in the least upset by finding herself in possession of the treasures of the Grand Turk. What changed her was what changes all women at fifty: the transfer from the active service of life—with a pension or the honors of war, as the case may be—to the mere passive state of a looker-on. A weight fell away from her; she flew up to a higher perch and cackled a little. Her fortune helped her only in so far as it provided the puff of air under her wings that enabled her to fly a little higher and cackle a little louder, although it also did away with all criticism from her surroundings. In her laughter of liberation there certainly was a little madness.

This madness took, as already said, the curious form of a firm faith in a past of colossal licentiousness. She believed herself to have been the grand courtesan of her time, if not the great whore of the Revelation. She took her fortune, her house, and her jewels as the wages of sin, collected in her long career of falls, and because of this she was extremely generous with her money, considering that what had been frivolously gathered must be frivolously spent. She could not open her mouth without referring to her days of debauchery. Even Prince Ernest Theodore, the chaste young lover whom she had refused even a parting kiss, figured in her waxwork collection as a victim of her siren's arts and ferocity.

It is doubtful whether any spectacle can be enjoyed in the same way by those people who may, after all, run a risk of becoming part of it and by those who are by circumstance entirely cut off from any such possibility. The Emperor of Rome himself might, after a particularly exciting show, see the trident and the net in a nightmare. But the Vestal Virgins would lie on their marble couches and, with the knowledge of connoisseurs, go over every detail in the fight, and imagine themselves in the place of their favorite gladiator. In the same way it is unlikely that even the most pious old lady would attend the trial and burning of a witch with quite the untroubled mind of the male audience around the stake.

No young woman could, even from a nun's cell, have thrown herself into the imaginary excesses of Miss Malin without fear and trembling. But the old woman, who had seen to her safety, could dive down into any abyss of corruption with the grace of a crested grebe. Faithful by nature, she stuck to the point of view of her youth with regard to the Gospel's words concerning adultery. She had the word of the Bible for it that a multitude of young men had indeed committed it with her. But she resolutely turned them inside out, as a woman will a frock the colors of which have disappointed her by fading. She was the catoptric image of the great repenting sinner whose sins are made white as wool, and was here taking a genuine pleasure in dyeing the pretty lamb's wool of her life in sundry fierce dyes. Jealousy, deceit, seduction, rape, infanticide, and senile cruelty, with all the perversities of the human world of passion, even to the *maladies galantes,* of which she exhibited a surprising knowledge, were to her little sweetmeats which she would pick, one by one, out of the *bonbonnière* of her mind, and crunch with true *gourmandise.* In all her fantasies she was her own heroine, and she ran through the spheres of the seven deadly sins with the ecstasy of a little boy who gallops through the great races of the world upon his rocking-horse. No danger could possibly put fear into her, nor any anguish of conscience spoil her peace. If there was one person of whom she spoke with contempt it was the Mary Magdalene of the Gospel, who could no better carry the burden of her sweet sins than to retire to the desert of Libya in the company of a skull. She herself carried the weight of hers with the skill of an athlete, and was up to playing a graceful game of bilboquet with it.

Her face itself changed under her great spiritual revolution, and at the time when other women resort to rouge and belladonna, her lenience with human weakness produced in her a heightened color and sweet brilliancy of eye. She was nearer to being a pretty woman than she had ever been before. Like a witch she had always looked, but in her second childhood her appearance had more of the wicked fairy of the children's tales than of the Medusa, the revenging angel with her flaming sword who had held her own against Prince Ernest. She had preserved her elfin leanness and lightness, and as for her skill as a dancer, she might still be the belle of any great ball. The little cloven hoof beneath was now daintily gilded, like that of Esmeralda's goat itself. It was in this glow of mild madness and second youth that she now sat, marooned in the hayloft of the peasant's barn, conversing vivaciously with the Cardinal Hamilcar.

"When, as a boy, I stayed for some time at Coblentz, at the court of the emigrant Duke of Chartres," the Cardinal said, after a little pause, pensively, "I knew the great painter Abildgaard, and used to spend my mornings in his studio. When the ladies of the court came to him to have their portraits painted—for he was much sought by such fair women who wanted their beauty immortalized—how many times have I not heard him tell them: 'Wash your faces, Mesdames. Take the powder, rouge, and kohl off them. For if you will paint your faces yourselves I cannot paint you.' Often, in the course of my life, have I thought of his words. It has seemed to me that this is what the Lord is continually telling the too weak and vain mortals: 'Wash your faces. For if you will do the painting of them yourselves, laying on humility and renunciation, charity and chastity one inch thick, I can do nothing about them.' Tonight, indeed," the old man went on, smiling, as a deep movement of the sea seemed to shake the building, "the Lord is doing the washing for us with his own hands, and he is using a great deal of water for it. But we will seek comfort in the thought that there is no higher honor or happiness for us than this: to have our portraits painted by the hand of the Lord. That alone is what we have ever longed for and named immortality."

Seeing that the face of the speaker was covered with blood-stained bandages, Miss Malin was about to make a remark, but she restrained herself, for she did not know what lasting disfigurements of a noble presence they might conceal. The Cardinal understood her thought and expressed it with a smile. "Yes, Madame," he said, "my face the Lord has seen fit to wash in a more ardent spirit. But have we not been taught of the cleansing power of blood? Madame, I know now that it is stronger even than we thought. And perhaps my face needed it. Who, but the Lord, knows what rouge and powder I have put on it in the course of seventy years? Verily, Madame, in these bandages I feel that I am nearer to posing for my portrait by him than I ever have been before."

Miss Malin blushed slightly at being detected in a lack of tact, and nimbly put back the conversation a little, as one sets back a clock. "I am thankful," she said, "that I have in my life had neither rouge nor powder on my face, and Monsieur Abildgaard might have painted it at any moment. But as to this divine portrait of me, which is, I suppose, to be hung in the galleries of heaven, when I myself am dead and gone—allow me to say, My Lord, that here my ideas differ from yours a little.

"The ideas of art critics," said the Cardinal, "are likely to differ; that much I learned in the studio. I have seen the master himself strike the face of a great French painter with a badger's-hair brush full of cadmium, because they disagreed about the laws of perspective. Impart to me your views, Madame. I may learn from you."

"Well, then," said Miss Malin, "where in all the world did you get the idea that the Lord wants the truth from us? It is a strange, a most original, idea of yours, My Lord. Why, he knows it already, and may even have found it a little bit dull. Truth is for tailors and shoemakers, My Lord. I, on the contrary, have always held that the Lord has a penchant for masquerades. Do you not yourself tell us, my lords spiritual, that our trials are really blessings in disguise? And so they are. I, too, have found them to be so, at midnight, at the hour when the mask falls. But at the same time nobody can deny that they have been dressed up by the hand of an unrivaled expert. The Lord himself—with your permission—seems to me to have been masquerading pretty freely at the time when he took on flesh and dwelt amongst us. Indeed, had I been the hostess of the wedding of Cana, I might have resented the feat a little—I might, I tell you, My Lord—had I there asked that brilliant youth, the carpenter's son, in order to give him a treat on my best Berncastler Doktor, and he had, at the moment when it suited him, changed pure water into a far finer vintage! And still the lady did not know, of course, of what things he was really capable, being God Almighty.

"Indeed, My Lord," she went on, "of all monarchs of whom I have ever heard, the one who came, to my mind, nearest to the true spirit of God was the Caliph Haroun of Bagdad, who, as you know, had a taste for disguise. Ah, ah! had I lived in his day I should have played the game with him to his own taste, should I have had to pick up five hundred beggars before knocking against the Commander of the Faithful under the beggar's robe. And when I have, in my life, come nearest to playing the rôle of a goddess, the very last thing which I have wanted from my worshipers has been the truth. 'Make poetry,' I have said to them, 'use your imagination, disguise the truth to me. Your truth comes out quite early enough'—under your favor, My Lord—'and that is the end of the game.'

"And now, what, My Lord," said the old lady, "do you think of womanly modesty? Surely, that is a divine quality; and what is it but deceit on principle? Since here a youth and a maiden are present, you and I, who have observed life from the best of observatories—you from the confessional, and I from the alcove—will take pains to disregard the truth; we will talk only of legs. I can tell you, then, that you may divide all women according to the beauty of their legs. Those who have pretty legs, and who know the concealed truth to be sweeter than all illusions, are the truly gallant women, who look you in the face, who have the genuine courage of a good conscience. But if they took to wearing trousers, where would their gallantry be? The young men of our days, who wear tight trousers which oblige them to keep two valets for drawing them on, one for each leg——"

"And a difficult job even at that," said the Cardinal thoughtfully.

"To walk about as true missionaries of the truth, Miss Malin resumed, "may be more human, but surely they have nothing divine. They may have the facts of life on their side, while the legs of the women, under their petticoats, are ideas. But the people who go forth on ideas are the ones who have the true heroism. For it is the consciousness of hidden power which gives courage. But I beg your pardon, My Lord, for speaking so long."

"Madame," said the Cardinal gently, "do not apologize. I have profited by your speech. But it has not convinced me that you and I are not really of one mind. This world of ours is like the children's game of bread and cheese; there is always something underneath—truth, deceit; truth, deceit! When the Caliph masqueraded as one of his own poor subjects, all his hidden splendor could not have saved the jest from being in pretty poor taste, had he not had beneath it a fraternal heart for his poor people. Likewise, when our Lord did, for some thirty years, masquerade as a son of man, there would have been no really good sense in the thing had he not had, after all, a humane heart, and even, Madame, a sympathy with lovers of good wine. The witty woman, Madame, chooses for her carnival costume one which ingeniously reveals something in her spirit or heart which the conventions of her everyday life conceal; and when she puts on the hideous long-nosed Venetian mask, she tells us, not only that she has a classic nose behind it, but that she has much more, and may well be adored for things other than her mere beauty. So speaketh the Arbiter of the masquerade: 'By thy mask I shall know thee.'

"But let us agree, Madame," he went on, "that the day of judgment shall not be, as insipid preachers will have us believe, the moment of unveiling of our own poor little attempts at deceit, about which the Lord does indeed already know all, but, on the contrary, that it shall be the hour in which the Almighty God himself lets fall the mask. And what a moment! Oh, Madame, it will not be too much to have waited for it a million years. Heaven will ring and resound with laughter, pure and innocent as that of a child, clear as that of a bride, triumphant as that of a faithful warrior who lays down the enemy's banners at his sovereign's feet, or who is at last lifted from the dungeon and the chains, cleared of his slanderer's calumnies!

"Still, Madame, has not the Lord arranged for us here a day of judgment in miniature? It will be soon midnight. Let it be the hour of the falling of the mask. If it be not your mask, or mine, which is to fall, let it be the mask of fate and life. Death we may soon have to face, without any mask. In the meantime we have nothing to do but to remember what life be really like. Come, Madame, and my young brother and sister! As we shall not be able to sleep, and are still comfortably seated here, tell me who you are, and recount to me your stories without restraint.

"You," the old man said, addressing himself to Jonathan Mærsk, "rose up in the boat, with danger of capsizing it, at the sight of the falling granary. Thus, I believe, some proud building of your life has fallen, and has gone to pieces under your eyes. Tell us which it was.

"Also, I noticed a short time ago," he went on, "when I spoke of the purity of our blood, that you shrank from my words as from the sight of the granary. You are, perhaps, a partisan of the revolutionary ideas of your generation. Do not imagine, then, that I am a stranger to those theories. I am indeed more closely in touch with them than you could know. But should we let any discrepancy in politics separate our hearts at this hour? Come, I shall speak to you in your own words: And now abideth liberty, equality, fraternity, these three, but the greatest of these is fraternity.

"Or," he said, "you may be, my dear son, groaning under the sad burden of the bastard. But who more than the bastard needs to cry out to ask who he is? So have faith in us. Tell us now, before morning, the story of your life."

The young man, whose countenance had all the time been stamped with the loneliness which is the hallmark of true melancholy, at these words looked up into the Cardinal's face. The great dignity of manner of the old man had impressed the others from the moment they came into his presence. Now the boy was fascinated by the strange lucidity of his eyes. For a few moments the two looked intensely at each other. The color rose in the pale cheeks of the young man. He drew a deep sigh.

"Yes," he said, as if inspired, "I will tell you my story. Perhaps I shall understand it all better when I can, at last, give words to it."

"Wash your face, my young friend," said Miss Malin, "and your portrait, within our hearts, will impart to you immortality."

"I will call my tale," said the young man, "The Story of Timon of Assens."

"If you had happened to live in Copenhagen," the young man began, "you would have heard of me, for there I was, at a time, much talked about. They even gave me a name. They called me Timon of Assens. And they were right in so far as I do indeed come from Assens, which is, as you may know, a small seaport town on the island of Funen. There I was born, the son of very respectable people, the skipper Clement Mærsk and his wife, Magdalena, who owned a pretty house with a garden in the town.

"I do not know whether you will think it curious that all the time I lived at Assens it never occurred to me that anything could or would harm me. I never, indeed, thought that anything at all might occupy itself with me. It seemed to me that it was, on the contrary, my task to look after the world. My father sailed, and for many summers I sailed with him, and came to Portugal and Greece. When we were on the sea, the ship and the cargo had to be looked after by us, and to both of us they seemed the important things in the world.

"My mother was a lovely woman. Although I have for some time moved in the highest society, I never have seen her equal either in looks or in manners. But she kept no company with the other skippers' wives, and never went to other people's houses. Her father had been assistant to the great Swedish botanist, Linné, and to her the flowers, and what happened to them, and the bees, and their hives and works, seemed more important than anything which had to do with human beings. While I was with her I held the belief that the plants, flowers, and insects of the world were the really important things in it, and that human beings were here only to look after them.

"In the garden at Assens my mother and I lived in what I think is called an idyll. Our days were filled with nothing but innocence and pleasure."

Miss Malin, who had been listening attentively, always keen for any kind of narrative, here interrupted the narrator, sighing a little. "Ah" she said, "I know about idylls. *Mais moi je n'aime pas les plaisirs innocents.*"

"I had a friend in Assens, or so I thought," Jonathan went on, "a clever boy by the name of Rasmus Petersen, a couple of years older than I, and taller by a head. He was to have been a parson, but he got into some trouble and never succeeded, but when he was a student in Copenhagen he was a tutor in many great houses. He always took a great interest in me, but though I admired him I never felt quite well in his company. He was very sharp, like a razor; you did not come away from him without having cut your fingers a little, although at the moment you might not feel it. When I was about sixteen he told my father that I ought to come with him to Copenhagen, to study under the learned people that he knew there, for he thought me a very brilliant boy."

"And were you very brilliant?" asked Miss Malin with surprise.

"Alas, no, Madame," said Jonathan.

"When I first came to Copenhagen," Jonathan went on, "I was very lonely, because there was nothing for me to do. It seemed to me that there was nothing but people there. They did not care for me, either. When I had talked to them for a little they generally walked away. But after a while my interest was caught by the expansive hothouses and nurseries of the royal palaces and of the great noblemen. Amongst these the most renowned were those of Baron Joachim von Gersdorff, who was High Steward of Denmark, and himself a great botanist, who had traveled all over Europe, India, Africa, and America and collected rare plants everywhere.

"Have you heard of this man before, or do you know him? He came of a Russian family, and his wealth was such as is otherwise unknown in Denmark. He was a poet and musician, a diplomat, a seducer of women, even then, when he was an old man. Still, all this was not what caught your mind about the man. But it was this: that he was a man of fashion. Or you might say that fashion itself was only, in Copenhagen at least, the footman of Baron Gersdorff. Whatever he did at once became the thing for everybody to do. Oh, I do not want to describe the man. You will know, I think, what a man of fashion means. I have learned it. Such a man was he.

"I had not been to his hothouses, to which Rasmus obtained admission for me, more than a few times when I met Baron Gersdorff himself there one afternoon. Rasmus presented me to him, and he greeted me in a very friendly way, and offered to show me the whole place, which he did with much patience and benevolence. After that day I nearly always found him there. He took me on to write a catalogue for his cactus house. We spent many days together in that hot glasshouse. I liked him much, because he had seen so much of the world, and could tell me about the flowers and insects of it. At times I noticed that my presence moved him strangely. One afternoon, as I was reading to him a treatise upon the mouth of the tube of the Epiphyllum, I saw that he had shut his eyes. He took my hand and held it, and as I finished he looked up and said: 'What am I to give you, Jonathan, as a finder's fee?' I laughed and answered that I did not think that I had found out anything exceptional yet. 'Oh, God,' he said, 'a finder's fee for the summer of 1814!' Shortly after that day he began to talk to me of my voice. He told me that I had a remarkably sweet voice, and asked me to let him arrange for Monsieur Dupuy to give me singing lessons."

"And did you have a lovely voice?" asked Miss Malin with some incredulity, for the voice of the narrator was low and hoarse.

"Yes, Madame," he said, "at that time I had a very pretty voice. I had been taught to sing by my mother."

"Ah," said Miss Malin, "there is nothing in the world more lovely than a lovely boy's voice. When I was in Rome there was a boy named Mario in the choir of the Jesu, who had a voice like an angel. The Pope himself told me to go and hear him, and I was well aware why, for he was hoping to convert me to Rome, and thought that this golden angel's song might break down all my resistance. From my pew I saw the Pope himself burst into tears when, like a swan taking the wing, this Mario lifted up his voice in Carissimi's immortal recitative: 'Get thee behind me, Satan!' Oh, that good Pius VIII. Two days later he was wickedly poisoned by three cantharide pills. I do not hold with popery, but I admit that he was a fine figure of a Pope, and died like a man. And so you had your lessons, and became a virtuoso, Monsieur Jonathan?"

"Yes, Madame," said Jonathan with a smile, "my lessons I had. And as I was always very fond of music I worked hard and made good progress. At the beginning of the third winter the Baron, who by this time never seemed to like to part with me, took me around to the great houses of his friends and made me sing for them. When I had first come to Copenhagen I used to stand outside the great houses on winter evenings, to see the flowers and chandeliers in the halls, and the young women as they got out of their carriages. Now I went in everywhere myself, and the ladies, old and young, were as kind to me as if I had been their child or young brother. I sang at Court, before King Frederick and Queen Marie, and the Queen smiled very kindly at me. I was very happy. I thought: How foolish those people are who tell you that the great people of the towns love nothing but riches and worldly honors. All these ladies and great gentlemen love music as much as I do—yes, more—and forget everything else for it, and what a great thing is the love of the beautiful."

"Did you fall in love?" Miss Malin asked.

"In a way I was in love with all of them," said Jonathan. "They had tears in their eyes when I sang; they accompanied me on the harp, or joined me in duets; they took flowers from their hair and gave them to me. But perhaps I was in love with the Countess Atalanta Danneskjold, who was the youngest of the sisters Danneskjold, whom they called the nine swans of Samsø. Her mother made us pose together in a charade, as Orpheus and Euridice. All that winter was very much like a dream, for do you not sometimes dream that you can sing whatever note you like, and run up and down the whole scale, like the angels on Jacob's ladder? I sometimes dream that even now.

"But toward spring there befell me what I took to be a great misfortune, not knowing then what misfortune means. I fell ill, and as I was getting well the court physician, who was attending me, told me that I had lost my voice and that I had no hope of getting it back. While I was still in bed I was much worried by this, not only by the loss of my voice itself, but by the thought of how I should now disappoint and lose my friends, and how sad my life would now become. I was even shedding tears about it when Rasmus Petersen came to see me. I opened my heart to him, to get his sympathy in my distress. He had to get up from his chair and pretend to look out of the window to hide his laughter. I thought it heartless of him, and did not say any more to him. 'Why, Jonathan,' he said, 'I have reason to laugh, for I have won my bet. I held that you were indeed the simpleton you look, which nobody else would believe. They think that you are a shrewd boy. It will not make the slightest difference in the world to you that you have lost that voice of yours.' I did not understand him. I think I grew pale, even though his words cheered me.

" 'Come,' he said, 'the Baron Gersdorff is your father. I guessed as much, before I ever brought you to his hothouses, from looking at a portrait of him as a child, in which he also has the head of an angel. When he knew it himself he was more pleased than I have ever seen him. He said: "I have never had a child in my life. It seems very curious to me that I should have got one. Still, I believe this boy to be indeed the son of my body, and I shall reward him for that. But should I find that my soul is going to live on, in him—as God liveth I will legitimatize him, and leave him all that I own. If it be not possible to have him made a Baron Gersdorff, I will at least have him a Knight of Malta under the name of De Résurrection."

" 'It is on this account,' Rasmus said, 'that the fine people of Copenhagen have all been spoiling you, Jonathan. They have been watching you all the time to see if the soul of Baron Gersdorff was showing itself in you, in which case you would be the richest man, and the best match, Jonathan, in all northern Europe.' Then he proceeded to recount to me a conversation that he had had with Baron Gersdorff about me:

" 'You know me, my good Rasmus, to be a poet,' the Baron had said to him. 'Well, I will tell you what sort of poet I am. I have never in my life written a line without imagining myself in the place of some poet or other that I know of. I have written poems in the manner of Horace or Lamartine. Likewise I am not capable of writing a love letter to a woman without representing to myself in my own mind either Lovelace, the Corsaire or Eugene Onegine. The ladies have been flattered, adored, and seduced by all the heroes of Chateaubriand and Lord Byron in turn. There is nothing that I have ever done unconsciously, without knowing well what I did. But this boy, this Jonathan, I have really made without thinking of it. He is bound to be, not any figure out of Firdousi, or even Oehlenschlaeger, but a true and genuine work of Joachim Gersdorff. That is a curious thing, a very curious thing, for Joachim Gersdorff to be watching. That is a phenomenon of extreme importance to Joachim Gersdorff. Let him but show me what a Joachim Gersdorff is in reality, and no reward of mine shall be too great. Riches, houses, jewels, women, wines, and the honors of the land shall be his for it.'

"All this I heard as I was lying in my bed.

"I do not know if you will think it strange, My Lord, or you, Miss Nat-og-Dag, that the strongest emotion which these words aroused in me was a feeling of deep shame. Such a strong feeling I had never, in all my life, experienced.

"If the Baron had seduced me, as I believe that he did seduce other pretty boys, I should have had to blush before the faces of honest people. But I might have found refuge from that shame in my own heart, for in a way I loved the man. For the shame which I now felt it seemed to me that there was no refuge anywhere. Upon the very bottom of my soul, I felt, and that for the first time in my life, the eyes of all the world.

"God made the world, My Lord, and looked at it, and saw that it was good. Yes. But what if the world had looked back at him, to see whether he was good or not? This was, I thought, what Lucifer had really done to God: he had looked at him, and had made the Lord feel that he himself was being judged by a critic. Was he good? I—I had been innocent as God. Now I was made a true Joachim Gersdorff. I had in all my veins the blood of this man, of a man of fashion, the sort of man who attracts the eyes of all the world. God could not stand it. He hurled down Lucifer, as you remember, into the abyss. God was right; he should not have stood it. I could not stand it either, but I had to.

"To find out whether Rasmus was right I did, I think, a brave, even a heroic, thing, which proves to my mind that I had been well brought up, after all, by the skipper and his wife. I went to a big party at the house of Countess Danneskjold, and sang to them again. I sang my old songs, and I heard my own voice, or what was left of it. You will understand, who are listening to me now, how poor that must have been. I had sung to them before, and done my best, and it seemed to me that I had then given them the very best which I had in me. As I now sang there was not one of the faces around me which showed the slightest disappointment or regret. All the people were kind and complimentary to me, as they had always been. I felt then that I had never given them anything, had never done anything to them at all. It was the world around me which was watching me, and meant to do something to me. All eyes were on me, for I was a genuine Joachim Gersdorff, a young man of fashion. I came away from that house at midnight, and that was the hour, My Lord, of which the fall of the granary reminded me.

"The same night I wrote a letter to the Baron, to take leave of him. I was so filled with abhorrence of him and all his world that, on reading my letter through, I found the word 'fashion' recurring nine times. I gave my letter to Rasmus to hand to him. As he was leaving I remembered that I had said nothing of the fortune which the Baron meant to leave to me. I now charged my friend to communicate to him my refusal of any of it.

"I could not stand the sight of the streets. Leaving my pretty rooms in the neighborhood of the Gersdorff Palace, I went in a boat across the harbor to the small fortified island of Trekroner, and took lodgings with the quartermaster, where I could see nothing but the sea. Rasmus walked down with me, and carried my bag. All the time he was trying to hold me back. We had to pass the door of the Gersdorff Palace, and such a sudden loathing of the whole place filled me at the sight of it that I spat at it, as my father—alas, as the skipper Clement Mærsk of Assens—had taught me to spit when I was a boy.

"For a few days I lived at Trekroner, trying to find again there the world as it had once been mine—not myself, for I wanted nothing less than myself. I thought of the garden of Assens, but it was closed to me forever. Once you have eaten of the tree of knowledge, and have seen yourself, gardens close themselves to you. You become a person of fashion, even as did Adam and Eve when they began to occupy themselves with their appearance.

"But only a few days later Rasmus came over to see me. He had taken a small yawl to get to me, he who was so terrified of the sea.

"'Ah, my friend,' he said, rubbing his hands, 'you were born under a lucky star. I gave your letter to the Baron, and as he read it he became to the highest degree excited and delighted. He got up and walked to and fro, and exclaimed: "God, this misanthropy, this melancholy! How I know them. They are my own altogether! For the first week after I had become the lover of the Empress Catherine I felt all that he feels now. I meant to enter a monastery. It is young Joachim Gersdorff to a turn, but done all in black, an etching from the colored original. But good God, what power the boy has got in him, what a fine deep black! I had not thought it of him with his high voice. This is the winter night of Russia, the wolves upon the steppes." After he had read your letter a second time he said: "He will not be a man of fashion? But so we all are, we Gersdorffs; so was my father at the court of the young Empress. Why should not my son be the same? Surely he shall be our heir, the glass of fashion, and the mold of form."

"'I tell you, Jonathan,' said Rasmus, 'that your melancholy is the highest fashion of the day. The elegant young men of Copenhagen wear black and speak with bitterness of the world, and the ladies talk of the grave.'

"And this was the time when they took to calling me Timon of Assens.

"'Did you tell him,' I asked Rasmus, 'that I will on no account have any of his money?' And Rasmus answered, 'Yes, I did; and he was so pleased that I thought that he might have a stroke and leave you his heir there and then. "Good," he said, "good, my son Timon. Let me see you throw it away. Scatter it well. Show the world your contempt of it in the true Gersdorff way Let the hetæra have it; there is no better advertisement for a melancholy man of fashion. They will follow you everywhere and make a charming contrast to your deep black. How I love that boy," he said. "I have," he added, "a collection of emeralds, unmatched in all Europe. I will send him that to start with." And here, indeed, it is,' said Rasmus, handing me, with great care, a case of jewels.

"'But when the Baron heard,' Rasmus said, 'of your spitting at the door of his house, he became very grave. "That," he said, "I did to my father's door, to the door of the Gersdorff Palace of St. Petersburg." He at once sent for his lawyer, and drew up a document to acknowledge you as his son, and to leave you all his fortune. Likewise he has written to obtain for you the title of Knight of Malta, and the name of De Résurrection.'

"By this time I was so depressed that I thought of death with a true longing and nostalgia. I returned with Rasmus to town, to pay my debts, so that my tailor and my hatter should not talk of me when I was dead, and I walked out upon the bridge of Langebro, looking at the water and the boats lying there, some of which came from Assens. I waited until there were not so many people about. It was one of the blue April evenings of Copenhagen. A barcarole by Salvadore that I had used to sing ran into my mind. It gave me much ease, together with the thought that I would soon disappear. As I was standing there a carriage, driving by, slackened its pace, and a little later a lady dressed in black lace came up, looked around, and spoke to me in a low voice, quite out of breath. 'You are Jonathan Mærsk?' she asked me, and as I said yes, she came up close to me. 'Oh, Jonathan Mærsk,' she said, 'I know you. I have followed you. I see what you are about. Let me die with you. I have long meant to seek death, but I dare not go alone. Let me go in your company. I am as great a sinner as Judas,' she said, 'like him I have betrayed, betrayed. Come, let us go.' In the spring twilight she seized my hand and held it. I had to shake her off and run away.

"I thought: There are probably always in Copenhagen four or five women who are on the verge of suicide; perhaps there are more. If I have become the man of fashion amongst them, how shall I escape them, to die in peace? Must I die, now, in fashionable company, and give the tone of fashion to the bridge of Langebro? Must I go down to the bottom of the sea in the society of women who do not know a major from a minor key, and is my last moan to be——"

"*Le dernier cri*," said Miss Malin, with a truly witchlike little laugh.

"I went back to Trekroner," said Jonathan after a short pause, "and sat in my room. I could neither eat nor drink.

"At this moment I unexpectedly received a visit from skipper Clement Mærsk of Assens. He had been away to Trankebar, and had just returned, and had looked me up.

"'What is this,' he said, 'that I hear of you, Jonathanner!? Are they to make you a Knight of Malta? I know Malta well. As you go into the entrance and have got the Castle of San Angelo on your right hand, you have to be careful about a rock to port.'

"'Father,' I said, remembering again how we had sailed together, 'is Baron Gersdorff my father? Do you know that man?'

"'Leave the women's business alone,' he said. 'Here you are, Jonathan, a seaworthy ship, whoever built you.'

"I told him then all that had happened to me.

"'Little Jonathan,' he said, 'you have fallen amongst women.' I said that I really did not know many women. 'That does not signify,' he said, 'I have seen the men of Copenhagen. Those people who want things to happen are all of them women, masquerading in a new model of wax noses. I tell you, in regard to ships, if it were not for the women sitting in ports waiting for silks, tea, cochineal, and pepper—all things which they want for making things happen—the ships would sail on quietly, content to be on the sea and never thinking of land. Your mother,' he went on after a little while, 'was the only woman I ever knew who did not want things to happen.' I said, 'But even she, Father, did not succeed in it, and God help me now.'

"I told him how Baron Gersdorff had wanted to leave me his fortune. Father had become hard of hearing. Only after a time he said, 'Did you speak of money? Do you want money, Jonathan? It would be curious if you did, for I know where there is a lot of it. Three years ago,' he recounted, 'I was becalmed off a small island near Haiti. I went ashore to see the place, and to dig up some rare plants which I meant to bring your mother, and there I struck upon the buried treasure of Captain l'Olonnais, who was one of the *Filibustiers*. I dug it all up, and as I wanted exercise I dug it all down again, in better order than the Captain had done. I know the exact place of it. If you want it I will get it for you some time, and if you cannot stop the Baron from giving you his money, you might make him a present of it. It is more than he has got.'

" 'Father!' I cried, 'you do not know what you say. You have not lived in this town. What a gesture that would be. It would make me a man of fashion forever—I should indeed be Timon of Assens. Bring me a parrot from Haiti, Father, but not money.'

" 'I believe you are unhappy, Jonathan,' he said.

" 'I am unhappy, Father,' I said. 'I have loved this town and the people in it. I have drunk them down with delight. But they have some poison in them which I cannot stand. If I think of them now, I vomit up my soul. Do you know of a cure for me?'

" 'Why, yes,' he said, 'I know of a cure for everything: salt water.'

" 'Salt water?' I asked him.

" 'Yes,' he said, 'in one way or the other. Sweat, or tears, or the salt sea.'

"I said: 'I have tried sweat and tears. The salt sea I meant to try, but a woman in black lace prevented me.'

" 'You speak wildly. Jonathan,' he said.

" 'You might come with me,' he said after a little time. 'I am bound for St. Petersburg.'

" 'No,' I said, 'to St. Petersburg I will not go.'

" 'Well,' he said, 'I am bound for it. But go and get well while I am there, for you are looking very sick. I will take you when I come back, into open sea.'

" 'I cannot stay in Copenhagen,' I said.

"'Good,' he said, 'go to some place of which the doctors can tell you, and I will pick you up at Hamburg.'

"And in this way, My Lord, and Miss Nat-og-Dag," the young man said, "I was sent here, by skipper Mærsk, whether he be my father or not, to get cured by salt water."

"Ah, ah, ah," said Miss Malin, when the young man had finished his tale, in which she had by this time become quite absorbed. She rubbed her small hands together, as pleased as a child with a new toy. "What a story, Monsieur Timon. What a place this is! What people we are! I myself have by now become aware of my identity: I am Mademoiselle Diogenes, and this little lantern, which the fat old peasant woman left us, that is my famous lamp, by the light of which I have sought a man, and by which I have found him. You are the man, Timon! If I had searched all Europe with lamp and lantern I should not have found more precisely what I wanted."

"What do you want me for, Madame?" Jonathan asked her.

"Oh, not for myself," said Miss Malin. "I am not in a mood for love-making tonight. In fact, I might have had, for supper, a decoction of the tree agnus castus, of which a specimen is shown in Guinenne. I want you for Calypso.

"You see this girl?" she asked him, looking with pride and tenderness at the fair young creature by her side. "She is not my own daughter, and still, by the Holy Ghost, I am making her, as much as my old friend Baron Gersdorff ever made you. I have carried her in my heart and my mind, and sighed under her weight. Now the days are accomplished when I shall be delivered, and here we have the stable and the manger. But when I have brought her forth, I shall want a nurse; further, I shall want a governess, a tutor, a *maestro* for her, and you are to be all that."

"Alas, to teach her what?" asked Jonathan.

"To teach her to be seen," said Miss Malin. "You complain of people looking at you. But what if you were bent down by the opposite misfortune? What if nobody could or would see you, although you were, yourself, firmly convinced of your own existence? There are more martyrdoms than yours, Misanthrope of Assens. You may have read the tale of the Emperor's new clothes, by that brilliant, rising young author, Hans Andersen. But here we have it the other way around: the Emperor is walking along in all his splendor, scepter and orb in hand, and no one in the whole town dares to see him, for they believe that they shall then be thought unfit for their offices, or impossibly dull. This is my little Emperor; the procession a bad man made, about whom I shall tell you; and you, Monsieur Timon, you are the innocent child who cries out: 'But there *is* an Emperor!'

"The motto of the Nat-og-Dag family," went on Miss Malin, "runs thus: 'The sour with the sweet.' Out of piety to my ancestors I have partaken of many of the mixed dishes of life: the giblet soup of Mr. Swedenborg, the salad of platonic love, even the sauerkraut of the divine Marquis. I have developed the palate of a true Nat-og-Dag; I have come to relish them. But the bitterness of life, that is bad nourishment, particularly to a young heart. Upon the meadows of the Westerlands they raise a sort of mutton which, fed on salt grass, produces an excellent-tasting meat known in the culinary world as *pré-salé*. This girl has been fed on such salt plains and on brine and bitter herbs. Her little heart has had nothing else to eat. She is indeed, spiritually, an *agneau pré-salé*, my salted little ewe lamb."

The girl, who had all the time sat crouching near her old friend, drew herself up when Miss Malin began to tell her story. She sat up straight then, her amber-colored eyes below their delicate, long-drawn eyebrows that were like the markings on a butterfly's wings, or themselves like a pair of low extended wings, were fixed on the air, too haughty to turn toward her audience. In spite of her gentle brow she was a dangerous animal, ready to spring. But at what? At life altogether.

"Have you ever heard," asked Miss Malin, "of Count August Platen-Hallermund?" At the sound of the name the girl shuddered and became pale. A threatening dusk sank over her clear eyes. "Hush," said Miss Malin, "we shall not name him again. As he is not a man, but an angel, we shall call him the Count Seraphina. We shall sit, tonight, in a *lit de justice* on the Count. The truth must be told about him just this one time. When I was a little girl and was taught French," the old lady addressed herself, above the heads of the young people, in a sudden little fit of familiarity, to the Cardinal, "the very first phrase in my reading book ran thus: *Le lit est une bonne chose; si l'on n'y dort pas, l'on s'y repose.* Like much else which we were taught as children, it was proved by life to be a complete fallacy. But it may still apply to the bed of justice."

"Indeed I have read the poetry and philosophy of Count August," said the Cardinal.

"Not I," said Miss Malin. "When, on doomsday, I am called to account for many hours spent in the wrong places, I shall still be able to plead: 'But I have not read the poems of Count August von Platen.' How many poems has he written, My Lord?"

"Ah, I could not tell," said the Cardinal. Miss Malin said: "*Cinq ou six milles? C'est beaucoup. Combien en a-t-il de bons? Quinze ou seize. C'est beaucoup, dit Martin.*"

"You have read, My Lord," she went on, "of the unhappy young man who had been changed into a pug by a witch, and who could not be transformed back unless a pure virgin, who had known no man, should, upon a St. Sylvester's night, read the poems of Gustav Pfizer without falling asleep? And his sympathetic friend, when he is told all this, answers: 'Then, alas, I cannot help you. First of all, I am no virgin. Secondly, I never could, reading Gustav Pfizer's poems, keep from falling into slumber.' If Count August is turned into a pug, for exactly the same reasons I shall not be able to help him."

"This man, then, this Count Seraphina," she took up the thread of her tale, after her little flutter of thought, "was the uncle of this girl, and she was brought up in his house after the death of her parents. So now, my good friends, I will lighten the darkness of this night to you, by impressing upon it the deeper darkness of Calypso's story:

"Count Seraphina," said Miss Malin, "meditated much upon celestial matters. And, as you must be aware, who have read his poems, he was convinced that no woman was ever allowed to enter heaven. He disliked and mistrusted everything female; it gave him goose flesh.

"His idea of paradise was, then, a long row of lovely young boys, in transparent robes of white, walking two by two, singing his poems to his music, in such lovely trebles as you yourself once possessed, Mr. Jonathan, or otherwise discussing his philosophy, or absorbed in his books upon arithmetics. The estate which he owned at Angelshorn in Mechlenburg he endeavored to turn into such a heaven, a Von Platen waxwork elysium, and in the very center of it he had, most awkwardly for himself and for her, this little girl, about whom he had doubts as to whether or not she might pass as an angel.

"As long as she was a child he took pleasure in her company, for he had an eye for beauty and grace. He had her dressed up in boy's clothes, all of velvet and lace, and he allowed her hair to grow into such hyacinthine locks as young Ganymede wore at the court of Jove. He was much occupied by the thought of showing himself to the world as a conjurer, a high white Magian, capable of transforming that drop of blood of the devil himself, a girl, into that sweet object nearest to the angels, which was a boy. Or perhaps he even dreamed of creating a being of its own kind, an object of art which was neither boy nor girl, but a pure Von Platen. There may have been times, then, when his delicate artist's blood stirred a little in his veins at the idea. He taught the little girl Greek and Latin. He tried to convey to her the idea of the beauty of higher mathematics. But when he lectured to her upon the infinite loveliness of the circle, she asked him: if it were really so fair, what color was it—was it not blue? Ah, no, he said, it had no color at all. From that moment he began to fear that she would not become a boy.

"He kept looking at her, with terrible doubts, more and more virtuously indignant at the signs of his mistake. And when he found that there was no longer any doubt, but that his failure was a certainty, with a shiver he turned his eyes away from her forever, and annihilated her. Her girl's beauty was her sentence of death. This happened two or three years ago. Since then she has not existed. Mr. Timon, you are free to envy her.

"The Count Seraphina had a great predilection for the Middle Ages. His huge castle of Angelshorn dated from that time, and he had taken pains to bring it back inside, as outside, to the times of the Crusades. It was not constructed, no more than was the Count himself, to spread itself much on earth, but the tall towers aspired to heaven, with a flight of jackdaws like a thin smoke around their heads, and the deep vaults seemed to dig themselves down toward the pit. The daylight was let in, between fathom-thick walls, through old stained glass, like cinnamon and blood of oxen, along the sides of the rooms, where, upon faded tapestries, unicorns were killed and the Magians and their retinue carried gold and myrrh to Bethlehem. Here the Count listened to, and himself played, the *viol de gamba* and the *viol d'amore,* and practiced archery. He never read a printed book, but had his authors of the day copied by hand in ultramarine and scarlet letters.

"He liked to imagine himself the abbot of a highly exclusive monastery, whereto only fair young monks of brilliant talent and soft manners were admitted. He and his circle of young friends sat down to dinner in old sculptured oak pews, and wore cowls of purple silk. His house was an abbey upon the northern soil, a Mount Athos to which no hen or cow is allowed to come, not even the wild bees, on account of their queen bee. Aye, the Count was more zealous than the monks of Athos, for when he and his seraglio of lovely youths sometimes drank wine out of a skull, to keep present the thought of death and eternity, he took care that it should not be the skull of a lady. Oh, that the name of that man must dishonor my lips! It were better for a man that he should kill a lady, in order to procure her skull to drink his wine from, than that he should excite himself by drinking it, so to say, out of his own skull.

"In this dark castle the annihilated girl would walk about. She was the loveliest thing in the place, and would have adorned the court of Queen Venus, who would very likely have made her keeper of her doves, dove as she is herself. But here she knew that she did not exist, for nobody ever looked at her. Where, My Lord, is music bred—upon the instrument or within the ear that listens? The loveliness of woman is created in the eye of man. You talk, Timon, of Lucifer offending God by looking at him to see what he was like. That shows that you worship a male deity. A goddess would ask her worshiper first of all: 'How am I looking?'

"You might well ask me now: 'Did not one of the castellan's sleek minions look for himself, and find out how sweet she was?' But no; this is the story of the Emperor's new clothes, and is told to prove to you the power of human vanity. These beautiful boys were too fearful of being found impossibly dull, and unfit for their office. They were busy discussing Aristotle and lecturing upon the doctrines and mysteries of ancient and medieval scholastics.

"The Emperor himself, you will remember, believed that he was finely attired. So also the maid herself believed that she was not worth looking at. Still, in her heart she could hardly believe it, and this everlasting struggle between instinct and reason devoured her, as much as it did Hercules himself, or any other traditional hero of tragedy. Sometimes she would stand and look at the mighty coats of armor in the corridors of Angelshorn. These looked like real men. She felt that they would have been partisans of hers, had they not all been hollow. She became shy of all people, and wild, in the loneliness of the brilliant circle of the house. But she became also fierce, and might well, on a dark night, have put fire to the castle.

"In the end, as you, Timon, could not stand your existence, but meant to jump into the water from Langebro, she could no longer stand her nonexistence at Angelshorn. But your task was easier. You wanted only to disappear, while she had to create herself. She had been for such a long time brought up in the wicked heresies of those falsifiers of truth, and so thoroughly tortured and threatened with the stake, that she was by now ready to deny any god. Abu Mirrah had a ring which made him invisible, but when he wanted to marry the Princess Ebadu, and could not get it off his finger, he cut off the finger with it. In this way Calypso resolved to cut off her long hair, and to chop off her young breasts, so as to be like her acquaintances. This deed of darkness she made up her mind to commit one summer night."

At this point of Miss Malin's narrative, the girl, who had hitherto stared straight in front of her, turned her wild eyes toward the narrator, and began to listen with a new kind of interest, as if she herself were hearing the tale for the first time. Miss Malin had an opulent power of imagination. But still the story, correct or not, was to the heroine herself a symbol, a dressed-up image of what she had in reality gone through, and she acknowledged it by her clear deep glance at the old woman.

"At midnight, My Lord," Miss Malin went on, "the maiden got up to go to this dismal rendezvous. She took a candlestick in one hand, and a sharp hatchet in the other, like to Judith when she went to kill Holophernes. But what darkness, my friends, what darkness in the castle of Angelshorn, compared to that of the tent of Dothaim. The angels must have turned away and wept.

"She walked all through the house to a room in which she knew there was a long looking-glass on the wall. It was a room that was never used; nobody would come there. The lost girl swept down her clothes to her waist, and fixed her eyes on the glass, not allowing herself any thought, lest it should frighten her from her purpose.

"In that same midnight hour newly married young men, within nuptial chambers, were trembling, unveiling, fondling and kissing the bodies of their young brides. In the light of five hundred wax candles great ladies were turning the destinies of nations by lifting their shoulders in their low frocks. Even in the houses of ill fame of Naples, the old brown *madamas,* dragging their girls to the little candle on the bed-table, and pulling down their bodices, were bargaining with their customers for higher fees. Calypso, while lowering her eyes to the whiteness of her bosom within the dim mirror, for she had never seen herself naked in a mirror, was trying the edge of her ax upon her little finger.

"At that moment she saw in the looking-glass a big figure behind her own. It seemed to move, and she turned around. There was nobody there, but on the wall was an enormous old painting which had grown dark with age, but in which the lighter parts, illuminated by her candle, sprang out. It represented a scene out of the life of the nymphs, fauns, and satyrs, with the centaurs, playing in groves and on the flowery plains. It had been brought, many years ago, from Italy by one of the old lords of the house, but it had been thought a very indecent picture even before the time of the present Count, and had been removed from the living-rooms. It was not a well-painted picture, but there were a lot of figures in it. In the foreground three young naked nymphs, silvery as white roses, were holding up branches of trees.

"Calypso walked all along the huge picture, holding up her candle, and gazing gravely at it. That it was a scandalous picture she lacked knowledge to see; neither did she doubt that it was a true representation of beings actually existing. She looked with great interest at the satyrs and centaurs. In her lonely existence she had developed a passionate tenderness for animals. To the mind of Count August the existence of the brute creation was an enigma and a tragedy, and there were no animals at Angelshorn. But to the girl they seemed sweeter than human beings, and she was delighted to find that there were people who possessed so many of their characteristics. But what surprised and overwhelmed her was the fact that these strong and lovely beings were obviously concentrating their attention upon following, adoring, and embracing young girls of her own age, and of her own figure and face, that the whole thing was done in their honor and inspired by their charms.

"She looked at them for a very long time. In the end she returned to her mirror and stood there contemplating herself within it. She had the sense of art of her uncle himself, and knew by instinct what things harmonized together. Now a hitherto unexperienced feeling of a great harmony came upon her.

"She knew now that she had friends in the world. By right of her looks she might step into the mellow golden light, the blue sky and gray clouds, and the deep brown shadows of these plains and olive groves. Her heart swelled with gratitude and pride, for here they all looked at her and recognized her as their own. The god Dionysos himself, who was present, looked her, laughingly, straight into the eyes.

"She looked around the room and saw, in showcases, what she had never seen before at Angelshorn: woman's clothes, fans, jewels, and little shoes. All these had belonged to her great-grandmother. For, strange to say, the Count had had a grandmother. He had even had a mother, and there had been a time, when, *bon gré mal gré*, he had made a close acquaintance with the body of a fair young woman. He had a tenderness for his grandmother, who had birched him when he was a child. In the very center of his abbey he had left her boudoir untouched. A faint perfume of attar of roses still lived here.

"The girl spent the night in the room. She put on and took off one after the other of the court robes, the pearl strings, and diamonds. She looked from the glass to the painting for the applause of the centaurs—in what attire did they like her best? She could have no doubt about it. At last she left the room to go to the room of the castellan. Before she closed the door she gently kissed the nymphs, as high up as she could place her kiss, as if they had been her beloved friends.

"She walked up the stairs very gently, and went close to the great bed of her uncle. There he was, between the yellow silk hangings, his eyes shut, his nose in the air, white in a fine white nightshirt. The girl still had on a great yellow-brocade frock, and she stood by his bedside like Psyche beside the couch of Eros. Psyche had feared to see a monster, and had found the god of love. But Calypso had held her uncle to be a minister of truth, an arbiter of taste, an Apollo himself, and what did she find? A poor little doll stuffed with sawdust, a caricature of a skull. She blushed deeply. Had she been afraid of this creature—she, who was the sister of the nymphs and had centaurs for playmates? She was a hundred times as strong as he.

"Had he woke up then, and seen her by his bedside, still with her hatchet in her hand, he might have died from fear, or it might have done him good in some other way. But he slept on—God knows what his dreams were—and she did not cut off his head. She gave him instead a little swift epigram out of her French book, which had once been made about a king who also imagined himself much-beloved:

> *Ci-git Louis, ce pauvre roi.*
> *L'on dit qu'il fut bon—mais à quoi?*

And she did not bear him the slightest grudge; for she was not a freed slave, but a conqueror with a mighty train, who could afford to forget.

"She left the room as quietly as she had come, and blew out the candle, for in the summer night she could find her way without it. All around her the whole seraglio was silent; only as she passed a door she heard two of the young boys arguing upon divine love. They might all have been dead as far as she was concerned. As she lifted the heavy medieval lock of the front door she lifted their weight off her heart.

"When she came out it was raining. The night itself wanted to touch her.

"She walked over the moors, grave as Ceres herself with a thunderbolt borrowed from Jove in her hand, who, even as she knits her brows, smells of strawberries and honey. Around the horizon the corn-lightnings were playing in her honor. She let her frock trail over the heather. Why should she not? Had a young highwayman met her, she might have made him her husband then and there, until death had them parted; or she might have chopped off his head, and God knows which fate would have been more to be envied him.

"She had no gay ditty on her lips. She had been seriously brought up as a good Protestant, and life had taught her no frivolity. In her heart she repeated the hymn of good Paul Gerhardt, altering it as to the personal pronoun only:

> *Against me who can stand?*
> *The lightning's in my hand.*
> *Who dares to bring distress*
> *Where I decide to bless?*

"In the early morning she came to the house where I was staying. She was wet all through like a tree in the garden. She knew of me, for I am her godmother, and she felt that I had knowledge of, and might tell her more about, nymphs and centaurs. She found me getting into my carriage to go to the bath of Norderney. In this way fate drove us together, to be, in the end, like yourself, Mr. Timon, cured by salt water."

"And to shine above them," the Cardinal said, as gently as he had all the time been listening to the tale of the old woman, "a Stella Maris in the darkness of our loft."

"Madame, indeed," said Jonathan, "I do not know if you will think it strange, but I have never in my life, until you told me so now, thought that fair women could suffer. I held them to be precious flowers, which must be looked after carefully."

"And what do you feel now that I have told you so?" Miss Malin asked him.

"Madame," said the young man after having thought it over, "I feel how edifying is the thought that toward women we are always in the wrong."

"You are an honest young man," said Miss Malin. "Your side hurts you now, where your rib was once taken out of you."

"If I had been in the castle of Angelshorn," he went on, in high agitation, "I should not have minded dying to serve this lady."

"Come, Jonathan and Calypso," said Miss Malin, "it would be sinful and blasphemous were you two to die unmarried. You have been brought here from Angelshorn and Assens, into each other's arms. You are hers, and she is yours, and the Cardinal and I, who stand you in parents' stead, will give you our blessing." The two young people stared at each other. "If anybody will say," said Miss Malin, "that you are not her equal in birth, I shall answer him that you belong to the order of knighthood of the hayloft of Norderney, outside of which no member of it can marry." The girl, in great excitement, rose half up and stood on her knees. "Did you not see, Calypso," Miss Malin addressed herself kindly to her, "how he followed you here, and how, the moment he heard that you were staying here with me, nothing in the world could induce him to go with the boat? Many waters cannot quench love, neither can the floods drown it."

"Is that true?" asked the girl, turning her eyes upon the boy with such an intense and frantic look as if life and death for her depended upon his answer.

"Yes, that is true," said Jonathan. It was not in the least true. He had not even, at the time, been aware of the girl's existence. But the power of imagination of the old woman was enough to sway anybody off his feet. The girl's face, at his words, suddenly paled into a rare pearly white. Her eyes grew bigger and darker.

They shone at him like stars with a moisture deeper than tears, and at the sight of her changed face Jonathan sank upon his knees before her in the hay.

"Oh, Jonathan," said Miss Malin, "are you going to thank the Baron, upon your knees, that he took the trouble about you?"

"Yes, Madame," said the young man.

"And you, Calypso," she asked the girl, "do you want him to look at you forever and ever?"

"Yes," said the girl.

Miss Malin looked at them triumphantly. "Then, My Lord," she said to the Cardinal, "will you consent to marry these two people, who stand in great need of it?"

The Cardinal's eyes gravely sought their faces, which had now colored as strongly as if they had been in front of a high fire. "Yes," he said. "Lift me up." The bridegroom-to-be helped him to rise.

"You will," said Miss Malin, "have a Cardinal to marry you, and a Nat-og-Dag for a bridesmaid, which no one will have hereafter. Your marriage must be in every way a more intense affair than the lukewarm unions generally celebrated around us, for you must see her, listen to her, feel her, know her with the energy which you meant to use for jumping into the sea from Langebro. One kiss will make it out for the birth of twins, and at dawn you shall celebrate your golden wedding."

"My Lord," she said to the Cardinal, "the circumstances being so unusual—for we have no need of procreation, seeing that the boat can hold no more than we are, and we run but little risk of fornication, I feel; and as to the company of one another, we cannot escape it if we would—I think that you will have to make us out a new marriage rite."

"I am aware of that," said the Cardinal.

To make a clear space in the middle of the circle, Miss Malin lifted up the little lamp in her clawlike hand, and Calypso moved the bread and the keg away. The dog, at this rearrangement of the group, got up and walked around them uneasily. In the end it settled down close to the young bride.

"Kneel down, my children," said the old priest.

He stood up, his huge and heavy figure looming over them in the large, half-dark room. At this moment, as the wind had risen a little, they heard the sighing of the waters all around and beneath them.

"I cannot," said the Cardinal very slowly, "here tonight call upon the magnificence of the cathedral, or the presence of a congregation, to sanction this covenant. I have no time to teach or prepare you. You must, therefore, accept my profession to you solely on my authority. You two, I have seen," he went on after a pause, "have had your faith in the cohesion and justice of life shaken. Have faith in me now; I will help you. Have you a ring?"

The young people had no ring, and were much put out by the lack of it, but Miss Malin took off a very magnificent diamond, which she handed to the old man.

"Jonathan," said he, "place this ring on this girl's finger." The boy did so, and the Cardinal placed a hand on the head of each of the kneeling people. "Jonathan," said the Cardinal again, "do you now believe that you are married?"

"Yes," said Jonathan.

"And you, Calypso?" the Cardinal asked the girl.

"Yes," she whispered.

"And that you will," said the Cardinal, "from now, love and honor each other until the end of your lives, and even in death and eternity?"

"Yes," they said.

"Then," said the Cardinal, "you are married."

Miss Malin stood by, erect, holding the lamp like a sibyl.

The hours of rest in the hayloft had not strengthened the Cardinal, who was probably past all his strength. He was less steady in his movements than when he had come out of the boat.

His figure seemed to sway, strangely, in time to the sound of the water.

"As to the state of marriage," he said, "and the matter of love, I suppose that neither of you knows anything at all about these things?" The two young people shook their heads. "I cannot," said the Cardinal again, "here make the Scripture and the Fathers of the Church bear witness to my words to you. I cannot even, for I am very tired, call up the texts and examples wherewith to enlighten and instruct you. You will, again, accept my profession on my authority as a very old man who has been throughout a long and strange life a student of divine matters. These matters, I tell you, are divine. Do you, Jonathan, expect and hold them to be so?"

"Yes," said Jonathan.

"And you, Calypso?" he asked the bride.

"Yes," she said.

"Then that is all," said the Cardinal.

As he did not appear to be going to say any more, the married young people, after a moment, got up, but they were too strongly moved to be able to get away. Standing there, they looked at each other for the first time since they had been called out to be married, and this one look took away all self-consciousness from both of them. They went back to their places in the hay.

"As to you and me, Madame," said the Cardinal, speaking over their heads to Miss Malin, but apparently forgetting that he was no longer in the pulpit, for he went on talking as solemnly as he had done when performing the marriage ceremony, "who are only onlookers upon this occasion, and who know more about the matters of love and marriage, we will consider the lesson which they, above and before all other things, teach us about the tremendous courage of the Creator of this world. Every human being has, I believe, at times given room to the idea of creating a world himself. The Pope, in a flattering way, encouraged these thoughts in me when I was a young man. I reflected then that I might, had

I been given omnipotence and a free hand, have made a fine world. I might have bethought me of the trees and rivers, of the different keys in music, of friendship, and innocence; but upon my word and honor, I should not have dared to arrange these matters of love and marriage as they are, and my world should have lost sadly thereby. What an overwhelming lesson to all artists! Be not afraid of absurdity; do not shrink from the fantastic. Within a dilemma, choose the most unheard-of, the most dangerous, solution. Be brave, be brave! Ah, Madame, we have got much to learn."

Upon this, he fell into deep thought.

As they sat down, their former positions were not much changed, except that the newly married people now sat closer together, and held each other's hands. Sometimes they also turned their faces toward each other. The lantern stood on the floor in front of them. Miss Malin and the Cardinal, after their effort in marrying them, remained silent for about half an hour, and drank a few drops out of the keg of gin.

Miss Malin sat up straight, but by now she looked like a corpse of twenty-four hours. She was deeply moved and happy, as if she had really given away a daughter in marriage. Long shudders ran through her from head to feet. When she at last took up the conversation again, her voice was faint, but she smiled. She had probably been reflecting upon marriage and the Garden of Eden.

"Do you, My Lord," she asked, "believe in the fall of man?"

The Cardinal thought over her question for some time, then he bent forward, his elbows on his knees, and pushed back the bandage a little from his brow.

"This is a question," he said, in a voice slightly changed, thicker than before, but also with a great deal more energy in it, as if he had at the same time pushed back ten years of his age, "upon which I have thought much. It is pleasant that I shall get an opportunity for talking of it tonight.

"I am convinced," he declared, "that there has been a fall, but

I do not hold that it is man who has fallen. I believe that there has been a fall of the divinity. We are now serving an inferior dynasty of heaven."

Miss Malin had been prepared for an ingenious argument, but at this speech she was shocked, and for a moment held her little hands to her ears. "These are terrible words to the ear of a Legitimist," she cried.

"What are they, then," asked the Cardinal solemnly, "to the lips of a Legitimist? I have detained them for seventy years. But you asked me, Madame, and, if the truth must out, this is a good place and night for it. At some time there has taken place, in heaven, a tremendous overturning, equal to the French Revolution upon earth, and its after-effects. The world of today is, like the France of today, in the hands of a Louis Philippe."

"There are traditions still," he went on, "from *le Grand Monarque* and *le Grand Siècle*. But no human being with a feeling for greatness can possibly believe that the God who created the stars, the sea, and the desert, the poet Homer and the giraffe, is the same God who is now making, and upholding, the King of Belgium, the Poetical School of Schwaben, and the moral ideas of our day. We two may at last speak about it. We are serving Louis Philippe, a human God, much as the King of France is a bourgeois King."

Miss Malin stared at him, pale, her mouth a little open.

"Madame," he said, "we who are by birth the grandees of the King, and hereditary office-holders of his court, and who have the code of *le Grand Monarque* in our veins, have a duty toward the legitimate king, whatever we think of him. We must keep up his glory. For the people must not doubt the greatness of the king, or suspect any weakness of his, and the responsibility for keeping up their faith rests upon you and me, Madame. The barber of the court was not capable of keeping his own counsel; he had to whisper to the reeds of the king's asses' ears. But we—are we barbers? No, Madame, we are no barbers."

"Have we not done our best?" asked Miss Malin proudly.

"Yes," said the Cardinal, "we have done our best. When you look around, Madame, you see everywhere the achievements of the faithful, who have worked, nameless, for the king's honor. I could name you many examples out of history, of which I have thought. I shall give you a few only. God made the shell, which is a pretty object, but not more than what even Louis Philippe might have hit upon when he was playing with a pair of dividers. Out of the shell we made all the art of the rococo, which is a charming jest, in the true spirit of the *Grand Monarque*. And if you read the history of great people, you will find that the lords and ladies of the bedchamber have been at work, serving our master of blessed memory. The Pope Alexander and his children, according to the latest historical researches, were a group of pleasant people, given to gardening and house decoration, and full of family affection, *et voilà tout*—obviously the handwork of Louis Philippe. But out of that indifferent material we have made our figures of the Borgias. You will find very nearly the same thing if you go into the facts about the great reputations of history. Or even, Madame, if you do not mind," the old man went on, "death: What is it, nowadays, at the hand of Louis Philippe? A negation, a decay, not even in the best of taste. But look at what we have made of it, faithful to our gone Lord: the Imperial Mausoleum of Escurial, Madame, the 'Funeral March' of Herr Ludwig von Beethoven. How could we ever have made those— poor human beings as we are, and, moreover, ourselves bound to be part in this meager affair—if we had not in our hearts the unquenchable love for our departed Lord, the great adventurer, to whom our family did first swear its oath of allegiance."

"But with all that," he went on, very gravely, "the end is nearing. I hear the cocks crow. King Louis Philippe cannot last. In his cause the blood of Roland himself would be shed in vain. He has all the qualities of a good bourgeois, and none of the vices of a *Grand Seigneur*. He claims no rank except that of the first citizen of his kingdom, and no privileges except on account of his loyalty to the bourgeois code of morals. When it comes to that, the days of royalty are counted. I will pronounce a prophecy, Madame: that good King of France will not last another thirteen years. And the good God, whom Louis Philippe and his bourgeoisie worship today, he has all the virtues of a righteous human being; he claims no divine privileges except by virtue of his virtues. We, we no more expected a moral attitude in our God than we meant to hold our great King responsible to the penal law. The humane God must share the fate of the bourgeois King. I was myself brought up by humane people to have faith in a humane God. It was to the highest extent intolerable to me. Ah, Madame, what a revelation, what a bliss to my heart, when, in the nights of Mexico, I felt the great traditions rise up again of a God who did not give a pin for our commandments. In this manner, Madame, we are dying for a lost cause."

"To get our reward in paradise," said Miss Malin.

"Oh, no, Madame," said the old man, "we shall not get into paradise, you or I. Look at the people whom the King Louis Philippe today decorates, elevates to peer's rank and places in the great offices. They are safely bourgeois, all of them; no name of the old aristocracy appears in the list. Neither you nor I succeed in pleasing the Lord nowadays; we even irritate him a little, and he is not beyond showing it in his behavior toward us. The old nobility, whose manner and very names bring back the traditions of the Great Monarch, must needs be a little trying to King Louis Philippe."

"So we have no hope of heaven, you or I?" asked Miss Malin proudly.

"I wonder if you would be keen to get in there," said the old Cardinal, "if you were first allowed a peep into the place. It must be the rendezvous of the bourgeoisie. Madame, to my mind there never was a great artist who was not a bit of a charlatan;

nor a great king, nor a god. The quality of charlatanry is indispensable in a court, or a theater, or in paradise. Thunder and lightning, the new moon, a nightingale, a young girl—all these are bits of charlatanry, of a divine swank. So is the *gallérie de glaces* at Versailles. But King Louis Philippe has no drop of blood of the charlatan in him; he is genuinely reliable all through. Paradise, these days, is very likely the same. You and I, Madame, were not brought up to a reasonable content. We shall cut a finer figure in hell. We were trained for it.

"It is a satisfaction, Madame, to do a thing that one has learned well. It must be a satisfaction to you, I am sure, to dance the minuet. Let us take an example. Let us say that I have been trained from a child to do something. For argument's sake, let us say to do rope-dancing. I have been taught it, beaten to learn it. If I fall down and break my bones, I still have to get up again on my rope. My mother has wept over me, and has still encouraged me. She has had to go without bread to pay the vaulter who teaches me. And I have become a good rope-dancer, say the best rope-dancer in the world. It is a fine thing, then, to be a rope-dancer. And I shall be amply rewarded when, upon some great occasion, at the entertainment of a great foreign monarch, my King says to his royal guest: 'You must really see this, Sire and my Brother; this is my finest show, my servant Hamilcar, the rope-dancer!' But what if he should say, Madame, 'There is not much sense in rope-dancing. It is a rough performance; I am going to stop it'? What sort of performance, on the part of the King, should that be to me?

"Have you been to Spain, Madame?" he asked the old lady.

"Oh, yes," said Miss Malin, "a beautiful country, My Lord. I had serenades sung under my window, and my portrait painted by Monsieur Goya himself."

"Have you seen a bullfight there?" the Cardinal asked.

"Yes," said Miss Malin. "It is a very picturesque thing, though not to my taste."

"It is a picturesque thing," said the Cardinal. "And what do you imagine, Madame, that the bull thinks of it? The plebeian bull may well think: 'God have mercy on me, what terrible conditions here. What disasters, what a run of bad luck. But it must be endured.' And he would be deeply thankful, moved even to humble tears, were the King, in the midst of the bullfight, to send directions to have it stopped, out of compassion for him. But the purebred fighting bull falls in with it, and says: 'Lo, this is a bullfight.' He will have his blood up straight away, and he will fight and die, because otherwise there would be no bullfight out of the thing at all. He will also be known for many years as that black bull which put up such a fine fight, and killed the matador. But if, in the middle of it, when this bull's blood had already flowed, the King chose to stop it, what would the true fighting bull think of it? He might go for the audience, even for the master of ceremonies then. He would roar at them: 'You should have thought of this before!' Madame, the King should have his show. He has bred and reared me for it, and I am ready to fight and die before the Great Monarch, when he comes in state to see me. But I am hanged," he said after a moment, with great energy, "if I care to perform before Louis Philippe."

"Ah, but wait," said Miss Malin. "I have thought of something else. Perhaps you are mistaken in your ideas of the sense of humor of King Louis Philippe. He may have a quite different taste from yours and mine, and may like a world turned upside down, like that Empress of Russia who, to amuse herself, made her old Councilors, the tears running down their faces, dance in a ballet before her, and her ballet-dancers sit in council. That, My Lord, might well be his idea of a joke. I will tell you a little story to make myself clear, and it fits in well, since we have been talking of rope-dancing.

"When I was in Vienna twenty years ago," she began, "a pretty boy with big blue eyes made a great stir there by dancing on a rope blindfolded. He danced with wonderful grace and skill, and the blindfolding was genuine, the cloth being tied around his eyes by a person out of the audience. His performance was the great sensation of the season, and he was sent for to dance before the Emperor and Empress, the archdukes and archduchesses, and the court. The great oculist, Professor Heimholz, was present. He had been sent for by the Emperor, since everybody was discussing the problem of clairvoyance. But at the end of the show he rose up and called out: 'Your Majesty,' he said, in great agitation, 'and your Imperial Highnesses, this is all humbug, and a cheat.'

" 'It cannot be humbug,' said the court oculist, 'I have myself tied the cloth around the boy's eyes most conscientiously.'

" 'It is all humbug and a cheat,' the great professor indignantly insisted. 'That child was born blind.' "

Miss Malin made a little pause. "What," she said, "if your Louis Philippe shall say, on seeing us cutting such fine figures in hell: This is all humbug. These people have been in hell from their birth." She laughed a little.

"Madame," said the Cardinal after a silence, "you have a great power of imagination, and a fine courage."

"Oh, I am a Nat-og-Dag," said Miss Malin modestly.

"But are you not," said the Cardinal, "a little——"

"Mad?" asked the old lady. "I thought that you were aware of that, My Lord."

"No," said he, "that was not what I meant to say. But a little hard on the King of France. I may perhaps be in a position to understand him better than you. Bourgeois he is, but not canaille.

"I shall also tell you a story," went on the old man, "seeing that I have not yet contributed to the night's entertainment. I shall tell it just to illustrate that there are—with your permission, Madame—worse things than perdition, and I shall call it—" he reflected a moment—"I shall call it 'The Wine of the Tetrarch'."

"As, then, upon the first Wednesday after Easter," the Cardinal began, "the Apostle Simon, called Peter, was walking down the streets of Jerusalem, so deeply absorbed in the thought of the resurrection that he did not know whether he was walking upon the pavement or was being carried along in the air, he noticed, in passing the Temple, that a man was standing by a pillar waiting for him. As their eyes met, the stranger stepped forward and addressed him. 'Wast thou not also,' he asked, 'with Jesus of Nazareth?'

" 'Yes, yes, yes,' Peter replied quickly.

" 'Then I should much like to have speech with you,' said the man. 'I do not know what to do. Will you come inside the inn close hereby, and have a drink with me?' Peter, because he could not disengage himself from his thoughts sufficiently to find an excuse, accepted, and soon the two were seated together inside the inn.

"The stranger seemed to be well known there. He at once obtained a table to himself at the end of the room and out of earshot of the other guests who from time to time entered the inn and went out again, and he also ordered the best wine for himself and the Apostle. Peter now looked at the man, and found him an impressive figure. He was a swarthy, strongly built, proud young man. He was badly dressed and had on a much-patched goatskin cloak, but with it he wore a fine crimson silk scarf, and he had a gold chain around his neck, and upon his hands many heavy gold rings, one of which had a large emerald in it. It now seemed to Peter that he had seen the man before, in the midst of terrible fear and turbulence; still, he did not remember where.

" 'If you are indeed one of the followers of the Nazarene,' he said, 'I want to ask you two questions. I will tell you my reasons, too, for asking them, as we go on.'

" 'I shall be glad if I can help you in any way,' said Peter, still absent-minded.

" 'Well,' said the man, 'first: Is it true, what they tell of this Rabbi whom you served, that he has risen from the dead?'

" 'Yes, it is true,' said Peter, even feeling his own heart to swell at his proclamation.

" 'Nay, I heard rumors about it,' said the man, 'but I did not know for sure. And is it true that he told you himself, before he was crucified, that he would rise?'

" 'Yes,' said the Apostle, 'he told us. We knew that it would happen.'

" 'Do you think, then,' the stranger asked, 'that every word which he has spoken is certain to come true?'

" 'Nothing in the world is as sure as that,' Peter answered. The man sat silent for a while.

" 'I will tell you why I ask you this,' he suddenly said. 'It is because a friend of mine was crucified with him on Friday at the place of a skull. You saw him there, I think. To him this Rabbi of yours promised that he should be with him in paradise on the very same day. Do you then believe that he did go to paradise on Friday?'

" 'Yes, he is sure to have gone there and he is there now,' said Peter. The man again was silent.

" 'Well, that is good,' he said. 'He was my friend.'

"Here a young boy of the inn brought the wine which the man had ordered. The man poured some of it out into their glasses, looked at it, and put it down again. 'And this,' he said, 'is the other thing that I wanted to speak with you about. I have tried many wines within the last few days, and they all tasted bad to me. I do not know what has happened to the wine of Jerusalem. It has neither flavor nor body any longer. I think it may be due to the earthquake which we had on Friday afternoon; it has turned it all bad.'

" 'I do not think that this wine is bad,' said Peter, to encourage the stranger, for he looked sad as death.

" 'Is it not?' the man said hopefully, and drank a little of it. 'Yes, this also is bad,' he said, as he put down his glass. 'If you call it good, perhaps you have not much knowledge of wine? I have, and good wine is my great pleasure. Now I do not know what to do.

"'Now about that friend of mine, Phares,' he took up the thread of the conversation, 'I will tell you all about how he was taken prisoner, and put to death. He was a robber on the road between Jericho and Jerusalem. On that road there came along a transport of wine which the Emperor of Rome sent as a present to the tetrarch Herodes, and amongst it was a hogshead of red Capri wine, which was beyond price. One evening, in this same place where we are now, I was talking to Phares. I said to him: "I would give my heart to drink that red wine of the tetrarch's." He said: "For the sake of my love of you, and to show you that I am not a much lesser man than you, I will kill the overseer of this transport and have the hogshead of red wine buried under such and such a cedar on the mountain, and you and I will drink the wine of the tetrarch together." He did indeed do all this, but as he came into Jerusalem to find me, he was recognized by one of the people of the transport, who had escaped, and thrown into prison, and condemned to be crucified.

"'I was told of it, and I walked about in Jerusalem in the night, thinking of a means to help him escape. In the morning, on passing the steps of the Temple, I saw there an old beggar, whom I had seen many times before, who had a bad leg, all bandaged up, and was also mad. In his madness he would scream out, and prophesy, complaining of his fate and cursing the governors of the town, proclaiming many bad things against the tetrarch and his wife. As he was mad, people only used to laugh at him. But this morning it happened that a centurion was passing with his men, and when he heard what the beggar said of the tetrarch's wife he was angry. He told the beggar that if he did this again he would make him sleep in the prison of Jerusalem, and he would have him dealt twenty-five strokes of a stick in the evening, and twenty-five in the morning, to teach him to speak reverently about high people.

"'I listened, and thought: this is the opportunity for me. So in the course of the day I had my beard and hair shaved off, I dyed my face in nut oil, and dressed myself in rags, and I also bandaged up my right leg, but in those bandages I had hidden a strong, sharp file and a long rope. In the evening, when I went to the steps of the Temple, the old beggar had been so frightened that he had not come, so I took his place there myself. Just as the watch was passing, I cried out loudly, in the voice of the mad beggar, the worst curses I could think of against Cæsar in Rome himself, and, as I had thought, the watch took hold of me and brought me to the prison, and no one could recognize me in my rags. I was given, there, twenty-five strokes, and I took note of the face of the man who beat me, for the sake of the future; but with a piece of silver I bribed the turnkey to shut me up for the night in the prison where Phares was kept, which was very high up in the prison, the which, as you know, is built into the rock.

" 'Phares fell down and kissed my feet, and he gave me some water that he had, but later we set to work to file through the iron bar of the window. It was high up, and he had to stand upon my shoulders, or I upon his, but by early morning we broke it, and then tied the rope onto the broken bar. Phares lowered himself down first, until he came to the end of the rope, which was not quite long enough, and then he let himself fall. Then I got out, but I was weak, and too slow at it, and it happened that just at that hour a batch of soldiers came to the place with a prisoner. They had torches with them, and one of them caught sight of me as I was hanging onto the rope on the wall. Now Phares could have got away, if he had run, but he would not go before he had seen what would happen to me, and in this way we were both taken once more, and they saw who I was.

" 'That is how it happened,' said the stranger. 'But then you tell me that Phares is now in paradise.'

" 'All this,' said Peter, who had, though, been listening only with half an ear, 'I hold to be very brave of you, and it was well done to risk your life for your friend.' At that he sighed deeply.

'Oh, I have lived too long in the woods to be frightened of an owl,' said the stranger. 'Has anybody told you of me that I was the sort that runs away from danger?'

" 'No,' said Peter. 'But then you tell me,' he said after a moment, 'that you, too, were made prisoner. Still, since you are here, you got off somehow?'

" 'Yes; I got off,' said the man, and gave Peter a strange deep glance. 'I meant, then, to revenge Phares's death. But since he is in paradise I do not see that I need to worry. And now I do not know what to do. Shall I dig up this hogshead of the tetrarch's wine and drink it?'

" 'It will be sad to you without your friend,' said Peter, and his eyes filled with such tears as were still left in him after this last week. He thought that he ought perhaps to reproach the man with the theft of the tetrarch's wine, but too many recollections welled up in his own heart.

" 'No, it is not that of which I am thinking,' said the stranger, 'but if that wine also has gone bad and gives me no pleasure, what am I to do then?'

"Peter sat for a little while in his own thoughts. 'Friend,' he said, 'there are other things in life to give you pleasure than the wine of the tetrarch.'

" 'Yes, I know,' said the stranger, 'but what if the same thing has happened to them? I have two lovely wives waiting for me at home, and just before this happened I purchased a virgin of twelve years. I have not seen her since. I could try them, if I chose. But the earthquake may have affected them as well, so that they may have neither flavor nor body, and what shall I do then?'

"Now Peter began to wish that this man would stop his complaints and leave him to himself. 'Why,' he asked, 'do you come to me about this?'

" 'You remind me,' said the stranger. 'I will tell you. I have been informed that your Rabbi, on the night before he died, gave a party to his followers, and that at that time a special wine was served, which was very rare and had some highly precious body in it. Have you, now, any more of this wine, and will you consent to sell it to me? I will give you your price.'

"Peter stared at the stranger. 'Oh, God, oh, God,' he cried, so highly affected that he upset his wine, which ran onto the floor, 'you do not know what you are saying. This wine which we drank on Thursday night, the Emperor of Rome cannot pay for one drop of it.' His heart was so terribly wrung that he rocked to and fro in his seat. Still, in the midst of his grief the words of the Lord, that he was to be a fisher of men, were brought back to him, and he reflected that it might be his duty to help this man, who seemed in some deep distress. He turned to him again, but as he was looking at him it came over him that of all people in the world, this young man was the one whom he could not help. To strengthen himself he called up one of the words of the Lord himself.

"'My son,' he said kindly and gravely, 'take up thine cross and follow him.' The stranger, just at the same moment as the Apostle, had been about to speak. Now he stopped and looked very darkly at Peter. 'My cross!' he cried. 'Where is my cross? Who is to take up my cross?'

"'No one but yourself can take up your cross,' said Peter, 'but He will help you to carry it. Have patience and strength. I will tell you much more about all this.'

"'What have you to tell me about it?' said the stranger. 'It seems to me that you know nothing of it. Help? Who is it who wants help to carry the sort of cross which the carpenters of Jerusalem make in these days? Not I, you may be sure. That bow-legged Cyrenean would never have had the opportunity to exhibit his strength on my behalf. You talk of strength and patience,' he went on after a moment, still highly agitated, 'but I have never known a man as strong as myself. Look,' he said, and pulling back his cloak he showed Peter his chest and shoulders, crossed by many terrible deep white scars. 'My cross! The cross of Phares was to the right, and the cross of the man Achaz, who was never worth much, to the left. I should have taken up my cross better than any of them. Do you not think that I should have lasted more than six hours? I do not think much of that, I tell you. Wherever I have been, I have been a leader of men, and they have looked to me. Do not believe, because now I do not know what to do, that I have not been used to telling others to come and go as I liked.'

"At the disdainful tone of this speech Peter was about to lose his patience with the stranger, but he had promised himself, since he cut off Malchus's ear, to control his temper, so he said nothing.

"After a while the man looked at him, as if impressed by his silence. 'And you,' he said, 'who are a follower of this Prophet, what do you think is likely to happen to yourself now?' Peter's face, marred by sorrow, cleared and softened. His whole countenance radiated hope. 'I trust and believe,' he said, 'that my faith, though it be tried with fire, be found unto praise and honor. I hope that it may be granted to me to suffer and die for my Lord. Sometimes, even, in these last nights,' he went on, speaking in a low voice, 'I have thought that at the end of the road a cross might await me.' Having spoken thus he dared not look up to meet the other's eyes. He added quickly, 'Although you may think that I am boasting, and that I am too low for that.'

" 'No,' said the stranger, 'I think it very likely that all this of which you have spoken will indeed happen to you.'

"This confidence in his own hopes struck Peter as a most unexpected and generous piece of friendliness in the stranger. His heat melted with gratitude. He blushed like a young bride. For the first time he felt a real interest in his companion, and it seemed to him that he ought to do something for him in return for the lovely things that he had said to him. 'I am sorry,' he said gently, 'that I have not been able to help you in what weighs upon your soul. But indeed I am hardly in command of myself, so much has happened to me in these last days.'

"'Oh,' said the stranger, 'I hardly expected anything better.'

"'In the course of our talk,' Peter said, 'you said a couple of times that you did not know what to do. Tell me in what matter it is that you are in such doubts. Even about this wine, of which you speak, I will try to advise you.' The stranger looked at him. 'I have not been talking of any particular matter,' he said. 'I do not know what to do at all. I do not know where such wine is found that will gladden my heart again. But I suppose,' he went on, after a little while, 'that I had better go and dig up that wine of the tetrarch's, and sleep with this girl that I told you of. I may as well try.'

"With these words he got up from the table and draped his cloak around him.

"'Do not go yet,' Peter said. 'It seems to me that there are many things of which we ought to talk together.'

"'I have to go in any case,' said the man. 'There is a transport of oil on its way from Hebron, which I must meet.'

"'Are you trading in oil, then?' Peter asked. 'In a way,' said the man.

"'But tell me, before you go,' said Peter, 'what is your name? For we might speak again together, some time, if I knew where to find you?' The stranger was already standing in the door. He turned around and looked at Peter with hauteur and a slight scorn. He looked a magnificent figure. 'Did you not know my name?' he asked him. 'My name was cried all over the town. There was not one of the tame burghers of Jerusalem who did not shout it with all his might. "Barabbas," they cried, "Barabbas! Barabbas! Give us Barabbas." My name is Barabbas. I have been a great chief, and, as you said yourself, a brave man. My name shall be remembered.'

"And with these words he walked away."

As the Cardinal had finished his tale, Jonathan got up and changed the tallow candle in the lantern, for it had burned quite down, and was now flickering wildly up and down in its last convulsions.

He had no sooner done this than the girl at his side became deadly pale. Her eyes closed, and her whole figure seemed to sink together. Miss Malin asked her kindly if she felt sleepy, but she denied it with great energy, and might well do so. She had lived during this night as she had never lived before. She had faced death and had thrown herself nobly into the jaws of danger for the sake of her fellow-creatures. She had been the center of a brilliant circle, and she had even been married. She did not want to miss a single moment of these pregnant hours. But during the next ten minutes she fell asleep time after time in spite of her efforts to keep awake, her young head rocking forward and back.

She at last consented to lie down to rest for a moment, and her husband arranged a couch for her in the hay, and took off his coat to spread over her. Still holding his hand she sank down, and looked, on the dark ground, like a lovely marble figure of the angel of death. The dog, which had stayed near her for the last hour, at once followed her, and, curling itself up, pressed close to her, its head on her knees.

Her young husband sat for some time watching her sleep, but after a little while he could no longer keep awake himself, and lay down at a little distance from her, but close enough so that he could still hold her hand. For a while he did not sleep, but looked sometimes at her, and sometimes at the erect figures of Miss Malin and the Cardinal. When he did at last fall asleep, in his sleep he made a sudden movement, thrusting himself forward, so that his head nearly touched the head of the girl, and their hair, upon the pillow of the hay, was mingled together. A moment later he sank into the same slumber as had his wife.

The two old people sat silent before the light of the new candle, which, to begin with, burned only feebly. Miss Malin, who now looked as if she were not going to sleep for all eternity, regarded the sleepers with the benevolence of a successful creator. The

Cardinal looked at her for a moment and then he evaded her eyes. After a while he began to undo the bandages around his head, and in doing so he kept his eyes fixed upon the face of the old lady in a strange stare.

"I had better get rid of these," he said, "now that morning is almost here."

"But will it not hurt you?" Miss Malin asked anxiously.

"No," he said, and went on with his occupation. After a moment he added: "It is not even my blood. You, Miss Nat-og-Dag, who have such an eye for the true noble blood, you ought to recognize the blue blood of Cardinal Hamilcar."

Miss Malin did not move, but her white face changed a little.

"The blood of Cardinal Hamilcar?" she asked in a slightly less steady voice. "Yes," he said, "the blood of that noble old man. On my head. And on my hands as well. For I struck him on the head with a beam which had fallen down, before the boat arrived to rescue us early this morning."

For quite two or three minutes there was a deep silence in the hayloft. Only the dog stirred, whining a little in its sleep as it poked its head further into the clothes of the young girl. The bandaged man and the old woman did not let go the hold of each other's eyes. He slowly finished taking off the long, red-stained linen strips, and laid them down. Freed of these, he had a broad, red, puffed face, and dark hair.

"God rest the soul of that noble man," said Miss Malin at last. "And who are you?"

The man's face changed a little at her words. "Is that what you ask me?" he said. "Is it of me that you are thinking, and not of him?"

"Oh, we need not think of him, you and I," she said. "Who are you?"

"My name," said the man, "is Kasparson. I am the Cardinal's valet."

"You must tell me more," said Miss Malin with firmness. "I still want to know with whom I have passed the night."

"I will tell you much more, if it amuses you," Kaparson said, "for I have been to many continents, and I myself like to dwell in the past.

"I am an actor, Madame, as you are a Nat-og Dag; that is, we remain so whatever else we take on, and fall back upon this one thing when the others fail us.

"But when I was a child I danced in ballet, and when I was thirteen years old I was taken up—because of being so extraordinarily graceful, and particularly because I had to an unusual extent what in the technique of the ballet is termed *ballon,* which means the capacity for soaring, for rising above the ground and the laws of gravitation—by the great elderly noblemen of Berlin. My stepfather, the famous tenor, Herr Eunicke, introduced me to them, and believed that I was to be a gold mine to him. For five years I have known what it is to be a lovely woman, fed upon dainties, dressed in silks and a golden turban, whose caprices are law to everyone. But Herr Eunicke, like all tenors, forgot to reckon with the laws of passing time. Age stole upon us before we dreamed of it, and my career as a courtesan was a short one.

"Then I went to Spain, and became a barber. I was a barber in Seville for seven years, and I liked that, for I have always had a partiality toward soap and toilet waters, and have liked all sorts of clean and neat things. For this reason it often surprised me in the Cardinal that he did not object to dirtying his hands with his black and red inks. I became, Madame, a very good barber indeed.

"But I have also been a printer of revolutionary papers in Paris, a dog-seller in London, a slavetrader in Algiers, and the lover of a dowager principezza of Pisa. Through her I came to travel with Professor Rosellini, and the great French orientalist Champollion, upon their Egyptian expedition. I have been to Egypt, Madame. I have stood in the great triangular shadow of the great pyramid, and from the top of it four thousand years gazed down upon me."

Miss Malin, outshone as a world traveler by the valet, quickly took refuge in the wide world of her imagination. "Ah," she said, "in Egypt, in the great triangular shadow of the great pyramid, while the ass was grazing, St. Joseph said to the Virgin: 'Oh, my sweet young dear, could you not just for a moment shut your eyes and make believe that I am the Holy Ghost?'"

Kasparson went on with his account. "I have even lived in Copenhagen," he said, "but toward the end I had but a poor time of it. I became a hostler in the night-lodgings of the fat old man called Bolle Bandeat—which means, with your permission, the cursed, or damned—where, for the fee of a penny, you could sleep on the floor, and for a halfpenny standing up, with a rope under your arms. When at last I had to flee from the hands of the law there, I changed my name to that of Kasparson, in remembrance of that proud and unfortunate boy of Nürnberg who stabbed himself to death in order to make Lord Stanhope believe that he was the illegitimate son of Grand Duchess Stephanie of Baden.

"But if it be about my family that you want to hear, I have the honor to inform you that I am a bastard of the purest bastard blood extant. My mother was a true daughter of the people, an honest artisan's child, that lovely actress Johanna Handel-Schutz, who made all the classic ideals live upon the stage. She had a melancholy disposition nevertheless. Of my sixteen brothers and sisters, five have committed suicide. But if I tell you who was my father, that will be sure to interest you. When Johanna came to Paris, sixteen years old, to study art, she found favor in the eyes of a great lord.

"I am the son of that Duke of Orléans—who shortly after took up with the people in still another way—who insisted on being addressed as a *citoyen,* voted for the death of the King of France, and changed his name to that of Égalité. The bastard of Égalité! Can one be more bastard than that, Madame?"

"No," said the old woman, with white and stiff lips, unable to give a word of comfort to the pale man before her.

"That poor King Louis Philippe," said Kasparson, "for whom I feel sorry, and about whom I regret having spoken so harshly to-night—he is my little brother."

Miss Malin, even face to face with the greatest misfortunes, was never speechless for long. She said after a silence:

"Tell me now, for we may not have much time, first, why did you murder the Cardinal? And secondly, why did you take the trouble to deceive me, after you came here with me, and to make a fool of me on what may be the last night of my life? You were in no danger here. Did you think that I had not sufficient spirit myself, or sympathy with the dark places of the heart, to understand you?"

"Ah," said Kasparson, "why did I not tell you? That moment, in which I killed the Cardinal, that was the mating of my soul with destiny, with eternity, with the soul of God. Do we not still impose silence at the threshold of the nuptial chamber? Or even, does the Emperor demand publicity, may not Pythagoras have a taste for decorum?

"And why did I kill my master?" he went on. "Madame, there was little hope that both of us could be saved, and he would have sacrificed his life for mine. Should I have lived on as the servant for whom the lord had died, or should I have been simply drowned and lost, a sad adventurer?

"I told you: I am an actor. Shall not an actor have a rôle? If all the time the manager of the theater holds back the good rôles from us, may we not insist upon understudying the stars? The proof of our undertaking is in the success or fiasco. I have played the part well. The Cardinal would have applauded me, for he was a fine connoisseur of the art. Sir Walter Scott, Madame, took much pleasure in Wilibald Alexis's novel, *Walladmor,* which he published in his name, and which he called the most delightful mystery of the century. The Cardinal would have recognized himself in me. Quoting the great tragedy, *Axel and Walborg,* he said, slowly:

> *"My honored Lord, St. Olaf comes in person,*
> *He puts me on, he drapes himself in me.*
> *I am his ghost, the larva of his spirit;*
> *The transient shell of an immortal mind. . . .*

"The only thing," he went on after a pause, "which he might have criticized is this: he might have held that I overdid my rôle. I stayed in this hayloft to save the lives of those sottish peasants, who preferred the salvation of their cattle to their own. It is doubtful whether the Cardinal would ever have done that, for he was a man of excellent sense. That may be so. But a little charlatanry there must needs be in all great art, and the Cardinal himself was not free from it.

"But in any case," he concluded, lifting his voice and his body, "at the day of judgment God shall not say to me now: 'Kasparson, you bad actor! How was it that you could not, not even with death in your own heart, play me the dying Gaul?'"

Again Miss Malin sat for a long time in the deep silence of the huge dark room.

"And why," she said at last, "did you want this rôle so much?"

"I will confide in you," said Kasparson, speaking slowly. "Not by the face shall the man be known, but by the mask. I said so at the beginning of the night.

"I am a bastard. I have upon me the bastard's curse, of which you know not. The blood of Égalité is an arrogant blood, full of vanity—difficult, difficult for you, when you have it in your veins. It claimed splendor, Madame; it will stand no equivalence; it makes you suffer greatly at the least slight.

"But these peasants and fishermen are my mother's people. Do you not think that I have wept blood over the hardness of their lives and their pale children? At the thought of their hard crusts and thin-worn breadknives, their patched clothes and patient faces, my heart is wrung. Nothing in the world have I ever loved, except them. If they would have made me their master I would have served them all my life. If they would only have fallen down and worshiped me, I would have died for them. But they would not. That they reserved for the Cardinal. Only tonight have they come around. They have seen the face of God in my face. They will tell you, after tonight, that there was a white light over the boat in which I went out with them. Yes, even so, Madame.

"Do you know," he said, "do you know why I look to, why I cleave to, God? Why I cannot do without him? Because he is the only being toward whom I need not, I cannot, I must not, feel pity. Looking at all the other creatures of this life I am tortured, I am devoured by pity, and I am bent and crushed under the weight of their sorrows. I was sorry for the Cardinal, very sorry for that old man who had to be great and good, and who wrote a book on the Holy Ghost like a little spider hanging in the great space. But in the relation of God and me, if there is any pitying to be done, it is for him to do it. He will be sorry for me.

"Why, Madame, so it should have been with our kings. But, God help me, I feel sorry for my brother the King of France. My heart aches a little for the little man.

"Only God I shall keep, to have no mercy upon him. Let me, at least, keep God, you tender-hearted humans."

"But in that case," said Miss Malin suddenly, "it cannot possibly mean much to you whether we are saved or not. Forgive me for saying so, Kasparson, but it will not make much difference to your fate if this house holds on until the boat comes back for us, or not."

Kasparson, at these words, laughed a little, softly and congenially. It was clear by now that he was under the influence of the peasants' keg of gin, but in this matter Miss Malin was not far behind him.

"You are right, Miss Nat-og-Dag," he said, "your sharp wits have hit the nail on the head. And so much for my fine courage. But have patience just a little longer, and I will explain the case to you.

"Few people, I said, could say of themselves that they were free of the belief that they could have made the world. Nay, go further, Madame: few people can say of themselves that they are free of the belief that this world which they see around them is in reality the work of their own imagination. Are we pleased with it, proud of it, then? Yes, at times. In the evenings, in early spring, in the company of children and of beautiful, witty women, I have been pleased with and proud of my creation. At other times, when I have been with ordinary people, I have had a very bad conscience over my producing of such vulgar, insipid, dull stuff. I may have tried to do away with them, as the monk, in his cell, tries to drive out the degrading pictures which disturb his peace of mind and his pride in being a servant of the Lord. Now, Madame, I am pleased to have made this night here. I am genuinely proud of having made you, I assure you. But what about this one figure within the picture, this man Kasparson? Is he a success? Is he worth keeping? May he not be pronounced a blot in the picture? The monk may go to the extent of flagellating himself to drive out the image which offends him. My five brothers and sisters, who, of my mother's sixteen children, have committed suicide, may have felt in this way, for, as I have already said, my mother had a deep feeling and instinct for the classics, for the harmonious cosmos. They may have said: 'This work is in itself rather brilliant. My only failure is this one figure within it, which I will now have removed, even at a cost."

"Well," said Miss Malin after a pause, "and did you enjoy playing the rôle of the Cardinal when you had your chance at last? Did you have a pleasant time?"

"As God liveth, Madame, I had that," said Kasparson, "a good night and day. For I have lived long enough, by now, to have learned, when the devil grins at me, to grin back. And what now if this—to grin back when the devil grins at you—be in reality the

highest, the only true fun in all the world? And what if everything else, which people have named fun, be only a presentiment,
a foreshadowing, of it? It is an art worth learning, then."

"And I too, I too," said Miss Malin in a voice which, although
it was subdued, was rich and shrill, and which seemed to rise in
the flight of a lark. As if she wanted to accompany in person the
soaring course of it, she rose straight up, with the lightness and
dignity of a lady who has had, by now, enough of a pleasant
entertainment, and is taking her leave. "I have grinned back at
him too. It is an art worth learning."

The actor had risen with her, her *cavalière servante,* and now
stood up. She looked at him with radiant eyes.

"Kasparson, you great actor," she said, "Bastard of Egalité,
kiss me."

"Ah, no, Madame," said Kasparson, "I am ill; there is poison in
my mouth."

Miss Malin laughed. "A fig for that tonight," she said. She
looked, indeed, past any sort of poison. She had on her shoulders
that death's-head by which druggists label their poison bottles, an
unengaging object for any man to kiss. But looking straight at the
man before her, she said slowly and with much grace: *"Fils de
St. Louis, montez au ciel!"*

The actor took her in his arms, held her even in a strong embrace, and kissed her. So the proud old maid did not go unkissed
into her grave.

With a majestic and graceful movement she lifted up the hem
of her skirt and placed it in his hand. The silk, which had been
trailing over the floor, was dripping wet. He understood that this
was the reason why she had got up from her seat.

Their eyes, together, sought the floor of the loft. A dark figure,
like that of a long thick snake, was lying upon the boards, and a
little lower down, where the floor slanted slightly, it widened to a
black pool which nearly touched the feet of the sleeping girl. The
water had risen to the level of the hayloft. Indeed, as they moved,

they felt the heavy boards gently rocking, floating upon the waters.

The dog suddenly sat up with a jerk. It threw its head back, its ears flattened and its nose in the air, and gave a low whine.

"Hush, Passup," said Miss Malin, who had learned its name from the fishermen.

She took one of the actor's hands in hers. "Wait a moment," she said softly, so as not to waken the sleepers. "I want to tell you. I, too, was once a young girl. I walked in the woods and looked at the birds, and I thought: How dreadful that people shut up birds in cages. I thought: If I could so live and so serve the world that after me there should never again be any birds in cages, they should all be free——"

She stopped and looked toward the wall. Between the boards a strip of fresh deep blue was showing, against which the little lamp seemed to make a red stain. The dawn was breaking.

The old woman slowly drew her fingers out of the man's hand, and placed one upon her lips.

"*A ce moment de sa narration,*" she said, "*Scheherazade vit paraître le matin, et, discrète, se tut.*"

The
Old Chevalier

MY father had a friend, old Baron von Brackel, who had in his day traveled much and known many cities and men. Otherwise he was not at all like Odysseus, and could least of all be called ingenious, for he had shown very little skill in managing his own affairs. Probably from a sense of failure in this respect he carefully kept from discussing practical matters with an efficient younger generation, keen on their careers and success in life. But on theology, the opera, moral right and wrong, and other unprofitable pursuits he was a pleasant talker.

He had been a singularly good-looking young man, a sort of ideally handsome youth, and although no trace of this past beauty could be found in his face, the history of it could be traced in a certain light-hearted dignity and self-reliance which are the product of a career of good looks, and which will be found, unaccountably, in the carriage of those shaking ruins who used to look into the mirrors of the last century with delight. In this way one should be able to point out, at a *danse macabre,* the skeletons of the real great beauties of their time.

One night he and I came to discuss an old theme, which has done its duty in the literature of the past: namely, whether one is ever likely to get any real benefit, any lasting moral satisfaction, out of forsaking an inclination for the sake of principle, and in the course of our talk he told me the following story:

On a rainy night in the winter of 1874, on an avenue in Paris, a drunken young girl came up and spoke to me. I was then, as you will understand, quite a young man. I was very upset and unhappy, and was sitting bareheaded in the rain on a seat along the avenue because I had just parted from a lady whom, as we said then, I did adore, and who had within this last hour tried to poison me.

This, though it has nothing to do with what I was going to tell you, was in itself a curious story. I had not thought of it for many years until, when I was last in Paris, I saw the lady in her box at the opera, now a very old woman, with two charming little girls in pink who were, I was told, her great-granddaughters. She was lovely no more, but I had never, in the time that I have known her, seen her look so contented. I was sorry afterward that I had not gone up and called on her in her box, for though there had been but little happiness for either of us in that old love affair of ours, I think that she would have been as pleased to be reminded of the beautiful young woman, who made men unhappy, as I had been to remember, vaguely as it was, the young man who had been so unhappy that long time ago.

Her great beauty, unless some rare artist has been able to preserve it in color or clay, now probably exists only within a few very old brains like mine. It was in its day something very wonderful. She was a blonde, the fairest, I think, that I have ever seen, but not one of your pink-and-white beauties. She was pale, colorless, all through, like an old pastel or the image of a woman in a dim mirror. Within that cool and frail form there was an unrivaled energy, and a distinction such as women have no more, or no more care to have.

I had met her and had fallen in love with her in the autumn, at the château of a friend where we were both staying together with a large party of other gay young people who are now, if they are alive, faded and crooked and deaf. We were there to hunt, and I think that I shall be able to remember to the last of my days how she used to look on a big bay horse that she had, and that autumn air, just touched with frost, when we came home in the evenings, warm in cold clothes, tired, riding side by side over an old stone bridge. My love was both humble and audacious, like that of a page for his lady, for she was so much admired, and her beauty had in itself a sort of disdain which might well give sad dreams to a boy of twenty, poor and a stranger in her set. So that every hour of our rides, dances and *tableaux vivants* was exuberant with ecstasy and pain, the sort of thing you will know yourself: a whole orchestra in the heart. When she made me happy, as one says, I thought that I was happy indeed. I remembered smoking a cigar on the terrace one morning, looking out over the large view of low, wood-covered blue hills, and giving the Lord a sort of receipt for all the happiness that I should ever have any claim to in my life. Whatever would happen to me now, I had had my due, and declared myself satisfied.

Love, with very young people, is a heartless business. We drink at that age from thirst, or to get drunk; it is only later in life that we occupy ourselves with the individuality of our wine. A young man in love is essentially enraptured by the forces within himself. You may come back to that view again, in a second adolescence. I knew a very old Russian in Paris, enormously rich, who used to keep the most charming young dancers, and who, when once asked whether he had, or needed to have, any illusions as to their feelings for him, thought the question over and said: "I do not think, if my chef succeeds in making me a good omelette, that I bother much whether he loves me or not." A young man could not have put his answer into those words, but he might say that he did not care whether his wine merchant was of his own religion or not, and imagine that he had got close to the truth of things. In middle age, though, you arrive at a deeper humility, and you come to consider it of importance that the person who sells or grows your wine shall be of the same religion as you yourself. In this case of my own, of which I am telling you, my youthful vanity, if I had too much of it, was to be taught a lesson very soon. For during the months of that winter, while we were both living in Paris, where her house was the meeting place of many *bel-esprits,* and she herself the admired dilettante in music and arts, I began to think that she was making use of me, or of her own love for me, if such can be said, to make her husband jealous. This has happened, I suppose, to many young men down through the ages, without the total sum of their experience being much use to the young man who finds himself in the same position today. I began to wonder what the relations between those two were really like, and what strange forces there might be in her or in him, to toss me about between them in this way, and I think that I began to be afraid. She was jealous of me, too, and would scold me with a sort of moral indignation, as if I had been a groom failing in his duties. I thought that I could not live without her, and also that she did not want to live without me, but exactly what she wanted me for I did not know. Her contact hurt me as one is hurt by touching iron on a winter day: you do not know whether the pain comes from heat or from cold.

Before I had ever met her I had read about her family, whose name ran down for centuries through the history of France, and learned that there used to be werewolves amongst them, and I sometimes thought that I should have been happier to see her really go down on all fours and snarl at me, for then I should have known where I was. And even up to the end we had hours together of a particular charm, for which I shall always be thankful to her. During my first year in Paris, before I knew any people there, I had taken up studying the history of the old hotels of the town, and this hobby of mine appealed to her, so that we used to dive into old quarters and ages of Paris, and dwell together in the age of Abélard or of Molière, and while we were playing in this way she was serious and gentle with me, like a little girl. But at other times I thought that I could stand it no longer, and would try to get away from her, and any suspicion of this was enough, I imagine, to make her lie awake at night thinking out new methods of punishing me. It was between us the old game of the cat and the mouse—probably the original model of all the games of the world. But because the cat has more passion in it, and the mouse only the plain interest of existence, the mouse is bound to become tired first. Toward the end I thought that she wished us to be found out, she was so careless in this *liaison* of ours; and in those days a love affair had to be managed with prudence.

I remember during this period coming to her hotel on the night of a ball to which she was going, while I had not been asked, disguised as a hairdresser. In the 'seventies ladies had large chignons and the work of a *coiffeur* took time. And through everything the thought of her husband would follow me, like, I thought, the gigantic shadow, upon the white back-curtain, of an absurd little punchinello. I began to feel so tired—not exactly of her, but really exhausted in myself—that I was making up my mind to have a scene and an explanation from her, even if I should lose her by it, when suddenly, on the night of which I am telling you, she herself produced both the scene and the explanation, such a hurricane as I have never again been out in; and all with exactly the same weapons as I had myself had ready: with the accusation that I thought more of her husband than I did of her. And when she said this to me, in that pale blue boudoir of hers that I knew so well—the silk-lined, upholstered and scented box, such as the ladies of that time liked to keep themselves in, with, I remember, some paintings of flowers on the walls, and very soft silk cushions everywhere, and a lot of lilacs in the corner behind me, with the lamp subdued by a large red shade—I had no reply, for I knew that she was right.

You would know his name if I told you, for he is still talked about, though he has been dead for many years. Or you would find it in any of the memoirs of that period, for he was the idol of our generation. Later on, great unhappiness came upon him, but at that moment—I believe that he was then thirty-three years old—he was walking quietly in the full splendor of his strange power. I once, about that time, heard two old men talk about his mother, who had been one of the beauties of the Restoration, and one of them said of her that she carried all her famous jewels as lightly and gracefully as other young ladies would wear garlands of field flowers. "Yes," the other said after he had thought it over for a moment, "and she scattered them about her. in the end, like flowers, *à la* Ophelia." Therefore I think that this rare lightness of his must have been, together with the weakness, a family trait. Even in his wildest whims, and in a sort of mannerism which we then named *fin de siècle* and were rather proud of, he had something of *le grand siècle* about him: a straight nobility that belonged to the old France.

I have looked since at those great buildings of the seventeenth century which seem altogether inexpedient as dwellings for human beings, and have thought that they must have been built for him—and his mother, I suppose—to live in. He had a confidence in life, independent of the successes which we envied him, as if he knew that he could draw upon greater forces, unknown to us, if he wanted to. It gave me much to think about, on the fate of man, when many years later I was told how this young man had, toward the end of his tragic destiny, answered the friends who implored him in the name of God, in the words of Sophocles's Ajax: "You worry me too much, woman. Do you not know that I am no longer a debtor of the gods?"

I see that I ought not to have started talking about him, even after all these years; but an ideal of one's youth will always be a landmark amongst happenings and feelings long gone. He himself has nothing to do with this story.

I told you that I myself felt it to be true that my feelings for the lovely young woman, whom I adored, were really light of weight compared to my feelings for the young man. If he had been with her when we first met, or if I had known him before I met her, I do not think that I should ever have dreamed of falling in love with his wife.

But his wife's love for him, and her jealousy, were indeed of a strange nature. For that she was in love with him I knew from the moment that she began to speak of him. Probably I had known it a long time before. And she was jealous. She suffered, she cried—she was, as I have told you, ready to kill if nothing else would help her—and all the time that fight, which was very likely the only reality in her life, was not a struggle for possession, but a competition. She was jealous of him as if he had been another young woman of fashion, her rival, or as if she herself had been a young man who envied him his triumphs. I think that she was, in herself, always alone with him in a world that she despised. When she rode so madly, when she surrounded herself with admirers, she had her eye on him, as a competitor in a chariot race would have his eyes only on the driver just beside him. As for the rest of us, we only existed for her in so far as we were to belong to her or to him, and she took her lovers as she took her fences, to pile up more conquests than the man with whom she was in love.

I cannot, of course, know how this had begun between them. Afterward I tried to believe that it must have arisen from a desire for revenge, on her side, for something that he had done to her in the past. But I had the feeling that it was this barren passion which had burned all the color out of her.

Now you will know that all this happened in the early days of what we called then the "emancipation of woman." Many strange things took place then. I do not think that at the time the movement went very deep down in the social world, but here were the young women of the highest intelligence, and the most daring and ingenious of them, coming out of the chiaroscuro of a thousand years, blinking at the sun and wild with desire to try their wings. I believe that some of them put on the armor and the halo of St. Joan of Arc, who was herself an emancipated virgin, and became like white-hot angels. But most women, when they feel free to experiment with life, will go straight to the witches' Sabbath. I myself respect them for it, and do not think that I could ever really love a woman who had not, at some time or other, been up on a broomstick.

I have always thought it unfair to woman that she has never been alone in the world. Adam had a time, whether long or short, when he could wander about on a fresh and peaceful earth,

among the beasts, in full possession of his soul, and most men
are born with a memory of that period. But poor Eve found him
there, with all his claims upon her, the moment she looked into
the world. That is a grudge that woman has always had against
the Creator: she feels that she is entitled to have that epoch of
paradise back for herself. Only, worse luck, when chasing a time
that has gone, one is bound to get hold of it by the tail, the wrong
way around. Thus these young witches got everything they wanted
as in a catoptric image.

Old ladies of those days, patronesses of the church and of home,
said that emancipation was turning the heads of the young women.
Probably there were more young ladies than my mistress galloping
high up above the ground, with their fair faces at the backs of
their necks, after the manner of the wild huntsman in the tale.
And in the air there was a theory, which caught hold of them
there, that the jealousy of lovers was an ignoble affair, and that
no woman should allow herself to be possessed by any male but
the devil. On their way to him they were proud of being, according to Doctor Faust, always a hundred steps ahead of man. But
the jealousy of competition was, as between Adam and Lilith, a
noble striving. So there you would find, not only the old witches
of Macbeth, of whom one might have expected it, but even young
ladies with faces smooth as flowers, wild and mad with jealousy
of their lovers' mustachios. All this they got from reading—in
the orthodox witches' manner—the book of Genesis backwards.
Left to themselves, they might have got a lot out of it. It was the
poor, tame, male preachers of emancipation, cutting, as warlocks
always will, a miserable figure at the Sabbath, who spoiled the
style and flight of the whole thing by bringing it down to earth
and under laws of earthly reason. I believe, though, that things
have changed by now, and that at the present day, when males
have likewise emancipated themselves, you may find the young
lover on the hearth, following the track of the witch's shadow

along the ground, and, with infinitely less imagination, blending the deadly brew for his mistress, out of envy of her breasts.

The part which had been granted to me, in the story of my emancipated young witch, was not in itself flattering. Still I believe that she was desperately fond of me, probably with the kind of passion which a little girl has for her favorite doll. And as far as that goes I was really the central figure of our drama. If she would be Othello, it was I, and not her husband, who must take the part of Desdemona, and I can well imagine her sighing, "Oh, the pity of it, the pity of it, Iago," over this unfortunate business, even wanting to give me a kiss and yet another before finishing it altogether. Only she did not want to kill me out of a feeling of justice or revenge. She wished to destroy me so that she should not have to lose me and to see a very dear possession belong to her rival, in the manner of a determined general, who will blow up a fortress which he can no longer hold, rather than see it in the hands of the enemy.

It was toward the end of our interview that she tried to poison me. I believe that this was really against her program, and that she had meant to tell me what she thought of me when I already had the poison in me, but had been unable to control herself for so long. There was, as you will understand, something unnatural in drinking coffee at that stage of our dialogue. The way in which she insisted upon it, and her sudden deadly silence as I raised the cup to my mouth, gave her away. I can still, although I only just touched it, recall the mortal, insipid taste of the opium, and had I emptied the cup, it could not have made my stomach rise and the marrow in my bones turn to water more than did the abrupt and fatal conviction that she wanted me to die. I let the cup drop, faint as a drowning man, and stood and stared at her, and she made one wild movement, as if she meant to throw herself at me still. Then we stood quite immovable for a minute, both knowing that all was lost. And after a little while she began to rock and whimper, with her hands at her mouth, sud denly changed into a very old woman. For my own part, I was not able to utter a sound, and I think that I just ran from the house as soon as I had strength enough to move. The air, the rain, and the street itself met me like old forgotten friends, faithful still in the hour of need.

And there I sat on a seat of the Avenue Montaigne, with the entire building of my pride and happiness lying around me in ruins, sick to death with horror and humiliation, when this girl, of whom I was telling you, came up to me.

I think that I must have been sitting there for some time, and that she must have stood and watched me before she could summon up her courage to approach. She probably felt herself in sympathy with me, thinking that I was drunk too, as sensible people do not sit without a hat in the rain, perhaps also because I was so near her own age. I did not hear what she said, neither the first nor the second time. I was not in a mood to enter into talk with a little girl of the streets. I think that it must have been from sheer instinct of self-preservation that I did in the end come to look at her and to listen. I had to get away from my own thoughts, and any human being was welcome to assist me. But there was at the same time something extraordinarily graceful and expressive about the girl, which may have attracted my attention. She stood there in the rain, highly rouged, with radiant eyes like stars, very erect though only just steady on her legs. When I kept on staring at her, she laughed at me, a low, clear laughter. She was very young. She was holding up her dress with one hand—in those days ladies wore long trains in the streets. On her head she had a black hat with ostrich feathers drooping sadly in the rain and overshadowing her forehead and eyes. The firm gentle curve of her chin, and her round young neck shone in the light of the gas lamp. Thus I can see her still, though I have another picture of her as well.

What impressed me about her was that she seemed altogether so strangely moved, intoxicated by the situation. Hers was not the conventional advance. She looked like a person out on a great adventure, or someone keeping a secret. I think that on looking at her I began to smile, some sort of bitter and wild smile, known only to young people, and that this encouraged her. She came nearer. I fumbled in my pocket for some money to give her, but I had no money on me. I got up and started to walk, and she came on, walking beside me. There was, I remember, a certain comfort in having her near me, for I did not want to be alone. In this way it happened that I let her come with me.

I asked her what her name was. She told me that it was Nathalie.

At this time I had a job at the Legation, and I was living in an apartment on the Place François I, so we had not far to go. I was prepared to come back late, and in those days, when I would come home at all sorts of hours, I used to keep a fire and a cold supper waiting for me. When we came into the room it was lighted and warm, and the table was laid for me in front of the fire. There was a bottle of champagne on ice. I used to keep a bottle of champagne to drink when I returned from my shepherd's hours.

The young girl looked around the room with a contented face. Here in the light of my lamp I could see how she really looked She had soft brown curls and blue eyes. Her face was round, with a broad forehead. She was wonderfully pretty and graceful. I think that I just wondered at her, as one would wonder at finding a fresh bunch of roses in a gutter, no more. If I had been normally balanced I suppose I should have tried to get from her some explanation of the sort of mystery that she seemed to be, but now I do not think that this occurred to me at all.

The truth was that we must both have been in quite a peculiar sort of mood, such as will hardly ever have repeated itself for either of us. I knew as little of what moved her as she could have known about my state of mind, but, highly excited and strained, we met in a special sort of sympathy. I, partly stunned and partly abnormally wide awake and sensitive, took her quite selfishly, without any thought of where she came from or where she would disappear to again, as if she were a gift to me, and her presence a kind and friendly act of fate at this moment when I could not be alone. She seemed to me to have come as a little wild spirit from the great town outside—Paris—which may at any moment bestow unexpected favors on one, and which had in the right moment sent her to me. What she thought of me or what she felt about me, of that I can say nothing. At the moment I did not think about it, but on looking back now I should say that I must also have symbolized something to her, and that I hardly existed for her as an individual.

I felt it as a great happiness, a warmth all through me, that she was so young and lovely. It made me laugh again after those weird and dismal hours. I pulled off her hat, lifted her face up, and kissed her. Then I felt how wet she was. She must have walked for a long time on the streets in the rain, for her clothes were like the feathers of a wet hen. I went over and opened the bottle on the table, poured her out a glass, and handed it to her. She took it, standing in front of the fire, her tumbled wet curls falling down over her forehead. With her red cheeks and shining eyes she looked like a child that has just awakened from sleep, or like a doll. She drank half the glass of wine quite slowly, with her eyes on my face, and, as if this half-glass of champagne had brought her to a point where she could no longer be silent, she started to sing, in a low, gentle voice, hardly moving her lips, the first lines of a song, a waltz, which was then sung in all the music halls. She broke it off, emptied her glass, and handed it back to me. *A votre santé,* she said.

Her voice was so merry, so pure, like the song of a bird in a bush, and of all things music at that time went most directly to my heart. Her song increased the feeling I had, that something special and more than natural had been sent to me. I filled her glass again, put my hand on her round white neck, and brushed the damp ringlets back from her face. "How on earth have you come to be so wet, Nathalie?" I said, as if I had been her grandmother. "You must take off your clothes and get warm." As I spoke my voice changed. I began to laugh again. She fixed her starlike eyes on me. Her face quivered for a moment. Then she started to unbutton her cloak, and let it fall onto the floor. Underneath this cloak of black lace, badly suited for the season and faded at the edges into a rusty brown, she had a black silk frock, tightly fitted over the bust, waist and hips, and pleated and draped below, with flounces and ruffles such as ladies wore at that time, in the early days of the bustle. Its folds shone in the light of my fire. I began to undress her, as I might have undressed a doll, very slowly and clumsily, and she stood up straight and let me do it. Her fresh face had a grave and childlike expression. Once or twice she colored under my hands, but as I undid her tight bodice and my hands touched her cool shoulders and bosom, her face broke into a gentle and wide smile, and she lifted up her hand and touched my fingers.

The old Baron von Brackel made a long pause. "I think that I must explain to you," he said, "so that you may be able to understand this tale aright, that to undress a woman was then a very different thing from what it must be now. What are the clothes that your ladies of these days are wearing? In themselves as little as possible—a few perpendicular lines, cut off again before they have had time to develop any sense. There is no plan about them. They exist for the sake of the body, and have no career of their own, or, if they have any mission at all, it is to reveal.

"But in those days a woman's body was a secret which her clothes did their utmost to keep. We would walk about in the streets in bad weather in order to catch a glimpse of an ankle, the sight of which must be as familiar to you young men of the present day as the stems of these wineglasses of ours. Clothes then had a being, an idea of their own. With a serenity that it was not easy to look through, they made it their object to transform the body which they encircled, and to create a silhouette so far from its real form as to make it a mystery which it was a divine privilege to solve. The long tight stays, the whalebones, skirts and petticoats, bustle and draperies, all that mass of material under which the women of my day were buried where they were not laced together as tightly as they could possibly stand it—all aimed at one thing: to disguise.

"Out of a tremendous froth of trains, pleatings, lace, and flounces which waved and undulated, *secundum artem,* at every movement of the bearer, the waist would shoot up like the chalice of a flower, carrying the bust, high and rounded as a rose, but imprisoned in whalebone up to the shoulder. Imagine now how different life must have appeared and felt to creatures living in those tight corsets within which they could just manage to breathe, and in those fathoms of clothes which they dragged along with them wherever they walked or sat, and who never dreamed that it could be otherwise, compared to the existence of your young women, whose clothes hardly touch them and take up no room. A woman was then a work of art, the product of centuries of civilization, and you talked of her figure as you talked of her salon, with the admiration which one gives to the achievement of a skilled and untiring artist.

"And underneath all this Eve herself breathed and moved, to be indeed a revelation to us every time she stepped out of her disguise, with her waist still delicately marked by the stays, as with a girdle of rose petals.

"To you young people who laugh at the ideas, as at the bustles, of the 'seventies, and who will tell me that in spite of all our artificiality there can have been but little mystery left to any of us, may I be allowed to say that you do not, perhaps, quite understand the meaning of the word? Nothing is mysterious until it symbolizes something. The bread and wine of the church itself has to be baked and bottled, I suppose. The women of those days were more than a collection of individuals. They symbolized, or represented, Woman. I understand that the word itself, in that sense, has gone out of the language. Where we talked of woman —pretty cynically, we liked to think—you talk of women, and all the difference lies there.

"Do you remember the scholars of the middle ages who discussed the question of which had been created first: the idea of a dog, or the individual dogs? To you, who are taught statistics in your kindergartens, there is no doubt, I suppose. And it is but justice to say that your world does in reality look as if it had been made experimentally. But to us even the ideas of old Mr. Darwin were new and strange. We had our ideas from such undertakings as symphonies and ceremonials of court, and had been brought up with strong feelings about the distinction between legitimate and illegitimate birth. We had faith in purpose. The idea of Woman—of *das ewig weibliche,* about which you yourself will not deny that there is some mystery—had to us been created in the beginning, and our women made it their mission to represent it worthily, as I suppose the mission of the individual dog must have been worthily to represent the Creator's idea of a dog.

"You could follow, then, the development of this idea in a little girl, as she was growing up and was gradually, no doubt in accordance with very ancient rules, inaugurated into the rites of the cult, and finally ordained. Slowly the center of gravity of her being would be shifted from individuality to symbol, and you would be met with that particular pride and modesty characteristic of the representative of the great powers—such as you may find again in a really great artist. Indeed, the haughtiness of the pretty young girl, or the old ladies' majesty, existed no more on account of personal vanity, or on any personal account whatever, than did the pride of Michelangelo himself, or the Spanish Ambassador to France. However much greeted at the banks of the Styx by the indignation of his individual victims with flowing hair and naked breasts, Don Giovanni would have been acquitted by a board of women of my day, sitting in judgment on him, for the sake of his great faith in the idea of Woman. But they would have agreed with the masters of Oxford in condemning Shelley as an atheist; and they managed to master Christ himself only by representing him forever as an infant in arms, dependent upon the Virgin.

"The multitude outside the temple of mystery is not very interesting. The real interest lies with the priest inside. The crowd waiting at the porch for the fulfillment of the miracle of the boiling blood of St. Pantaleone—that I have seen many times and in many places. But very rarely have I had admittance to the cool vaults behind, or the chance of seeing the priests, old and young, down to the choirboys, who feel themselves to be the most important persons at the ceremony, and are both scared and impudent, occupying themselves, in a measure of their own, with the preparations, guardians of a mystery that they know all about. What was the cynicism of Lord Byron, or of Baudelaire, whom we were just reading then with the *frisson nouveau*, to the cynicism of these little priestesses, augurs all of them, performing with the utmost conscientiousness all the rites of a religion which they knew all about and did not believe in, upholding, I feel sure, the doctrine of their mystery even amongst themselves. Our poets of those days would tell us how a party of young beauties, behind the curtains of the bathing-machine, would blush and giggle as they 'put lilies in water.'

"I do not know if you remember the tale of the girl who saves the ship under mutiny by sitting on the powder barrel with her lighted torch, threatening to put fire to it, and all the time knowing herself that it is empty? This has seemed to me a charming image of the woman of my time. There they were, keeping the world in order, and preserving the balance and rhythm of it, by sitting upon the mystery of life, and knowing themselves that there was no mystery. I have heard you young people saying that the women of old days had no sense of humor. Thinking of the face of my young girl upon the barrel, with severely down-cast eyes, I have wondered if our famous male humor be not a little insipid compared to theirs. If we were more thankful to them for existing than you are to your women of the present day, I think that we had good reason for it.

"I trust that you will not mind," he said, "an old man lingering over these pictures of an age gone by. It will be, I suppose, like being detained a little in a museum, before a *montre* showing its fashions. You may laugh at them, if you like."

The old chevalier then resumed his story:

As I then undressed this young girl, and the layers of clothes which so severely dominated and concealed her fell one by one there in front of my fire, in the light of my large lamp, itself swathed in layers of silk—all, my dear, was thus draped in those days, and my large chairs had, I remember, long silk fringes all around them and on the tops of those little velvet pompons, other-wise they would not have been thought really pretty—until she stood naked, I had before me the greatest masterpiece of nature that my eyes have ever been privileged to rest upon, a sight to take away your breath. I know that there may be something very lovable in the little imperfections of the female form, and I have myself worshiped a knock-kneed Venus, but this young figure was pathetic, was heart-piercing, by reason of its pure fault-lessness. She was so young that you felt, in the midst of your deep admiration, the anticipation of a still higher perfection, and that was all there was to be said.

All her body shone in the light, delicately rounded and smooth as marble. One straight line ran through it from neck to ankle, as though the heaven-aspiring column of a young tree. The same character was expressed in the high instep of the foot, as she pushed off her old shoes, as in the curve of the chin, as in the straight, gentle glance of her eyes, and the delicate and strong lines of her shoulder and wrist.

The comfort of the warmth of the fire on her skin, after the clinging of her wet and tumbled clothes, made her sigh with pleasure and turn a little, like a cat. She laughed softly, like a child who quits the doorstep of school for a holiday. She stood up erect before the fire; her wet curls fell down over her forehead and she did not try to push them back; her bright painted cheeks looked even more like a doll's above her fair naked body.

I think that all my soul was in my eyes. Reality had met me, such a short time ago, in such an ugly shape, that I had no wish to come into contact with it again. Somewhere in me a dark fear was still crouching, and I took refuge within the fantastic like a distressed child in his book of fairy tales. I did not want to look ahead, and not at all to look back. I felt the moment close over me, like a wave. I drank a large glass of wine to catch up with her, looking at her.

I was so young then that I could no more than other young people give up the deep faith in my own star, in a power that loved me and looked after me in preference to all other human beings. No miracle was incredible to me as long as it happened to myself. It is when this faith begins to wear out, and when you conceive the possibility of being in the same position as other people, that youth is really over. I was not surprised or suspicious of this act of favor on the part of the gods, but I think that my heart was filled with a very sweet gratitude toward them. I thought it after all only reasonable, only to be expected, that the great friendly power of the universe should manifest itself again, and send me, out of the night, as a help and consolation, this naked and drunk young girl, a miracle of gracefulness.

We sat down to supper, Nathalie and I, high up there in my warm and quiet room, with the great town below us and my heavy silk curtains drawn upon the wet night, like two owls in a ruined tower within the depth of the forest, and nobody in the world knew about us. She leaned one arm on the table and rested her head on it. I think that she was very hungry, under the influence of the food. We had some caviar, I remember, and a cold bird. She began to beam on me, to laugh, to talk to me, and to listen to what I said to her.

I do not remember what we talked about. I think we were very open-hearted, and that I told her, what I could not have mentioned to anybody else, of how I had come near to being poisoned just before I met her. I also think that I must have told her about my country, for I know that at a time afterwards the idea came to me that she would write to me there, or even come to look for me. I remember that she told me, rather sadly to begin with, a story of a very old monkey which could do tricks, and had belonged to an Armenian organ-grinder. Its master had died, and now it wanted to do its tricks and was always waiting for the catchword, but nobody knew it. In the course of this tale she imitated the monkey in the funniest and most gracefully inspired manner that one can imagine. But I remember most of her movements. Sometimes I have thought that the understanding of some pieces of music for violin and piano has come to me through the contemplation of the contrast, or the harmony, between her long slim hand and her short rounded chin as she held the glass to her mouth.

I have never in any other love affair—if this can be called a love affair—had the same feeling of freedom and security. In my last adventure I had all the time been worrying to find out what my mistress really thought of me, and what part I was playing in the eyes of the world. But no such doubts or fears could possibly penetrate into our little room here. I believe that this feeling of safety and perfect freedom must be what happily married people mean when they talk about the two being one. I wonder if that understanding can possibly, in marriage, be as harmonious as when you meet as strangers; but this, I suppose, is a matter of taste.

One thing did play in to both of us, though we were not conscious of it. The world outside was bad, was dreadful. Life had made a very nasty face at me, and must have made a worse at her.

But this room and this night were ours, and were faithful to us. Although we did not think about it, ours was in reality a supper of the Girondists.

The wine helped us. I had not drunk much, but my head was fairly light before I began. Champagne is a very kind and friendly thing on a rainy night. I remember an old Danish bishop's saying to me that there are many ways to the recognition of truth, and that Burgundy is one of them. This is, I know, very well for an old man within his paneled study. But young people, who have seen the devil face to face, need a stronger helping hand. Over our softly hissing glasses we were brought back to seeing ourselves and this night of ours as a great artist might have seen us and it, worthy of the genius of a god.

I had a guitar lying on my sofa, for I was to serenade, in a *tableau vivant,* a romantic beauty—in real life an American woman from the Embassy who could not have given you an echo back from whatever angle you would have cried to her. Nathalie reached out for it, a little later in our supper. She shuddered slightly at the first sound, for I had not had time or thought for playing it, and crossing her knees, in my large low chair, she began to tune it. Then she sang two little songs to me. In my quiet room her low voice, a little hoarse, was clear as a bell, faintly giddy with happiness, like a bee's in a flower. She sang first a song from the music halls, a gay tune with a striking rhythm. Then she thought for a moment and changed over into a strange plaintive little song in a language that I did not understand. She had a great sense of music. That strong and delicate personality which showed itself in all her body came out again in her voice. The light metallic timbre, the straightness and ease of it, corresponded with her eyes, knees, and fingers. Only it was a little richer and fuller, as if it had grown up faster or had stolen a march somehow upon her body. Her voice knew more than she did herself, as did the bow of Mischa Elman when he played as a *Wunderkind.*

All my balance, which I had kept somehow while looking at

her, suddenly left me at the sound of her voice. These words that I did not understand seemed to me more directly meaningful than any I had ever understood. I sat in another low chair, opposite her. I remember the silence when her song was finished, and that I pushed the table away, and how I came slowly down on one knee before her. She looked at me with such a clear, severe, wild look as I think that a hawk's eyes must have when they lift off his hood. I went down on my other knee and put my arms around her legs. I do not know what there was in my face to convince her, but her own face changed and lighted up with a kind of heroic gentleness. Altogether there had been from the beginning something heroic about her. That was, I think, what had made her put up with the young fool that I was. For *du ridicule jusqu'au sublime,* surely, *il n'y a qu'un pas.*

My friend, she was as innocent as she looked. She was the first young girl who had been mine. There is a theory that a very young man should not make love to a virgin, but ought to have a more experienced partner. That is not true; it is the only natural thing.

It must have been an hour or two later in the night that I woke up to the feeling that something was wrong, or dangerous. We say when we turn suddenly cold that someone is walking over our grave—the future brings itself into memory. And as *l'on meurt en plein bonheur de ses malheurs passés,* so do we let go our hold of our present happiness on account of coming misfortune. It was not the *omne animal* affair only; it was a distrust of the future as if I had heard myself asking it: "I am to pay for this; what am I to pay?" But at the time I may have believed that what I felt was only fear of her going away.

Once before she had sat up and moved as if to leave me, and I had dragged her back. Now she said: "I must go back," and got up. The lamp was still burning, the fire was smoldering. It seemed to me natural that she should be taken away by the same mysterious forces which had brought her, like Cinderella, or a little spirit out of the *Arabian Nights*. I was waiting for her to come up and let me know when she would come back to me, and what I was to do. All the same I was more silent now.

She dressed and got back into her black shabby disguise. She put on her hat and stood there just as I had seen her first in the rain on the avenue. Then she came up to me where I was sitting on the arm of my chair, and said: "And you will give me twenty francs, will you not?" As I did not answer, she repeated her question and said: "Marie said that—she said that I should get twenty francs."

I did not speak. I sat there looking at her. Her clear and light eyes met mine.

A great clearness came upon me then, as if all the illusions and arts with which we try to transform our world, coloring and music and dreams, had been drawn aside, and reality was shown to me, waste as a burnt house. This was the end of the play. There was no room for any superfluous word.

This was the first moment, I think, since I had met her those few hours ago, in which I saw her as a human being, within an existence of her own, and not as a gift to me. I believe that all thoughts of myself left me at the sight, but now it was too late.

We two had played. A rare jest had been offered me and I had accepted it; now it was up to me to keep the spirit of our game until the end. Her own demand was well within the spirit of the night. For the palace which he builds, for four hundred white and four hundred black slaves all loaded with jewels, the djinn asks for an old copper lamp; and the forest-witch who moves three towns and creates for the woodcutter's son an army of horse-soldiers demands for herself the heart of a hare. The girl asked me for her pay in the voice and manner of the djinn and the forest-witch, and if I were to give her twenty francs she might still be safe within the magic circle of her free and graceful and defiant spirit. It was I who was out of character, as I sat there in silence, with all the weight of the cold and real world upon me, knowing well that I should have to answer her or I might, even within these few seconds, pass it on to her.

Later on I reflected that I might have had it in me to invent something which would have kept her safe, and still have allowed me to keep her. I thought then that I should only have had to give her twenty francs and to have said: "And if you want another twenty, come back tomorrow night." If she had been less lovely to me, if she had not been so young and so innocent, I might perhaps have done it. But this young girl had called, during our few hours, on all the chivalrousness that I had in my nature. And chivalrousness, I think, means this: to love, or cherish, the pride of your partner, or of your adversary, as you will define it, as highly, or higher than, your own. Or if I had been as innocent of heart as she was, I might perhaps have thought of it, but I had kept company with this deadly world of reality. I was practiced in its laws and had the mortal bacilli of its ways in my blood. Now it did not enter my head any more than it ever has to alter my answers in church. When the priest says: "O God, make clean our hearts within us," I have never thought of telling him that it is not needed, or to answer anything whatever but, "And take not your holy spirit from us."

So, as if it were the only natural and reasonable thing to do, I took out twenty francs and gave them to her.

Before she went she did a thing that I have never forgotten. With my note in her left hand she stood close to me. She did not kiss me or take my hand to say good-by, but with the three fingers of her right hand she lifted my chin up a little and looked at me, gave me an encouraging, consoling glance, such as a sister might give her brother in farewell. Then she went away.

In the days that followed—not the first days, but later—I tried to construct for myself some theory and explanation of my adventure.

This happened only a short time after the fall of the Second Empire, that strange sham millennium, and the Commune of Paris. The atmosphere had been filled with catastrophe. A world had fallen. The Empress herself, whom, on a visit to Paris as a child, I had envisaged as a female deity resting upon clouds, smilingly conducting the ways of humanity, had flown in the night, in a carriage with her American dentist, miserable for the lack of a handkerchief. The members of her court were crowded into lodgings in Brussels and London while their country houses served as stables for the Prussians' horses. The Commune had followed, and the massacres in Paris by the Versailles army. A whole world must have tumbled down within these months of disaster.

This was also the time of Nihilism in Russia, when the revolutionaries had lost all and were fleeing into exile. I thought of them because of the little song that Nathalie had sung to me, of which I had not understood the words.

Whatever it was that had happened to her, it must have been a catastrophe of an extraordinary violent nature. She must have gone down with a unique swiftness, or she would have known something of the resignation, the dreadful reconciliation to fate which life works upon us when it gets time to impress us drop by drop.

Also, I thought, she must have been tied to, and dragged down with, somebody else, for if she had been alone it could not have happened. It would have been, I reflected, somebody who held her, and yet was unable to help her, someone either very old, helpless from shock and ruin, or very young, children or a child, a little brother or sister. Left to herself she would have floated, or she would have been picked up near the surface by someone who would have valued her rare beauty, grace, and charm and have congratulated himself upon acquiring them; or, lower down, by somebody who might not have understood them, but whom they would still have impressed. Or, near the bottom, by people who would have thought of turning them to their own advantage. But she must have gone straight down from the world of beauty and harmony in which she had learned that confidence and radiance of hers, where they had taught her to sing, and to move and laugh as she did, where they had loved her, to a world where beauty and grace are of no account, and where the facts of life look you in the face, quite straight to ruin, desolation and starvation. And there, on the last step of the ladder, had been Marie, whoever she was, a friend who out of her narrow and dark knowledge of the world had given her advice, and lent her the miserable clothes, and poured some sort of spirit into her, to give her courage.

About all this I thought much, and for a long time; but of course I could not know.

As soon as she had gone and I was alone—so strange are the automatic movements which we make within the hands of fate— I had no thought but to go after her and get her back. I think that I went, in those minutes, through the exact experience, even to the sensation of suffocation, of a person who has been buried alive. But I had no clothes on. When I got into some clothes and came down to the street it was empty. I walked about in the streets for a long time. I came back, in the course of the early morning, to the seat on which I had been sitting when she first spoke to me, and to the hotel of my former mistress. I thought what a strange thing is a young man who runs about, within the selfsame night, driven by the mad passion and loss of two women. Mercutio's words to Romeo about it came into my mind, and, as if I had been shown a brilliant caricature of myself or of all young men, I laughed. When the day began to spring I walked back to my room, and there was the lamp, still burning, and the supper table.

This state of mine lasted for some time. During the first days it was not so bad, for I lived then in the thought of going down, at the same hour, to the same place where I had met her first. I thought that she might come there again. I attached much hope to this idea, which only slowly died away.

I tried many things to make it possible to live. One night I went to the opera, because I had heard other people talk about going there. It was clear that it was done, and there might be something in it. It happened to be a performance of *Orpheus*. Do you remember the music where he implores the shadows in Hades, and where

Euridice is for such a short time given back to him? There I sat, in the brilliant light of the *entr'actes,* a young man in a white tie and lavender gloves, with bright people who smiled and talked all around, some of them nodding to me, closely covered and wrapped up in the huge black wings of the Eumenides.

At this time I developed also another theory. I thought of the goddess Nemesis, and I believed that had I not had the moment of doubt and fear in the night, I might have felt, in the morning, the strength in me, and the right, to move her destiny and mine. It is said about the highwaymen who in the old days haunted the forests of Denmark that they used to have a wire stretched across the road with a bell attached. The coaches in passing would touch the wire and the bell would ring within their den and call out the robbers. I had touched the wire and a bell had rung somewhere. The girl had not been afraid, but I had been afraid. I had asked: "What am I to pay for this?" and the goddess herself had answered: "Twenty francs," and with her you cannot bargain. You think of many things, when you are young.

All this is now a long time ago. The Eumenides, if they will excuse me for saying so, are like fleas, by which I was also much worried as a child. They like young blood, and leave us alone later in life. I have had, however, the honor of having them on me once more, not very many years ago. I had sold a piece of my land to a neighbor, and when I saw it again, he had cut down the forest that had been on it. Where were now the green shades, the glades and the hidden footpaths? And when I then heard again the whistle of their wings in the air, it gave me, with the pain, also a strange feeling of hope and strength—it was, after all, music of my youth.

"And did you never see her again?" I asked him.

"No," he said, and then, after a little while, "but I had a fantasy about her, a *fantaisie macabre,* if you like.

"Fifteen years later, in 1889, I passed through Paris on my way to Rome, and stayed there for a few days to see the exhibition and the Eiffel Tower which they had just built. One afternoon I went to see a friend, a painter. He had been rather wild as a young artist, but later had turned about completely, and was at the time studying anatomy with great zeal, after the example of Leonardo. I stayed there over the evening, and after we had discussed his pictures, and art in general, he said that he would show me the prettiest thing that he had in his studio. It was a skull from which he was drawing. He was keen to explain its rare beauty to me. 'It is really,' he said, 'the skull of a young woman, but the skull of Antinoüs must have looked like that, if one had been able to get hold of it.'

"I had it in my hand, and as I was looking at the broad, low brow, the clear and noble line of the chin, and the clean deep sockets of the eyes, it seemed suddenly familiar to me. The white polished bone shone in the light of the lamp, so pure. And safe. In those few seconds I was taken back to my room in the Place François I, with the silk fringes and the heavy curtains, on a rainy night of fifteen years before."

"Did you ask your friend anything about it?" I said.

"No," said the old man, "what would have been the use? He would not have known."

The Monkey

I

IN a few of the Lutheran countries of northern Europe there are still in existence places which make use of the name convent, and are governed by a prioress or chanoiness, although they are of no religious nature. They are retreats for unmarried ladies and widows of noble birth who here pass the autumn and winter days of their lives in a dignified and comfortable routine, according to the traditions of the houses. Many of these institutions are extremely wealthy, own great stretches of land, and have had, during the centuries, inheritances and legacies bequested to them. A proud and kindly spirit of past feudal times seems to dwell in the stately buildings and to guide the existence of the communities.

The Virgin Prioress of Closter Seven, under whose hands the convent prospered from the year 1818 to that of 1845, had a little gray monkey which had been given her by her cousin, Admiral von Schreckenstein, on his return from Zanzibar, and of which she was very fond. When she was at her card table, a place where she spent some of her happiest hours, the monkey was wont to sit on the back of her chair, and to follow with its glittering eyes the course of the cards as they were dealt out and taken in. At other times it would be found, in the early mornings, on top of the stepladder in the library, pulling out brittle folios a hundred years old, and scattering over the black-and-white marble floor browned leaves dealing with strategy, princely marriage contracts, and witches' trials.

In a different society the monkey might not have been popular. But the convent of Closter Seven held, coördinately with its estimable female population, a whole world of pets of all sorts, and was well aware of the order of precedence therein. There were here parrots and cockatoos, small dogs, graceful cats from all parts of the world, a white Angora goat, like that of Esmeralda, and a purple-eyed young fallow deer. There was even a tortoise which was supposed to be more than a hundred years old. The old ladies therefore showed a forbearance with the whims of the Prioress's favorite, much like that which courtiers of a petticoat-governed court of the old days, conscious of their own frailty, might have shown toward the caprices of a royal *maîtresse-en-titre*.

From time to time, particularly in the autumn, when nuts were ripening in the hedges along the roads and in the large forests that surrounded the convent, it happened that the Prioress's monkey would feel the call of a freer life and would disappear for a few weeks or a month, to come back of its own accord when the night frosts set in. The children of the villages belonging to Closter Seven would then come upon it running across the road or sitting in a tree, from where it watched them attentively. But when they gathered around it and started to bombard it with chestnuts from their pockets, it would roll its eyes and grind its teeth at them, and finish by swiftly mounting the branches to disappear in the crowns of the forest.

It was the general opinion, or a standing joke amongst the ladies of the convent, that the Prioress, during these periods, would become silent and the victim of a particular restlessness, and would seem loth to act in the affairs of the house, in which at ordinary times she showed great vigor. Amongst themselves they called the monkey her *Geheimrat,* and they rejoiced when it was to be seen again in her drawing-room, a little chilled after its stay in the woods.

Upon a fine October day, when the monkey had in this way been missing for some weeks, the Prioress's young nephew and godson, who was a lieutenant in the Royal Guards, arrived unexpectedly at the convent.

The Prioress was held in high respect by all her relations, and had in her time presented at the font many babies of her own noble blood, but this young man was her favorite amongst them. He was a graceful boy of twenty-two, with dark hair and blue eyes. Although he was a younger son, he was fortunately situated in life. He was the preferred child of his mother, who had come from Russia and had been an heiress; he had made a fine career. He had friends, not everywhere in the world, but everywhere in that world, that is of any significance.

On his arrival at the convent he did not, however, look like a young man under a lucky star. He came, as already said, in head long hurry and unannounced, and the ladies with whom he ex changed a few words while waiting for admission to his aunt, and who were all fond of him, noticed that he was pale and looked deadly tired, as if under some great agitation of mind.

They were not unaware, either, that he might have reason to be so. Although Closter Seven was a small world of its own, and moved in a particular atmosphere of peace and immutability, news of the greater world outside reached it with surprising quickness, for each of the ladies had her own watchful and zealous cor respondents there. Thus these cloistered women knew, just as well as the people in the center of things, that during the last month clouds of strange and sinister nature had been gathering over the heads of that very regiment and circle of friends to which the boy belonged. A sanctimonious clique of the capital, led by the Court-Chaplain, of all people, who had the ear of high personages, had, under pretense of moral indignation, lifted their voices against these young flowers of the land, and nobody knew for certain, or could even imagine, what might come out of that.

The ladies had not discussed these happenings much amongst themselves, but the librarian of the convent, who was a theologian and a scholar, had been dragged away into more than one tête-à-tête, and encouraged to give his opinion on the problem. From him they had learnt to connect it somehow with those romantic and sacred shores of ancient Greece which they had till now held in high esteem. Remembering their young days, when everything Greek had been *le dernier cri,* and frocks and coiffures had been named *à la grecque,* they wondered—Could the expression be used also to designate anything so little related to their young ladies' dreams of refinement? They had loved those frocks, they had waltzed with princes in them; now they thought of them with un-easiness.

Few things could have stirred their natures more deeply. It was not only the impudence of the heroes of the pulpit and the quill attacking warriors which revolted the old daughters of a fighting race, or the presentiment of trouble and much woe that worried them, but something in the matter which went deeper than that. To all of them it had been a fundamental article of faith that woman's loveliness and charm, which they themselves represented in their own sphere and according to their gifts, must constitute the highest inspiration and prize of life. In their own individual cases the world might have spread snares in order to capture this prize of their being at less cost than they meant it to, or there might have been a strange misunderstanding, a lack of apprecia-tion, on the part of the world, but still the dogma held good. To hear it disputed now meant to them what it would mean to a miser to be told that gold no longer had absolute value, or to a mystic to have it asserted that the Lord was not present in the Eucharist. Had they known that it might ever be called into ques-tion, all these lives, which were now so nearly finished, might have come to look very different. To a few proud old maids, who had the strategic instincts of their breed developed to the full, these new conceptions came very hard. So might have come, to a gallant and faithful old general who through a long campaign, in loyalty to higher orders, had stood strictly upon the defensive, the informa-tion that an offensive would have been the right, and approved, move.

Still in the midst of their inquietude every one of the old women would have liked to have heard more of this strange heresy, as if, after all, the tender and dangerous emotions of the human heart were, even within their own safe reclusion, by right their domain. It was as if the tall bouquets of dried flowers in front of the convents' pier glasses had stirred and claimed authority when a question of floriculture was being raised.

They gave the pale boy an unsure welcome, as if he might have been either one of Herod's child martyrs, or a young priest of black magic, still within hope of conversion, and when he walked up the broad stair which led to the Prioress's rooms, they evaded one another's eyes.

The Prioress received her nephew within her lofty parlor. Its three tall windows looked out, between heavy curtains which had on them borders of flower garlands done in cross-stitch, over the lawns and avenues of the autumnal garden. From the damask-clad walls her long-departed father and mother gazed down, out of broad gilt frames, with military gravity and youthful grace, powdered and laced for some great court occasion. Those two had been the young man's friends since he was a baby, yet today he was struck and surprised by a puzzled, even a worried, look upon their faces. It seemed to him also, for a moment, that there was a certain strange and disquieting smell in the room, mixed with that of the incense sticks, which were being burned more amply than usual. Was this, he thought, a new aspect of the catastrophal tendencies of his existence?

The boy, while taking in the whole well-known and harmonious atmosphere, did not want or dare to waste time. After he had kissed his aunt's hand, inquired after her health and the monkey and given her the news of his own people in town, he came straight to the matter which had brought him to Closter Seven.

"Aunt Cathinka," he said, "I have come to you because you have always been so good to me. I should like"—here he swallowed to keep his rebellious heart in place, knowing how little indeed it would like it—"to marry, and I hope that you will give me your advice and help."

II

The boy was well aware that under ordinary circumstances nothing that he could have said could possibly have pleased the old woman better. Thus did life, he thought, manage to satisfy its taste for parody, even in relation to people like his aunt, whom in his own heart he had named after the Chinese goddess Kuan-Yin, the deity of mercy and of benignant subtlety. He thought that in this case she would suffer from the irony of destiny more than he himself, and it made him feel sorry for her.

On his way to the convent, driving through the forests and little villages, past long stretches of stubble-fields on which large flocks of geese were feeding, herded by bare-legged children and young girls, he had been trying to imagine how the meeting between his aunt and himself would be likely to develop. Knowing the old lady's weakness for little Latin phrases, he had wondered if he would get from her lips *Et tu, Brute,* or a decided *Discite justitiam moniti, et non temnere divos.* Perhaps she would say *Ad sanitatem gradus est novisse morbum*—that would be a better sign.

After a moment he looked straight at the old lady's face. Her high-backed chair was in the chiaroscuro of the lace curtain, while he had on him the full light of the afternoon sun. From the shade her luminous eyes met his, and made him look away, and this dumb play was repeated twice over.

"Mon cher enfant," she said at last in a gentle voice which gave him the impression of firmness, although it had in it a curious little shiver, "it has long been a prayer of my heart that you should make this decision. On what help an old woman, outside the world, can give you, dear Boris, you can surely rely."

Boris looked up with smiling eyes in a white face. After a terribly agitated week, and a row of wild scenes which his mother's love and jealousy had caused, he felt like a person who is, from a flooded town, taken up into a boat. As soon as he could speak he said: "It is all for you to decide, Aunt Cathinka," trusting that the sweetness of power would call out all the generosity of the old woman's nature.

She kept her eyes on him, kindly. They took possession of him as if she had actually been drawing him to her bosom, or even within the closer circle of her heart. She held her little handkerchief to her mouth, a gesture common with her when she was moved. She would help him, he felt, but she had something to say first.

"What is it," she said very slowly, in the manner of a sibylla, "which is bought dearly, offered for nothing, and then most often refused?—Experience, old people's experience. If the children of Adam and Eve had been prepared to make use of their parents' experience, the world would have been behaving sensibly six thousand years ago. I will give you my experience of life in a little pill, sugar-coated by poetry to make it go down: 'For as of all the ways of life but one—the path of duty—leads to happiness.'" Boris sat silent for a moment. "Aunt Cathinka," he said at last, "why should there be only one way? I know that good people think so, and I was taught it myself at my confirmation, but still the motto of our family is: 'Find a way or make it.' Neither can you read any cookery book which will not give you at least three or four ways of making a chicken ragout, or more. And when Columbus sailed out and discovered America," he went on, because these were thoughts which had occupied him lately, and the Prioress was a friend of his, to whom he could venture to express them, "he really did so to find the back way to the Indies, and it was considered a heroic exploit." "Ah," said the Prioress with great energy, "Dr. Sass, who was the parson of Closter Seven in the seventeenth century, maintained that in paradise, until the time of the fall, the whole world was flat, the back-curtain of the Lord, and that it was the devil who invented a third dimension. Thus are the words 'straight,' 'square,' and 'flat' the words of noblemen, but the apple was an orb, and the sin of our first parents, the attempt at getting around God. I myself much prefer the art of painting to sculpture." Boris did not contradict her. His own taste differed from hers here, but she might be right. Up to now he had congratulated himself upon his talent for enjoying life from all sides, but lately he had come to consider it a doubtful blessing.

It was to this, he thought, that he owed what seemed to be his fate: to get everything he wanted at a time when he no longer wanted it. He knew from experience how a wild craving for an orgy, or music, or the sea, or confidence might, before there had been time for its fulfillment, have ceased to exist—as in the case of a star, of which the light only reaches the earth long after it has itself gone under—so that at the moment when his wish was about to be granted him, only a bullfight, or the life of a peasant plowing his land in the rain, would satisfy the hunger of his soul.

The Prioress looked him up and down, and said:

> *Straight is the line of duty,*
> *Curved is the line of beauty.*
> *Follow the straight line, thou shalt see*
> *The curved line ever follows thee.*

The boy thought the poem over.

A decanter of wine and some fruit were at this moment brought in for him, and as he understood that she wanted him to keep quiet, he drank two glasses, which did him good, and in silence peeled the famous silky pears of Closter Seven, and picked the dim black grapes off their stems one by one. Without looking at his aunt he could follow all her thoughts. The dramatic urgency for quick action, which might have frightened another person of her age, did not upset her in the least. She had amongst her ancestors great lords of war who had prepared campaigns with skill, but who had also had it in them to give over at the right moment to pure inspiration.

He understood that for her in these moments her red parlor was filled with young virgins of high birth—dark and fair, slim and junoesque, good housekeepers, good horsewomen, grand-daughters of schoolmates and friends of her youth—a muster-roll of young femininity, who could hide no excellency or shortcoming from her clear eyes. Spiritually she was licking her lips, like an old connoisseur walking through his cellar, and Boris himself followed her in thought, like the butler who is holding the candle.

Just then the door opened and the Prioress's old servant came in again, this time with a letter on a silver tray, which he presented to her. She took it with a hand that trembled a little, as if she could not very well take in any more catastrophe, read it through, read it again, and colored faintly. "It is all right, Johann," she said, keeping the letter in her silken lap.

She sat for a little while in deep thought. Then she turned to the boy, her dark eyes clear as glass. "You have come through my new fir plantation," she said with the animation of a person talking about a hobby. "What do you think of it?" The planting and up-keep of forests were indeed among her greatest interests in life. They talked for some time pleasantly of trees. There was nothing for your health, she said, like forest air. She herself was never able to pass a good night in town or amongst fields, but to lie down at night knowing that you had the trees around you for miles, their roots so deep in the earth, their crowns moving in the dark, she considered to be one of the delights of life. The forest had always done Boris good when he had been staying at Closter Seven as a child. Even now he would notice a difference when he had been in town for a long time, and she wished that she could get him down more often.—"And who, Boris," she said with a sudden skip of thought and a bright and determined benevolence, "who, now that we come to talk about it, could indeed make you a better wife than that great friend of yours and mine, little Athena Hopbal-lehus?"

No name could in this connection have come more unexpectedly to Boris. He was too surprised to answer. The phrase itself sounded absurd to him. He had never heard Athena described as little, and he remembered her as being half an inch taller than himself. But that the Prioress should speak of her as a great friend showed a complete change of spirit, for he was sure that ever since their neighbor's daughter had grown up, his aunt and his mother, who were rarely of one mind, had been joining forces to keep him and Athena apart.

As his mind turned from this unaccountable veering on the part of the old lady to the effect which it might have upon his own destiny, he found that he did not dislike the idea. The burlesque he had always liked, and it might even be an extravaganza of the first water to bring Athena to town as his wife. So when he looked at his aunt he had the face of a child. "I have the greatest faith in your judgment, Aunt Cathinka," he said.

The Prioress now spoke very slowly, not looking at him, as if she did not want any impressions from other minds to intermingle with her own. "We will not waste time, Boris," she said. "That has never been my habit once my mind was made up." And that means, never at all, Boris thought. "You go and change into your uniform, and I will in the meantime write a letter to the old Count. I will tell him how you have made me your confidante in this matter of your heart, upon which the happiness of your life depends, and in which your dear mother has not been able to give you her sympathy. And you, you must be ready to go within half an hour."

"Do you think, Aunt Cathinka, that Athena will have me?" asked Boris as he rose to go. He was always quick to feel sorry for other people. Now, looking out over the garden, and seeing two of the old ladies emerge, in galoshes, from one of the avenues, wherein they had been taking their afternoon walk, he felt sorry for Athena for merely existing. "Athena," the Prioress was saying, "has never had an offer of marriage in her life. I doubt if, for the last year, she has seen any man but Pastor Rosenquist, who comes to play chess with her papa. She has heard my ladies discuss the brilliant marriages which you might have made if you had wanted to. If Athena will not have you, my little Boris," she said, and smiled at him very sweetly, "I will."

Boris kissed her hand for this, and reflected what an excellent arrangement it might prove to be, and then all at once he got

such a terrible impression of strength and cunning that it was as if
he had touched an electric eel. Women, he thought, when they are
old enough to have done with the business of being women, and
can let loose their strength, must be the most powerful creatures
in the whole world. He gazed at his aunt's refined face.

No, it would not do, he thought.

III

Boris drove from Closter Seven in the Prioress's britzska, with
her letter upon his heart, looking the ideal young hero of romance.
The news of his errand had spread mysteriously in the convent, as
if it had been a new kind of incense, and had gone straight to the
hearts of the old ladies. Two or three of them were sitting in the
sun on the long terrace to see him go, and a particular friend of
his, a corpulent old maid, bleached by having been kept for fifty
years from all the lights of life, stood beside his carriage to hand
him three long-stemmed white asters from her little winter garden.
Thus had gone away, thirty years ago, the young man she loved,
and then he had been killed at Jena. A gentle melancholy veiled
her always, and her lady companion said of her: "The Countess
Anastasia has a heavy cross. The love of eating is a heavy cross."
But it was the memory of this last parting of theirs that had kept
her eyes, in her puny face, bright like light blue enamel. She felt at
the moment the resurrection of an entire destiny, and handed him
her flowers as if they had been some part of it, mysteriously come
to life in a second round, as if they had been her three unborn
daughters, now tall and marriageable, joining his journey in the
quality of bridesmaids.

Boris had left his servant at the convent, for he knew him to be
in love with one of the lady's maids, and it seemed to him that he
ought now to show sympathy towards all legitimate lovemaking.
He wished to be alone. Solitude was always a pleasure to him, and

he never had much opportunity for it. Lately he seemed never to have been alone at all. When people were not at him, working upon his feelings with all their might, they had still succeeded in making him take up their line of thought, until he felt those convolutions of the brain which had to do with these matters aching as if they were worn out. Even on his way down to the convent he had been made to think the thoughts of other people. Now, he thought with great contentment, for an hour he could think whatever he liked.

The road from Closter Seven to Hopballehus rises more than five hundred feet and winds through tall pine forest. From time to time this opens and affords a magnificent view over large stretches of land below. Now in the afternoon sun the trunks of the fir trees were burning red, and the landscape far away seemed cool, all blue and pale gold. Boris was able now to believe what the old gardener at the convent had told him when he was a child: that he had once seen, about this time of the year and the day, a herd of unicorns come out of the woods to graze upon the sunny slopes, the white and dappled mares, rosy in the sun, treading daintily and looking around for their young, the old stallion, darker roan, sniffing and pawing the ground. The air here smelled of fir leaves and toadstools, and was so fresh that it made him yawn. And yet, he thought, it was different from the freshness of spring; the courage and gayety of it were tinged with despair. It was the finale of the symphony.

He remembered how he had, upon a May evening not six months ago, been taken into the young heart of spring, as now into the sad heart of autumn. He and a young friend of his had amused themselves by wandering for three weeks about the country, visiting places where nobody had known them to be. They had traveled in a caravan, carrying with them a little theater of dolls, and had given performances of plays which they made up themselves in the villages that they came through. The air had been filled with sweet smells, the nightingales had been raving within the bird cherries, the moon stood high, not much paler than the sky of those nights of spring.

One night they had come, very tired, to a farmhouse in a grass field, and had been given a large bed in a room that had in it a grandfather's clock and a dim looking-glass. Just as the clock was striking twelve, three quite young girls appeared on the threshold in their shifts, each with a lighted candle in her hand, but the night was so clear that the little flames looked only like little drops of the moon. They clearly did not know that two wayfaring young men had been taken in and given the large bedroom, and the guests watched them in deep silence from behind the hangings of the big bed. Without looking at one another, without a word, one by one they dropped their slight garments on the floor and quite naked they walked up to the mirror and looked into it, the candle held high overhead, absorbed in the picture. Then they blew out their candles, and in the same solemn silence they walked backward to the door, their long hair hanging down, got into their shifts, and disappeared. The nightingales kept on singing outside, in a green bush near the window. The two boys remembered that this was Walpurgis Night, and decided that what they had witnessed was some witchcraft by which these girls had hoped to catch a glimpse of their future husbands.

He had not been up this way for a long time, not since, as a child, he had gone with the Prioress in her landaulet to pay a call at her neighbors'. He recognized the curves, but they had shrunk, and he fell to meditating upon the subject of change.

The real difference between God and human beings, he thought, was that God cannot stand continuance. No sooner has he created a season of a year, or a time of the day, than he wishes for something quite different, and sweeps it all away. No sooner was one a young man, and happy at that, than the nature of things would rush one into marriage, martyrdom or old age. And human beings cleave to the existing state of things. All their lives they are striving to hold the moment fast, and are up against a *force majeure*. Their art itself is nothing but the attempt to catch by all means the one particular moment, one mood, one light, the momentary beauty of one woman or one flower, and make it everlasting. It is all wrong, he thought, to imagine paradise as a never-changing state of bliss. It will probably, on the contrary, turn out to be, in the true spirit of God, an incessant up and down, a whirlpool of change. Only you may yourself, by that time, have become one with God, and have taken to liking it. He thought with deep sadness of all the young men who had been, through the ages, perfect in beauty and vigor—young pharaohs with clean-cut faces hunting in chariots along the Nile, young Chinese sages, silk-clad, reading within the live shade of willows—who had been changed, against their wishes, into supporters of society, fathers-in-law, authorities on food and morals. All this was sad.

A turning of the road and a long vista cut through the wood brought him face to face with Hopballehus, still at a distance. The old architect of two hundred years ago had succeeded in building something so enormous that it fell in with nature, and might have been a little formation of the gray rock. To someone now standing on the terrace, Boris thought, I and the britzska and the gray and black horses would look diminutive, hardly distinguishable.

The sight of the house turned his thoughts toward it. It had always appealed to his imagination. Even now, when he had not seen it for years, it would happen that he would dream of it at night. It was in itself a fantastic place, resting upon a large plateau, with miles of avenues around it, rows of statues and fountains, built in late baroque and now baroquely dilapidated and more than half a ruin. It seemed a sort of Olympus, more Olympic still for the doom which was hanging over it. The existence therein of the old Count and his daughter had about it something Olympic as well. They lived, but how they got through the twenty-four hours of their day and night must remain a mystery to humans. The old Count, who had once been a brilliant diplomatist, a scientist and a poet, had for many years been absorbed in a great lawsuit which he had going on in Poland, and which he had inherited from his father and grandfather. If he could win it, it would give him back the immense riches and estates that had once belonged to his family, but it was known that he could never win it, and it was only ruining him with ever greater speed. He lived in those gigantic worries as in clouds which made all his movements dim. Boris had at times wondered what the world looked like to his daughter. Money, if she had ever seen it, he knew to hold no place in her life; no more did society or what is called the pleasures of life, and he wondered if she had ever heard of love. God knows, he thought, if she has ever looked at herself in a glass.

The light carriage swished through the layers of fallen leaves upon the terrace. In places they lay so thick that they half covered the stone balusters and reached the knees of Diana's stag. But the trees were bare; only here and there a single golden leaf trembled high upon the black twigs. Following the curve of the road, Boris's carriage came straight upon the main terrace and the house, majestic as the Sphinx herself in the sunset. The light of the setting sun seemed to have soaked into the dull masses of stone. They reddened and glowed with it until the whole place became a mysterious, a glorified, abode, in which the tall windows shone like a row of evening stars.

Boris got out of the britzska in front of the mighty stone stairs and walked toward them, feeling for his letter. Nothing stirred in the house. It was like walking into a cathedral. And, he thought, by the time that I get into that carriage once more, what will everything be like to me?

IV

At this moment the heavy doors above the stairs were flung open, and the old Count appeared at the top step, standing like

Samson when in his wrath he broke down the temple of the Philistines.

He was always a striking figure, short in the legs and with the torso of a giant, his mighty head surrounded by a mane of wild gray hair, like a poet's or a lion's. But today he seemed strangely inspired, in the grip of some tremendous emotion, swaying where he stood. He remained for a moment immovable, scrutinizing his visitor, like an old man gorilla outside his lair, ready for the attack; then he came down the stairs upon the young man, imposing upon him a presence such as the Lord himself might have shown had he descended, for once, the ladder of Jacob.

Good God, thought Boris, as he walked up the steps to meet him, this old man knows all, and is going to kill me. He had a glimpse of the old Count's face, filled with wild triumph, the light eyes aflame. The next moment he felt his arms around him, and his body trembling against his own.

"Boris!" he cried, "Boris, my child," for he had known the boy from childhood, and had, Boris was aware, once been one of his beautiful mother's adorers, "welcome. Welcome here today. Do you know?" "Know?" said Boris. "I have won my case," said the old man. Boris stared at him. "I have won my case in Poland," he repeated. "Lariki, Lipnika, Parnov Grabovo—they are all mine, as they were the old people's."

"I congratulate you," said Boris, slowly, his thoughts strangely put into motion. "With all my heart. This is unexpected news indeed!" The old Count thanked him many times, and showed him the letter from his lawyer, which he had just received, and was still holding in his hand. As he was talking to the boy he spoke slowly at first, seeking for his words, as a man out of the habit of speech, but as he went on he recovered his old voice and speech that had in the old days charmed so many people. "A great passion, Boris," he said, "such as does really and truly devour your heart and soul, you cannot feel for individual beings. Perhaps you cannot feel it for anything which is capable of loving you in return. Those officers who have loved their armies, those lords who have loved their soil, they can talk about passion. My God, I have had the whole weight of the land of Hopballehus upon my chest at night, when I imagined that I had been leading it into a lost battle. But this," he said, drawing a deep breath, "this is happiness." Boris understood that it was not the thought of his riches which filled the soul of the old man, but the triumph of right over wrong, the righteousness of the entire universe being, to him, concentrated in his own figure. He began to explain the judgment in detail, still with one hand upon the young man's shoulder, and Boris felt that he was welcome to his heart as a friend who could listen. "Come in, come in, Boris," he said, "we will drink a glass together, you and I, from the wine which I have put aside for today. Our good Pastor is here. I sent for him when I got the letter, to keep me company, as I did not know that you would be coming."

Within the prodigious hall, richly ornamented with black marble, a small corner was made habitable by a few chairs and a table, covered with the Count's books and papers. Above it was a gigantic picture, much darkened by age, an equestrian portrait of an old lord of the house, holding himself very calm upon a rearing horse with a small head, and pointing with a roll of paper toward a battlefield depicted in the distance under the belly of the horse. Pastor Rosenquist, a short man with red cheeks, who had for many years been the spiritual guide of the family, and whom Boris knew well, was sitting in one of the chairs, apparently in deep thought. The happenings of the day had brought disorder in his theories, which was to him a more serious disaster than if the parsonage had burnt down. He had suffered from poverty and misfortunes all his life, and had in the course of time come to live upon a system of spiritual bookkeeping according to which earthly trials became an investment, drawing interest in the other world. His own personal account, he knew, was made up in very small change, but he had taken a great interest in the old Count's sorrows, and had looked upon him as a favorite of the Lord's, whose treasures were all the time accumulating in the new Jerusalem, like to sapphires, chrysoprase and amethyst propagating on their own. Now he was upset and did not know what to think, which to him was a terrible condition. He had sought comfort in the book of Job, but even there the figures would not agree, Behemoth and Leviathan coming in upon an account of losses and profits of their own. The whole affair seemed to him in the nature of a gift, which, according to Ecclesiastes, destroyeth the heart, and he could not get away from the thought that this old man, whom he loved, was in the bad way of anticipating his income.

"Now I would," said the old Count, when he had fetched and opened the golden bottle, "that my poor father and my dear grandfather were here with us to drink this wine. I have felt, as I have lain awake at night, that they have kept awake with me within their sarcophagi below. I am happy," he went on as, still standing, he lifted his glass, "that it be the son of Abunde"—that was his old name for Boris's mother—"who drinks here with me tonight." In the exuberance of his heart he patted Boris's cheek with tenderness, while his face radiated a gentleness which had been in exile for years; and the boy, who knew a good thing when he saw it, envied the old man his innocence of heart. "And to our good Pastor," the Count said, turning to him. "My friend, you have shed tears of sympathy in this house. They arise now as wine."

The old Count's manner heightened Pastor Rosenquist's uneasiness. It seemed to him that only a frivolous heart could move with such ease in a new atmosphere, forgetting the old. Brought up himself upon a system of examinations and promotions, he was not prepared to understand a race reared upon the laws of luck in war and court favor, adjusted for the unforeseen and accustomed to the unexpected, for whom to be safe, or even saved, seems the least necessary of all things. Then again came into his mind the words of the Scripture—"He saith amongst the trumpets, ha, ha!"—and he thought that perhaps after all his old friend was all right. "Yes,

yes," he said, smiling, "water has certainly been changed into wine, once. It is without doubt a good drink. But you know what our good peasants hold: that wine-begotten children will end badly. So, we have reason to fear, will wine-begotten hopes and moods. Though that," he added, "would not, of course, apply to the children of the wedding of Cana, of which I was just speaking."

"At Lariki," said the Count, "there is hung, in the ceiling of the gateway, a hunting horn in an iron chain. My grandfather's grandfather was a man of herculean strength. When in the evening he rode through the gate, he used to take hold of the horn, and, lifting himself and his horse from the ground, he blew it. I have known that I could do the same, but I thought I should never ride through that gate. Athena might do it, too," he added thoughtfully.

He refilled his glasses. "How is it that you came here today?" he asked Boris, beaming upon him and his gala uniform, as if his coming had been a unique exploit. "What brings you to Hopballehus?" Boris felt the old man's openness reflected in his own heart, like a blue sky in the sea. He looked into his friend's face. "I came here today," he said, "to ask Athena to marry me." The old man gave him a great, luminous glance. "To ask Athena to marry you!" he exclaimed. "You came here today for that?" He stood for a moment, deeply moved. "The ways of God are strange indeed," he said. Pastor Rosenquist rose from his chair and sat down again, to arrange his accounts.

When the old Count spoke again he was much changed. The intoxication was gone, and he seemed to have collected the forces of his nature in good order. It was this balance which had given him a name in the old days, when he had, as a young man of the Embassy in Paris, upon the first night of his tragedy, *The Undine*, fought a duel with pistols in the *entr'acte*.

"Boris, my child," he said, "you have come here to change my heart. I have been living with my face toward the past, or for this hour of victory. This moment is the first in which I have thought

of the future. I see that I shall have to come down from a pinnacle
to walk along a road. Your words are opening up a great vista to
me. What am I to be? The patriarch of Hopballehus, crowning
virtuous village maidens? Grandpapa, planting apple trees? Ave,
Hopballehus. *Naturi te salutem."*

Boris remembered the Prioress's letter, and told the old man
how he had called at Closter Seven on his way. The Count inquired after the lady, and, always keen on all sorts of papers, he
put on his glasses and became absorbed in the letter. Boris sat and
drank his wine in a happy mood. During the last week he had
come to doubt whether life ever held anything pleasant at all. Now
his reception in the old Count's house was to him a show of the
most enjoyable kind, and he always moved with ease from one
mood to another.

When the Count had finished the reading, he laid the letter
down and, keeping his folded hands upon it, he sat for a long time
silent.

"I give you," he said at last slowly and solemnly, "my blessing.
First I give it to the son of your mother—and of your father—secondly to the young man who, as I see now, has loved so long
against all. And finally I feel that you have been sent, Boris, by
stronger hands than your own tonight.

"I give you, in Athena, the key of my whole world. Athena," he
repeated, as if it gave him joy to pronounce his daughter's name,
"is herself like a hunting-horn in the woods." And as if, without
knowing it himself, some strange and sad memory of his youth
had taken possession of him, he added, almost in a whisper, *"Dieu,
que le son du cor est triste au fond du bois."*

V

While they had been talking, a strong wind had sprung up outside. The day had been still. This blowing weather had come with

the dusk, like an animal of the night. It swept along the long walls, around the corners of the house, and whirled the dead leaves up in the air. In the midst of it, Athena, who had been outspanning the horse from Pastor Rosenquist's trap in the stables, was heard to cross the terrace and come up the stairs.

The old Count, whose eyes had been dwelling on Boris's face, made a sudden movement, as if he had been alarmed by something he did not himself understand. "Do not speak to her to-night," he said. "You will understand: our friend, the Pastor, Athena and myself have had so many evenings here, together. Let this be the last of them. I will tell her myself, and you, my dear son, come back to Hopballehus tomorrow morning." Boris thought this a good plan. As the Count spoke, his daughter came into the room, still in her big cloak.

Athena was a strong young woman of eighteen, six feet high and broad in proportion, with a pair of shoulders which could lift and carry a sack of wheat. At forty she would be enormous, but now she was too young to be fat, and straight as a larch tree. Beneath her flaming hair her noble forehead was white as milk; lower down her face was, like her broad wrists, covered with freckles. Still she was so fair and clear of skin that she seemed to lighten up the hall on entering it, with the light that you will get inside a room when the snow is lying outside. Her clear eyes had a darker ring around the iris—a pair of eyes for a young lioness or eagle—otherwise the strong young creature's countenance was peaceful, and her round face had that expression of attention and reserve which is ordinarily found in the faces of people who are hard of hearing. When he had been with her, Boris had sometimes thought of the old ballad about the giant's daughter, who finds a man in the wood, and, surprised and pleased, takes him home to play with. The giant orders her to let him go, telling her that she will only break him.

The giant himself, the old Count, showed her an old-fashioned chivalrousness which appeared to Boris like a rather noble old

coin, dug out of the ground, and keeping its gold value, even
when no more current. It was said that the Count had been, in
his young days, one of the lovers of Princess Pauline Borghese,
who was the loveliest woman of her time. He had seen Venus
Anadyomene face to face, and for the sake of that vision gave
homage to the likeness of the goddess, even where it was more
clumsily cut in wood or stone. With no claim to beauty, Athena
had grown up in an atmosphere of incense burnt to woman's loveliness.

She blinked a little at the light and the stranger, and indeed
Boris, in his white uniform and high golden collar, his pomatumed
curls like a halo in the light, was a striking meteor in the great
dim room. Still, safe in her great strength, she asked him—standing, as was her habit, on one leg, like a big stork—of news of his
aunt, and the ladies of Closter Seven. She knew very few people,
and for these old women, who had given her much good advice,
though she had shocked them a little by growing up so unromanti-
cally big, she had, Boris thought, the sort of admiration that a
peasant's child at a fair has for the skilled and spangled tight-rope
dancers. If she marries me, he thought, as he stood and talked to
her, his voice sweet as a song, with the fond gaze of the old Count
upon her face and his, she will be susceptible to my tricks; but is
my married life to be an everlasting fair? And if ever I drop from
my rope, will she pick me up, or just turn her back and leave?

She bid him let the Prioress know that she had seen her monkey
a few nights ago, on the terrace of Hopballehus, sitting upon the
socle of Venus's statue, in the place where a small Cupid, now
broken, used to be. Talking about the monkey, she asked him if
he did not think it curious that her father's solicitor in Poland had
a monkey of the same kind, which had also come from Zanzibar.
The old Count started to speak of the Wendish idols, from whose
country his own family originally came, and of which the goddess
of love had the face and façade of a beautiful woman, while, if
you turned her around, she presented at the back the image of a

monkey. How, he asked, had these wild Nordic tribes come to know about monkeys? Might there have lived monkeys in the somber pine forests of Wenden a thousand years ago?

"No, that is not possible," said Pastor Rosenquist. "It would always have been too cold. But there are certain symbols which seem to have been the common property of all pagan iconoclasts. It would be worth studying; it might be due to the idea of original sin."

But how, asked Athena, did they know, in the case of that goddess of love, which was the front and which the back?

Boris here ordered his carriage, and took leave of the party. The old Count seemed to be sorry to send him away and repentant of his hardness to a lover. He apologized for the bad weather of Hopballehus, held the youth's hand with tears in his eyes, and told Athena to see him out. Pastor Rosenquist, on the other hand, could not but be pleased by the departure of anyone who looked so much like an angel without being one.

Athena walked out on the terrace with Boris. In the light of his carriage lanterns her big cloak, blowing about her, threw strange shadows upon the gravel, like a pair of large wings. Over the vast lawn, iron gray in the moonlight, the moon herself appeared and disappeared in a stormy sky.

Boris felt at this moment really sorry to be leaving Hopballehus. The chaotic world of the place had reminded him of his childhood, and seemed to him infinitely preferable to the existence of clockwork order which he would find at the convent. He stood a little in silence, near Athena. The clouds were parted, and a few of the constellations of stars stood clear in the sky. The Great Bear preached its lesson: Keep your individuality in the crowd. "Do you ever think of the bear hunt?" Boris asked Athena. The children had not been allowed to take part in it, but they had stolen away together, and had joined the Count's huntsmen, on a very hot July day, high up in the hills. Two spotted dogs had been killed, and he remembered the terrible tumult of the fight, and the quick movements of the huge ragged brown beast within the thicket of firs and ferns, and one glimpse of its furious roaring face, the red tongue hanging out..

"Yes, I do, sometimes," said Athena, her eyes, with his, in the skies, on a stellar bear hunt. "It was the bear which the peasants called the Empress Catherine. She had killed five men."

"Are you still a Republican, Athena?" he asked. "One time you wanted to cut off the heads of all the tyrants of Europe."

The color of Athena's face, in the light of the lamp, heightened. "Yes," she said, "I am a Republican. I have read the history of the French Revolution. The kings and priests were lazy and licentious, cruel to the people, but those men who called themselves 'the Mountain' and put on the red Phrygian bonnet were courageous. Danton was a true patriot, and I should have liked to meet him; so was the Abbé Sieyès." She warmed to her subject in the night air. "I should like to see that place in Paris where the guillotine stood," she said.

"And to wear the Phrygian bonnet?" Boris asked her. Athena nodded shortly, collecting her thoughts. Then, as if meaning to be sure to bring the truth home to him, she broke into some lines of verse, herself, as she went on, carried away by the pathos of the words:

> O Corse à cheveux plats, que la France était belle
> au grand soleil de Messidor.
> C'était une cavale indomptable et rebelle,
> sans freins d'acier, ni rênes d'or.
> Une jument sauvage, à la croupe rustique,
> fumant encore du sang des rois.
> Mais fière, et d'un pied libre heurtant le sol antique,
> Libre, pour la première fois!

As Boris drove away from Hopballehus the wind was blowing strong. The moon was racing the heavens behind wild thin clouds; the air was cold. It must be near the freezing point, he thought. His lanterns chased the trees and their shadows and threw them to all sides around him. A large dry branch from a tree was suddenly blown down, and crashed in front of his shying horses. He thought, alone in the dark, of the three people in the hall of Hopballehus, and laughed.

As he drove on, below him in the valley lights leapt up. As if they were playing with him they appeared between the trees, looked him straight in the face and went off again. A large group of lights came in sight, like a reflection, on the earth, of the Pleiades. Those were the lamps of Closter Seven.

And suddenly it came upon him that somewhere something was not right, was quite wrong and out of order. Strange powers were out tonight. The feeling was so strong and distinct that it was as if an ice-cold hand had passed for a moment over his scalp. His hair rose a little upon his head. For a few minutes he was really and genuinely afraid, struck by an extraordinary terror. In this strange turbulence of the night, and the wild life of dead things all around him, he felt himself, his britzska, and his gray and black horses terribly and absurdly small, exposed and unsafe.

As he turned into the long avenue of Closter Seven, his lamps suddenly shone into a pair of glinting eyes. A very small shadow ran across the road and was gone into the deeper black shadows of the Prioress's shrubbery.

On his arrival at the convent he was told that the Prioress had gone to bed. To have, Boris thought, all her strength on hand in the morning.

The supper table was laid for him in his aunt's private dining-room, which she had just lately redecorated. Before it had been white, with ornaments of stucco perhaps a hundred years old. Now it was prettily covered with a wall paper whose pattern, upon a buff background, presented various scenes of oriental life. A girl danced under a palm tree, beating a tambourine, while old men in red and blue turbans and long beards looked on. A sultan held his court of justice under a golden canopy, and a hunting party on

horseback, preceded by its greyhounds and Negro dog-boys, passed
a ruin. The Prioress had also done away with the old-fashioned
candlesticks, and had the table lighted by tall, brightly modern,
Carcel lamps of blue china, painted with pink roses. In the warm
and cozy room he supped by himself. Like, he thought, Don
Giovanni in the last act of the opera. "Until the Commandante
comes," his thoughts added on their own. He stole a glance at the
window. The wind was still singing outside, but the disquieting
night had been shut out by the heavy drawn curtains.

VI

The aunt and the nephew had breakfast together in pleasant
harmony, from time to time gazing, within the Prioress's silver
samovar, at their own faces curiously distorted. A little shining sun
also showed itself therein, for the day that followed the stormy
night was clear and serene. The wind had wandered on to other
neighborhoods, leaving the gardens of Closter Seven airy and
bare.

Boris had recorded to the old lady the happenings at Hopballehus, and she had listened with great content and a deep interest
in the fate of her old neighbor and friend. She could hardly refrain
from letting her imagination flutter amongst the glories of the
boy's future, but it was done so gracefully that the old Count and
Athena might have been present.

"I feel, my dear," she said, "that now Athena ought to travel and
see a little of the world. When I was her age, Papa took me to
Rome and Paris, and I met many celebrities. What a pleasure to a
man of talent to accompany that highly gifted child to those places,
and show her life."

"Yes," said Boris, pouring himself out some more coffee, "she
told me yesterday that she wanted to see Paris."

"Naturally," said the Prioress. "The dear child has never owned a Paris bonnet in her life. At Lariki," she went on, her thoughts running pleasantly to and fro, "there is splendid bear-hunting, and wild boars. I can well imagine your divinity, spear in hand. At Lipnika the cellar is stored with Tokay, presented to one old lord by the Empress Maria Theresa. Athena will pour it out with the generous hand of her family. At Patnov Grabovo are found the famous row of *jets d'eaux*, which were constructed by the great Danish astronomer Ole Roemer, the same who made the *grandes eaux* of Versailles."

While they were thus playing about with the happy possibilities of life, old Johann had brought in two letters, which had arrived at the same time, although the one for the Prioress had come by post, and Boris's letter had been brought by a groom from Hopballehus. Boris, on looking up after having read a few lines, noticed the hard and fine little smile on the face of the old lady, absorbed in her reading. She will not smile for long, he thought.

The old Count's letter ran as follows:

I am writing to you, my dear Boris, because Athena refuses to do so. I am taking hold of my pen in deep distress and repentance; indeed I have come to know that desire to cover my head with ashes, of which the old writers talk.

I have to tell you that my daughter has rejected your suit, which last night seemed to me to crown the benefactions of destiny toward my house. She surely feels no reluctance toward this alliance in particular, but she tells me that she will never marry, and that it is even impossible for her to consider the question at all.

In a way it is right that it should be I who write you this letter. For in this misfortune the guilt is mine, the responsibility rests with me.

I, who have had this young life in my hand, have made her strong youth my torchbearer on my descent to the sepulchral chamber. Step by step, as I have gone downwards, her shoulder

*has been my support, and she has never failed me. Now she will
not—she cannot—look up.*

*The peasants of our province have the saying that no child born
in wedlock can look straight at the sun; only bastards are capable
of it. Alas, how much is my poor Athena my legitimate child, the
legitimate child of my race and its fate! She is so far from being
able to look straight at the sun, that she fears no darkness whatever, but her eyes are hurt by light. I have made, of my young
dove, a bird of the night.*

*She has been to me both son and daughter, and I have in my
mind seen her wearing the old coats of armor of Hopballehus. Too
late I now realize that she is wearing it, not as the young St.
George fighting the dragons, but as Azrael, the angel of death, of
our house. Indeed, she has shut herself up therein, and for all the
coming years of her life, she will refuse to lay it aside.*

*I have never sinned against the past, but I see now that I have
been sinning against the future; rightly it will have none of me.
Upon Athena's maiden grave I shall be laying down flowers for
those unborn generations in whose faces I had for a moment, my
dear child, thought to see your features. In asking your forgiveness I shall be asking the forgiveness of much doomed energy,
talent and beauty, of lost laurels and myrtles. The ashes which I
strew on my head is theirs! . . .*

Boris handed the letter to the Prioress without words, and leaned
his chin in his hand to watch her face while she read it. He nearly
got more than he asked for. She became so deadly white that he
feared that she was going to faint or die, while red flames sprang
out on her face as if somebody had struck her across it with a
whip. King Solomon, it is known, shut up the most prominent
demons of Jewry in bottles, sealed them, and had them sunk to the
bottom of the sea. What goings on, down there, of impotent fury!
Alike, Boris thought, to the dumb struggles within the narrow and
wooden chests of old women, sealed up by the Solomonic wax of

their education. Probably her sight failed her, and the red damask parlor grew black before her eyes, for she laid down the letter before she could have had time to finish it.

"What! what!" she said in a hoarse and hardly audible voice, "what does the Poet write to you?" She gasped for air, raised her right hand, and shook her trembling forefinger in the air. "She will not marry you!" she exclaimed.

"She will not marry at all, Aunt," said Boris to console her.

"No? Not at all?" sneered the old lady. "A Diana, is she that? But would you not have made a nice little Actæon, my poor Boris? And all that you have offered her—the position, the influence, the future—that means nothing to her? What is it she wants to be?" She looked into the letter, but in her agony she was holding it, bewildered, upside down. "A stone figure upon a sarcophagus—in the dark, in silence, forever? Here we have a fanatical virgin, *en plein dixneuvième siècle? Vraiment tu n'as pas de la chance!* There is no *horror vaccui* here."

"The law of the *horror vaccui*," Boris, who was really frightened, said to distract her, "does not hold good more than thirty two feet up."

"More than what?" asked the Prioress.

"Thirty-two feet," he said. The Prioress shrugged her shoulders. She turned her glinting eyes on him, pulling the letter, which she had received by the post, half up from her silk pocket, and putting it back again. "She will have nothing," she said slowly, "and you will give nothing. It seems to me, in all modesty, that you are well paired. I myself, giving you my blessing, have got nothing to say. That was already in the rules of my forefathers: 'Where nothing is, *le Seigneur a perdu son droit.*' You, Boris, you will have to go back to Court, and to the old Dowager Queen and her Chaplain, by the way you came. For," she added, still more slowly, "where we have entered in, there also we withdraw." These words impressed the old woman herself more than they did her nephew, who had heard them before. She became very silent.

Boris began to feel really uncomfortable, and desired to put an end to the conversation. He could understand quite well that she wanted him to suffer. While she had been happy she had liked to have happy people around her. Now, tortured, she had to surround herself with the sort of substance which was within herself, or, as in the vacuum of which she had been talking, she would be crushed. But in his particular case she had such strong allies in the very circumstances. It was true that he had not yet realized what Athena's refusal would mean to him. If the old woman would go on beating him like this with all her might, all the misery of the last weeks would be returned upon his head again. Suddenly the Prioress turned from him and went up to the window, as if she meant to throw herself out.

In the midst of his own individual distress Boris could not hold his thoughts from the other two persons within this trinity of theirs. Perhaps Athena was walking the pine forests of Hopballehus, her face as wildly set as that of the old woman in her parlor. In his mind he saw himself, in his white uniform, as a marionette, pulled alternately by the deadly determined old lady and the deadly determined young lady. How was it that things meant so much to them? What forces did these impassionate people have within them to make them prefer death to surrender? Very likely he had himself as strong tastes in the matter of this marriage as anybody, but still he did not clench his hands or lose his power of speech.

The Prioress turned from the window and came up to him. She was all changed, and carried no implements of the rack with her. On the contrary she seemed to bring a garland to crown his head. She looked so much lighter, that it was really as if she had been throwing a weight away, out of the window, and was now gracefully floating an inch above the ground.

"Dear Boris," she said, "Athena still has a heart. She owes it to the old playfellow of her childhood to see him, to give him a chance of speaking to her, and to answer him by word of mouth.

I will tell her all this, and send the letter back at once. The daughter of Hopballehus has a sense of duty. She will come."

"Where?" asked Boris.

"Here," said the Prioress.

"When?" asked Boris, looking around.

"This evening, for supper," said his aunt. She was smiling, a gentle, even waggish little smile, and still her mouth seemed to get smaller and smaller, like a very dainty little rosebud. "Athena," she said, "must not leave Closter Seven tomorrow without being——" She paused a little, looked to the right and left, and then at him. "Ours!" she said, smiling, in a little whisper. Boris looked at her. Her face was fresh as that of a young girl.

"My child, my dear child," she exclaimed, in a sudden outburst of deep, gentle passion, "nothing, nothing must stand in the way of your happiness!"

VII

This great supper of seduction, which was to remain a landmark in the existence of the banqueters, was served in the Prioress's dining-room, and groups of oriental statesmen and dancers watched it from the walls. The table was prettily decorated with camellias from the orangery, and upon the snow-white tablecloth, amongst the clear crystal glasses, the old green wineglasses threw delicate little shadows, like the spirit of a pine forest in summer. The Prioress had on a gray taffeta frock with very rare lace, a white lace cap with streamers, and her large old diamond eardrops and brooches. The heroic strength of soul of old women, Boris thought, who with great taste and trouble make themselves beautiful—more beautiful, perhaps, than they have ever been as young women—and who still can hold no hope of awakening any desire in the hearts of men, is like that of a righteous man working at his good deeds even after he has abandoned his faith in a heavenly reward.

The food was very good, and they had one of the famous carp of Closter Seven, cooked in a way which was kept a secret of the convent. Old Johann poured out the wine very freely, and before they had come to the marzipan and crystallized fruit, the convives of this quiet and dignified meal of an old and a young maid and a rejected lover, were all three of them more than a little drunk.

Athena was slightly drunk in the everyday sense of the word. She had drunk very little wine in her life, and had never tasted champagne, and with the amounts which the hostess of the supper party poured into her, she ought rightly not to have been able to stand on her legs. But she had behind her a long row of ancestors who had in their time lain under all the heavy old oak tables of the province, and who now came to the assistance of the daughter of their race. Still the wine went to her head. It gave her a rose on each cheek, and very bright eyes, and let loose new forces of her nature. She came to swell over a little in her feeling of invincibility, like a young captain advancing into fire, with a high courage, overbearingly.

Boris, who could drink more than most people, and who till the end remained the most sober of the party, was drunk in a more spiritual way. The deepest and truest thing in the nature of the young man was his great love for the stage and all its ways. His mother, as a maiden, had had the same grand passion, and had fought a mighty combat with her parents in Russia to go onto the stage, and lost it. Her son had no need to fight anybody. He was not dogmatic enough to believe that you must have boards and footlights to be within the theater; he carried the stage with him in his heart. As a very young boy he had played many ladies' rôles in amateur theatricals, and the famous old stage manager Paccazina had burst into tears on seeing him as Antigone, so much did he remind him of Mars. To him the theater was real life. As long as he could not act, he was puzzled by the world and uncertain what to do with it; but as an actor he was his true self, and as soon as he could see a situation in the light of the theater, he would feel at home in it. He did not shirk tragedy, and would perform with good grace in a pastoral, if it were asked of him.

There was something in this way of thinking that he had which exasperated his mother, in spite of her old sympathies for the art, for she suspected him of having in his heart very little preference for the rôle of a promising and popular young officer. He was, she thought, prepared to give it up at any moment should a rôle that would appeal more strongly to him present itself, be it that of an outcast or martyr, or, possibly, the tragic part of a youth ascending the scaffold. She had sometimes wanted to cry to him, contrarily to the Old Cordelier: Oh, my child, you fear too little unpopularity, exile and death! Still she could not herself help admiring him in his favorite rôles, nor, even, at times taking up a rôle herself in an ensemble with him, and these performances of theirs might embrace a very wide scale.

Tonight Paccazina would have delighted in him; he had never played better. Out of gratitude to his godmother, he had resolved to do his best. He had laid his mask with great care in front of his mirror, and had exchanged his uniform for that black color which he considered more appropriate to his part. In itself he always preferred the rôle of the unhappy, to that of the successful, lover. The wine helped him on, as did the faces of his fellow-players, including old Johann, who wore on his closed countenance a discreet shine of happiness. But he was himself in his own heart carried away by the situation, by the action of the play and by his own talents. He was on the boards, the curtain was up, every moment was precious, and he needed no *souffleur*.

As he looked at Athena on his left hand, he was pleased with his *jeune première* of the night. Now that they were upon the stage together he read her like a book.

He quite understood the deep impression which his proposal had made upon the mind of the girl. It had not flattered her; it had probably at the moment made her very angry. And the fact that any live person could in this way break in upon the proud isolation of her life had given her a shock. He agreed with her about it. Having lived all his life with people who were never alone, he had become sensitive to her atmosphere of solitude. It had happened to himself, at times, to be entirely alone on a night, dreaming, not of familiar persons or things, but of scenes and people wholly his own creation, and the recollection of such nights he would cherish in his mind. What was now at the moment bewildering the girl was the fact that the enemy approached her in such an extremely gentle manner, and that the offender was asking for consolation. As Boris grew conscious of these feelings of hers, he accentuated the sweetness and sadness of his behavior.

It was probably such a new thing to Athena to feel fear that it had a strange attraction for her. It was doubtful, he thought, whether anything but the scent of some sort of danger could have brought her to Closter Seven on this night. Of what is she afraid? he thought. Of being made happy by my aunt and me? This is this tragic maiden's prayer: From being a success at court, a happy, congratulated bride, a mother of a promising family, good Lord, deliver me. As a tragic actor of a high standard himself, he applauded her.

The presence of some unknown danger, he felt, was impressed upon the girl by the Prioress's manner toward her. The old woman had been her friend before, but a severe friend. Most of what the girl had said and done had till now been wrong here at the convent, and she had always known that in a benevolent way the old lady had wanted to put her in a cage. Tonight the old eyes dwelt upon her with sweet content, what she said was received with little smiles as gentle as caresses. The cage had been put out of sight. This special sort of incense, offered to her individually, was as unknown to Athena as the champagne itself, and as it was now being burnt at her from her right and her left, she might have felt a difficulty in breathing within the comfortable dining-room of Closter Seven, had she not felt so sure that the door behind her would open, whenever she wanted it, to the woods of Hopballehus.

Boris, who knew more about that door, lifted his eyelashes, soft as mimosa leaves, upon her flaming face. Had her father called her a bird of the night, the eyes of which are hurt by the light? He himself was now walking, slowly, backwards in front of her, carrying some sort of chandelier which twinkled at her. She blinked a little at the light, but she came on.

The Prioress was drunk with some secret joy which remained a mystery to the other convives of her supper party and which glinted in the dark. From time to time she dabbed her eyes or her mouth with her little, delicately perfumed, lace handkerchief.

VIII

"My great-grandmother," said the Prioress in the course of the conversation, "was, in her second marriage, ambassadress to Paris, and lived there for twenty years. This was under the Regency. She has written down in her memoirs, how, during the Christmas of 1727, the Holy Family came to Paris and were known to stay there for twelve hours. The entire building of the stable of Bethlehem had mysteriously been moved, even with the crib and the pots in which St. Joseph had been cooking the spiced beer for the Virgin, to a garden of a small convent, called du Saint Esprit. The ox and the ass were themselves transported, together with the straw upon the floor. When the nuns reported the miracle at the Court of Versailles, it was kept from the public, for they feared that it might presage a judgment upon the lewdness of the rulers of France. But the Regent went in great state, with all his jewels on, together with his daughter, the Duchess of Berri, the Cardinal Dubois, and a few selected ladies and gentlemen of the Court, to do homage to the Mother of God and her husband. My great-grandmother was allowed, because of the high esteem in which she was held at Court, to come with them as the only foreigner, and she preserved to the end of her days the furred robe of brocade, with a long train, which she wore on the occasion.

"The Regent had been highly moved and agitated by the news. At the sight of the Virgin he went into a strange ecstasy. He swayed and uttered little screams. You will know that the beauty of the Mother of the Lord, while without equal, was of such a kind that it could awaken no sort of earthly desire. This the Duke of Orléans had never experienced before, and he did not know what to do. At last he asked her, in turn blushing scarlet and deadly pale, to come to a supper at the Berri's, where he would have such food and wine served as had never been seen before, and to which he would make the Comte de Noircy come, and Madame de Parabere.

"The Duchess of Berri was at the time in *grossesse*, and evil tongues had it that this was by her father, the Regent. She threw herself at the feet of the Virgin. 'Oh, dear sweet Virgin,' she cried, 'forgive me. You would never have done it, I know. But if I could only tell you what a deadly, what a damnably dull Court this is!' Fascinated by the beauty of the child she dried her tears and asked for permission to touch it. 'Like strawberries and cream,' she exclaimed, 'like strawberries à la Zelma Kuntz.' Cardinal Dubois saluted St. Joseph with extreme politeness. He considered that this saint would not often be bothering the Almighty with supplications, but when he did so, he would be heard, as the Lord owed him much. The Regent fell upon my great-grandmother's neck, all in tears, and cried: 'She will never, never come. Oh, Madame—you, who are a virtuous woman, tell me what in the world to do.' All this is in my great-grandmother's memoirs."

They talked about travels, and the Prioress entertained them with many pleasant reminiscences of her young days. She was in high spirits, her old face freshly colored under the lace of her cap. From time to time she made use of a little gesture peculiar to her, of daintily scratching herself here and there with her delicately pointed little finger. "You are lucky, my little friend," she said to Athena. "To you the world is like a bride, and each particular unveiling is a surprise and a delight. Alas, we, who have celebrated our golden wedding with it, are prudent in our inquisitiveness."

"I should like," said Athena, "to go to India, where the King of Ava is now fighting the English General Amhurst. He has, Pastor Rosenquist has told me, tigers with his army, which are taught to fight the enemy along with it." In her excited state of mind she overturned her glass, breaking the stem of it, and the wine flowed over the tablecloth.

"I should like," said Boris, who did not want to talk of Pastor Rosenquist, in whom he suspected an antagonist—beware, his mind told him, of people who have in the course of their lives neither taken part in an orgy nor gone through the experience of childbirth, for they are dangerous people—"to go away and live upon a forlorn island, far from other people. There is nothing for which you feel such a great longing as for the sea. The passion of man for the sea," he went on, his dark eyes on Athena's face, "is unselfish. He cannot cultivate it; its water he cannot drink; in it he dies. Still, far from the sea you feel part of your own soul dying, disappearing, like a jellyfish thrown on dry land."

"On the sea!" the Prioress cried. "Going on the sea! Ah, never, never." Her deep disgust drove the blood to her face until it became quite pink and her eyes shone. Boris was impressed, as he had been before, by the intensity of all women's aversion to anything nautical. He had himself as a boy tried to run away from home to be a sailor. But nothing, he thought, makes a woman flare up in a deadly hostility as quickly as talk of the sea. From the first smell of sea water to the contact with salted and tarred ropes, they loath and shun it and all its ways; and perhaps the church might have kept the sex in order by painting them a maritime, an ashen-gray and frigid waving hell. For fire they fear not, looking upon it as an ally to whom they have long done service. But to talk to them of the sea is like talking of the devil. By the time when the rule of woman shall have made the land inhabitable to man, he will have to take to the sea for peace, for women will rather die than follow him there.

A sweet pudding was served to them, and the Prioress, with a neat *gourmandise,* picked out a few of the cloves in it and ate them. "This is a very lovable smell and taste," she said, "and the fragrance of a clove grove unbelievably delightful in the midday sun, or when the evening breeze fans the spiced currents of air all over the land. Try a few of them. It is incense to the stomach."

"Where do they come from, Madame my Aunt?" asked Athena, who, in accordance with the tradition of the province, was used to address her in this way.

"From Zanzibar," said the Prioress. A gentle melancholy seemed for a few minutes to sink over her as she sat in deep thought, nibbling at her cloves.

Boris, in the meantime, had been looking at Athena, and had let a fantasy take hold of his mind. He thought that she must have a lovely, an exquisitely beautiful, skeleton. She would lie in the ground like a piece of matchless lace, a work of art in ivory, and in a hundred years might be dug up and turn the heads of old archeologists. Every bone was in place, as finely finished as a violin. Less frivolous than the traditional old libertine who in his thoughts undresses the women with whom he sups Boris liberated the maiden of her strong and fresh flesh together with her clothes, and imagined that he might be very happy with her, that he might even fall in love with her, could he have her in her beautiful bones alone. He fancied her thus, creating a sensation on horseback, or trailing her long dresses through the halls and galleries at Court, with the famous tiara of her family, now in Poland, upon her polished skull. Many human relations, he thought, would be infinitely easier if they could be carried out in the bones only.

"The King of Ava," said the Prioress, awakening from the soft reverie into which she had been sunk, "had, in the city of

Yandabu—so I have been told by those who have been there —a large menagerie. As in all his country he had none but the elephants of India, the Sultan of Zanzibar presented him with an African elephant, which is much bigger and more magnificent than the rotund, domesticated Indian beasts. They are indeed wonderful animals. They rule the highlands of East Africa, and the ivory traders who sell their mighty tusks at the ivory markets have many tales of their strength and ferocity. The elephants of Yandabu and their herdsmen were terrified of the Sultan's elephants—such as Africa always frightens Asia—and in the end they made the King have him put in chains and a barred house built for him in the menagerie. But from that time, on moonlit nights, the whole city of Yandabu began to swarm with the shades of the elephants of Africa, wandering about the place and waving their large shadow-ears in the streets. The natives of Yandabu believed that these shadow-elephants were able to walk along the bottom of the ocean, and to come up beside the landing place of the boats. No people dared any more be out in the town after dark had fallen. Still they could not break the cage of the captive elephant.

"The hearts of animals in cages," the Prioress went on, "become grated, as upon a grill, upon the shadow of the bars. Oh, the grated hearts of caged animals!" she exclaimed with terrible energy.

"Still," she said after a moment, her face changing, with a little giggle at the bottom of her voice, "it served those elephants right. They were great tyrants when in their own country. No other animal could have its own way for them."

"And what became of the Sultan's elephant?" Athena asked.

"He died, he died," said the old woman, licking her lips.

"In the cage?" asked Athena.

"Yes. In the cage," the Prioress answered.

Athena laid her folded hands upon the table, with exactly the gesture of the old Count after he had read the Prioress's letter.

She looked around the room. The bright color sank from her face. The supper was finished, and they had nearly emptied their glasses of port.

"I think, my Aunt," she said, "that with your permission I will now go to bed. I feel very tired."

"What?" said the Prioress. "Indeed you must not deprive us of the pleasure of your company yet, my nutmeg. I was going to withdraw myself now, but I want you two old friends to have a little talk on this night. Surely you promised Boris that —the dear boy."

"Yes, but that must be tomorrow morning," Athena said, "for I believe that I have drunk too much of the good wine. Look, my hand is not even steady when I put it on this table." The Prioress stared at the girl. She probably felt, Boris thought, that she ought not to have talked about cages, that she had here made her one *faux pas* of the evening.

Athena looked at Boris, and he felt that he had obtained this slight success: that she was sorry to part from him. Altogether she probably realized that she was making an abrupt retreat from the battle, and regretted it, but under the circumstances she considered it the best move. Boris felt her straight glance as a decoration received before the front. It was not a high decoration, but in this campaign he could not expect more. The girl bid a very kind goodnight to the Prioress, curtseyed to her, and was gone.

The Prioress turned in great agitation to her nephew. "Do not let her go away," she said to him. "Follow her. Take hold of her. Do not waste your time."

"Let us leave her alone," said Boris. "That girl has spoken the truth. She will not have me."

The double rebelliousness in the two young people, the happiness of whose lives she was arranging, seemed to make the Prioress lose speech, or faith in speech. She and Boris remained together in the room for perhaps five minutes more, and it seemed to Boris, when he afterward thought of it, that their intercourse had been carried out entirely in pantomime.

The Prioress stood quite still and looked at the young man, and he really did not know whether within the next seconds she would kill him or kiss him. She did neither. She laughed a little in his face, and fumbling in her pocket she drew out the letter which she had received in the morning, and gave it to him to read.

This letter was a last deadly blow upon the boy's head. It was written by the Prioress's friend, who was the first lady of honor of the Dowager Queen. With deep compassion for his aunt she gave, in very dark colors, the latest news of the capital. His name had been brought up, he had even been pointed out particularly by the Court Chaplain, as one of the corrupters of youth in the case. It was clear that he was at this moment standing upon the brink of an abyss, and that unless he could get this marriage of his through, he should fall over and disappear.

He stood for a little while, his face changed by pain. His whole being rose against being dragged from his star part of the evening, and the elegiac mood of a lover, back to this reality that he loathed. As he looked up to give back the letter to his aunt he found her standing quite close to him. She lifted one hand, keeping her elbow close to her body, and pointed toward the door.

"Aunt Cathinka," said Boris, "you do not know, perhaps, but there is a limit to the effects of will-power in a man."

The old woman kept staring at him. She stretched out her dry delicate little hand and touched him. Her face twisted in a wry little grimace. After a moment she moved around to the back of the room and brought back a bottle and a small glass. Very carefully she filled the glass, handed it to him, and nodded her head two or three times. In sheer despair he emptied it.

The glass was filled with a liquor of the color of very old dark amber. It had an acrid and rank taste. Acrid and rank were also the old dark-amber eyes of the woman, watching him over the rim of the glass. As he drank, she laughed. Then she spoke. Boris, strangely enough, afterward remembered these words, which he did not understand: "Help him now, you good Faru," she said.

When he had left the room, after a second or two she very gently closed the door after him.

IX

Now this might be the hour for tears, to move the proud beauty's heart, Boris thought. He remembered the tales of that gruesome gang of pilgrims, the old hangmen, who are said to have been wandering over Europe in the twelfth century, visiting the holy places. They carried with them the attributes of their trade: thumbscrews, whips, irons and tongs, and these people, it was said, were able to weep whenever they wanted to. "Yes," the boy said to himself, "but I have not hewed up, flayed and fried alive enough people for that. A few I have, of course, as we all have; but I am only a young hangman for all that—a hangman's apprentice—and the gift of weeping whenever I want to, I have not attained."

He walked down the long white corridor, which led to Athena's room. It had on his left hand a row of old portraits of ladies, and on the right a row of tall windows. The floor was laid with black and white marble tiles, and the whole place looked seriously at him in the nocturnal light. He heard his own footfall, fatal to others and to himself. He looked out of one of the windows as he passed it. The moon stood high in the heavens, clear and cold, but the trees of the park and the lawns lay in a silvery mist. There outside was the whole noble blue universe, full of things, in which the earth swam onward amongst thousands of stars, some near and others far away. O world, he thought, O rich world. Into his hot brain was thrown a long-forgotten verse:

> *Athena, my high mistress, on Apollon's bidding,*
> *Here I come to thee.*
> *Much experienced, and tried in many things.*
> *A house, inhabited by strangers, strangely changed.*
> *Thus have I wandered far on land, and on the sea. . . .*

He had come to the door. He turned the handle, and went in.

Of all the memories which afterward Boris carried with him from this night, the memory of the transition from the coloring and light of the corridor to that of the room was the longest lasting.

The Prioress's state guest room was large and square, with windows, upon which the curtains were now drawn, on the two walls. The whole room was hung with rose silks, and in the depths of it the crimson draperies of the four-poster bed glowed in the shade. There were two pink-globed lamps, solicitously lighted by the Prioress's maid. The floor had a wine-colored carpet with roses in it, which, near the lamps, seemed to be drinking in the light, and farther from them looked like pools of dark crimson into which one would not like to walk. The room was filled with the scent of incense and flowers. A large bouquet decorated the table near the bed.

Boris knew at once what it was that he felt like. He had at one time, when he had been on a visit to Madrid, been much addicted to bull fights. He was familiar with the moment when the bull is, from his dark waiting-room underneath the tribune, rushed into the dazzling sunlight of the arena, with the many hundred eyes around it. So was he himself in a moment hurled from the black and white corridor, of quiet moonlight, into this red atmosphere. His blood leapt up to his brain; he hardly knew where he was. With failing breath he wondered if this was an effect of the Prioress's love potion. He did not know either whether Athena was now to be the disemboweled horse, which would be dragged out of the arena, having no more will of its own, or the matador who was to lay him low. One or the other she would be—he could meet nobody else in this place.

Athena was standing in the middle of the room. She had taken off her frock and was dressed only in a white chemise and white pantalettes. She looked like a sturdy young sailor boy about to swab the deck. She turned as he came in, and stared at him.

Boris had been afraid, when imagining the development of the situation, that he would not be able to keep himself from laughing. This risibility of his had before now been his ruin in tender situations. But at the moment he ran no such risk. He was as much in earnest as the girl herself. He had, before he knew where he was, taken hold of one of her wrists and drawn her toward him. Their breaths met and mingled, they were both baring their teeth a little in a sort of perplexed smile or challenge.

"Athena," he said, "I have loved you all my life. You know that without you I shall dry up and shrink, there shall be nothing left of me. Stoop to me, throw me back in the deep. Have mercy on me."

For a moment the light-eyed girl stared at him, bewildered. Then she drew herself up as a snake does when it is ready to strike. That she did not attempt to cry for help showed him that she had a clearer understanding of the situation, and of the fact that she had no friend in the house, than he had given her credit for; or perhaps her young broad breast harbored sheer love of combat. The next moment she struck out. Her powerful, swift and direct fist hit him in the mouth and knocked out two of his teeth. The pain and the smell and taste of the blood which filled his mouth sent him beside himself. He let her go to try for a stronger hold, and immediately they were in each other's arms, in an embrace of life and death.

At this same moment Boris's heart leapt up within him and sang aloud, like a bird which swings itself to the top of a tree and there bursts into song. Nothing happier in all the world could have happened to him. He had not known how this conflict between them was to be solved, but she had known it; and as a coast sinks around a ship which takes the open sea, so did all the worries of his life sink around this release of all his being. His existence up to now had given him very little opportunity for fury. Now he gave his heart up to the rapture of it. His soul laughed like the souls of those old Teutons to whom the lust of anger was in itself the highest voluptuousness, and who demanded nothing better of their paradise than the capacity for being killed once a day.

He could not have fought another young man, were he one of the Einherjar of Valhalla, as he fought this girl. All hunters of big game will know that there is a difference between hunting the wild boar or buffalo, however dangerous they may be, and hunting the carnivora, who, if successful, will eat you up at the end of the contest. Boris, on a visit to his Russian relations, had seen his horse devoured by a pack of wolves. After that, none of the Prioress's raging wild elephants could have called forth the same feeling in him. The old, wild love, which sympathy cannot grant, which contrast and adversity inspire, filled him altogether.

If the shadows of the young women who had clung to him, and out of whose soft arms the fickle lover had torn himself, had been at this moment gathered within the Prioress's rose-colored guest room, they would have felt the pride of their sex satisfied in the contemplation of his mortal pursuit of this maiden who now strove less to escape than to kill him. They tumbled to and fro for a few seconds, and one of the lamps was turned over, fell down, and went out Then the struggle stabilized itself. They ceased moving and stood clasped together, swaying a little until they found their foothold, the balance of the one so dependent upon and amalgamated with that of the other that neither knew clearly where his own body ended and that of his adversary began. They were breathing hard. Her breath in his face was fragrant as an apple. The blood kept coming into his mouth.

The girl had no feminine inspiration to scratch or bite. Like a young she bear, she relied on her great strength, and in weight she scored a little. Against his attempts to bend her knees she stood up as straight as a tree. By a sudden movement she got her hands on his throat. He was holding her close to him, her elbows pressed to her sides. Her posture was that of a warrior, clinging to the hilt of his lifted sword, taking a vital vow. He had not known the power of her hands and wrists. Gasping for air, his mouth full of blood, he saw the whole room swaying from one side to another. Red and black flecks swam in front of him. At this moment he struck out for a last triumph. He forced her head forward with the hand that he had at the back of her neck, and pressed his mouth to hers. His teeth grated against her teeth.

Instantly he felt, through his whole body, which was clinging to hers from the knees to the lips, the terrible effect which his kiss had on the girl. She, surely, had never been kissed in her life, she had not even heard or read of a kiss. The force used against her made her whole being rise in a mortal disgust. As if he had run a rapier straight through her, the blood sank from her face, her body stiffened in his arms like that of a slowworm, when you hit it. Then all the strength and suppleness which he had been fighting seemed to roll back and withdraw, as a wave withdraws from a bather. He saw her eyes grow dim, her face, so close to his, fade to a dead white. She went down so suddenly that he came down with her, like a drowning man tied to a weight. His face was thrown against hers.

He got up on his knees, wondering if she were dead. As he found that she was not, he lifted her, after a moment, with difficulty, and laid her upon her bed. She was indeed now like a stone effigy of a mail-clad knight, felled in battle. Her face had preserved its expression of deadly disgust. He watched her for a little while, very still himself. He did not know that his own face had the same expression. Had the thought of the Court Chaplain been with him, had the Court Chaplain been with him in the flesh, it could not have stirred him. His spirit had gone almost as definitely as hers. There was no more effect of the wine in him; none, either, of the Prioress's love philter, which perhaps was not calculated for more than one great effort. He wiped his bleeding mouth and left the room.

Within his own room and bed he came to wonder whether the maiden would, upon her awakening, lament her lost innocence. He laughed to himself in the dark, and it seemed to him that a thin, shrill laughter, like to the shoot of hot steam from a boiling kettle, was echoing his own somewhere in the great house, in the dark.

X

In the morning the Prioress sent for Boris. He was a little frightened when he saw her, for she seemed to have shrunk. She filled up neither her clothes nor her armchair, and he wondered what sort of night hours had passed over her head in her lonely bed to have squeezed out her strength like this. If all this, he thought, is to go on much longer, there will be nothing left of her. But probably I am looking worse than she myself. Still, she appeared to be in high spirits, and pleased to have got hold of him, as if she had been, somehow, in fear that he might have run away. She told him to sit down. "I have sent for Athena as well," she said.

Boris was content that she did not ask him any questions. His mouth had swelled badly, and hurt him when he had to speak. While waiting he thought of the Vicomte de Valmont, who loved *de passion, les mines de lendemain*. Would the unusual in the circumstances have given this particular morrow an additional charm in the eyes of the matter-of-fact old conqueror of a hundred years ago? Or was it not more likely that he would have considered the romantic values of the situation to be all nonsense? Athena's arrival put an end to his reflections.

She was wearing the same great gray cloak in which he had seen her at Hopballehus, and seemed about to depart. She did indeed so much give the impression of having turned her back on Closter Seven, and of being already away from it, that he felt somehow left out in the cold. As she looked slowly around, he was deeply struck by her appearance. She seemed to be well on her way to that purified state of the skeleton in which he had imagined her on the night before. She had in reality a death's-head upon her strong shoulders. Her eyes, grown paler in themselves, lay in black holes. She had given up her habit of standing on one leg, as if it now required both her legs to keep her upright and in balance. Confronted by the Prioress, who had still much keen life in her face, she might well have been an accused in the felon's dock, brought straight from the vaults of a dungeon, and from the rack.

Boris at this moment wondered whether it would be better for her that he should tell her all, and assure her that he had done her no harm and would not be likely ever to do her any; in fact, that she had come out of their trial of strength with the honors of war. But he thought it would not. If you prepare yourself, he considered, for lifting a leaden weight, and are deceived by a painted cardboard, your arms come out of joint. In his admiration for her skeleton he was the last person to wish this to happen to her. It was better for her to carry the weight. This maiden, he thought, who could not, who would not, be made happy, let her now have her fill. Like to an artist who has got his statue in the crucible and finds himself short of metals, and who seizes the gold and silver from his treasury, from his table, from his women's caskets to hurl it in, so he had thrown his being, body and soul, into the fatal soundings of her nature. Now she must make out of it what she could.

The Prioress, looking in turn at one and then at the other of the young people, spoke to the girl.

"I have been informed," she said in a dull and hard voice, "by Boris of what has happened here in the night. I do not forgive him. It is a horrible deed to seduce a maiden. But I know that he was goaded on, and also that a candid repentance extenuates the crime. But you, Athena, a girl of your blood and your upbringing—what have you done? You, who must have known your own nature, you ought never to have come here."

"No, no, Madame my Aunt," said Athena, looking straight at the old woman, "I came here because you invited me, and you told me that it was my duty to come. Now I go away again, and if you do not like to think of me, you need not."

"Ah, no," said the Prioress, "such a thing you cannot do. It is terrible to me that this has happened within the walls of Closter Seven. You know me very little if you think that I shall not have it repaired. Would I show so little friendship toward your father, who is a nobleman? Till this wrong has been expiated, you shall not depart."

Athena first seemed to let this pass for what it was worth and did not answer. Then she asked: "How is it to be repaired?"

"We must be thankful," said the Prioress, "that Boris, guilty as he be, has still a sense of duty left. He will marry you even now." With these words she shot at her nephew a little hard and shining glance, which startled him, as if she had touched him once more.

"Yes, but I will not marry him," said Athena.

The Prioress had by now a highly glowing color in her face. "How is it," she asked in a shrill voice, "that you refuse an honorable offer, of which your father approves, to accept, in the middle of the night, the love that you had rejected?"

"I do not think," said Athena, "that it matters whether a thing happens in the day or the night."

"And if you have a child?" cried the Prioress.

"What!" said Athena.

The Prioress subdued her blazing passion with a wonderful strength of spirit. "I pity you as much as I condemn you," she said. "And if you have a child, unfortunate girl?"

Athena's world was evidently tumbling down to the right and left of her, like a position under heavy gun fire, but still she stood up straight. "What?" she asked. "Shall I have a child from that?"

The old woman looked hard at her. "Athena," she said after a moment, with the first particle of gentleness which she had, during the conversation, shown toward the girl, "the last thing I wish is to destroy what innocence you may still have left. But it is more than likely that you will have a child."

"If I have a child," said Athena, from her quaking earth thrusting at the heavens, "my father will teach him astronomy."

Boris leaned his elbow on the table and his face in his hand to hide it. For the life of him he could not help laughing. This deadly pale and still maiden was not beaten. A good deal of her pallor and immobility might be due to the wine and the exertion of the night, and God only knew if they would ever get her into their power. She had in her the magnet, the maelstrom quality of drawing everything which came inside her circle of consciousness into her own being and making it one with herself. It was a capacity, he thought, which had very likely been a characteristic of the martyrs, and which may well have aggravated the Great Inquisitor, and even the Emperor Nero himself, to the brink of madness. The tortures, the stake, the lions, they made their own, and thereby conveyed to them a great harmonious beauty; but the torturer they left outside. No matter what efforts he made to possess them, they stood in no relation to him, and in fact deprived him of existence. They were like the lion's den, into which all tracks were seen to lead, while none came out; or like the river, which drowns blood or filth in its own being, and flows on. Here, just as the conquering old woman and young man had believed the situation to be closing around her, the girl was about to ride away from Closter Seven, like to Samson when he lifted upon his shoulders the doors of Gazi, the two posts, bars and all, and carried them to the top of the hill that is before Hebron. And if she should really become aware of him, would the giant's daughter, he wondered, carry him with her upon the palm of her hand to Hopballehus, and make him groom her unicorns? Again a verse from Euripides ran through his head, and he felt that it must be the wine of the previous night and the whole agitation around him which now caused him, in this way, to mix up the classics with Scripture and with the legends of his province, for ordinarily he did not do that sort of thing:

Oh, Pallas, savior of my house, I was bereft
of Fatherland, and thou hast given me a home again therein.
It shall be said
in Hellas: Lo, the man is an Argive once more,
and dwells again within his father's heritance. . . .

"And what of the honor of your house?" asked the Prioress with a deadly calm. "Who do you think, Athena, of the daughters of Hopballehus, has, before you, been breeding bastards?"

At these words all Athena's blood rushed to her face until it flamed darker than her flaming hair. She took a step toward the old lady.

"My child," she cried in a low tone, but with the lioness's roar deep within her voice, from head to foot the offended daughter of a mighty race, "would my child be that?"

"You are ignorant, Athena," said the old woman. "Unless Boris marries you, what can your child be but a bastard?" Brave as the Prioress was, she probably realized that the girl, if she wished to, could crush her between her fingers. She kept her quick eyes on Boris, who did not feel called upon to interfere in the women's discussion of his child.

Athena did not move. She stood for a few moments quite still. "Now," she said at length, "I will go back to Hopballehus, and speak with my father, and ask his advice about all this."

"No," said the Prioress again, "that is not as it should be. If you tell your father of what you have done, you will break his heart. I will not let that happen. And who knows, if you go now, if Boris will still be ready to marry you when you meet again? No, Athena, you must marry Boris, and you must never let your father know of what has happened here. These two things you shall promise me. Then you can go."

"Good," said Athena. "I will never tell Papa of anything. And as to Boris, I promise you that I shall marry him. But, Madame my Aunt, when we are married, and whenever I can do so, I shall kill him. I came near to killing him last night, he can tell you that. These three things I promise·you. Then I will go."

After Athena's words there was a long pause. The three people in the room had enough in their own thoughts, without speech, to occupy them.

In this silence was heard a hard and sharp knocking upon the pane of one of the windows. Boris now realized that he had heard it before, during the course of their talk, without paying any attention to it. Now it was repeated three or four times.

He became really aware of it at sight of the extraordinary effect which the sound had upon his aunt. She had, like himself, been too absorbed in the debate to listen. Now it attracted her attention and she was immediately struck by a deadly terror. She glanced toward the window and grew white as a corpse. Her arms and legs moved in little jerks, her eyes darted up and down the walls, like a rat that is shut up and·cannot get out.

Boris turned to the window to find out what was frightening her. He had not known that anything could really do so. Upon the stone sill outside, the monkey was crouching together, its face close to the glass.

He rose to open the window for it. "No! No!" shrieked the old woman in a paroxysm of horror. The knocking went on. The monkey obviously had something in its hand with which it was beating against the pane. The Prioress got up from her chair. She swayed in raising herself, but once on her legs she seemed alert and ready to run. But at the next moment the glass of the window fell crashing to the floor, and the monkey jumped into the room.

Instantly, without looking around, as if escaping from the flames of an advancing fire, the Prioress, gathering up the front of her silk frock with her two hands, ran, threw herself, toward the door. On finding it closed, she did not give herself time to open it. With the most surprising, most wonderful, lightness and swiftness she heaved herself straight up along the frame, and at the next moment was sitting squeezed together upon the sculptured cornice, shivering in a horrible passion, and grinding her teeth at the party on the floor. But the monkey followed her. As quickly as she had done it, it squirmed up the doorcase and was stretching out its hand to seize her when she deftly slid down the opposite side of the doorframe. Still holding her frock with both hands, and bending double, as if ready to drop on all fours, madly, as if blinded by fright, she dashed along the wall. But still the monkey followed her, and it was quicker than she. It jumped upon her, got hold of her lace cap, and tore it from her head. The face which she turned toward the young people was already transformed, shriveled and wrinkled, and of dark-brown color. There was a few moments' wild whirling fight. Boris made a movement to throw himself into it, to save his aunt. But already at the next moment, in the middle of the red damask parlor, under the eyes of the old powdered general and his wife, in the broad daylight and before their eyes, a change, a metamorphosis, was taking place and was consummated.

The old woman with whom they had been talking was, writhing and disheveled, forced to the floor; she was scrunched and changed. Where she had been, a monkey was now crouching and whining, altogether beaten, trying to take refuge in a corner of the room. And where the monkey had been jumping about, rose, a little out of breath from the effort, her face still a deep rose, the true Prioress of Closter Seven.

The monkey crawled into the shade of the back of the room and for a little while continued its whimpering and twitching. Then, shaking off its misfortunes, it jumped in a light and graceful leap onto a pedestal, which supported the marble head of the philosopher Immanuel Kant, and from there it watched, with its glittering eyes, the behavior of the three people in the room.

The Prioress took up her little handkerchief and held it to her eyes. For a few minutes she found no words, but her deportment was as quietly dignified and kindly as the young people had always remembered it.

They had been following the course of events, too much paralyzed by surprise to speak, move, or even look at each other. Now, as out of the terrible .tornado which had been reigning in the room, calm was again descending, they found themselves close to each other. They turned around and looked into each other's faces.

This time Athena's luciferous eyes within their deep dark sockets did not exactly take Boris into possession. She was aware of him as a being outside herself; even the memory of their fight was clearly to be found in her clear limpid gaze. But she was, in this look, laying down another law, a command which was not to be broken: from now, between, on the one side, her and him, who had been present together at the happenings of the last minutes, and, on the other side, the rest of the world, which had not been there, an insurmountable line would be forever drawn.

The Prioress lowered the handkerchief from her face, and in a soft and sweeping movement sat down in her large armchair. She looked at the young man and the girl.

"*Discite justitiam, et non temnere divos,*" she said.

The
Roads Round
Pisa

I. THE SMELLING-BOTTLE

COUNT AUGUSTUS VON SCHIMMELMANN, a young Danish nobleman of a melancholy disposition, who would have been very good-looking if he had not been a little too fat, was writing a letter on a table made out of a millstone in the garden of an *osteria* near Pisa on a fine May evening of 1823. He could not get it finished, so he got up and went for a stroll down the highroad while the people of the inn were getting his supper ready inside. The sun was nearly down. Its golden rays fell in between the tall poplars along the road. The air was warm and pure and filled with the sweet smell of grass and trees, and innumerable swallows were cruising about high and low, as if wanting to make the most of the last half-hour of daylight.

Count Augustus's thoughts were still with his letter. It was addressed to a friend in Germany, a schoolfellow of his happy student days in Ingolstadt, and the only person to whom he could open his heart. But have I been, he thought, really truthful in my letter to him? I would give a year of my life to be able to talk to him tonight and, while talking, to watch his face. How difficult it is to know the truth. I wonder if it is really possible to be absolutely truthful when you are alone. Truth, like time, is an idea arising from, and dependent upon, human intercourse. What is the truth about a mountain in Africa that has no name and not even a footpath across it? The truth about this road is that it leads to Pisa, and the truth about Pisa can be found within books written and read by human beings. What is the truth about a man on a desert island? And I, I am like a man on a desert island. When I was a student my friends used to laugh at me because I was in the habit of looking at myself in the looking-glasses, and had my own rooms decorated with mirrors. They attributed this to personal vanity. But it was not really so. I looked into the glasses to see what I was like. A glass tells you the truth about yourself. With a shudder of disgust he remembered how he had been taken, as a child, to see the mirror-room of the Panoptikon, in Copenhagen, where you see yourself reflected, to the right and the left, in the ceiling and even on the floor, in a hundred glasses each of which distorts and perverts your face and figure in a different way—shortening, lengthening, broadening, compressing their shape, and still keeping some sort of likeness—and thought how much this was like real life. So your own self, your personality and existence are reflected within the mind of each of the people whom you meet and live with, into a likeness, a caricature of yourself, which still lives on and pretends to be, in some way, the truth about you. Even a flattering picture is a caricature and a lie. A friendly and sympathetic mind, like Karl's, he thought, is like a true mirror to the soul, and that is what made his friendship so precious to me. Love ought to be even more so. It ought to mean, along the roads of life, the companionship of another mind, reflecting your own fortune and misfortunes, and proving to you that all is not a dream. The idea of marriage has been to me the presence in my life of a person with whom I could talk, tomorrow, of the things that happened yesterday.

He sighed, and his thoughts returned to his letter. There he had tried to explain to his friend the reasons that had driven him from his home. He had the misfortune to have a very jealous wife. It is not, he thought, that she is jealous of other women. In fact she is that least of all, and the reason is, first, that she knows that she can hold her own with most of them, being the most charming and accomplished of them all; secondly, that she feels how little they mean to me. Karl himself will remember that the little adventures which I had at Ingolstadt meant less to me than the opera, when a company of singers came along and gave us *Alceste* or *Don Giovanni*—less even than my studies. But she is jealous of my friends, of my dogs, of the forests of Lindenburg, of my guns and books. She is jealous of the most absurd things.

He remembered something that had happened some six months after his wedding. He had come into his wife's room to bring her a pair of eardrops which he had made a friend in Paris buy for him from the estate of the Duke of Berri. He had always been fond of jewels himself, and had good knowledge of their quality and cut. It had even at times annoyed him that men should not be free to wear them, and after his marriage it had given him pleasure to make them set off the beauty of his young wife, who wore them so well. These were very fine, and he had been so pleased to have got them that he had fastened them in her ears himself, and held up the mirror for her to see them. She watched him, and was aware that his eyes were on the diamonds and not on her face. She quickly took them off and handed them to him. "I am afraid," she said, with dry eyes more tragic than if they had been filled with tears, "that I have not your taste for pretty things." From that day she had given up wearing jewels, and had adopted a style of dress as severe as that of a nun, and she was so elegant and graceful that she had created a sensation and made a whole school of imitators.

Can I make Karl understand, Augustus thought, that she is indeed jealous of her own jewels? Surely nobody can understand such folly. I know that I do not understand her myself, and I often think that I make her as unhappy as she makes me. I had hoped to find, in my wife, somebody to whom I could be perfectly truthful, with whom I could share every motion of my mind. But with Malvina that is the most impossible thing of all. She has made me lie to her twenty times a day, and deceive her even in looks and voice. No, I am certain that it could not go on, and that I have been right in leaving her, for while I was with her it would have been the same thing always.

But what will happen to me now? I do not know what to do with myself or my life. Can I trust to fate to hold out a helping hand to me just for once?

He took a small object from his waistcoat pocket and looked at it. It was a smelling-bottle, such as ladies of an earlier generation had been wont to use, made in the shape of a heart. It had painted on it a landscape with large trees and a bridge across a river. In the background, on a high hill or rock, was a pink castle with a tower, and on a ribbon below it all was written *Amitié sincère*.

He smiled as he thought that this little bottle had played its part in making him go to Italy. It had belonged to a maiden aunt of his father's, who had been the beauty of her time, and to whom he had been devoted. As a girl she had traveled in Italy, and had been a guest in that same rose-colored palace, and every dream of romance and adventure was in her mind attached to it. She had faith in her little smelling-bottle, thinking that it would cure any ache of the teeth or the heart. When he had been a little boy he had shared these fancies of hers, and had himself made up tales of the beautiful things to be found in the house and the happy life to be led there. Now that she was many years dead, nobody would know where it was to be found. Perhaps, he thought, some day I shall come across the bridge under the trees and see the rock and the castle before me.

How mysterious and difficult it is to live, he thought, and what does it all mean? Why does my life seem to me so terribly important, more important than anything that has ever happened? Perhaps in a hundred years people will be reading about me, and about my sadness tonight, and think it only entertaining, if even that.

II. THE ACCIDENT

At that moment he was interrupted in his thoughts by a terrible noise behind him. He turned around and the sinking sun shone straight into his eyes so that he was blinded and for a few seconds saw the world as all silver, gold and flames. In a cloud of dust a large coach was coming toward him at a terrifying speed, the horses running in a wild gallop and hurling the carriage from one side of the road to the other. While he was looking at it he seemed to see two human forms being whirled down and out.

They were, in fact, the coachman and lackey who were thrown from their seats to the road. For a moment Augustus thought of throwing himself in the way of the horses to stop them, but before the carriage reached him something gave way; first one and then the other of the horses detached itself from the carriage and came galloping past him. The carriage was thrown to one side of the road, stopping dead there, with one of the back wheels off. He ran toward it.

Leaning against the seat of the smashed carriage now lying in the dust was a bald old man with a refined face and a large nose. He stared straight at Augustus, but was so deadly pale and kept so still that Augustus wondered if he had not really been killed after all. "Allow me to help you, Sir," Augustus said. "You have had a horrible accident, but I hope you are not badly hurt." The old man looked at him as before, with bewildered eyes.

A broad young woman who had sat in the opposite seat and had been thrown down on her hands and knees between cushions and boxes, now began disentangling herself with loud lamentations. The old man turned his eyes upon her. "Put on my bonnet," he said. The maid, as Augustus found her to be, after some struggle got hold of a large bonnet with ostrich feathers, and managed to get it fixed on the old bald head. Fastened inside the bonnet was an abundance of silvery curls, and in a moment the old man was transformed into a fine old lady of imposing appearance. The bonnet seemed to set her at ease. She even found the shadow of a sweet and thankful smile for Augustus.

The coachman now came running up, all covered with dust, while the lackey was still lying in a dead faint in the middle of the road. Also the people of the *osteria* had come out with uplifted arms and loud exclamations of sympathy. One of them brought one of the horses back, and at a distance two peasants were seen trying to get hold of the other. Between them they carried the old lady out of the wreckage of the coach and into the best bed-room of the inn, which was adorned with an enormous bed with red curtains. She was still pale as a corpse, and breathed with difficulty. Her right arm seemed to have been broken above the wrist, but what other injuries she had received they could not tell. The maid, who had large round eyes like big black buttons, turned toward Augustus and asked: "Are you a doctor?"

"No," said the old lady from the bed, in a very faint voice, hoarse with pain. "No, he is neither a doctor nor a priest, of which I want none. He is a nobleman, and that is the only person I need. Leave the room, all of you, and let me speak to him alone."

When they were alone her face changed and she shut her eyes; then she told him to come nearer and asked his name. "Count," she said, after a short silence, "do you believe in God?"

Such a direct question threw Augustus into confusion, but as he found her pale old eyes fixed on him, he answered: "That was in fact the very question which I was asking myself at the moment when your horses ran away. I cannot tell."

"There is a God," she said, "and even very young people will realize it some day. I am going to die," she went on, "but I cannot, I will not, die till I have seen my granddaughter once more. Will you, as a man of noble birth and high mind, undertake to find her and bring her here?" She paused, and a strange series of expressions passed over her face. "Tell her," she said, "that I cannot lift my right hand, and that I will bless her."

Augustus, after wondering a moment, asked her where the young lady could be found. "She is in Pisa," said the grandmother, "and her name is Donna Rosina di Gampocorta. If you had been in the country nine months ago you would have known her name, for then nobody talked of anything else." She spoke so feebly that he had to keep his head close to her pillow, and for a moment he thought that all was over. Then she seemed to collect her strength. Her voice changed and became at times very high and clear, but he was not sure that she saw him or knew where she was. A faint color rose into her cheeks; her eyelids, like thick crape, trembled slightly. Strange and deep emotions seemed to shake her whole being. "I will tell you my whole story," she said, "so that you will understand what I want you to do for me."

III. THE OLD LADY'S STORY

"I am an old woman," she said, "and I know the world. I do not cling to it, for I know enough about it to realize that whatever you cling to will either patronize you or get tired of you. I do not even cling to God, for that same reason. Do not pretend to be sorry for me because I am going to die, for I feel that it is really more *comme il faut* to be dead than alive.

"I have had lovers, a husband, hundreds of friends and admirers. I have myself in my life loved three people, and of those I have now only one left, this girl Rosina.

"Her mother was not my own child—I was her stepmother. But we were more devoted to each other than any mother and daughter ever have been. It was all meant to be so, for from my girlhood I have had the greatest terror of childbearing, and when I was demanded in marriage by a widower, whose first wife had died in childbirth, I made it a condition that I should never bear him any children myself, and because of my beauty and wealth he agreed. The girl Anna was so lovely that I have with my own eyes seen the statue of St. Joseph at the Basilica turn his head to look at her, remembering the appearance of the Virgin at the time that they were betrothed. Her feet were like swan's bills, and the shoemaker made us our shoes over the same last. I brought her up to know that a woman's beauty is the crowning masterpiece of God, and is not to be given away, but when she was seventeen years old she fell in love with a man, a soldier, at that—for this was the time of the wars of the French and their dreadful Emperor. She married him and followed him, and a year later she died in great agonies, like her mother.

"Though I have never had it in me really to care for any male,

I had hoped that the child would be a boy. But it was a girl, and she was given into my care, for her father could not stand the sight of her, and in fact he died of a broken heart only a few months later, leaving her the heiress of his great riches, of which most was booty of war.

"Now as my granddaughter grew up, you will understand that I was all the time thinking of how I could best arrange the future for her. Did I say that her mother's beauty was the Almighty's highest work? No, it proved to be but his probation work, Rosina herself being the masterpiece of his craft. She was so fair that it was said in Pisa that when she drank red wine you could follow its course as it ran down her throat and chest. I did not want her to marry, so I was for a long time well pleased to see the hardness and contempt that the child showed toward all men, and especially toward the brilliant young swains who surrounded her with their adoration. But I was getting old, and I did not want to die and leave her alone in the world, either. Upon the morning of her seventeenth birthday I took to the Church of Santa Maria della Spina a great treasure that had been in my mother's family for many hundred years, a belt of chastity that one of her ancestors had had made in Spain when he went to fight the infidels. And because his wife was a niece of St. Ferdinand of Castile, it was set with crosses of rubies. This I gave so that the saints should help me to think of what to do.

"That same evening I gave a great ball, at which the Prince Pozentiani saw Rosina, and applied for her hand. Now I will ask you, Count, was this not an answer to my prayer? For the Prince was a magnificent match. He is today the richest man in the province, for it is well known that his family can never keep their hands from making money in one way or another. Although he is a little advanced in years he is the most charming person, a Mæcenas, a man of refined tastes and many talents, and an old friend of mine. And I knew also that a caprice of nature had made him, although an admirer of our sex, incapable of being a lover or a husband. It was his vanity or his weakness not to like this to be known, and he used to keep the most expensive courtesans with him, and people were afraid of him, so that the secret did not get out. But I happened to know, because he had at a time many years ago been one of my greatest admirers, and I had liked him very much. I was so happy and thankful that I saw my own face smile to me in the mirror, like the face of a blessed spirit.

"The child Rosina herself was pleased with the Prince's proposal, and for a time she liked him very much because of his wit and charming manners and the rich gifts which he showered upon her. The betrothal had been announced when one night, after I had already retired to bed, Rosina came into my room in her frock of high-red satin. She stood in the light of the candles, as lovely as the young St. Michele himself commanding the heavenly hosts, and told me, as if it might have been welcome news to me, that she had fallen in love with her cousin Mario, and would never marry anybody but him. Already at that moment I felt my heart faint within me. But I controlled my face, and only reminded her that the Prince was a deadly shot, and that, whatever she thought of her cousin, she had better keep him out of his way if she really liked him. She only answered as if she had been in love with death itself.

"I did not dislike Mario for I have always had a curious weakness for my husband's family, although they have all in them a sort of eccentricity, which has in this boy come out in a passion for astronomy. But as a husband he could not be compared to the Prince, and moreover I had only to see Rosina and him together to realize that any weakness of mine here would, within nine months, lead her straight into her mother's tomb. Rosina had had her head turned by the Prince's flatteries. She imagined that should she want the moon, she was to have it, much more her young cousin. When I saw her holding on to her fancy I took her before me and explained to her the facts of life. But God alone knows what has come over the generation of women who have been born after the Revolution of the French and the novels of that woman de Staël—wealth, position and a tolerant husband are not enough to them, they want to make love as we took the Sacrament."

Here the old lady interrupted her tale. "Are you married?" she asked.

"Yes, I am married," the young man answered her.

"I need not then," she went on, as if satisfied with the accent of his reply, "develop to you the folly of these ideas. Rosina was so obstinate that I could not reason with her. If in the end she had told me that what she wanted was to have nine children, I should not have been surprised.

"I have arrived at an age when I cannot very well stand to be crossed. I got furious with her, as furious as I would have been with a brigand whom I had seen slinging her over his horse to carry her off to wild mountains. I told the Prince that we must hurry with the wedding, and I kept Rosina shut up in the house. I lived through these months in such a state of deadly worry that I hardly ever slept, and each night was like a journey around the world.

"Rosina had a friend, Agnese della Gherardesci, whom all her life she had loved next to me. Once, when the girls were doing needlework together, they had pricked their fingers, mixed their blood, and vowed sisterhood. This girl had been allowed to grow up wild and had become a real child of the age. She got into her head the notion that she looked like the Milord Byron, of whom so much is talked, and she used to dress and ride as a man, and to write poetry. To make Rosina happier I made Agnese come and stay with her the last week before the wedding. But there is a demon in girls when they believe a love affair to be at stake, and I think that she managed somehow to bring letters to Mario.

"On the morning before the wedding, when the Prince and I thought that all was safe, Agnese got hold of a hackney coach,

Rosina slipped out of the house and got into it, and they started on the road to Pisa. A faithful maid gave them away to me, and I got into my own coach and followed them at once. By midday I overtook the miserable little carriage on the road, Agnese driving it, dressed in a coachman's cloak, and the horses ready to drop, while mine were as fresh as ever.

"When Rosina saw me approaching at full speed she got out, and I also, when I came up to her, descended on the road, but neither of us spoke a word. I took her into my coach, paying no attention whatever to her friend, and told my coachman to turn back. On that road there is a little chapel amongst some trees. As we came up to it Rosina asked me for permission to stop the coach and enter it for a moment. I said to myself, 'She is going to make a vow of some sort,' and I got out and went with her into the little church. But in that dark room, smelling from the cold incense, I felt with despair that the heart of a maid is a dark church, a place of mystery, and that it is no use for an old woman to try to find her way in it. Rosina went straight to the altar and dropped on her knees. She looked into the face of the Virgin and then walked up, as if I had been an old peasant woman praying in the chapel on my own. I was in great pain, since for the life of me I could not make up a prayer. It was as if I had been informed that the Virgin and the saints had gone deaf. When I came out and saw her standing beside the coach looking toward Pisa, I spoke to her. 'I know, if you do not,' I said, 'what madness it is to let the thought of any man come between you and me. Now, I can make a vow as well as you can. As I hope that we shall some day walk together in paradise, I swear that as long as I can lift my right hand I am not going to give my blessing to any marriage of yours, except with the Prince.' Rosina looked at me and courtesied as when she was a child, and never spoke. The next day the marriage was celebrated with much splendor.

"A month after the wedding Rosina petitioned the Pope for an annulment of her marriage on the ground that it had not been consummated.

"This was a very great scandal. The Prince had mighty friends and she was all alone to begin with, and quite young and inexperienced; but she held out with a wonderful strength till in the end it was the only thing that anybody talked about, and she got the whole people with her. The Prince was not popular, mostly on account of his unhappy passion for money; and romance, you will know, appeals to the lower classes. They ended by looking upon her as some sort of saint, and when she had at last been assisted to get to Rome, the population there surrounded her in the streets and applauded her as if she had been a prima donna of the opera. The Prince behaved like a fool and used his influence to chase Mario out of Pisa, which under the circumstances was probably the most stupid thing he could have done, and he mocked the church and shocked the people.

"Rosina threw herself at the feet of the Holy Father with her certificates from all the doctors and midwives of Rome. The Prince fell down like dead when he was told about it, and for three days could not speak. He had to shut the windows so as not to hear them sing in the streets about the Virgin of Pisa, and would keep on biting his fingers while imagining the happiness of the young people—at which I think that he would be good—for as soon as she had the Pope's letter of annulment they were married.

"During all this time, while I had heard the very air around me humming with her name, I had refused to see her, and had tried not to think of her. But what is there left in the world to take an old woman's mind off the things she has thought about for seventeen years, when she does not want to think about them any longer?

"Two months ago I was told that my granddaughter was to have a child. Although I had of course been prepared for this, it was like the last blow to me. It nearly killed me. I thought of her mother and of my vow. I failed to believe in the saints any longer. Rosina's picture was before me day and night as she had looked in the chapel, and my heart was filled with such bitterness as it is not right that a woman shall endure at my time of life. In the end I gave up thinking of paradise, for I thought that a hundred years there would not be worth a week within her house in Italy. For a long time I have been too ill to travel, but yesterday I set out for Pisa.

"Now, my friend, you have heard all my story, and I leave it to you to make your reflections upon the ways of providence."

Here she made a long pause. When, frightened by it, he looked up at her face, he saw that it had fallen. She seemed to have shrunk, but beneath her waxen eyelids her clear eyes were still fixed upon his face.

"I am ready to leave this world," she said. "It must by now know me by heart as I know it. We have nothing more to say to each other. It seems curious to me myself that I should still feel so much affection for, and take so much interest in, this old Carlotta de Gampocorta, who will soon have disappeared altogether, that I cannot let her go out without giving her the chance of assembling, and forgiving, those who have trespassed against her. But what will you—habits are not easily changed at my age. Will you go and find her for me?"

Her left arm moved on the sheet as if trying to reach his hand. Augustus touched the cold fingers. "I am at your service, Madame," he said. She drew a deep sigh and closed her eyes. He hastened to get hold of the doctor, who had been sent for from the village.

He ordered his servants to have everything ready for an early start in the morning, and as he wanted to get his letter off before leaving, he took it up again to finish it. On reading through his reflections on life, he thought that their sadness might upset his good Karl, so he took his pen and added two lines out of Goethe's

Faust, a favorite quotation of his friend's, by which he had many times, in Ingolstadt, closed one of their discussions:

> *A good man, through obscurest aspirations,*
> *Has still the instinct of the one true way. . . .*

And half smiling, he sealed the letter.

IV. THE YOUNG LADY'S SORROWS

At the next inn to which he came—which was the last before Pisa, and had more houses, carts and people around it, so that one felt already in the air the nearness of a great town—a phaëton drove up just in front of Augustus, from which descended a slim young man in a large dark cloak and an old major-domo who looked like Pantalone. It was getting dark. A few stars had sprung out upon the deep blue sky, and there was a slight breeze in the air. Augustus had that feeling of being really on the road in which lies so much of the happiness of all true travelers. He had passed so many wayfarers in the course of the day—riders on horses and donkeys, coaches, oxcarts and mule carts—that there seemed to be a direction in life, and it would be strange if there should be none for him. The lamplight, the noise, and the smell of wood-smoke, grease and cheese from the house pleased him. The air of Italy seemed to have come down from mountains and across rivers to lay itself gently against his face.

The *osteria* had at one time been the lodge of a great villa; it had a large fine room with frescoes on the walls. Entering it, he found the old landlord with two attendants laying the table at the open window, and at the same time having a heated discussion, from which the old man tore himself away to welcome the guest and assure him that he would do anything to make him happy. But all these honored guests arriving at the same moment, unexpected, to a house so keen to maintain its *renommé* nearly overwhelmed him. For Prince Pozentiani was arriving within half an hour, and with him his young friend, the Prince Giovanni Gastone. These were people who could judge a meal, and they had ordered quails, but the cook had made a mistake in the cooking. Augustus asked if the boy whom he had just seen arrive would be the Prince Giovanni. Ah, no, said the old man, that undoubtedly was another rich and fastidious customer. But was it possible that the Milord had never heard of Prince Nino? He was such a young man the like of whom one would not find outside of Tuscany. When he was a baby his beauty had made him the model of the infant Jesus on the painting in the cathedral. Wherever he went the people loved him. For he was a patriot, a true son of Tuscany. Though he had been sent by his ambitious mother to the courts of both Vienna and St. Petersburg, he had come back unwilling to speak any language but that of the great poets. His *palazzi* were run in the old Tuscan manner: he kept an orchestra to play Italian music only; he ran his horses in the classical races; and when his vintage was finished, the festivals—at which the old dances were performed, the virgins of the villages pressed the grapes, naked, and the *improvvisatori* recited in the old way—called back the ancient happy days.

With a greasy towel under his arm and his little black eyes upon every movement of the servants, the old man had still sufficient vivacity of spirit to entertain his foreign guest with great charm. Had not Prince Nino, when a German singer had the audacity to appear in Cimarosa's opera, *Ballerina Amante,* chased him off the stage and himself sung the entire part to an enraptured audience? As to the fair sex—here the broad face of the landlord seemed to draw itself together actually into a point, so concentrated did it become in the communication—the Milord must know for himself, if they choose to throw themselves in the way of a man, what is it possible for him to do? And even there he had shown himself a true son of his country. For he might have married an archduchess, and the sister of the Czar of Russia herself had gone mad with love of him when he had been at the Court of St. Petersburg, but he had quoted the exquisite Redi in his *Bacco in Tuscany,* saying that only the barrels of the wine of Tuscany should come to groan under his caresses. Also it was said that the husbands of Tuscany did not always mind his invincibility as much as one would have thought, for a woman who had belonged to Prince Nino would never afterward condescend to take another lover, and more than one coquettish lady had, when he had left her, settled down to her husband and her memories. It was a great pity that the way in which he had scattered the riches of his house, and even of his mother, had delivered him to the mercy of the old Prince Pozentiani, who lent out money. It was said that of late he had changed. He had been known to say that a miracle had crossed his way and made him believe in miracles. Some people thought that the sainted Queen Mathilda, of his own house, had shown herself to him in a dream and turned his heart from this world. Here one of the waiters made such a grave mistake in the laying of the table that the old man, as in a terrific spiritual bound, flew off from the conversation. He came back a little later, smiling but silent, with the wine that Augustus had ordered, and left him to it with a deep bow.

Two old priests sat over their wine near the glowing coals on the fireplace, which shone on their greasy black frocks, and the boy who had driven the phaëton was thoughtfully drinking coffee out of a glass which his old servant brought him, on a low seat under a picture of the angels visiting Abraham. His young figure there was so graceful that Augustus, always an admirer of beauty, and finding in his pure pensive face a likeness to his friend Karl's as a boy, found his eyes wandering back to it. When the old major-domo, returning, reported on a quarrel between the young man's groom and his own over the best stabling places, Augustus profited by the opportunity to ask him a few questions about the road to Pisa, and prayed him to have a glass of wine with him. The boy very courteously declined, saying that he never drank

wine, but finding that Augustus was a foreigner and ignorant of
the road, he sat down with him for a moment to give him the information he wanted. While talking, the youth rested his left arm
on the table, and Augustus, looking at it, thought how plainly one
must realize, in meeting the people of this country, that they had
been living in marble palaces and writing about philosophy while
his own ancestors in the large forests had been making themselves weapons of stone and had dressed in the furs of the bears
whose warm blood they drank. To form a hand and wrist like
these must surely take a thousand years, he reflected. In Denmark
everybody has thick ankles and wrists, and the higher up you go,
the thicker they are.

The boy colored with pleasure on learning that Augustus came
from Denmark, and told him that he was the first person from
the country of Prince Hamlet that he had ever met. He appeared
to know the English tragedy very well, and talked as if Augustus
must have come straight from the court of King Claudius. His
Italian courtesy kept him from dwelling upon the tragic happenings, as if Ophelia might have been the recently lost cousin of
the other young man, but he quoted the soliloquy with great
charm, and said that he had often in his thoughts stood at Elsinore, upon the dreadful summit of the cliff that beetles o'er his
base into the sea. Augustus did not want to tell him that Elsinore
is quite flat, so asked him instead if he did not write poetry himself.

"Ah, no," said the boy, shaking his soft brown curls, "I used to,
but I gave it up a year ago."

"You were wrong, I think," said Augustus, smiling. "Surely
poetry is one of the delights of life, and helps us to endure the
monotony of the world."

The boy seemed to feel that he had here met a brother or friend
of the unhappy Danish Prince, and to open his heart to the stranger on this account.

"Something happened to me," he said after a short silence, "that

I could not turn into poetry. I have written both comedies and tragedies, but I could not fit it into either." Again after a short pause he added: "I am now going to Pisa to study astronomy."

He had a grave and friendly manner that attracted Augustus, who had himself at Ingolstadt given much time to the study of the stars. They talked for some time of them, and he told the boy how the great Danish astronomer Tycho Brahe had ordered at Augsburg the construction of a nineteen-foot quadrant and of a celestial globe five feet in diameter.

"I want to study astronomy," said the boy, "because I can no longer stand the thought of time. It feels like a prison to me, and if I could only get away from it altogether I think I should be happy."

"I have thought that myself," Augustus said pensively, "and still I have reflected that if at any single moment of our lives, even such as we ourselves call the happiest, we were told that it was to go on forever, we would conclude that we had been brought, not to eternal bliss, but to everlasting suffering." He remembered with sadness how this old reflection of his had come back to him even on a certain moment of his wedding night. The young man seemed to follow the train of his thought with sympathy.

"I have had the misfortune, Signore," he said after a moment, his young face looking somehow paler and his eyes darker than before, "to have always on my mind the recollection of one single hour of my life. Up to that hour I used to think with pleasure of both the past and the future, as well as of the present itself, and time was like a road through a pleasant landscape on which I could wander to and fro as I fancied. But now I cannot get my thoughts away from that one hour. Every second of it seems bigger than whole years of the rest of my life. I must escape from it to where there is no time. I know," he said, "that some people would recommend the idea of moral infinity, as given to us in religion, as the right refuge, but I have already tried it and it is of no use to me—on the contrary, the thought of the omnipotence of

God, man's free will, heaven and hell, all bring back to me the thoughts from which I want to get away. I want to turn to the infinity of space, and from what I have heard it seems to me that the roads of the planets and stars, their elipses and circles within the infinite space, must have the power to turn the mind into new ways. Do you not think so, Signore?"

Augustus thought of the time, not many years ago, when he had himself felt the spheres his right home. "I think," he said sadly, "that life has its law of gravitation spiritually as well as physically. Landed property, women——" He looked out through the window. On the blue sky of the spring evening Venus stood, radiant as a diamond.

The boy turned toward him. "You do not," he said, "really think that I am a man? I am not, and under your favor, I am happy not to be. I know, of course, that great work has been achieved by men, but still I think that the world would be a more tranquil place if men did not come in to break up, very often, the things that we cherish."

Augustus became confused to find that he had been treating a young lady as a boy, but he could not apologize for it, as it was not his fault. He made haste to introduce himself and to ask if he could be of any assistance to her on her journey. The girl, however, did not alter her manner toward him in the least, and seemed quite indifferent to any change in his attitude toward her which her information might have caused. She sat in the same position, with her slender knees crossed under her cloak and her hands folded around one knee. Augustus thought that he had hardly ever talked to a young woman whose chief interest in the conversation had not been the impression that she herself was making on him, and he reflected that this must be what generally made converse with women awkward and dull to him. The way in which this young woman seemed to take a friendly and confident interest in him, without apparently giving any thought to what he thought of her, seemed to him new and sweet, as if he suddenly realized that he had all his life been looking for such an attitude in a woman. He wished that he could now himself keep away from the conventional accent of male and female conversation.

"It is very sad," he said thoughtfully, "that you should think so little of us, for I am sure that all men that you have met have tried to please you. Will you not tell me why it should be so? For it has happened to me many times that a lady has told me that I was making her unhappy, and that she wished that she and I were dead, at a time when I have tried hardest to make her happy. It is so many years now since Adam and Eve"—he looked across the room to a picture of them—"were first together in the garden, that it seems a great pity that we have not learned better how to please one another."

"And did you not ask her?" said the girl.

"Yes," he answered, "but it seemed to be our fate that we should never take up these questions in cold blood. For myself, I think that women, for some reason, will not let us know. They do not want an understanding. They want to mobilize for war. But I wish that once, in all the time of men and women, two ambassadors could meet in a friendly mind and come to understand each other. It is true," he added after a moment, "that I did once meet, in Paris, a woman, a great courtesan, who might have been such an ambassador. But you would hardly have given her your letters of credence or have submitted to her decisions. I do not even know if you would not have considered her a traitor to your sex."

The girl thought for a time of what he had said. "I suppose," she then said, "that even in your country you have parties, balls and *conversazione?*"

"Yes," he said, "we have those."

"Then you will know," she went on slowly, "that the part of a guest is different from that of a host or hostess, and that people do not want or expect the same things in the two different capacities?"

"I think you are right," said Augustus.

"Now God," she said, "when he created Adam and Eve"—she also looked at them across the room—"arranged it so that man takes, in these matters, the part of a guest, and woman that of a hostess. Therefore man takes love lightly, for the honor and dignity of his house is not involved therein. And you can also, surely, be a guest to many people to whom you would never want to be a host. Now, tell me, Count, what does a guest want?"

"I believe," said Augustus when he had thought for a moment, "that if we do, as I think we ought to here, leave out the crude guest, who comes to be regaled, takes what he can get and goes away, a guest wants first of all to be diverted, to get out of his daily monotony or worry. Secondly the decent guest wants to shine, to expand himself and impress his own personality upon his surroundings. And thirdly, perhaps, he wants to find some justification for his existence altogether. But since you put it so charmingly, Signora, please tell me now: What does a hostess want?"

"The hostess," said the young lady, "wants to be thanked."

Here loud voices outside put an end to their conversation.

V. THE STORY OF THE BRAVO

The landlord of the *osteria* came in first, walking backwards with a three-armed candlestick in each hand, with surprising grace and lightness for an old man. Following him came the party of three gentlemen for whom the table had been laid, the first two walking arm in arm. Their arrival changed the whole room in a moment, they brought with them so much light, loud talk and color—even so much plain matter, for two of them were very big men.

The one who attracted Augustus's attention, as he would always attract the attention of anybody near him, was a man of about fifty, very tall and broad, and enormously fat. He was dressed very elegantly in black, his white linen shining, and wore some heavy rings and in his large stock a brilliantly sparkling diamond. His hair was dyed jet black, and his face was painted and powdered. In spite of his fatness and his stays, he moved with a peculiar grace, as if he had in him a rhythm of his own. Altogether, Augustus thought, if one could get quite away from the conventional idea of how a human being ought to look, he would be a very handsome object and a fine ornament in any place, and would have made, for instance, a most powerful and impressive idol. It was he who spoke, in a high and piercing, and at the same time strangely pleasing, voice.

"Oh, charming, charming, my Nino," he said, "to be together again. But I have heard about you last week only, and how you have bought a Danaë by Correggio, and sixteen piebald horses from Cascine, to drive with your coach."

The young man to whom he spoke and whose arm he was holding seemed to pay very little attention to him. On looking at him Augustus understood that the people of the country should think highly of his beauty. He had been looking over many galleries of paintings lately, and reflected that any young St. Sebastian or John the Baptist, living on wild honey and locust, or even a young angel from the opened sepulcher, might have come down from his frame, dressed in modern clothes with elegance and carelessness, and looked like that. He even had in the pronounced brown color-tones of his hair, face and eyes something of the patina of old paintings, and he had withal the appearance of thinking of nothing at all which must be natural in paradise where there is no need of thought.

The third of the party was a tall young man, also very richly dressed, with fair curly hair and a pink face like a sheep's, which continued down into his fat throat without any sign of a jawbone. He was absorbed in listening to the old man and never took his eyes off him. All three sat down to their meal, with the light of the candles on them.

The young lady looked at the newly arrived party for a few seconds, then got up and, draping her cloak around her, left the room. Augustus followed her out, where her old servant was waiting for her with a candle.

As he came back his own supper was being brought in, and he sat down to a capon and a cake decorated with pink whipped cream. The supper party at the larger table was so noisy that he was disturbed in his thoughts and from time to time had his eyes drawn toward them. He noticed that the old man, while all the time making his guests drink, drank himself only lemonade, but nevertheless kept pace with them in their rising spirits, as if he had within him a sort of natural intoxication upon which he could draw without outward assistance. Once his voice, talking for a long time, caught Augustus's ear as he was telling the others a story.

"At Pisa," he said, "I was, many years ago, present when our glorious Monti, the poet, drew out his pistol and shot down Monsignor Talbot. It happened at a supper party, just like ours here with only the three of us present. And it all arose from an argument on eternal damnation.

"Monti, who had then just finished his *Don Giovanni,* had for some time been sunk in a deep melancholy, and would neither drink nor talk, and Monsignor Talbot asked him what was the matter with him, and wondered that he was not happy after having achieved so great a success. So Monti asked him whether he did not think that it might weigh upon the mind of a man to have created a human being who was to burn through eternity in hell. Talbot smiled at him and declared that this could only happen to real people. Whereupon the poet cried out and asked him if his Don Giovanni were not real, and the *monsignore,* still smiling at him for taking it so seriously, and leaning back in his chair, explained that he meant beings who had really been in the flesh. 'The flesh!' the poet cried. 'Can you doubt that he was in the flesh when in Spain alone there can be found one thousand

and three ladies to give evidence to that effect?' Monsignor Talbot asked him if he did really believe himself a creator in the same sense as God.

" 'God!' Monti cried, 'God! Do you not know that what God really wants to create is my Don Giovanni, and the Odysseus of Homer, and Cervantes's knight? Very likely those are the only people for whom heaven and hell have ever been made, for you cannot imagine that an Almighty God would go on forever and ever, world without end, with my mother-in-law and the Emperor of Austria? Humanity, the men and women of this earth, are only the plaster of God, and we, the artists, are his tools, and when the statue is finished in marble or bronze, he breaks us all up. When you die you will probably go out like a candle, with nothing left, but in the mansions of eternity will walk Orlando, the Misanthrope and my Donna Elvira. Such is God's plan of work, and if we find it somehow slow, who are we that we should criticize him, seeing that we know nothing whatever of time or eternity?'

"Monsignor Talbot, although himself a great admirer of the arts, began to feel uncomfortable about such heretical views, and took the poet to task over them. 'Oh, go and find out for yourself then!' Monti cried, and resting the barrel of the pistol, with which he had been playing, upon the edge of the table, he fired straight at the *monsignore,* who sat opposite him, so that he fell down in his blood. It was a serious affair, for Monsignor Talbot had to have a grave operation, and hovered for a long time between life and death."

The young men, who had by this time had a good deal to drink, began to make jests over this idea, holding up to the narrator the various forms of immortality which he might obtain under the hands of different poets. In this they used many names and expressions unknown to Augustus; also their voices were less distinct than that of the old man, so he only began to give their conversation his attention when the latter was again talking alone.

"No, no, my children," he said, "I have other hopes than that. But as it may be good for you to occupy yourselves a little with the idea of the other world, and may even dissipate that new melancholy of our sweet Nino, about which the whole province grieves, I will tell you another story."

He leaned back in his chair, and throughout his narrative he did not again touch food or drink. Augustus noticed that as he proceeded his dark young neighbor, whom he had called his Nino, took to the same manner, so that of the three it was only the fair young man with the sheep's face who went on enjoying the pleasures of the table.

"In Pisa lived, my dear friends," the old man began, "at the time of my grandfather, a nobleman of high rank and great wealth, who had the sad experience of having a young friend, on whom he had bestowed every benefaction, turn upon him with the common ingratitude of youth and inflict upon him a deadly insult, one which, moreover, turned him into an object of ridicule in the eyes of the world. The nobleman was a philosopher, and valued beyond everything in life his peace of mind. When he realized that this matter was about to spoil his sleep, and that he would not get any pleasure, or recover his balance, till he had had the blood of his young enemy, he decided to have it. Now because of his position and other circumstances he did not see his way to do it himself, so addressed himself to a young bravo of the town. In those days such people were still to be found. This young man was of an extravagant disposition, and thereby had got himself into heavy debt and such a miserable position that he could hardly see any way out of it but marriage. My grandfather's friend said to him: 'I want everybody to come out of this affair perfectly satisfied. I will pay you for my peace of soul what I think it worth, which is a great deal. Do me this service, and I will have your debts wiped out, even down to your grandmother's little rosary of coral beads, which you had pawned.' Upon this the bravo agreed, and everything was arranged between them."

A big cat that had been walking about the room, here sprang up on the knee of the old man who was telling the story. Without looking at it he kept on stroking it while he continued his tale.

"The clock struck midnight when the bravo left him, and as he knew that he should not be able to sleep until he had made sure that the business had been settled, he kept awake in his room, waiting for the young man's return, and had a very dainty supper prepared for him there. Just as the clock struck the hour of one the young man entered, looking like death. 'Is my enemy dead?' the nobleman asked. 'Yes,' said the bravo. 'And is it sure?' said his employer, whose heart began to dance within his breast. 'Yes,' said the bravo, 'if a man be dead who has had my stiletto in his heart three times, up to the hilt. Everybody ought, as you have said, to come out of this affair perfectly satisfied. Now I will have a bottle of champagne with you.' So the two had a very pleasant supper together. 'Do you know,' said the bravo, 'what I think a great pity? It is this: that we have all become such skeptics that we hardly believe what our pious grandmothers told us. For it would give me great pleasure to think that both you and I shall be eternally damned.'

"The nobleman was surprised, and sorry for the young man, for he looked as if he were out of his senses. He also felt very kindly disposed toward him, so he tried to comfort him. 'This has been too much for you,' he said. 'I took you for a stronger man. As to this business of damnation, I see what you mean, and believe that very likely you are right. The murder that you have committed tonight I have myself committed many times already in my heart, and the Scripture has it that it is then as good as done. Sophistical thinkers may even prove your part in it to be entirely illusory, and you may very well still wash your robes in the blood of the Lamb and make them white. Still, I must say that what I paid you, I paid for the trouble which you had to take and for the risk you are running with regard to the law of Pisa and the relations of my dead enemy. Of your soul I had not thought. Against this risk, small as I consider it to be, I will give you, in addition to what you have already, this ring of mine.' With these words he took from his hand a ring with a large ruby in it, a very valuable stone, and handed it to the young man, who laughed at him as if they had never been talking of sacred things, and went away. Our nobleman went to bed, and slept well for the first time in many months, in the consciousness of having had his wish fulfilled at last, and also of having behaved with great generosity toward his bravo."

At this point in the tale the cat walked across the table and jumped into the lap of the young Prince. As if he had been the reflection, within a looking-glass, of his neighbor, he began to stroke the beast softly while leaning back in his chair and listening.

"But it was his fate," the old man went on, "to have his faith in human beings shaken. It was only a few weeks later, and while he was still enjoying, as in a second youth, the society of his friends, music, and the beauty of the scenery around Pisa, that he had a letter from a friend in Rome who wrote to tell him that his enemy, for whose death he had paid so high a price, was there, fresher than ever, and highly admired in Roman society and at the papal court.

"This last proof of human perfidy, and of the foolishness of having faith in friends or employees, hit the unsuspecting man hard. He fell ill and suffered for a long time from pains in his eyes and his right arm, so that he had to go to the baths of Pyrmont to recover. But I will pass over this sad period. Only, as he was a man given to thinking, he began to speculate upon the future of himself and his bravo as they had discussed it over their supper table. Is it really, he thought, the intention only which weighs down the scale, and saves us or condemns us, and has the action nothing to do with it all? The more he thought of this the more he realized that it must be so. Probably even, he thought, the intention only carries this weight in so far as it remains an intention and nothing else. For the action wipes out the desire. The surest way to leave off coveting your neighbor's wife is, without doubt, to have her, and we can love our enemies and pray for them which despitefully use us, if only they be dead. He remembered how kindly he had thought of his young enemy during that short period when he believed him to have been killed.

"Therefore, he thought, hell is very likely filled with people who have not carried out what they had meant to do. Theirs is the worm that never dies. And so," said the old man, his voice suddenly becoming very slow and gentle as a caress, "having lost his faith in bravoes, he decided, in the future, to carry out his intentions himself. But there was one thing," he went on in the same soft voice, "which he thought he should have liked to know, before he put the whole tragedy out of his mind: How much, he wondered, did this bravo of his, who had been so handsomely paid by him, make out of the affair from the other side?

"This, my sweet Nino, is my story, and I hope that I have not bored you with it. You would do me a great service if you would tell me what you think of it."

There was a silence. The dark young Prince leaned forward, put his arm upon the table and his chin in his hand, and looked at the old man. This movement had in it so much of the cat which he was holding that it gave Augustus quite a shock.

"Yes, under your favor," he said, "I have been a little bored, for I think that as a story yours was too long, and even yet it has had no end. Let us make an end tonight."

He refilled his glass with his left hand and half emptied it Then, with a gentle movement, as if he had drunk too much to make a more violent effort, he tossed the glass across the table into the old man's face. The wine ran down the scarlet mouth and powdered chin. The glass rolled onto his lap and from there fell to the floor and was broken.

The young man with the fair curly hair gave a scream. He jumped up and, producing a small lace handkerchief, tried to wipe the wine from the other's face as if it had been blood. But the fat old man pushed him away. His face remained for a moment quite immovable, like a mask. Then it began to glow, as if from inside, with a strange triumphant brightness. It would have been impossible to say whether his face really colored under the paint, but it showed suddenly the same effect of heightened primitive vitality. He had looked old while he was telling his tale. Now he gave the impression of youth or childhood. Augustus now saw who he was really like: he had the soft fullness, and the great power behind it, of the ancient statues of Bacchus. The atmosphere of the room became resplendent with his rays, as if the old god had suddenly revealed himself, vine-crowned, to mortals. He took up a handkerchief and carefully dabbed his mouth with it, then, looking at it, he spoke in a low and sweet voice, such as a god would use in speaking to human beings, aware that his natural strength is too much for them.

"It is a tradition of your family, Nino, I know," he said, "this exquisite *savoir-mourir.*" He sipped a little of his lemonade to take away the taste of the wine which had touched his mouth. "What an excellent critic you are," he went on, "not only of your own Tuscan songs, but of modern prose as well. That exactly was the fault of my story: that it had no end. A charming thing, an end. Will you come tomorrow at sunrise to the terrace at the back of this house? I know the place; it is a very good spot."

"Yes," said Nino, still in the same position, with his chin in his hand. "Thank you," said the old man, "thank you, my dear. And now," he went on with quiet dignity, "with your permission I shall retire. I cannot," he said, with a glance downward at his soiled shirt, "remain in your company in these clothes. Arture, give me your arm. I will send him back to arrange with you, Nino. Good night, sleep you well!"

When he had gone away on the arm of the fair young man, who was now deadly pale and seemed stricken with panic, the other young man sat for a time without moving, as if he had fallen asleep over the table. Then, turning, he looked straight at

Augustus, of whose presence he had not before seemed to be aware, got up, came over to him, and greeted him very politely. He was not quite steady on his feet, but nevertheless looked as if he would, mentally, be able to take a part in any ballet.

"Signore," he said, "you have been the witness of a quarrel between myself and my friend, the Prince Pozentiani, whom I shall have to give satisfaction. Will you, as a nobleman, show me the favor of acting as my second tomorrow morning? I am Giovanni Gastone, of Tuscany, at your service." Augustus told the Prince that he had never had anything to do with a duel and the idea now made him uneasy.

"I should be glad to be of assistance to you," he said, "but I cannot help thinking that it would be better to settle such a quarrel, between friends and over a supper table, in a friendly way, and that you cannot have any wish to fight a man so much older than yourself over nothing."

Giovanni smiled very sweetly at him. "Set your conscience at rest, Count," he said, "the Prince is the affronted party and will choose the weapons. If you had lived in Tuscany you would have heard something of his shooting. As to his being old, it is true that he has lived for twice as many years as either you or I, but for all that he is in himself a child compared to any of us. It will be as natural to him to live for two hundred years as for us to live sixty. The things that wear us down do not touch him. He is very wonderful."

"What you have said," Augustus replied, "does not seem to me to make your duel more reasonable. Might he not then kill you?"

"No, no," said the young man, "but he has been my best friend for many years. We want to find out which of us does really stand best with God."

The low and clear cry of a bird sounded from the garden, like the voice of the night itself. "Do you hear the aziola cry?" asked Giovanni. "That used to mean that something fortunate was going to happen to me. I do not know," he added after a while, "what it would be now, unless God has very much more power of imagination than I myself have—that is, unless he is very much more like my friend the Prince than he is like me. But that, of course, I trust him to be." He sat in thought for some time. "Those horses which I bought—" he said, "I have not yet given them names. The Prince, now, could so easily have found names for them. Can you think of any?"

VI. THE MARIONETTES

As the young Prince had, with repeated thanks, said good night to his second and left him, the old servant whom he had seen in the phaëton came up behind Augustus, noiseless as a cat, and touched his sleeve. His mistress, he said, had been disturbed by the noises in the house and wished the Count to tell her what was happening. She was, in fact, waiting for him at the end of the house, where the light from a window fell out upon a stone seat. The old servant remained in attendance, near a large tree a little way off.

Augustus hesitated to inform the young lady of the duel, but he found that she knew all about it already, her old major-domo having, with the host of the inn, been listening outside the door. What she wanted to know, and seemed in a highly excited state about, was how the quarrel had arisen. Augustus thought that he might as well tell her, in case there should be an inquest later on, so declaring that he was himself quite unable to see how it could have brought on a fight of life and death, he repeated to her as much of the conversation of the supper party as he could remember. She listened to him without a word, standing as still and erect as a statue, but in the midst of the narrative she took hold of his arm and led him into the circle of light. When he had finished she begged him to tell her the old Prince's story of the bravo all over again, and stopped him to have certain words and figures repeated to her.

As he came to the end the second time she suddenly turned toward the light, and he was startled to see in her face, as if reflected within a mirror, the expression in the face of the old Prince when he had been so deeply insulted. She did not use either powder or paint, so that he could follow the course of her blood as it slowly rose to her forehead until her whole face glowed as from violent exercise or strong wine. In a lighter manner—since she did not carry any of his weight, either physically or morally—she partook at this moment of his divine metamorphosis, and might well have passed, in the train of that old Dionysus, for a young bacchante, or possibly, with the light in her big eyes, for one of his panthers.

She drew her breath deeply. "From the moment I first saw you, Signore," she said, "I knew that something fortunate was going to happen to me. Please tell me now: Is it possible, if they both fire at the same moment, and both take good aim, that the two bullets would hit their hearts at the same instant and that they would both be killed?"

Augustus thought this young lady to be, for a student of the stars and of philosophy, of a sanguinary turn of mind. "I have never heard of such a thing happening," he said, "though I cannot say that it would not be possible. I am myself uneasy about the result of this duel, and it is a strange coincidence that I should have been told, only yesterday, of this old Prince being such a deadly shot."

"Everybody knows that," she said, "if he cannot frighten people in any other way, he frightens them with his pistols. But kindly tell me, Signore," she went on, "who is the young man whom the old Prince is going to kill? You did not tell me his name." Augustus told her. Again she stood silent and very quiet. "Giovanni Gastone," she repeated slowly, "then I have myself seen him. On the day of my first communion, five years ago, he accompanied his grandmother to the basilica, and held his umbrella over her from her carriage to the porch, for it was raining heavily."

"Let them go to bed," she said after a little while. "If this is to be the last night he will ever go to bed, let him sleep. But we, Signore, cannot possibly sleep, and what are we to do? My servant tells me that there is a marionette company at the inn, and as the wagoners from Pisa come back late, they are giving a performance within this hour. Let us go and see them."

Augustus felt himself that he was not likely to sleep. In fact, he had not often been more wide awake or more pleasantly so. He felt his own body lighter, as when he had been a boy. With the happy wonder of a searcher for gold who strikes a vein of the metal in the rock, he reflected that he had come upon a vein of events in life. The company of the girl also pleased him in a particular way, and he was thinking whether it might not be, partly, because she was dressed like himself in those long black trousers which seemed to him the normal costume for a human being. The fluffs and trains with which women in general accentuate their femininity are bound, he thought, to make talking with them much like conversation with officers in uniform or clergymen in their robes, neither of which you are likely to get much out of. He followed her into the large whitewashed barn where the theater had been erected and the play had just started.

The air in there was hot and stifling, though high up in the roof a window had been opened to the powder-blue nocturnal sky. The building was half filled with people and very dimly lighted by some old lanterns which hung from the ceiling. Around the stage itself the candles of the footlights were creating a magic oasis of light, and making the crimson, orange and bright green of the puppets' little costumes, probably faded and dull in the daylight, shine and glow like jewels. Their shadows, much larger than themselves, reflected all their movements upon the white cloth of the back-curtain.

The performer stopped his speech upon the arrival of the distinguished spectators, and brought them two armchairs to sit in near the stage, in front of the audience. Then he took up the thread where he had interrupted it, speaking loudly in the various voices of his characters.

The play which was being acted was the immortal *Revenge of Truth,* that most charming of marionette comedies. Everybody will remember how the plot is created by a witch pronouncing, upon the house wherein all the characters are collected, a curse to the effect that any lie told within it will become true. Thus the mercenary young woman who tries to catch a rich husband by making him believe that she loves him, does fall in love with him; the braggart becomes a hero; the hypocrites finish by becoming really virtuous; the old miser who tells people that he is poor loses all his money. When the women are alone they speak in verse, but the language of the men is very coarse in parts; only a young boy, the one innocent person in the comedy, has some very fine songs which are accompanied by a mandolin behind the stage.

The moral of the play pleased the audience, and their tired, dusty faces lighted up as they laughed at Mopsus, the clown. The girl followed the development of the plot in the spirit of a fellow author. Augustus felt, in his present mood, some of the speeches go strangely to his heart. When the lover says to his mistress that a piece of dry bread satiates one's hunger better than a whole cookery book, he took it, somehow, as advice to himself. The unsuspecting victim discourses to his intended murderer upon the loveliness of the moonlight, and the villain answers by lecturing on the absurdity of the power of God to make us delight in things which are of no advantage whatever to us, which may even be quite the contrary; and he goes on saying that God therefore likes us in the same way as we like our dogs: because when he is in high spirits, we are in high spirits; and when he is depressed, we are depressed; and when he, in a romantic mood, makes the moonlight night, we trot at his heels as well as we can. This made Augustus smile. He thought that he would like to feel once more, as when he was a child, like one of the dogs of God.

At the end the witch appears again, and on being asked what is really the truth, answers: "The truth, my children, is that we are, all of us, acting in a marionette comedy. What is important more than anything else in a marionette comedy, is keeping the ideas of the author clear. This is the real happiness of life, and now that I have at last come into a marionette play, I will never go out of it again. But you, my fellow actors, keep the ideas of the author clear. Aye, drive them to their utmost consequences." This speech seemed to him suddenly to hold a lot of truth. Yes, he thought, if my life were only a marionette comedy in which I had my part and knew it well, then it might be very easy and sweet. The people of this country seemed, somehow, to be practicing this ideal. They were as immune to the terrors, the crimes and miracles of the life in which they took part as were the little actors upon the old player's stage. To the people of the North the strong agitations of the soul come each time as a strange thing, and when they are in a state of excitement their speech comes by fits and starts. But these people spoke fluently under the wildest passions, as if life were, in any of her whims, a comedy which they had already rehearsed. If I have now at last, he thought, come into a marionette play, I will not go out of it again.

During the last scene, when all the puppets were on the stage to receive the applause of the house, Augustus heard a door open at the back of the room, and on turning saw the Prince Giovanni and his servant come in and look around the audience as if searching for somebody. As he thought that they might be looking for him, he went up to them, a little away from the noise of the theater. He felt somehow shy for having gone away to amuse himself on what might be the last night of this young man's life, but Giovanni did not appear to be surprised, and asked if the play had been good. "An unfortunate thing has happened," he said. "The young friend of the Prince, who was to have been his second, has been taken with fits. He is very sick and cannot stop crying. I remembered having seen you, in the evening, in the company of a

boy whom I took, from your manner toward him, to be a young
gentleman of high rank, perhaps from your own country. I came
to beg you to make him take the part of second tomorrow morning, for neither the Prince nor I wish the affair delayed."

The speech of the Prince brought Augustus into a dilemma. He
did not want to give away the young lady's secret, and reflected
that he had perhaps better let Giovanni remain in the belief that
she was really a boy of his own country, of whom he was somehow in charge. "This young gentleman," he said, "seems to me to
be very young to take part in so sinister an affair. But as he is here
with me, if you will wait I will go and speak with him."

As he came back to the young lady she was still looking at the
stage, but just then the curtain went down for the last time. He
repeated to her his conversation with the Prince and suggested
that they should find some excuse which would enable her to get
away early in the morning, so that she might keep out of the
affair. She thought this over for a moment, and got up and looked
at Giovanni, who was himself, from the other end of the room,
looking at her and Augustus.

"Signore," she said slowly and gravely, "I wish to meet your
friend the Prince Nino, and nothing could give me greater pleasure than to be a second at this duel. Our families have never been
friendly to one another, but in an affair of honor it is a duty to disregard any matters of the past. Have the goodness to tell him that
my name is Daniele delle Gherardesci, and that I am at his
service."

Prince Giovanni, seeing them looking at him, came up to them,
and as Augustus introduced them to each other the young people
exchanged a greeting of extreme politeness. She was standing with
her back to the stage, and the footlights of the theater made a halo
around her head, so that in her easy and arrogant attitude she
looked like a young saint masquerading as a dandy. The people in
the audience, who had been getting up, on recognizing the Prince
stopped to look at him, holding back a little from the group.

The Prince expressed his gratitude for the courtesy shown to him. "Sir," said the girl, "in Egypt, when she was an old lady and he prime minister, Potiphar's wife once obtained an audience with Joseph to ask him for the high order, the star of paradise, for her son-in-law. 'I much dislike being exacting,' she said, 'still, I feel that it is now such a long time since I asked Your Excellency for anything that I hope that you will lend me a favorable ear.'

" 'Madame,' said the Prime Minister, 'once upon a time I happened to be in a prison. There I could not see the stars, but I used to dream about them. I dreamed that because I could not watch them they were running wild all over heaven, and the shepherds and the camelherds driving their flocks at night would lose their way. I even once dreamed about you, Madame, and that when I found the star Aldebaran fallen from the sky, I picked it up and gave it to you. You pinned it in your fichu and said: "A thousand thanks, Joseph." I am glad that my dream has more or less come true. The order which you want for your son-in-law is already his.' "

Soon after they parted.

VII. THE DUEL

The sun was not up as yet, but there was a wonderful promise of light in the air, and not a cloud in the sky. The stone pavement of the terrace was still wet with dew; a bird, and then another, started singing within the trees of the garden, and from the road came the shouts of the wagon drivers, who were afoot early, walking beside their long-horned bullocks.

Augustus was the first to come out of the house. The coolness of the morning air, pure as a glass of water, made him draw his breath deeply, slowly taking in the smell of smoke, flowering trees, and the dust of the road. It seemed strange to him that there should be death in this air, and yet he could not doubt that the adversaries were in dead earnest; and from the rules of the duel, as they had made them up the previous night, he thought it very likely that one of them would not be alive to see the sun high up upon this cloudless sky.

The thought of death grew stronger in him as he walked slowly up to the end of the long terrace. From there he had a wide view of the road with its rows of trees, winding up and down through the landscape. On the horizon he distinguished a low, broken, blue line over which a little cloud was hovering in the air. He thought that when the sun came up this would prove to be Pisa. So 'here was the first station on his journey, for he had letters of introduction to people there. But these people were hurrying to the last station of their entire journey, and he reflected that they must have traveled, in a way, much farther than himself, and have seen more on the road, to be prepared to make an end to it in this way.

As he turned again he saw Giovanni come out, accompanied by his valet, and stop to look at the sky just as he himself had done. On seeing the young Dane, he came up and bade him good morning, and they walked up and down the terrace together, talking of indifferent matters. If the duelist was nervous, this was deep down in him and showed itself only in a new softness and playfulness of manner. At the same time Augustus had the feeling that he was clinging to the fatefulness of the coming hour with a passionate tenderness, so that he would not have allowed anything in the world to take it away from him.

Two of the old Prince's servants came out, carrying a large armchair. The Prince was too fat to stand up for his duel, and was accustomed to do his shooting practice sitting down. They asked Augustus where to put the chair, and they all began to look for a perfectly level place on the ground. There was to be ten paces between the combatants, and they measured the distance out carefully, and marked the place where Giovanni was to stand. The old Prince's servants also brought out a pair of pistols in a very elegant case, and placed it, together with a glass of lemonade and a silk handkerchief, on a small table near the old man's chair. Then they went back into the house. While they were arranging this, the girl and her old servant came up the long terrace. She looked pale in her large cloak, and kept a little away from the others. The doctor, who had been sent for from the village—an old man who smelled of peppermint and still wore the pigtail and bag of the last generation—arrived at the same time, and kept standing close to her, entertaining her with tales of duels of which he had heard and read, and which had all ended with death. The young Prince, at a distance, looked at them from time to time. The air seemed to be slowly filling with light; the song of the birds was suddenly very clear In a moment, it was felt, something would happen. Upon the road a large flock of sheep passed in a cloud of dust which was already tinged with gold.

They were looking toward the door of the *osteria* when it was opened and the old Prince walked out, leaning upon his servant's arm. He was very elegantly dressed in a bottle-green coat, and made up with great care, and he carried himself with the utmost grace and dignity. It was plain that he was deeply moved. The sun rose at this moment above the horizon, but it did not change or dominate the scene any more than did his arrival. All the others were in some way repressing or disguising their real feelings, whereas he showed his distress with the simplicity of an unspoiled child, perfectly confident of the sympathy of his surroundings. His dark eyes were moist, but frank and gentle, as if everything in life were natural and sweet to him, and he gave the same impression of assurance and mastery as a great virtuoso who on his violin runs up and down all the scales, even to the devil's own thrill, as if it were child's play. This equilibrium of his mind was as striking and surprising as the balance of his great body upon his extraordinarily small and elegant feet. The moment Augustus met his eyes, on that morning on the terrace, he felt convinced that the shot of this old man would be deadly. Jupiter himself, with his thunderbolt within the pocket of his coat-tail, could not have given a stronger impression of insuperability.

He spoke with courtesy and friendliness to them all, and seemed to make the doctor his slave from the first instant. The fish-like eyes of the latter followed the great man's slightest movement. He was in no hurry, but obviously did not want to draw things out, either. It was clear, from the moment when he came in, that everything would proceed with the measure and grace of a perfectly performed minuet.

After a few remarks on the weather and the surroundings, and and on his gratitude to the two seconds, he offered, still standing, the choice of pistols to his friend, and as Giovanni, with one of them in his hand, withdrew a little to the place marked for him, he freed himself of his servant's arm, made a deep bow to his adversary and a sort of great movement of relief, as if he had now happily come to the end of everyday existence and the beginning of real life, and, holding the other pistol, he seated himself in the large armchair, resting, for a moment, the weapon on his knee. Augustus took up his position at an equal distance from both duelists, so that each of them should be able to hear his signal. A faint breeze at this moment ran through the leaves of the trees in the garden, shaking down the blossoms and spreading their fragrance.

At the moment when Augustus was clearing his throat to pronounce the one—two—three of the moment, the slim figure of the girl, who stood with her face toward him, stepped up to the old Prince, and, lifting one hand to her hip, she spoke to him in a clear low voice, as if a bird of the garden had descended on his shoulder to sing to him.

"Allow me, Prince," she said, "to speak to you before you shoot. I have something to tell you. If I were quite sure about the issue of your duel I would wait till you have killed your friend, but nobody can know certainly the ways of providence, and I do not wish you to die before you have heard what I have to say." All faces had turned toward her, but she looked only into the still and sorrowful face of the old man. She looked very young and small, but her deep gravity and great self-possession gave her figure a terrible importance, as if a young destroying angel had rushed from the blue sky above them onto the stone terrace, to stand in judgment there.

"A year ago," she said, "Rosina, your wife, went in the middle of the night to see her cousin Mario, who was to leave Pisa in the morning, at the house of her old nurse near the harbor. It was necessary to those two to meet and decide what they were to do, and Rosina also felt that her strength was giving way, and that she must see her lover again or she thought that she might die.

"Rosina, as you know, always had a night lamp burning in her bedroom, and she dared not put it out on this night for fear that you yourself might walk through the room, or that one of your spies, her maids, might look in, and, on finding the room empty, might wake up all the house. So she asked her best friend, a virgin like herself, one who, by virtue of a sacred vow, would always be ready to serve her, to take her place in the bed for this one hour. Between them they bribed your negro servant, Baba, with twelve yards of crimson velvet and a little Bologna dog belonging to Rosina's friend—which was all that they possessed in the world to give away—to let them in and out of the house. They came and went away dressed like the apothecary's assistant, who would sometimes be called for to give a clyster to your old housekeeper. Rosina went to her nurse's house and talked to Mario in the old woman's presence, for so it had to be. They pledged eternal fidelity and she gave him a letter to her great-uncle in Rome, and she came back to the *palazzo* a little after one o'clock. This, Prince, was my tale, which I wanted you to know."

They all stood perfectly immobile, like a party of little wooden dolls placed on that terrace of the inn, in the middle of the great landscape—Augustus and the old doctor, because they did not know what this speech meant; the old Prince and Giovanni, because they were too deeply impressed to move.

At last the old man spoke. "Who," said he, "has sent you to tell me this today, my pretty young signore?" The girl looked him straight in the eyes.

"Do you not recognize me, Prince?" she asked. "I am that girl, Agnese della Gherardesci, who did your wife this service. You have seen me at your wedding, where I was a bridesmaid, dressed in yellow. Also at one time you came into Rosina's rooms, and I was playing chess with the Professor Pacchiani, whom you had sent to talk to her about her duties. She stood at the window so as not to show that she was crying." After she had spoken these words the Prince Giovanni never took his eyes off her face; during all that happened later he kept quite still, like one of the trees in the garden.

The old Prince sat in the large chair, looking more than ever like a beautiful and severe old idol made in a mosaic of gold, ivory and ebony. He looked with interest at the young girl. "I am extremely sorry, Signora," he said with a deep courtesy. Then again he sat silent.

"And so," he said very slowly after a time, "if Baba had been faithful to me I should have found the two together at that house near the harbor, in the night, and I should have had them in my hand?"

"Yes, that you would," said the girl. "But they would not have minded being killed by you if they had died together."

"No, no, no," said the old Prince, "by no means. How can you imagine that I would have killed either of them? But I would have taken their clothes away and told them that I was going to have them killed in a terrible way, in the morning, and I would have had them shut up together alone over the night. When she was frightened or angry her face, her whole body, blushed like an oleander flower." This gave him stuff for thought for a long time. He seemed to stiffen more and more into something inanimate, until suddenly a great wave of high color spread over his old face.

"And," he exclaimed with deep emotion, "I should have had her, my lovely child, to play with still!"

There was a long silence; nobody dared to speak in the presence of so great a pain.

Suddenly he smiled at them all, a very gentle and sweet smile. "Always," he said in a high and clear voice, "we fail because we are too small. I grudged the boy Mario that, in a petty grudge. And in my vanity I thought that I should prefer an heir to my name, if it was to be, out of a ducal house. Too small I have been, too small for the ways of God."

"Nino," he said after a minute, "Nino, my friend, forgive me. Give me your hand." Deeply moved, Giovanni put away his pistol and took the hand of his old friend. But the old Prince, after having squeezed the young man's fingers, again took hold of his pistol, as if on guard against a greater enemy.

His deep dark eyes looked straight in front of him. His mouth was slightly open, as if he were going to sing. "Carlotta," he said.

Then, with a strange, as if weary, movement, he turned to the right and fell, with the chair, sideways onto the ground, his heavy weight striking the stone pavement with a dull thud. The chair lay with its two legs in the air as he rolled out of it onto the pavement and remained still. At that moment his pistol, which he was still holding in his hand, went off, the bullet, taking a wild line up in the air, passed so close to Augustus's head that he heard its whistle as it passed, like a bird's singing. It stunned him for a second, and brought back the image of his wife. When he felt steady on his feet again he saw the doctor, kneeling beside the old Prince, lifting both arms toward heaven. The face of the old man slowly took on an ashen color. The paint on his cheeks and mouth looked like rose and crimson enamel upon silver.

The doctor dropped his arms and put one hand on the breast of the still figure. After a minute he turned his head and looked back at the people behind him, his face so terrified that it had no expression in it at all. Meeting their eyes, it changed. He got up and solemnly declared to them, "All is over."

They remained quite still around him. The figure of the old Prince, lying immovably on the ground, still held the center of the picture as much as if he had been slowly ascending to heaven, and they his disciples, left behind, gazing up toward him. Only Nino, like one of those figures which were put into sacred pictures as the portrait of the man on whose order they were painted, kept somehow his own direction.

The sun, rising in the blue morning sky, lent a misty bloom to the green broadcloth covering the heavy curves of the old man's body upon the stone terrace.

VIII. THE FREED CAPTIVE

When the old Prince's servants had lifted him up and carried him into the house, Giovanni and Agnese found themselves face to face on the deserted terrace. Their dark eyes met, and as if this were the most fatal of her missions on this spring morning, she looked straight at him for as long a time as it took the landlady's cock—which was a descendant of the cock in the house of the high priest Caiaphas, and whose ancestors had been brought to Pisa by the Crusaders—to raise and finish a long crow. Then she turned to follow the others into the house. At that he spoke, standing quite still. "Do not go away," he said. She stood for a moment, waiting, but did not speak to him. "Do not go away," he said again, "before you have let me speak to you."

"I cannot think," said she, "that you can have anything to say to me." He stood for a long time, very pale, as if making a great effort to collect his voice, then he spoke in a changed and low voice:

> *Lo spirito mio, che già cotanto*
> *tempo era stato ch'alla sua presenza*

non era di stupor tremando affranto
sanza degli occhi aver più conoscenza,
per occulta virtù che da lei mosse
d'antico amor sentì la gran potenza.

There was a long and deep silence. She might have been a little statue in the garden, except for the light morning wind playing with and lifting her soft locks.

"I had left you," he said, speaking altogether like a person in a dream, "and was going away, but I turned back at the door. You were sitting up in the bed. Your face was in the shadow, but the lamp shone on your shoulders and your back. You were naked, for I had torn off your clothes. The bed had green and golden curtains, like my forests in the mountains, and you were like my picture of Daphne, who turns away and is changed into a laurel. And I was standing in the dark. Then the clock struck one. For a year," he cried, "I have thought of nothing but that one moment."

Again the two young people stood quite still. Like the marionettes of the night before, they were within stronger hands than their own, and had no idea what was going to happen to them. He spoke again:

Di penter sì mi punse ivi l'ortica
che di tutt'altre cose, qual mi torse
più nel suo amor, più mi si fe' nemica.
Tanta riconoscenza il cuor mi morse
ch' io caddi vinto. . . .

He stopped because, though he had repeated these lines to himself many times, at the moment he could not remember any more. It was as if he might have dropped down dead, like his old adversary.

She turned again and looked at him, very severely, and yet her face expressed the clearness and calm which the sound of poetry

produces in the people who love it. She spoke very slowly to him,
in her clear and sweet voice, like a bird's:

> . . . *da tema e da vergogna*
> *voglio che tu omai ti disviluppe*
> *e che non parli più com' uom che sogna.*

She looked away for a moment, drew a deep breath, and her
voice took on more force.

> *Sappi che il vaso che il serpente ruppe*
> *fu e non è, ma chi n'ha colpa creda*
> *che vendetta di Dio non teme suppe.*

With these words she walked away, and though she passed so
near to him that he might have held her back by stretching out his
hand, he did not move or try to touch her, but stood upon the
same spot as if he intended to remain there forever, and followed
her with his eyes as she walked up to the house.

Augustus came out of the door at that same moment, and walked
up to meet her. Though he was deeply affected by the happenings
of the morning, and last of all by the sight of the old Prince, now
lying in peace and dignity on a large bed within the inn, his conscience told him that he ought to make an effort to get the message of the old lady to Pisa, and he wanted the girl to help him
and guide him there. At the same time he was, now that he understood more of the whole affair which had brought on the morning's tragedy, shy of approaching her, as one of the principal figures in it, and talking to her of such trivial matters as roads and
coaches. She met him, however, as if he had been an old friend
whom she was happy to meet again. She took his hand and looked
at him. She was changed, like a statue come to life, he thought.

She listened with great interest to all he had to tell her, and was
naturally eager to bring the message to her friend as soon as possible. She suggested that they travel together in her phaëton, which

would be quicker than his coach. She told him that she would drive it herself.

"My friend," she said, "let us go away. Let us go to Pisa as quickly as we can. For I am free. I can choose where I will go, I can think of tomorrow. I think that tomorrow is going to be lovely. I can remember that I am seventeen, and that by the mercy of God I have sixty years more to live. I am no more shut up within one hour. God!" she said with a sudden deep shudder, "I cannot remember it now if I try."

She looked like a young charioteer who is confident of winning his race. It was clear that the idea of speed was at this moment the most attractive of all ideas to her. As they were going into the house she looked back at the terrace.

"We have all been wrong," she said. "That old man was great and might well have been loved. While he was alive we wished for his death, but now that he is dead I think that we all wish that he were back."

"That," said Augustus, who had been reflecting upon his own life, "may make us realize that every human being whom we meet and get to know is, after all, something in our minds, like a tree planted in our gardens or a piece of furniture within our house. It may be better to keep them and try to put them to some use, than to cast them away and have nothing at all there in the end." She thought of this for a little while. "Then the old Prince shall be," said she, "within the garden of my mind a great fountain, made of black marble, near which it is always cool and fresh, and from which great cascades of water are rushing and playing. I shall go and sit there sometimes, when I have much to think of. If I had been Rosina I would not have tried to get away from him. I would have made him happy. It would have been good if he had been happy; it is hard to make anybody unhappy."

Augustus, who thought he heard the note of a late regret in her voice, said in order to console her: "Remember now that you have saved the other's life." She changed color and was silent for a moment. Then she turned and looked at him with deep serenity. "Who," she said, "would have stood by and heard a man so unjustly accused?"

As soon as her carriage was ready they started for Pisa and went at a great speed. The day was beginning to get warm, the road was dusty, and the shadows of the trees were keeping close underneath them. Augustus had left his address with the old doctor in case there would have to be an inquest, but after all the old Prince had died a natural death.

IX. THE PARTING GIFT

Count Augustus von Schimmelmann had been staying in Pisa for more than three weeks and had come to like the place. He had had a love affair with a Swedish lady, some years older than himself, who lived in Pisa to keep away from her husband, and had a small opera stage on which she appeared to her friends. She was a disciple of Swedenborg, and told Augustus that she had had a vision of herself and him in the next world. What really interested him more were the attempts of two priests, one old and one young, to convert him to the Church of Rome. He had no intention of joining it, but it surprised and pleased him that anyone should chose to occupy himself so much with his soul, and he took much trouble in explaining to the churchmen his ideas and states of mind. He could, however, foresee that this affair of spiritual seduction could not go on forever, but would, like, worse luck, all affairs of seduction, have to come to an end one way or another, and he had begun to give much of his time to a secret political society to which he had been introduced as coming from a freer country. At their séances he had met one of the genuine old Jacobins, an exile, a former member of the Mountain, who had been a friend of Robespierre. Augustus often visited him in a little dark and dirty room high up in an old house, and discussed tyranny and freedom with him. He was also taking painting lessons, and had begun to copy an old picture in the gallery.

One day he received a letter from the old Countess di Gampo-corta, who was at the time in residence at her villa close to Pisa and asked him to come and see her. She wrote with great friend-liness and gratitude and gave him her news. On being informed, at the same moment, of her grandmother's accident and the death of her former husband, the young Rosina had been brought to bed of a boy, who had been christened Carlo after his great grand-mother, and whom she described as a very wonderful baby. Both the old and the young woman were well again, though the old Countess wrote that she had given up all hope of getting back the use of her right hand, and they were longing to express to him their thanks for the service that he had done them in their hour of need.

Augustus drove out to the old lady's villa on the afternoon of an extremely hot day. As he was nearing the place a thunderstorm which had hung over Pisa for three days broke loose. A strange sulphurous color and smell filled the air, and the large dark trees near the road on which they were driving were bent down by the violent gusts of wind. A few tremendous flashings of lightning seemed to strike quite close to the carriage, and were followed by long wild roarings of thunder. Then came the rain in heavy warm drops, and in a moment the whole landscape was veiled to him, within his covered carriage, behind streaks of gray and luminous water. As they drove over a stone bridge with a low balustrade he saw the rain strike the dark river like many hundred arrowheads. They climbed up a road along a steep and rocky hill, now slip-pery with the rain, and as they came to a stop at the bottom of a long stone stair in front of the house, a servant with a large um-brella came running down to protect the visitor on his ascent to the house.

In the very large room opening onto a long stone terrace with a view over the river, the quick drumming of heavy raindrops upon the stones was as distinct as if it had been in the room itself. With it came, through the tall open windows, the smell of the sudden freshness and moisture of the air, and of hot stones cooling under water. The room itself smelled of roses. At the other end of it an old *abbate* had been giving a little girl a lesson on the piano, but they had stopped because the noise of the thunder and rain interfered with their counting their measures, and they were now looking out over the valley and the river.

The old Countess and the young mother, on a sofa, had had the baby brought in to look at. He was in the arms of his nurse, a very large magnificent young woman in pink and red, like an oleander flower, and there looked fantastically small, like a little roasted apple to which had been attached a great stream of lace and ribbons. Their attention was divided between the child and the storm, and the two had brought them into a state of exultation, as if their lives had at this hour reached their zenith.

The old lady, who had meant to get up to meet him, was so overcome with her feelings at the sight of Augustus that she could not move. Her eyes, under the old eyelids that were like crape, filled with tears, which from time to time during their conversation rolled down her face. She kissed him on both cheeks, and introduced him with deep emotion to her granddaughter, who was in reality as lovely as any Madonna he had seen in Italy, and to the baby. Augustus had never been able to feel anything but fear in the presence of very young children—though they might, he thought, be of some interest as a kind of promise—and he was surprised to realize that the women were all of the opinion that the baby at this stage had reached its very acme of perfection, and that it was a tragic thing that it should ever have to change. This view, that the human race culminates at birth to decline ever after, impressed him as being easier to live up to than his own.

The old lady had changed since the day when he had met her on the road. The love for a male creature, which she had told him that she had thus far been unable to feel, had rounded out her life in a great and sweet harmony. She told him so herself in the course of their talk. "When I was a little girl," she said, "I was told never to show a fool a thing half finished. But what else does the Lord himself do to us during all our lives? If I had been shown this child from the beginning I should have been docile and have let the Lord ride me in any direction he wanted. Life is a mosaic work of the Lord's, which he keeps filling in bit by bit. If I had seen this little bit of bright color as the centerpiece, I would have understood the pattern, and would not have shaken it all to pieces so many times, and given the good Lord so much trouble in putting it together again." Otherwise she talked mostly about her accident and the afternoon that they had spent together at the inn. She talked with that great delight in remembering which gives value to any occurrence of the past, however insignificant it may have been at the moment.

A servant brought wine and some very beautiful peaches, and the young father came in and was introduced to the guest; but he played no greater part in the picture than the youngest Magus of the adoration, the old Countess having taken for herself the part of Joseph.

When the rain had eased off the old lady took Augustus to the window to see the view. "My friend," she said, while they were standing there together, a little away from the others, "I can never rightly express my gratitude to you, but I want to give you a small token of it to remember me by, when you are far away, and I hope that you will give me the pleasure of accepting it."

Augustus was looking out at the landscape below. A vaguely familiar note within it struck him and made him feel slightly giddy.

"When we first met," she went on, "I told you that I had loved three persons in the course of my life. About the two you know. The third and first was a girl of my own age, a friend from a far country, whom I knew for a short time only and then lost. But we had promised to remember each other forever, and the memory of her has given me strength many times in the vicissitudes of life. When we parted, with many tears, we gave each other a gift of remembrance. Because this thing is precious to me and a token of a real friendship, I want you to take it with you."

With these words she took from her pocket a small object and handed it to him.

Augustus looked at it, and unconsciously his hand went up to his breast. It was a small smelling-bottle in the shape of a heart. On it was painted a landscape with trees, and in the background a white house. As he gazed at it he realized that the house was his own place in Denmark. He recognized the high roof of Lindenburg, even the two old oaks in front of the gate, and the long line of the lime-tree avenue behind the house. The stone seat under the oaks had been painted with great care. Underneath, on a painted ribbon, were the words *Amitié sincère*.

He could feel his own little bottle in his waistcoat pocket, and came near to taking it out and showing it to the old lady. He felt that this would have made a tale which she would forever have cherished and repeated; that it might even come to be her last thought on her deathbed. But he was held back by the feeling that there was, in this decision of fate, something which was meant for him only—a value, a depth, a resort even, in life which belonged to him alone, and which he could not share with anybody else any more than he would be able to share his dreams.

He thanked the old lady with much feeling, and as she realized how much her gift was being appreciated she answered him back with pride and dignity.

He parted from his old friend and the young couple with all the expressions of sincere friendship and took the road to Pisa.

The rain had stopped. The afternoon air was almost cold. Golden sunlight and deep quiet blue shadows divided the landscape between them. A rainbow stood low in the sky.

Augustus took a small mirror from his pocket. Holding it in the flat of his hand, he looked thoughtfully into it.

The Supper
at
Elsinore

PON the corner of a street of Elsinore, near the harbor, there stands a dignified old gray house, built early in the eighteenth century, and looking down reticently at the new times grown up around it. Through the long years it has been worked into a unity, and when the front door is opened on a day of north-north-west the door of the corridor upstairs will open out of sympathy. Also when you tread upon a certain step of the stair, a board of the floor in the parlor will answer with a faint echo, like a song.

It had been in the possession of the family De Coninck for many years, but after the state bankruptcy of 1813 and simultaneous tragic happenings within the family itself, they gave it up and moved to their house in Copenhagen. An old woman in a white cap looked after the old house for them, with a man to assist her, and, living in the old rooms, would think and talk of old days. The two daughters of the house had never married, and were now too old for it. The son was dead. But in summers of long ago— so Madam Bæk would recount—on Sunday afternoons when the weather was fine, the Papa and Mamma De Coninck, with the three children, used to drive in a landaulet to the country house of the old lady, the grandmother, where they would dine, as the custom was then, at three o'clock, outside on the lawn under a large elm tree which, in June, scattered its little round and flat brown seeds thickly upon the grass. They would partake of duck with green peas and of strawberries with cream, and the little boy would run to and fro, in white nankeens, to feed his grandmother's Bolognese dogs.

The two young sisters used to keep, in cages, the many birds presented to them by their seafaring admirers. When asked if they did not play the harp, old Madam Bæk would shrug her shoulders over the impossibility of giving any account of the many perfections of the young ladies. As to their adorers, and the proposals which had been made them, this was a hopeless theme to enter upon. There was no end to it.

Old Madam Bæk, who had herself been married for a short

time to a sailor, and had, when he was drowned, reëntered the service of the De Coninck family as a widow, thought it a great pity that neither of the lovely sisters had married. She could not quite get over it. Toward the world she held the theory that they had not been able to find any man worthy of them, except their brother. But she herself felt that her doctrine would not hold water. If this had been the two sisters' trouble, they ought to have put up with less than the ideal. She herself, on their behalf, would have done so, although it would have cost her much. Also, in her heart she knew better. She was seventeen years older than the elder sister, Fernande, whom they called Fanny, and eighteen years older than the younger, Eliza, who was born on the day of the fall of the Bastille, and she had been with them for the greater part of her life. Even if she was unable to put it into words, she felt keenly enough, as with her own body and soul, the doom which hung over the breed, and which tied these sisters and this brother together and made impossible for them any true relation to other human beings.

While they had been young, no event in the social world of Elsinore had been a success without the lovely De Coninck sisters. They were the heart and soul of all the gayety of the town. When they entered its ballrooms, the ceilings of sedate old merchants' houses seemed to lift a little, and the walls to spring out in luminous Ionian columns, bound with vine. When one of them opened the ball, light as a bird, bold as a thought, she consecrated the gathering to the gods of true joy of life, from whose presence care and envy are banished. They could sing duets like a pair of nightingales in a tree, and imitate without effort and without the slightest malice the voices of all the *beau monde* of Elsinore, so as to make the paunches of their father's friends, the matadors of the town, shake with laughter around their card tables. They could make up a charade or a game of forfeits in no time, and when they had been out for their music lessons, or to the Promenade, they came back brimful of tales of what had happened, or of tales out of their own imaginations, one whim stumbling over the other.

And then, within their own rooms, they would walk up and down the floor and weep, or sit in the window and look out over the harbor and wring their hands in their laps, or lie in bed at night and cry bitterly, for no reason in the world. They would talk, then, of life with the black bitterness of two Timons of Athens, and give Madam Bæk an uncanny feeling, as in an atmosphere of corrodent rust. Their mother, who did not have the curse in her blood, would have been badly frightened had she been present at these moments, and would have suspected some unhappy love affair. Their father would have understood them, and have grieved on their behalf, but he was occupied with his affairs, and did not come into his daughters' rooms. Only this elderly female servant, whose temperament was as different as possible from theirs, would understand them in her way, and would keep it all within her heart, as they did themselves, with mingled despair and pride. Sometimes she would try to comfort them. When they cried out, "Hanne, is it not terrible that there is so much lying, so much falsehood, in the world?" she said, "Well, what of it? It would be worse still if it were actually true, all that they tell."

Then again the girls would get up, dry their tears, try on their new bonnets before the glass, plan their theatricals and sleighing parties, shock and gladden the hearts of their friends, and have the whole thing over again. They seemed as unable to keep from one extremity as from the other. In short, they were born melancholiacs, such as make others happy and are themselves helplessly unhappy, creatures of playfulness, charm and salt tears, of fine fun and everlasting loneliness.

Whether they had ever been in love, old Madam Bæk herself could not tell. They used to drive her to despair by their hard skepticism as to any man being in love with them, when she, indeed, knew better, when she saw the swains of Elsinore grow pale and worn, go into exile or become old bachelors from love of them. She also felt that could they ever have been quite convinced of a man's love of them, that would have meant salvation to these young flying Dutchwomen. But they stood in a strange, distorted relation to the world, as if it had been only their reflection in a mirror which they had been showing it, while in the background and the shadow the real woman remained a looker-on. She would follow with keen attention the movements of the lover courting her image, laughing to herself at the impossibility of the consummation of their love, when the moment should come for it, her own heart hardening all the time. Did she wish that the man would break the glass and the lovely creature within it, and turn around toward herself? Oh, that she knew to be out of the question. Perhaps the lovely sisters derived a queer pleasure out of the adoration paid to their images in the mirror. They could not do without it in the end.

Because of this particular turn of mind they were predestined to be old maids. Now that they were real old maids, of fifty-two and fifty-three, they seemed to have come to better terms with life, as one bears up with a thing that will soon be over. That they were to disappear from the earth without leaving any trace whatever did not trouble them, for they had always known that it would be so. It gave them a certain satisfaction to feel that they were disappearing gracefully. They could not possibly putrefy, as would most of their friends, having already been, like elegant spiritual mummies, laid down with myrrh and aromatic herbs. When they were in their sweet moods, and particularly in their relations with the younger generation, the children of their friends, they even exhaled a spiced odor of sanctity, which the young people remembered all their lives.

The fatal melancholy of the family had come out in a different manner in Morten, the boy, and in him had fascinated Madam Bæk even to possession. She never lost patience with him, as she sometimes did with the girls, because of the fact that he was male and she female, and also by reason of the true romance which surrounded him as it had never surrounded his sisters. He had been, indeed, in Elsinore, as another highborn young dandy before him, the observed of all observers, the glass of fashion and the mold of form. Many were the girls of the town who had remained unmarried for his sake, or who had married late in life one having a likeness, perhaps not quite *en face* and not quite in profile, to that god-like young head which had, by then, forever disappeared from the horizon. And there was even the girl who had been, in the eyes of all the world, engaged to be married to Morten, herself married now, with children—*aber frage nur nicht wie!* She had lost that radiant fairness which had in his day given her the name, in Elsinore, of "golden lambkin," so that where that fairy creature had once pranced in the streets a pale and quiet lady now trod the pavement. But still this was the girl whom, when he had stepped out of his barge on a shining March day at the pier of Elsinore, with the whole population of the town waving and shouting to him, he had lifted from the ground and held in his arms, while all the world had swung up and down around her, had whirled fans and long streamers in all the hues of the rainbow.

Morten De Coninck had been more reticent of manner than his sisters. He had no need to exert himself. When he came into a room, in his quiet way, he owned and commanded it. He had all the beauty of limb and elegance of hands and feet of the ladies of the family, but not their fineness of feature. His nose and mouth seemed to have been cut by a rougher hand. But he had the most striking, extraordinarily noble and serene forehead. People talking to him lifted their eyes to that broad pure brow as if it had been radiant with the diamond tiara of a young emperor, or the halo of a saint. Morten De Coninck looked as if he could not possibly know either guilt or fear. Very likely he did not. He played the part of a hero to Elsinore for three years.

This was the time of the Napoleonic wars, when the world

was trembling on its foundations. Denmark, in the struggle of the Titans, had tried to remain free and to go her own ways, and had had to pay for it. Copenhagen had been bombarded and burned. On that September night, when the sky over the town had flamed red to all Sealand, the great chiming bells of Frue Kirke, set going by the fire, had played, on their own, Luther's hymn, *Ein fester Burg ist unser Gott,* just before the tall tower fell into ruins. To save the capital the government had had to surrender the fleet. The proud British frigates had led the warships of Denmark—the apples of her eye, a string of pearls, a flight of captive swans—up through the Sound. The empty ports cried to heaven, and shame and hatred were in all hearts.

It was in the course of the struggles and great events of the following years of 1807 and 1808 that the flotilla of privateers sprang up, like live sparks from a smoking ruin. Driven forth by patriotism, thirst of revenge, and hope of gain, the privateers came from all the coasts and little islands of Denmark, manned by gentlemen, ferrymen, and fishermen, idealists and adventurers—gallant seamen all of them. As you took out your letter of marque you made your own cause one with that of the bleeding country; you had the right to strike a blow at the enemy whenever you had the chance, and you might come out of the rencounter a rich man. The privateer stood in a curious relationship to the state: it was a sort of acknowledged maritime love-affair, a left-handed marriage, carried through with passionate devotion on both sides. If she did not wear the epaulets and sanctifying bright metal of legitimate union, she had at least the burning red kiss of the crown of Denmark on her lips, and the freedom of the concubine to enchant her lord by these wild whims which queens do not dream of. The royal navy itself—such as was left of it in those ships which had been away from Copenhagen that fatal September week—took a friendly view of the privateer flotilla and lived with it on congenial terms; on such terms, probably, as those on which Rachel lived with her maid Bilhah, who accomplished what she could not do herself. It was a great time for brave men. There were cannons singing once more in the Danish fairways, here and there, and where they were least expected, for the privateers very rarely worked together; every one of them was out on its own. Incredible, heroic deeds were performed, great prizes were snatched away under the very guns of the conveying frigates and were brought into port, by the triumphant wild little boats with their rigging hanging down in rags, amid shouts of exultation. Songs were made about it all. There can rarely have been a class of heroes who appealed more highly and deeply to the heart and imagination of the common people, and to all the boys, of a nation.

It was soon found that the larger type of ship did not do well for this traffic. The ferryboat or snow, with a station bill of twelve to twenty men, and with six to ten swivel guns, handy and quick in emergencies, was the right bird for the business. The nautical skill of the captain and his knowledge of the seaways played a great part, and the personal bravery of the crew, their artfulness with the guns, and, in boarding, with hand weapons, carried the point. Here were the honors of war to be won; and not only honor, but gold; and not gold alone, but revenge upon the violator, sweet to the heart. And when they came in, these old and young sea dogs, covered with snow, their whole rigging sometimes coated with ice until the ship looked as if it were drawn with chalk upon a dark sea, they had their hour of glory behind them, but a great excitement in front, for they made a tremendous stir in the little seaport towns. Then came the judgment of the prize, and the sale of the salved goods, which might be of great value. The government took its share, and each man on board came in for his, from the captain, gunner, and mate to the boys, who received one-third of a man's share. A boy might have gone to sea possessing nothing but his shirt, trousers and trouser-strap, and come back with those badly torn and red-stained, and a tale of danger and high seas to tell his friends and might be jingling

five hundred riksdaler in his pocket a fortnight later, when the
sale was over. The Jews of Copenhagen and Hamburg, each in
three tall hats, one on top of the other, made their appearance
upon the spot quickly, to play a great rôle at the sale, or, before-
hand, to coax the prize-marks out of the pockets of impatient
combatants.

Soon there shot up, like new comets, the names of popular
heroes and their boats, around whose fame myths gathered daily.
There was Jens Lind, of the *Cort Adeler,* the one they called "Velvet" Lind because he was such a swell, and who played the rôle
of a great nabob for some years, and then, when all gain was
spent, finished up as a bear-leader. There was Captain Raaber, of
The Revenger. who was something of a poet; the brothers Wulff-
sen, of *The Mackerel* and the *Madame Clark,* who were gentlemen of Copenhagen; and Christen Kock of the *Æolus,* whose
entire crew—every single man—was killed or wounded in her
fight with a British frigate off Læssø; and there was young Morten De Coninck, of the *Fortuna II.*

When Morten first came to his father and asked him to equip
a privateer for him, the heart of old Mr. De Coninck shrank a
little from the idea. There were many rich and respectable ship-
owners of Copenhagen, some of them greater merchants than he,
who had in these days launched their privateers, and Mr. De
Coninck, who yielded to no one in patriotic feeling, had himself
suffered heavy losses at the hands of the British. But the business
was painful to him. There was to his mind something revolting
in the idea of attacking merchant ships, even if they did carry
contraband. It seemed to him like assaulting ladies or shooting
albatrosses. Morten had to turn for support to his father's cousin,
Fernand De Coninck, a rich old bachelor of Elsinore whose
mother was French and who was an enthusiastic partisan of the
Emperor Napoleon. Morten's two sisters masterfully assisted him
in getting around Uncle Fernand, and in November, 1807, the
young man put to sea in his own boat. The uncle never regretted

his generosity. The whole business rejuvenated him by twenty years, and he possessed, in the end, a collection of souvenirs from the ships of the enemy that gave him great pleasure.

The *Fortuna II* of Elsinore, with a crew of twelve and four swivel guns, received her letter of marque on the second of November—was not this date, and the dates of exploits following it, written in Madam Bæk's heart, like the name of Calais in Queen Mary's, now, thirty-three years after? Already on the fourth the *Fortuna II* surprised an English brig off Hveen. An English man-of-war, hastening to the spot, shot at the privateer, but her crew managed to cut the cables of the prize and bring her into safety under the guns cf Kronborg.

On the twentieth of November the boat had a great day. From a convoy she cut off the British brig, *The William,* and the snow, *Jupiter,* which had a cargo of sail cloth, stoneware, wine, spirits, coffee, sugar and silks. The cargo was unloaded at Elsinore, but both prizes were brought to Copenhagen, where they were condemned. Two hundred Jews came to Elsinore to bid at the auction sale of the *Jupiter's* cargo, on the thirtieth of December. Morten himself bought in a piece of white brocade which was said to have been made in China and sent from England for the wedding dress of the Czar's sister. At this time Morten had just become engaged, and all Elsinore laughed and smiled at him as he walked away with the parcel under his arm.

Many times he was pursued by the enemy's men-of-war. Once, on the twenty-seventh of May, in flight from a British frigate, he ran ashore near Aarhus, but escaped by throwing his ballast of iron overboard, and got in under the guns of the Danish batteries. The burghers of Aarhus provided the illustrious young privateersman with new iron for his ballast, free of charge. It was said that the little seamstresses brought him their pressing-irons, and kissed them in parting with them, to bring him luck.

On the fifteenth of January the *Fortuna* had, together with the privateer *Three Friends,* captured six of the enemy's ships, and with these was bearing in with Drogden, to have them realized in Copenhagen, when one of the prizes ran ashore on the Middelgrund. It was a big British brig loaded with sail cloth, valued at 100,000 riksdaler, which the privateers had, on the morning of the same day, cut off from an English convoy. The British men-of-war were still pursuing them. At the sight of the accident the pursuing ships instantly dispatched a strong detachment of six longboats to recapture their brig. The privateers, on their side, were not disposed to give her up, and beat up against the British, who were driven away by a fire of grapeshot and had to give up the recapture. But the ship was to be lost all the same. The prize-master on board her, at the sight of the enemy's boats with their greatly superior forces, had put fire to the brig so that she should not fall again into the hands of the British. The fire spread so violently that the ship could not be saved, and all night the people of Copenhagen watched the tall, terrible beacon to the north. The five remaining prizes were taken to Copenhagen.

It was in the summer of the same year that the *Fortuna II* came in for a life-and-death fight off Elsinore. She had by then become a thorn in the flesh of the British, and on a dark night in August they made ready, from the men-of-war stationed on the Swedish coast, to capture her. Two big launches were sent off, their tholes bound with wool. The crew of the privateer had turned in, and only young Morten himself and his balker were on deck when the launches, manned by thirty-five sailors, grated against the *Fortuna's* sides, and the boarding pikes were planted in her boards. From the launches shots were fired, but on board the privateer there was neither time nor room for using the guns. It became a struggle of axes, broadswords and knives. The enemy swarmed on deck from all sides; men were cutting at the chain-cable and hanging in the figurehead. But it did not last long. The *Fortuna's* men put up a desperate fight, and in twenty minutes the deck was cleared. The enemy jumped into its boats and pushed off. The guns were used then, and three canister shots were fired after the retreating British. They left twelve dead and wounded men on the deck of the *Fortuna II*.

At Elsinore the people had heard the musketry fire from the longboats, but no reply from the *Fortuna*. They gathered at the harbor and along the ramparts of Kronborg, but the night was dark, and although the sky was just reddening in the east, no one could see what was happening. Then, just as the first light of morning was filling the dull air, three shots rang out, one after another, and the boys of Elsinore said that they could see the white smoke run along the dark waves. The *Fortuna II* bore in with Elsinore half an hour later. She looked black against the eastern sky. It was apparent that her rigging had been badly crippled, and gradually the people on land were able to distinguish the little dark figures on board, and the red on the deck. It was said that there was not a single broadsword or knife on board that was not red, and all the netting from stern to main chains had been soaked with blood. There was not one man on board, either, who had not been wounded, but only one was badly hurt. This was a West-Indian Negro, from the Danish colonies there—"black in skin but a Dane in heart," the newspapers of Elsinore said the next day. Morten himself, fouled with gunpowder, a bandage down over one eye, white in the morning light and wild still from the fight, lifted both his arms high in the air to the cheering crowd on shore.

In the autumn of that same year the whole privateer trade was suddenly prohibited. It was thought that it drew the enemy's frigates to the Danish seas, and constituted a danger to the country. Also, it was on many sides characterized as a wild and inhuman way of fighting. This broke the hearts of many gallant sailors, who left their decks to wander all over the world, unable to settle down again to their work in the little towns. The country grieved over her birds of prey.

To Morten De Coninck, all people agreed, the new order came

conveniently. He had gathered his laurels and could now marry and settle down in Elsinore.

He was then engaged to Adrienne Rosenstand, the falcon to the white dove. She was the bosom friend of his sisters, who treated her much as if they had created her themselves, and took pleasure in dressing up her loveliness to its greatest advantage. They had refined and decided tastes, and spent as much time on the choice of her trousseau as if it had been their own. Between themselves they were not always so lenient to their frail sister-in-law, but would passionately deplore to one another the mating of their brother with a little *bourgeoise*, an ornamental bird out of the poultry yard of Elsinore. Had they thought the matter over a little, they ought to have congratulated themselves. The timidity and conventionality of Adrienne still allowed them to shine unrivaled within their sphere of daring and fantasy; but what figures would the falcon's sisters have cut, had he, as might well have happened, brought home a young eagle-bride?

The wedding was to take place in May, when the country around Elsinore is at its loveliest, and all the town was looking forward to the day. But it did not come off in the end. On the morning of the marriage the bridegroom was found to be missing, and he was never seen again in Elsinore. The sisters, dissolved in tears of grief and shame, had to take the news to the bride, who fell down in a swoon, lay ill for a long time, and never quite recovered. The whole town seemed to have been struck dumb by the blow, and to wrap up its head in sorrow. No one made much out of this unique opportunity for gossip. Elsinore felt the loss its own, and the fall.

No direct message from Morten De Coninck ever reached Elsinore. But in the course of the years strange rumors of him drifted in from the West. He was a pirate, it was said first of all, and that was not an unheard-of fate for a homeless privateer. Then it was rumored that he was in the wars in America, and had distinguished himself. Later it was told that he had become a great planter and slave-owner in the Antilles. But even these rumors were lightly handled by the town. His name was hardly ever mentioned, until, after long years, he could be talked about as a figure out of a fairy tale, like Bluebeard or Sindbad the Sailor. In the drawing-rooms of the De Coninck house he ceased to exist after his wedding-day. They took his portrait down from the wall. Madame De Coninck took her death over the loss of her son. She had a great deal of life in her. She was a stringed instrument from which her children had many of their high and clear notes. If it were never again to be used, if no waltz, serenade, or martial march were ever to be played upon it again, it might as well be put away. Death was no more unnatural to her than silence.

To Morten's sisters the infrequent news of their brother was manna on which they kept their hearts alive in a desert. They did not serve it to their friends, nor to their parents; but within the distillery of their own rooms they concocted it according to many recipes. Their brother would come back an admiral in a foreign fleet, his breast covered with unknown stars, to marry the bride waiting for him, or come back wounded, broken in health, but highly honored, to die in Elsinore. He would land at the pier. Had he not done so, and had they not seen it with their own eyes? But even this spare food came in time to be seasoned with much pungent bitterness. They themselves, in the end, would rather have starved than have swallowed it, had they had the choice. Morten, it was told, far from being a distinguished naval officer or a rich planter, had indeed been a pirate in the waters around Cuba and Trinidad—one of the last of the breed. But, pursued by the ships *Albion* and *Triumph,* he had lost his ship near Port of Spain, and himself had a narrow escape. He had tried to make his living in many hard ways and had been seen by somebody in New Orleans, very poor and sick. The last thing that his sisters heard of him was that he had been hanged.

From Morten's wedding day, Madam Bæk had carried her

wound in silence for thirty years. The sophistries of his sisters she never chose to make use of; she let them go in at one ear and out at the other. She was very humble and attentive to the deserted bride, when she again visited the family, yet she never showed her much sympathy. Also she knew, as was ever the case in the house, more than any other inhabitant of it. It cannot be said that she had seen the catastrophe approach, but she had had strange warnings in her dreams. The bridegroom had been in the habit, from childhood, of coming and sitting with her in her little room from time to time. He had done that while they were making great preparations for his happiness. Over her needlework and her glasses she had watched his face. And she, who often worked late at night, and who would be up in the linen-room before the early summer sun was above the Sound, was aware of many comings and goings unknown to the rest of the household. Something had happened to the engaged people. Had he begged her to take him and hold him, so that it should no longer be in his power to leave her? Madam Bæk could not believe that any girl could refuse Morten anything. Or had she yielded, and found the magic ineffective? Or had she been watching him, daily slipping away from her, and still had not the strength to offer the sacrifice which might have held him?

Nobody would ever know, for Adrienne never talked of these things; indeed, she could not have done so if she had wanted to. Ever since her recovery from her long illness she seemed to be a little hard of hearing. She could only hear the things which could be talked about very loudly, and finished her life in an atmosphere of high-shrieked platitudes.

For fifteen years the lovely Adrienne waited for her bridegroom, then she married.

The two sisters De Coninck attended the wedding. They were magnificently attired. This was really the last occasion upon which they appeared as the belles of Elsinore, and although they were then in their thirties, they swept the floor with the young girls of the town. Their wedding present to the bride was no less imposing. They gave her their mother's diamond earrings and brooch, a *parure* unique in Elsinore. They had likewise robbed the windows of their drawing-rooms of all their flowers to adorn the altar, this being a December wedding. All the world thought that the two proud sisters were doing these honors to their friend to make amends for what she had suffered at their brother's hands. Madam Bæk knew better. She knew that they were acting out of deep gratitude, that the diamond *parure* was a thankoffering. For now the fair Adrienne was no longer their brother's virgin widow, and held no more the place next to him in the eyes of all the world. When the gentle intruder now walked out of their house, the least they could do was to follow her to the door with deep courtesies. To her children, later in life, they also for the same reason showed the most excessive kindness, leaving them, in the end, most of their worldly goods; and to all this they were driven by their thankfulness to that pretty brood of ornamental chickens out of the poultry yard of Elsinore, because they were not their brother's children.

Madam Bæk herself had been asked to the wedding, and had a pleasant evening. When the ice was being served, she suddenly thought of the icebergs in the great black ocean, of which she had read, and of a lonely young man gazing at them from the deck of a ship, and at that moment her eyes met those of Miss Fanny, at the other end of the table. These dark eyes were all ablaze, and shone with tears. With all her De Coninck strength the distinguished old maid was suppressing something: a great longing, or shame, or triumph.

But there was another girl of Elsinore whose story may rightly be told, very briefly, in this place. That was an innkeeper's daughter of Sletten, by the name of Katrine, of the blood of the charcoal burners who live near Elsinore and are in many ways like gypsies. She was a big, handsome, dark and red-cheeked girl, and was said to have been, at a time, the sweetheart of Morten De Coninck.

This young woman had a sad fate. She was thought to have gone a little out of her head. She took to drink and to worse ways, and died young. To this girl, Eliza, the younger of the sisters, showed great kindness. Twice she started her in a little milliner's shop, for the girl was talented and had an eye for elegance, and advertised it herself by wearing no bonnets but hers, and to the end of her life she gave her money. When, after many scandals in Elsinore, Katrine moved to Copenhagen, and took up her residence in the street of Dybensgade, where, in general, the ladies of the town never set foot, Eliza De Coninck still went to see her, and seemed to come back having gathered strength and a secret joy from her visits. For this was the way in which a girl beloved and deserted by Morten De Coninck ought to behave. This plain ruin, misery and degradation were the only harmonious accompaniment to the happenings, which might resound in and rejoice the heart of the sister while she stopped her ears to the words of comfort of the world. Eliza sat at Katrine's deathbed like a witch attentively observing the working of the deadly potion, holding her breath for the fulfillment of it.

The winter of 1841 was unusually severe. The cold began before Christmas, but in January it turned into a deadly still, continuous frost. A little snow in spare hard grains came down from time to time, but there was no wind, no sun, no movement in air or water. The ice was thick upon the Sound, so that people could walk from Elsinore to Sweden to drink coffee with their friends, the fathers of whom had met their own fathers to the roar of cannons on the same waters, when the waves had gone high. They looked like little rows of small black tin soldiers upon the infinite gray plane. But at night, when the lights from the houses and the dull street lamps reached only a little way out on the ice, this flatness and whiteness of the sea was very strange, like the breath of death over the world. The smoke from the chimneys went straight up in the air. The oldest people did not remember another such winter.

Old Madam Bæk, like other people, was very proud of this extraordinarily cold weather, and much excited about it, but during these winter months she changed. She probably was near her end, and was going off quickly. It began by her fainting in the dining-room one morning when she had been out by herself to buy fish, and for some time she could hardly move. She became very silent. She seemed to shrink, and her eyes grew pale. She went about in the house as before, but now it seemed to her that she had to climb an endless steep hill when in the evenings, with her candlestick and her shadow, she walked up the stair; and she seemed to be listening to sounds from far away when, with her knitting, she sat close to the crackling tall porcelain stove. Her friends began to think that they should have to cut out a square hole for her in that iron ground before the thaw of spring would set in. But she still held on, and after a time she seemed to become stronger again, although more rigid, as if she herself had frozen in the hard winter with a frost that would not thaw. She never got back that gay and precise flow of speech which, during seventy years, had cheered so many people, kept servants in order, and promoted or checked the gossip of Elsinore.

One afternoon she confided to the man who assisted her in the house her decision to go to Copenhagen to see her ladies. The next day she went out to arrange for her trip with the hackney man. The news of her project spread, for the journey from Elsinore to Copenhagen is no joke. On a Thursday morning she was up by candlelight and descended the stone steps to the street, her carpetbag in her hand, while the morning light was still dim.

The journey was no joke. It is more than twenty-six miles from Elsinore to Copenhagen, and the road ran along the sea. In many places there was hardly any road; only a track that went along the seashore. Here the wind, blowing onto the land, had swept away the snow, so that no sledges could pass, and the old woman went in a carriage with straw on the floor. She was well wrapped up, still, as the carriage drove on and the winter day came up and showed all the landscape so silent and cold, it was as if nothing at all could keep alive here, least of all an old woman all by herself in a carriage. She sat perfectly quiet, looking around her. The plane of the frozen Sound showed gray in the gray light. Here and there seaweeds strewn upon the beach marked it with brown and black. Near the road, upon the sand, the crows were marching martially about, or fighting over a dead fish. The little fishermen's houses along the road had their doors and windows carefully shut. Sometimes she would see the fishermen themselves, in high boots that came above their knees, a long way out on the ice, where they were cutting holes to catch cod with a tin bait. The sky was the color of lead, but low along the horizon ran a broad stripe the color of old lemon peel or very old ivory.

It was many years since she had come along this road. As she drove on, long-forgotten figures came and ran alongside the carriage. It seemed strange to her that the indifferent coachman in a fur cap and the small bay horses should have it in their power to drive her into a world of which they knew nothing.

They came past Rungsted, where, as a little girl, she had served in the old inn, red-tiled, close to the road. From here to town the road was better. Here had lived, for the last years of his life, in sickness and poverty, the great poet Ewald, a genius, the swan of the North. Broken in health, deeply disappointed in his love for the faithless Arendse, badly given to drink, he still radiated a rare vitality, a bright light that had fascinated the little girl. Little Hanne, at the age of ten, had been sensitive to the magnetism of the great mysterious powers of life, which she did not understand. She was happy when she could be with him. Three things, she had learned from the talk of the landlady, he was always begging for: to get married, since to him life without women seemed unbearably cold and waste; alcohol of some sort—although he was a fine connoisseur of wine, he could drink down the crass gin of the country as well; and, lastly, to be taken to Holy Communion. All three were firmly denied him by his mother and stepfather, who were rich people of Copenhagen, and even by his friend, Pastor Schoenheyder, for they did not want him to be happy in either of the first two ways, and they considered that he must alter his ways before he could be made happy in the third. The landlady and Hanne were sorry for him. They would have married him and given him wine and taken him to Holy Communion, had it lain with them. Often, when the other children had been playing, Hanne had left them to pick early spring violets for him in the grass with cold fingers, looking forward to the sight of his face when he smelled the little bunches of flowers. There was something here which she could not understand, and which still held all her being strongly—that violets could mean so much. Generally he was very gay with her, and would take her on his knees and warm his cold hands on her. His breath sometimes smelled of gin, but she never told anybody. Even three years later, when she was confirmed, she imagined the Lord Jesus with his long hair in a queue, and with that rare, wild, broken and arrogant smile of the dying poet.

Madam Bæk came through the East Gate of Copenhagen just as people were about to light their lamps. She was held up and questioned by the toll collectors, but when they found her to be an honest woman in possession of no contraband they let her pass. So she would appear at the gate of heaven, ignorant of what was wanted of her, but confident that if she behaved correctly, according to her lights, others would behave correctly, according to theirs.

She drove through the streets of Copenhagen, looking around—for she had not been there for many years—as she would look around to form an opinion of the new Jerusalem. The streets here were not paved with gold or chrysoprase, and in places there was a little snow; but such as they were she accepted them. She likewise accepted the stables, where she was to get out, and the walk in the icy-cold blue evening of Copenhagen to Gammeltorv, where lay the house of her ladies.

Nevertheless she felt, as she took her way slowly through the streets, that she was an intruder and did not belong. She was not even noticed, except by two young men, deep in a political discussion, who had to separate to let her pass between them, and by a couple of boys, who remarked upon her bonnet. She did not like this sort of thing, it did not take place in Elsinore.

The windows of the first floor of the Misses De Conincks' house were brightly lighted. Remembering it to be Fernande's birthday, Madam Bæk, down in the square, reasoned that the ladies would be having a party.

This was the case, and while Madam Bæk was slowly ascending the stair, dragging her heavy feet and her message from step to step, the sisters were merrily entertaining their guests in their warm and cozy gray parlor with its green carpet and shining mahogany furniture.

The party was characteristic of the two old maids by being mostly composed of gentlemen. They existed, in their pretty house in Gammeltorv, like a pair of prominent spiritual courtesans of Copenhagen, leading their admirers into excesses and seducing them into scattering their spiritual wealth and health upon their charms. As a couple of corresponding young courtesans of the flesh would be out after the great people and princes of this world, so were they ever spreading their snares for the *honoratiori* of the world spiritual, and tonight could lay on the table no meaner acquisition than the Bishop of Sealand, the director of the Royal Theater of Copenhagen, who was himself a distinguished dramatic and philosophical scribe, and a famous old painter of animals, just back from Rome, where he had been shown great honor. An old commodore with a fresh face, who had carried a wound since 1807, and a lady-in-waiting to the Dowager Queen, elegant and a good listener, who looked as if her voluminous skirt was absolutely massive, from her waist down, completed the party, all of whom were old friends, but were there chiefly to hold the candle.

If these sisters could not live without men, it was because they

had the firm conviction, which, as an instinct, runs in the blood
of seafaring families, that the final word as to what you are really
worth lies with the other sex. You may ask the members of your
own sex for their opinion and advice as to your compass and
crew, your cuisine and garden, but when it comes to the matter
of what you yourself are worth, the words of even your best
friends are void and good for nothing, and you must address
yourself to the opposite sex. Old white skippers, who have been
round the Horn and out in a hundred hurricanes, know the law.
They may be highly respected on the deck or in the mess, and
honored by their staunch gray contemporaries, but it is, finally,
the girls who have the say as to whether they are worth keeping
alive or not. The old sailor's women are aware of this fact, and
will take a good deal of trouble to impress even the young boys
toward a favorable judgment. This doctrine, and this quick esti-
mating eye is developed in sailor's families because there the two
sexes have the chance to see each other at a distance. A sailor, or
a sailor's daughter, judges a person of the other sex as quickly
and surely as a hunter judges a horse; a farmer, a head of cattle;
and a soldier, a rifle. In the families of clergymen and scribes,
where the men sit in their houses all their days, people may judge
each other extremely well individually, but no man knows what
a woman is, and no woman what a man is; they cannot see the
wood for trees.

The two sisters, in caps with lace streamers, were doing the
honors of the house gracefully. In those days, when gentlemen did
not smoke in the presence of ladies, the atmosphere of an evening
party remained serene to the end, but a very delicate aromatic
and exotic stream of steam rose from the tumblers of rare old rum
with hot water, lemon, and sugar, upon the table in the soft glow
of the lamp. None of the company was quite uninfluenced by this
nectar. They had a moment before been conjuring forth their
youth by the singing of old songs which they themselves remembered their fathers' friends singing over their wine in the really

good old days. The Bishop, who had a very sweet voice, had been holding up his glass while giving the ancient toast to the old generation:

Let the old ones be remembered now; they once were gay and free.
And that they knew to love, my dear, the proof thereof are we!

The echo of the song—for she now declared that it was a five minutes' course from her ear to her mind—was making Miss Fanny De Coninck thoughtful and a little absentminded. What a strange proof, she thought, are these dry old bodies here tonight of the fact that young men and women, half a century ago, sighed and shivered and lost themselves in ecstasies. What a curious proof is this gray hand of the follies of young hands upon a night in May long, long ago.

As she was standing, her chin, in this intensive dreaming, pressed down a little upon the black velvet ribbon around her throat, it would have been difficult for anyone who had not known her in her youth to find any trace of beauty in Fanny's face. Time had played a little cruelly with her. A slight wryness of feature, which had been an adorable piquantry once, was now turned into an uncanny little disfigurement. Her birdlike lightness was caricatured into abrupt little movements in fits and starts. But she had her brilliant dark eyes still, and was, all in all, a distinguished, and slightly touching, figure.

After a moment she took up again the conversation with the bishop as animatedly as before. Even the little handkerchief in her fingers and the small crystal buttons down her narrow silk bosom seemed to take part in the argument. No pythoness on her tripod, her body filled with inspiring fumes, could look more prophetic. The theme under discussion was the question whether, if offered a pair of angel's wings which could not be removed, one would accept or refuse the gift.

"Ah, Your Right Worshipfulness," said Miss Fanny, "in walking up the aisle you would convert the entire congregation with your back. There would not be a sinner left in Copenhagen. But remember that even you descend from the pulpit at twelve o'clock every Sunday. It must be difficult enough for you as it is, but how would you, in a pair of white angels' wings, get out of——" What she really wanted to say was, "get out of using a chamber-pot?" Had she been forty years younger she would have said it. The De Coninck sisters had not been acquainted with sailors all of their lives for nothing. Very vigorous expressions, and oaths even, such as were never found in the mouths of the other young ladies of Elsinore, came naturally to their rosy lips, and used to charm their admirers into idolatry. They knew a good many names for the devil, and in moments of agitation would say, "Hell—to hell!" Now the long practice of being a lady and a hostess prevented Fanny, and she said instead very sweetly, "of eating a roast white turkey?" For that was what the Bishop had been doing at dinner with obvious delight. Still, her imagination was so vividly at work that it was curious that the prelate, gazing, at close quarters, with a fatherly smile into her clear eyes, did not see there the picture of himself, in his canonicals, making use of a chamber-pot in a pair of angels' wings.

The old man was so enlivened by the debate that he spilled a few drops from his glass onto the carpet. "My dear charming Miss Fanny," he said, "I am a good Protestant and flatter myself that I have not quite failed in making things celestial and terrestrial go well together. In that situation I should look down and see, in truth, my celestial individuality reflected in miniature, as you see yours every day in the little bit of glass in your fair hand."

The old professor of painting said: "When I was in Italy I was shown a small, curiously shaped bone, which is found only in the shoulder of the lion, and is the remains of a wing bone, from the time when lions had wings, such as we still see in the lion of St. Mark. It was very interesting."

"Ah, indeed, a fine monumental figure on that column," said

the Bishop, who had also been in Italy, and who knew that he had a leonine head.

"Oh, if I had a chance of those wings," said Miss Fanny, "I should not care a hang about my fine or monumental figure. But, by St. Anne, I should fly."

"Allow me," said the Bishop, "to hope, Miss Fanny, that you would not. We may have our reasons to mistrust a flying lady. You have, perhaps, heard of Adam's first wife, Lilith? She was, in contradistinction to Eve, made all out of earth, like himself. What was the first thing that she did? She seduced two angels and made them betray to her the secret word which opens heaven, and so she flew away from Adam. That goes to teach us that where there is too much of the earthly element in a woman, neither husband nor angels can master her.

"Indeed," he went on, warming to his subject, his glass still in his hand, "in woman, the particularly heavenly and angelic attributes, and those which we most look up to and worship, all go to weigh her down and keep her on the ground. The long tresses, the veils of pudicity, the trailing garments, even the adorable womanly forms in themselves, the swelling bosom and hip, are as little as possible in conformity with the idea of flying. We, all of us, willingly grant her the title of angel, and the white wings, and lift her up on our highest pedestal, on the one inevitable condition that she must not dream of, must even have been brought up in absolute ignorance of, the possibility of flight."

"Ah, la la," said Fanny, "we are aware of that, Bishop, and so it is ever the woman whom you gentlemen do not love or worship, who possesses neither the long lock nor the swelling bosom, and who has had to truss up her skirts to sweep the floor, who chuckles at the sight of the emblem of her very thraldom, and anoints her broomstick upon the eve of Walpurgis."

The director of the Royal Theater rubbed his delicate hands gently against each other. "When I hear the ladies complain of their hard task and restrictions in life," he said, "it sometimes reminds me of a dream that I once had. I was at the time writing a tragedy in verse. It seemed to me in my dream that the words and syllables of my poem made a rebellion and protested, 'Why must we take infinite trouble to stand, walk and behave according to difficult and painful laws which the words of your prose do not dream of obeying?' I answered, 'Mesdames, because you are meant to be poetry. Of prose we think, and demand, but little. It must exist, if only for the police regulations and the calendar. But a poem which is not lovely has no *raison d'être*.' God forgive me if I have ever made poems which had in them no loveliness, and treated ladies in a manner which prevented them from being perfectly lovely—my remaining sins I can shoulder easily then."

"How," said the old commodore, "could I entertain any doubts as to the reality of wings, who have grown up amongst sailing ships and amongst the ladies of the beginning of our century? The beastly steamships which go about these days may well be a species of witches of the sea—they are like self-supporting women. But if you ladies are contemplating giving up being white-sailed ships and poems—well, we must be perfectly lovely poems ourselves, then, and leave you to make up the police regulations. Without poetry no ship can be sailed. When I was a cadet, on the way to Greenland, and in the Indian Ocean, I used to console myself, on the middle watch, by thinking, in consecutive order, of all the women I knew, and by quoting poetry that I had learned by heart."

"But you have always been a poem, Julian," said Eliza, "a roundel." She felt tempted to put her arms round her cousin, they had always been great friends.

"Ah, in talking about Eve and Paradise," said Fanny, "you all still remain a little jealous of the snake."

"When I was in Italy," said the professor, "I often thought what a curious thing it is that the serpent, which, if I understand the Scripture, opened the eyes of man to the arts, should be, in itself, an object impossible to get into a picture. A snake is a lovely t Naples they had a large reptile house, and I used to study the snakes there for many hours. They have skins like jewels, and their movements are wonderful performances of art. But I have never seen a snake done successfully in a picture. I could not paint it myself."

"Do you remember," said the commodore, who had been following his own thoughts, "the swing that I put up for you, at Oregaard, on your seventeenth birthday, Eliza? I made a poem about it."

"Yes, I do, Julian," said Eliza, her face brightening, "it was made like a ship."

It was a curious thing about the two sisters, who had been so unhappy as young women, that they should take so much pleasure in dwelling upon the past. They could talk for hours of the most insignificant trifles of their young days, and these made them laugh and cry more heartily than any event of the present day. Perhaps to them the first condition for anything having real charm was this: that it must not really exist.

It was another curious phenomenon about them that they, to whom so very little had happened, should talk of their married friends who had husbands, children, and grandchildren with pity and slight contempt, as of poor timid creatures whose lives had been dull and uneventful. That they themselves had had no husbands, children, or lovers did not restrain them from feeling that they had chosen the more romantic and adventurous part. The explanation was that to them only possibilities had any interest; realities carried no weight. They had themselves had all possibilities in hand, and had never given them away in order to make a definite choice and come down to a limited reality. They might still take part in elopements by rope-ladder, and in secret marriages, if it came to that. No one could stop them. Thus their only intimate friends were old maids like themselves, or unhappily married women, dames of the round table of possibilities. For their happily married friends, fattened on realities, they had, with much kindness, a different language, as if these had been of a slightly lower caste, with whom intercourse had to be carried on with the assistance of interpreters.

Eliza's face had brightened, like a fine, pure jar of alabaster behind which a lamp is lighted, at mention of the swing, made like a boat, which had been given her for her seventeenth birthday. She had always been by far the loveliest of the De Coninck children. When they were young their old French aunt had named them *la Bonté, la Beauté,* and *l'Esprit,* Morten being *la Bonté.*

She was as fair as her sister was dark, and in Elsinore, where at the time a fashion for surnames had prevailed, they had called her "Ariel," or "The Swan of Elsinore." There had been that particular quality about her beauty that it seemed to hold promise, to be only the first step of the ladder of some extraordinary career. Here was this exceptional young female creature who had had the inspiration to be, from head to foot, strikingly lovely. But that was only the beginning of it. The next step was perhaps her clothes, for Eliza had always been a great swell, and had run up heavy debts—for which at times her brother had taken the responsibility before their father—on brocades, cashmeres, and plumes ordered from Copenhagen and Hamburg, and even from Paris. But that was also only the beginning of something. Then came the way in which she moved, and danced. There was about it an atmosphere of suspense which caused onlookers to hold their breaths. What was this extraordinary girl to do next? If at this time she had indeed unfolded a pair of large white wings, and had soared from the pier of Elsinore up into the summer air, it would have surprised no one. It was clear that she must do something extraordinary with such an abundance of gifts. "There is more strength in that girl," said the old boatswain of *La Fortuna,* when upon a spring day she came running down to the harbor, bareheaded, "than in all *Fortuna's* crew." Then in the end she had done nothing at all.

At Gammeltorv she was quietly, as if intentionally, fading day by day, into an even more marble-like loveliness. She could still span her waist with her two long slim hands, and moved with much pride and lightness, like an old Arab mare a little stiff, but unmistakably noble, at ease in the sphere of war and fantasias. And there was still that about her which kept open a perspective, the feeling that somewhere there were reserves and it was not out of the question that extraordinary things might happen.

"God, that swing, Eliza!" said the commodore. "You had been so hard on me in the evening that I actually went out into the garden of Oregaard, on that early July morning, resolved to hang myself. And as I was looking up into the crown of the great elm, I heard you saying behind me: 'That would be a good branch.' That, I thought, was cruelly said. But as I turned around, there you were, your hair still done up in curling papers, and I remembered that I had promised you a swing. I could not die, in any case, till you had had it. When I got it up, and saw you in it, I thought: If it shall be my lot in life to be forever only ballast to the white sails of fair girls, I still bless my lot."

"That is what we have loved you for all your life," said Eliza.

An extremely pretty young maid, with pale blue ribbons on her cap—kept by the pair of old spiritual courtesans to produce an equilibrium in the establishment, in the way in which two worldly young courtesans might have kept, to the same end, an ugly and misshapen servant, a dwarf with wit and imagination—brought in a tray filled with all sorts of delicacies: Chinese ginger, tangerines, and crystallized fruit. In passing Miss Fanny's chair she said softly, "Madam Bæk has come from Elsinore, and waits in the kitchen."

Fanny's color changed, she could never receive calmly the news that anybody had arrived, or had gone away. Her soul left her and flew straight to the kitchen, from where she had to drag it back again.

"In that summer of 1806," she said, "the *Odyssey* had been translated into Danish for the first time, I believe. Papa used to read it to us in the evenings. Ha, how we played, his gallant crew, braved the Cyclops and cruised, island of the Læstrygones and the Phæacian shores. I shall never be made to believe that we did not spend that summer in our ships, under brown sails."

Shortly after this the party broke up, and the sisters drew up the blinds of their window to wave to the four gentlemen who helped Miss Bardenfleth into her court carriage and proceeded in a gayly talking group across the little iron-gray desert of nocturnal Gammeltorv, remarking, in the midst of philosophical and poetic discussions, upon the extraordinary cold.

This moment at the end of their parties always went strangely to the sisters' hearts. They were happy to get rid of their guests; but a little silent, bitter minute accompanied the pleasure. For they could still make people fall in love with them. They had the radiance in them which could refract little rainbow effects in the atmosphere of Copenhagen existence. But who could make them feel in love? That glass of mental and sentimental alcohol which made for warmth and movement within the old phlebolitic veins of their guests—from where were they themselves to get it? From each other, they knew, and in general they were content with the fact. Still, at this moment, the *tristesse* of the eternal hostess stiffened them a little.

Not so tonight, for no sooner had they lowered the blind again than they were off to the kitchen, making haste to send their pretty maid to bed, as if they knew the real joy of life to be found solely amongst elderly women. They made Madam Bæk and themselves a fresh cup of coffee, lifting down the old copper kettle from the wall. Coffee, according to the women of Denmark, is to the body what the word of the Lord is to the soul.

Had it been in the old days that the sisters and their servant met again after a long separation, the girls would have started at once to entertain the widow with accounts of their admirers. The theme was ever fascinating to Madam Bæk, and dear to the ers by reason of the opportunity it gave them of shocking her. But these days were past. They gave her the news of the town— an old widower had married again, and another had gone mad— also a little gossip of the Court, such as she would understand, which they had heard from Miss Bardenfleth. But there was something in Madam Bæk's face which caught their attention. It was heavy with fate; she brought news herself. Very soon they paused to let her speak.

Madam Bæk allowed the pause to wax long.

"Master Morten," she said at last, and at the sound of her own thoughts of these last long days and nights she herself grew very pale, "is at Elsinore. He walks in the house."

At this news a deadly silence filled the kitchen. The two sisters felt their hair stand on end. The terror of the moment lay, for them, in this: that it was Madam Bæk who had recounted such news to them. They might have announced it to her, out of perversity and fancies, and it would not have meant much. But that Hanne, who was to them the principle of solidity and equilibrium for the whole world, should open her mouth to throw at them the end of all things—that made these seconds in their kitchen feel to the two younger women like the first seconds of a great earthquake.

Madam Bæk herself felt the unnatural in the situation, and all which was passing through the heads of her ladies. It would have terrified her as well, had she still had it in her to be terrified. Now she felt only a great triumph.

"I have seen him," she said, "seven times."

Here the sisters took to trembling so violently that they had to put down their coffee cups.

"The first time," said Madam Bæk, "he stood in the red dining room, looking at the big clock. But the clock had stopped. I had forgotten to wind it up."

Suddenly a rain of tears sprang out of Fanny's eyes, and bathed her pale face. "Oh, Hanne, Hanne," she said.

"Then I met him once on the stair," said Madam Bæk. "Three times he has come and sat with me. Once he picked up a ball of wool for me, which had rolled onto the floor, and threw it back in my lap."

"How did he look to you?" asked Fanny, in a broken, cracked voice, evading the glance of her sister, who sat immovable.

"He looks older than when he went away," said Madam Bæk. "He wears his hair longer than people do here; that will be the American fashion. His clothes are very old, too. But he smiled at me just as he always did. The third time that I saw him, before he went—for he goes in his own way, and just as you think he is there, he is gone—he blew me a kiss exactly as he used to do when he was a young man and I had scolded him a little."

Eliza lifted her eyes, very slowly, and the eyes of the two sisters met. Never in all their lives had Madam Bæk said anything to them which they had for a moment doubted.

"But," said Madam Bæk, "this last time I found him standing before your two pictures for a long time. And I thought that he wanted to see you, so I have come to fetch you to Elsinore."

At these words the sisters rose up like two grenadiers at parade. Madam Bæk herself, although terribly agitated, sat where she had sat, as ever the central figure of their gatherings.

"When was it that you saw him?" asked Fanny.

"The first time," said Madam Bæk, "was three weeks ago today. The last time was on Saturday. Then I thought: 'Now I must go and fetch the ladies.'"

Fanny's face was suddenly all ablaze. She looked at Madam Bæk with a great tenderness, the tenderness of their young days. She felt that this was a great sacrifice, which the old woman was bringing out of her devotion to them and her sense of duty. For these three weeks, during which she had been living with the ghost of the outcast son of the De Coninck house, all alone, must have been the great time of Madam Bæk's life, and would remain so for her forever. Now it was over.

It would have been difficult to say if, when she spoke, she came nearest to laughter or tears. "Oh, we will go, Hanne," she said, "we will go to Elsinore."

"Fanny, Fanny," said Eliza, "he is not there; it is not he."

Fanny made a step forward toward the fire, so violently that the streamers of her cap fluttered. "Why not, Lizzie?" she said. "God means to do something for you and me after all. And do you not remember, when Morten was to go back to school after the holiday, and did not want to go, that he made us tell Papa that he was dead? We made a grave under the apple tree, and laid him down in it. Do you remember?" The two sisters at this moment saw, with the eyes of their minds, exactly the same picture of the little ruddy boy, with earth in his curls, who had been lifted out of his grave by their angry young father, and of themselves, with their small spades and soiled muslin frocks, following the procession home like disappointed mourners. Their brother might play a trick on them this time.

As they turned to each other their two faces had the same expression of youthful waggishness. Madam Bæk, in her chair, felt at the sight like a happily delivered lady-in-the-straw. A weight and a fullness had been taken from her, and her importance had gone with it. That was ever the way of the gentry. They would lay their hands on everything you had, even to the ghosts.

Madam Bæk would not let the sisters come back with her to Elsinore. She made them stay behind for a day. She wanted to see for herself that the rooms were warm to receive them, and that there would be hot water bottles in those maiden beds in which they had not slept for so long. She went the next day, leaving them in Copenhagen till the morrow.

It was good for them that they had been given these hours in which to make up their minds and prepare themselves to meet the ghost of their brother. A storm had broken loose upon them, and their boats, which had been becalmed in back waters, were whirled in a blizzard, amongst waves as high as houses. Still they were, in their lappets of lace, no landlubbers in the tempests of life. They were still able to maneuver, and they held their sheets. They did not melt into tears either. Tears were never a solution for them. They came first and were a weakness only; now they were past them, out in the great dilemma. They were themselves acquainted with the old sailors' rule:

Comes wind before rain—Topsail down and up again.
Comes rain before wind—Topsail down and all sails in.

They did not speak together much while waiting for admission to their Elsinore house. Had the day been Sunday they would have gone to church, for they were keen churchgoers, and critics of the prominent preachers of the town, so that they generally came back holding that they could have done it better themselves. In the church they might have joined company; the house of the Lord alone of all houses might have held them both. Now they had to wander in opposite parts of the town, in snowy streets and parks, their small hands in muffs, gazing at cold naked statues and frozen birds in the trees.

How were two highly respected, wealthy, popular and petted ladies to welcome again the hanged boy of their own blood? Fanny walked up and down the linden avenue of the Royal Rose Gardens of Rosenborg. She could never revisit it later, not even in summer time, when it was a green and golden bower, filled like an aviary with children's voices. She carried with her, from one end of it to the other, the picture of her brother, looking at the clock, and the clock stopped and dead. The picture grew upon her. It was upon his mother's death from grief of him that he was gazing, and upon the broken heart of his bride. The picture still grew. It was upon all the betrayed and broken hearts of the world, all the sufferings of weak and dumb creatures, all injustice and despair on earth, that he was gazing. And she felt that it was all laid upon her shoulders. The responsibility was hers. That the world suffered and died was the fault of the De Conincks. Her misery drove her up and down the avenue like a dry leaf before the wind—a distinguished lady in furred boots, in her own heart a great, mad, wing-clipped bird, fluttering in the winter sunset. Looking askance she could see her own large nose, pink under her veil, like a terrible, cruel beak. From time to time a question came into her mind: What is Eliza thinking now? It was strange that the elder sister should feel thus, with bitterness and fear, that her younger sister had deserted her in her hour of need. She had herself fled her company, and yet she repeated to herself: "What, could she not watch with me one hour?" It had been so even in the old De Coninck home. If things began to grow really difficult, Morten and the Papa and Mamma De Coninck would turn to the quiet younger girl, so much less brilliant than herself: "What does Eliza think?"

Toward evening, as it grew dark, and as she reflected that Madam Bæk must by now be at home in Elsinore, Fanny suddenly stopped and thought, Am I to pray to God? Several of her friends, she knew, had found comfort in prayer. She herself had not prayed since she had been a child. Upon the occasions of her Sundays in church, which were visits of courtesy to the Lord, her little silences of bent head had been gestures of civility. Her prayer now, as she began to form it, did not please her either. She used, as a girl, to read out his correspondence to her papa, so she was well acquainted with the jargon of mendicant letters— ". . . Feeling deeply impressed with the magnificence of your noble and well-known loving-kindness . . ." She herself had had many mendicant letters in her days; also many young men had begged her, on their knees, for something. She had been highly generous to the poor, and hard on the lovers. She had not begged herself, nor would she begin it now on behalf of her proud young brother. As her prayer took on a certain likeness to a mendicant letter or to a proposal, she stopped it. "He shall not be ashamed," she thought, "for he has called upon me. He shall not be afraid of ten thousands of people that have set themselves against him round about." Upon this she walked home.

When upon Saturday afternoon the sisters arrived at the house in Elsinore, they went through much deep agitation of the heart. Even the air—even the smell in the hall, that atmosphere of salt and seaweed which ever braces up old seaside houses—went straight through them. They say, thought Miss Fanny, sniffing, that your body is changed completely within the course of seven years. How I have changed, and how I have forgotten! But my nose must be the same. My nose I have still kept and it remembers all. The house was as warm as a box, and this struck them as a sweet compliment, as if an old admirer had put on his gala uniform for them. Many people, in revisiting old places, sigh at the sight of change and age. The De Coninck sisters, on the contrary, felt that the old house might well have deplored the signs of age and decay at this meeting again of theirs, and have cried: Heavens, heavens! Are these the damask-cheeked, silver-voiced girls in dancing sandals who used to slide down the bannisters of my stairs?—sighing down its long chimneys, Oh, God! Fare away, fare away! When, then, it chose to pass over its feelings and pretend that they were the same, it was a fine piece of courtesy on its part.

Old Madam Bæk's great and ceremonious delight in their visit was also bound to touch them. She stood out on the steps to receive them; she changed their shoes and stockings for them, and had warm drinks ready. If we can make her happy so easily, they thought, how is it that we never came till now? Was it that the house of their childhood and young days had seemed to them a little empty and cold, a little grave-like, until it had a ghost in it?

Madam Bæk took them around to show them the spots where Morten had stood, and she repeated his gestures many times. The sisters did not care a pin what gestures he would make to anybody but themselves, but they valued the old woman's love of their brother, and listened patiently. In the end Madam Bæk felt very proud, as if she had been given a sacred relic out of the boy's beloved skeleton, a little bone that was hers to keep.

The room in which supper was made ready was a corner room. It turned two windows to the east, from which there was a view of the old gray castle of Kronborg, copper-spired, like a clenched fist out in the Sound. Above the ramparts departed commandants of the fortress had made a garden, in which, in their winter bareness, lindens now showed the world what loosely built trees they are when not drilled to walk, militarily, two by two. Two windows looked south out upon the harbor. It was strange to find the harbor of Elsinore motionless, with sailors walking back from their boats on the ice.

The walls of the room had once been painted crimson, but with time the color had faded into a richness of hues, like a glassful of dying red roses. In the candlelight these flat walls blushed and shone deeply, in places glowing like little pools of dry, burning, red lacquer. On one wall hung the portraits of the two young De Coninck sisters, the beauties of Elsinore. The third portrait, of their brother, had been taken down so long ago that only a faint shadow on the wall showed where it had once been. Some potpourri was being burned on the tall stove, on the sides of which Neptune, with a trident, steered his team of horses through high waves. But the dried rose-petals dated from summers of long ago. Only a very faint fragrance now spread from their funeral pile, a little rank, like the bouquet of fine claret kept too long. In front of the stove the table was laid with a white tablecloth and delicate Chinese cups and plates.

In this room the sisters and the brother De Coninck had in the old days celebrated many secret supper-parties, when preparing some theatrical or fancy-dress show, or when Morten had returned very late at night from an expedition in his sailing boat, of which their parents must know nothing. The eating and drinking at such times had to be carried on in a subdued manner, so as not to wake up the sleeping house. Thirty-five years ago the red room had seen much merriment caused by this precaution.

Faithful to tradition, the Misses De Coninck now came in and took their seats at table, opposite each other, on either side of the stove, and in silence. To these indefatigable old belles of a hundred balls, age and agitation all the same began to assert themselves. Their eyelids were heavy, and they could not have held out much longer if something had not happened.

They did not have to wait long. Just as they had poured out their tea, and were lifting the thin cups to their lips, there was a slight rustle in the quiet room. When they turned their heads a little, they saw their brother standing at the end of the table.

He stood there for a moment and nodded to them, smiling at them. Then he took the third chair and sat down, between them. He placed his hands upon the edge of the table, gently moving them sideward and back again, exactly as he always used to do.

Morten was poorly dressed in a dark gray coat that looked faded and much worn. Still it was clear that he had taken pains about his appearance for the meeting, he had on a white collar and a carefully tied high black stock, and his hair was neatly brushed back. Perhaps he had been afraid, Fanny for a moment thought, that after having lived so long in rough company he should impress his sisters as less refined and well mannered than before. He need not have worried; he would have looked a gentleman on the gallows. He was older than when they had seen him last, but not as old as they. He looked a man of forty.

His face was somehow coarser than before, weather-beaten and very pale. It had, with the dark, always somewhat sunken eyes, that same divine play of light and darkness which had long ago made maidens mad. His large mouth also had its old frankness and sweetness. But to his pure forehead a change had come. It was not that it was now crossed by a multitude of little horizontal lines, for the marble of it was too fine to be marred by such superficial wear. But time had revealed its true character. It was not the imperial tiara, that once had caught all eyes, above his dark brows. It was the grave and noble likeness to a skull. The radiance of it belonged to the possessor, not of the world, but of the grave and of eternity. Now, as his hair had withdrawn from it, it gave out the truth frankly and simply. Also, as you got, from the face of the brother, the key of understanding to this particular type of family beauty, you would recognize it at once in the appearance of the sisters, even in the two youthful portraits on the wall. The most striking characteristic in the three heads was the generic resemblance to the skull.

All in all, Morten's countenance was quiet, considerate, and dignified, as it had always been.

"Good evening, little sisters; well met, well met," he said, "it was very sweet and sisterly of you to come and see me here. You had a—" he stopped a moment, as if searching for his word, as if not in the habit of speaking much with other people—"a nice fresh drive to Elsinore, I should say," he concluded.

His sisters sat with their faces toward him, as pale as he. Morten had always been wont to speak very lowly, in contrast to themselves. Thus a discussion between the sisters might be carried on with the two speaking at the same time, on the chance of the one shrill voice drowning the other. But if you wanted to hear what Morten said, you had to listen. He spoke in just the same way now, and they had been prepared for his appearance, more or less, but not for his voice.

They listened then as they had done before. But they were longing to do more. As they had set eyes on him they had turned their slim torsos all around in their chairs. Could they not touch him? No, they knew that to be out of the question. They had not been reading ghost stories all their lives for nothing. And this very thing recalled to them the old days, when, for these private supper-parties of theirs, Morten had come in at times, his large cloak soaked with rain and sea water, shining, black and rough like a shark's skin, or glazed over with snow, or freshly tarred, so that they had, laughing, held him at arm's length off their frocks. Oh, how thoroughly had the tunes of thirty years ago been transposed from a major to a minor key! From what blizzards had he come in tonight? With what sort of tar was he tarred?

"How are you, my dears?" he asked. "Do you have as merry a time in Copenhagen as in the old days at Elsinore?"

"And how are you yourself, Morten?" asked Fanny, her voice a full octave higher than his. "You are looking a real, fine privateer captain. You are bringing all the full, spiced, trade winds into our nunnery of Elsinore."

"Yes, those are fine winds," said Morten.

"How far away you have been, Morten?" said Eliza, her voice trembling a little. "What a multitude of lovely places you have visited, that we have never seen! How I have wished, how I have wished that I were you."

Fanny gave her sister a quick strong glance. Had their thoughts gone up in a parallel motion from the snowy parks and streets of Copenhagen? Or did this quiet sister, younger than she, far less brilliant, speak the simple truth of her heart?

"Yes, Lizzie, my duck," said Morten. "I remember that. I have thought of that—how you used to cry and stamp your little feet and wring your hands shouting, 'Oh, I wish I were dead.'"

"Where do you come from, Morten?" Fanny asked him.

"I come from hell," said Morten. "I beg your pardon," he added, as he saw his sister wince. "I have come now, as you see, because the Sound is frozen over. I can come then. That is a rule."

Oh, how the heart of Fanny flew upward at his words. She felt it herself, as if she had screamed out, in a shout of deliverance, like a woman in the final moment of childbirth. When the Emperor, from Elba, set foot on the soil of France he brought back the old time with him. Forgotten was red-hot Moscow, and the deadly white and black winter marches. The tricolor was up in the air, unfolded, and the old grenadiers threw up their arms and cried once more: *Vive l'Empereur!* Her soul, like they, donned the old uniform. It was for the benefit of onlookers only, and for the fun of the thing, from now, that she was dressed up in the body of an old woman.

"Are we not looking a pair of old scarecrows, Morten?" she asked, her eyes shining at him. "Were not our old aunts right when they preached to us about our vanity, and the vanity of all things? Indeed, the people who impress on the young that they should purchase, in time, crutches and an ear-trumpet, do carry their point in the end."

"No, you are looking charming, Fanny," he said, his eyes shining gently back. "Like a bumblebee-hawkmoth."—For they used to collect butterflies together in their childhood. "And if you were really looking like a pair of old ladies I should like it very much. There have been few of them where I have been, for many years. Now when grandmamma had her birthday parties at Oregaard, that was where you would see a houseful of fine old ladies. Like a grand aviary, and grandmamma amongst them like a proud cockatoo."

"Yet you once said," said Fanny, "that you would give a year of your existence to be free from spending the afternoon with the old devils."

"Yes, I did that," said Morten, "but my ideas about a year of my existence have changed since then. But tell me, seriously, do they still tie weights to *billets-doux,* and throw them into your carriage when you drive home from the balls?"

"Oh!" said Eliza, drawing in her breath.

> *Was klaget aus dem dunkeln Thal*
> *Die Nachtigall?*
> *Was seuszt darein der Erlenbach*
> *Mit manchen Ach?*

She was quoting a long-forgotten poem by a long-forgotten lover.

"You are not married, my dears, are you?" said Morten, suddenly frightened at the absurd possibility of a stranger belonging to his sisters

"Why should we not be married?" asked Fanny. "We both of us have husbands and lovers at each finger-tip. I, I married the Bishop of Sealand—he lost his balance a little in our bridal bed because of his wings." She could not prevent a delicate thin little laughter coming out of her in small puffs, like steam from a kettle-spout. The Bishop looked, at the distance of forty-eight hours, ridiculously small, like a little doll seen from a tower. "Lizzie married——" she went on, and then stopped herself. When they were children the young De Conincks had lived under a special superstition, which they had from a marionette comedy. It came to this: that the lies which you tell are likely to become truth. On this account they had always been careful in their choice of what lies they would tell. Thus they would never say that they could not pay a Sunday visit to their old aunts because they had a toothache, for they would be afraid that Nemesis might be at their heels, and that they would indeed have a toothache. But they might safely say that their music master had told them not to practice their gavottes any longer, as they already played them with masterly art. The habit was still in their blood.

"No, to speak the truth, Morten," Fanny said, "we are old maids, all on your account. Nobody would have us. The De Conincks have had a bad name as consorts since you went off and took away the heart and soul and innocence of Adrienne."

She looked at him to see what he would say to this. She had followed his thoughts. They had been faithful, but he—what had he done? He had encumbered them with a lovely and gentle sister-in-law.

Their uncle, Fernand De Coninck, he who had helped Morten to get his ship, had in the old days lived in France during the Revolution. That was the place and the time for a De Coninck to live in. Also he had never got quite out of them again, not even when he had been an old bachelor in Elsinore, and he never felt quite at home in a peaceful life. He had been full of anecdotes and songs of the period, and when they had been children the brother and the sisters had known them by heart from him. After a moment Morten slowly and in a low voice began to quote one of Uncle Fernand's ditties. This had been made on a special occasion, when the old aunts of the King of France had been leaving the country, and the revolutionary police had ordered all their boxes to be opened and examined at the frontier, for fear of treachery.

He said:

> *Avez-vous ses chemises,*
> *à Marat?*
> *Avez-vous ses chemises?*
> *C'est pour vous un tres vilain cas*
> *si vous les avez prises.*

Fanny's face immediately reflected the expression of her brother's. Without searching her memory more than a moment she followed him with the next verse of the song. This time it is the King's old aunts speaking:

> *Avait-il de chemises,*
> *à Marat?*
> *Avait-il de chemises?*
> *Moi je crois qu'il n'en avait pas.*
> *Ou les avait-il prises?*

And Eliza took up the thread after her, laughing a little:

> *Il en avait trois grises,*
> *à Marat.*
> *Il en avait trois grises.*
> *Avec l'argent de son mandat*
> *sur le Pont Neuf acquises.*

With these words the brother and the sisters lightened their hearts and washed their hands forever of fair, unhappy Adrienne Rosenstand.

"But you were married, Morten?" said Eliza kindly, the laughter still in her voice.

"Yes," said Morten, "I had five wives. The Spanish are lovely women, you know, like a mosaic of jewels. One of them was a dancer, too. When she danced it was really like a swarm of butterflies whirling round, and being drawn into, the little central flame; you did not know what was up and what was down, and that seemed to me then, when I was young, a charming quality in a wife. One was an English skipper's daughter, an honest girl, and she will never have forgotten me. One was the young widow of a rich planter. She was a real lady. All her thoughts had some sort of long train trailing after them. She bore me two children. One was a Negress, and her I liked best."

"Did they go on board your ship?" Eliza asked.

"No, none of them ever came on board my ship," said Morten.

"And tell us," said Fanny, "which, out of all the things that you had, you liked the best?"

Morten thought her question over for a moment. "Out of all lives," he said, "the life of a pirate is the best."

"Finer than that of a privateer captain in the Sound?" asked Fanny.

"Yes, it is that," said Morten, "inasmuch as you are in the open sea."

"But what made you decide to become a pirate?" asked Fanny, much intrigued, for this was really like a book of romance and adventure.

"The heart, the heart," said Morten, "that which throws us into all our disasters. I fell in love. It was the *coup de foudre* of which Uncle Fernand spoke so much. He himself knew it to be no laughing matter. And she was somebody else's, so I could not have her without cheating law and order a little. She was built in Genoa, had been used by the French as a dispatch-carrier, and was known to be the quickest schooner that ever flew over the Atlantic. She was run ashore at the coast of the island of St. Martin, which is half French and half Dutch, and was sold by the Dutch at Philippsburg. Old Van Zandten, the ship-owner, who employed me then and loved me as a son, sent me to Philippsburg to buy her for him. She was the loveliest, yes, by far the loveliest thing I ever saw. She was like a swan. When she came along, carrying the press of her sails, she was light, gallant, noble, a great lady— like one of grandmamma's swans at Oregaard, when we teased them—pure, loyal, like a Damascene blade. And then, my dears, she was a little like *Fortuna II*. She had, like her, a very small foresail with an unusually large mainsail and high boom.

"I took all old Van Zandten's money then and bought her for myself, and after that we had, she and I, to keep off the respectable people of the country. What are you to do when love sets to at you? I made her a faithful lover, and she had a fine time with her loyal crew, adored and petted like a dainty lady who has her toe nails polished with henna. With me she became the fear of the Caribbean Sea, the little sea-eaglet who kept the tame birds on the stir. So I do not know for certain whether I did right or wrong. Shall not he have the fair woman who loves her most?"

"And was she in love with you as well?" asked Eliza, laughing.

"But who shall ask a woman if she is in love with him?" said Morten. "The question to ask about woman is this: 'What is her price, and will you pay it?' We should not cheat them, but should ask them courteously and pay with a good grace, whether it be cash, love, marriage, or our life or honor which they charge us; or else, if we are poor people and cannot pay, take off our hats to them and leave them for the wealthier man. That has been sound moral Latin with men and women since the world began. As to their loving us—for one thing, Can they love us?"

"And what of the women who have no price?" said Eliza, laughing still.

"What of those indeed, dear?" said Morten. "Whatever they ought to have been, they should not have been women. God may have them, and he may know what to do with them. They drive men into bad places, and afterward they cannot get us out even when they want to."

"What was the name of your ship?" asked Eliza, her eyes cast down.

Morten looked up at her, laughing. "The name of my ship was *La Belle Eliza*," he answered. "Did you not know?"

"Yes, I knew," said Eliza, her voice full of laughter once more. "A merchant captain of Papa's told me, many years ago in Copenhagen, how his crew had gone mad with fear and had made him turn back into port when, off St. Thomas, they spied the topsails of a pirate ship. They were as afraid of her, he said, as of Satan himself. And he told me that the name of the ship was *La Belle Eliza*. I thought then that she would be your boat."

So this was the secret which the old maid had guarded from all the world. She had not been marble all through. Somewhere within her this little flame of happiness had been kept alive. To this purpose—for it had been to no other—had she grown up so lovely in Elsinore. A ship was in blue water, as in a bed of hyacinths, in winds and warm air, her full white sails like to a bold chalk-cliff, baked by the sun, with much sharp steel in boards, not one of the broadswords or knives not red, and the name of the ship fairly and truly *La Belle Eliza*. Oh, you burghers of Elsinore, did you see me dance the minuet once? To those same measures did I tread the waves.

While he had been speaking the color had mounted to her face. She looked once more like a girl, and the white streamers of her cap were no longer the finery of an old lady, but the attire of a chaste, flaming bride.

"Yes, she was like a swan," Morten said, "sweet, sweet, like a song."

"Had I been in that merchant ship," said Eliza, "and you had boarded her, your ship should have been mine by right, Morten."

"Yes," said he, smiling at her, "and my whole *matelotage*. That was our custom when we took young women. You would have had an adoring seraglio."

"I lost her," he said, "through my own fault, at a river mouth of Venezuela. It is a long story. One of my men betrayed her anchoring place to the British governor of Port of Spain, in Trinidad. I was not with her then. I had gone myself the sixty miles to Port of Spain in a fishing boat, to get information about a Dutch cargo boat. I saw all my crew hanged there, and saw her for the last time.

"It was after that," he said after a pause, "that I never slept well again. I could not get down into sleep. Whenever I tried to dive down into it I was shoved upward again, like a piece of flotsam. From that time I began to lose weight, for I had thrown overboard my ballast. It was with her. I had become too light for anything. From that time on I was somehow without body. Do you remember how Papa and Uncle Fernand used to discuss, at dinner, the wines which they had bought together, and to talk of some of them having a fine enough bouquet, but no body to them? That was the case with me, then, my dears: a bouquet I should say that I may still have had, but no body. I could not sink into friendship, or fear, or any real delight any longer. And still I could not sleep."

The sisters had no need to pretend sympathy with this misfortune. It was their own. All the De Conincks suffered from sleeplessness. When they had been children they had laughed at their father and his sisters when they greeted one another in the morning first of all with minute inquiries and accounts of how they had slept at night. Now they did not laugh; the matter meant much to them also now.

"But when you cannot sleep at night," said Fanny, sighing, "is it that you wake up very early, or is it that you cannot fall asleep at all?"

"Nay, I cannot fall asleep at all," said Morten.

"Is it not, then," asked Fanny, "because you are——" She would have said "cold," but remembering where he had said he came from, she stopped herself.

"And I have known all the time," said Morten, who did not seem to have heard what she said to him, "that I shall never lay me down to rest until I can sleep once more on her, in her, *La Belle Eliza.*"

"But you lived ashore, too," said Fanny, her mind running after his, for she felt as if he were about to escape her.

"Yes, I did," said Morten. "I had for some time a tobacco plantation in Cuba. And that was a delightful place. I had a white house with pillars which you would have liked very much. The air of those islands is fine, delicate, like a glass of true rum. It was there that I had the lovely wife, the planter's widow, and two children. There were women to dance with there, at our balls, light like the trade winds—like you two. I had a very pretty pony to ride there, named Pegasus; a little like Papa's Zampa— Do you remember him?"

"And you were happy there?" Fanny asked.

"Yes, but it did not last," said Morten. "I spent too much money. I lived beyond my means, something which Papa had always warned me against. I had to clear out of it." He sat silent for a little while.

"I had to sell my slaves," he said.

At these words he grew so deadly pale, so ashen gray, that had they not known him to be dead for long they would have been afraid that he might be going to die. His eyes, all his features, seemed to sink into his face. It became the face of a man upon the stake, when the flames take hold.

The two women sat pale and rigid with him, in deep silence. It was as if the breath of the hoarfrost had dimmed three windows. They had no word of comfort for their brother in this situation. For no De Coninck had ever parted with a servant. It was a code to them that whoever entered their service must remain there and be looked after by them forever. They might make an exception with regard to marriage or death, but unwillingly. In fact it was the opinion of their circle of friends that in their old age the sisters had come to have only one real object in life, which was to amuse their servants.

Also they felt that secret contempt for all men, as beings unable to raise money at any fatal moment, which belongs to fair women with their consciousness of infinite resources. The sisters De Coninck, in Cuba, would never have allowed things to come to such a tragic point. Could they not easily have sold themselves three hundred times, and made three hundred Cubans happy, and so saved the welfare of their three hundred slaves? There was, therefore, a long pause.

"But the end," said Fanny finally, drawing in her breath deeply, "that was not yet, then?"

"No, no," said Morten, "not till quite a long time after that. When I had no more money I started an old brig in the carrying trade, from Havana to New Orleans first, and then from Havana to New York. Those are difficult seas." His sister had succeeded in turning his mind away from his distress, and as he began to explain to her the various routes of his trade he warmed to his subject. Altogether he had, during the meeting, become more and more sociable and had got back all his old manner of a man who is at ease in company and is in really good understanding with the minds of his convives. "But nothing would go right for me," he went on. "I had one run of bad luck after another. No, in the end, you see, my ship foundered near the Cay Sal bank, where she ran full of water and sank in a dead calm; and with one thing and another, in the end, if you do not mind my saying so, in Havana I was hanged. Did you know that?"

"Yes," said Fanny.

"Did you mind that, I wondered, you two?" he asked.

"No!" said his sisters with energy.

They might have answered him with their eyes turned away,

but they both looked back at him. And they thought that this might perhaps be the reason why he was wearing his collar and stock so unusually high; there might be a mark on that strong and delicate neck around which they had tied the cambric with great pains when they had been going to balls together.

There was a moment's silence in the red room, after which Fanny and Morten began to speak at the same time.

"I beg your pardon," said Morten.

"No," said Fanny, "no. What were you going to say?"

"I was asking about Uncle Fernand," said Morten. "Is he still alive?"

"Oh, no, Morten, my dear," said Fanny, "he died in 'thirty. He was an old man then. He was at Adrienne's wedding, and made a speech, but he was very tired. In the evening he took me aside and said to me: 'My dear, it is a *gênante fête*.' And he died only three weeks later. He left Eliza his money and furniture. In a drawer we found a little silver locket, set with rose diamonds, with a curl of fair hair, and on it was written, 'The hair of Charlotte Corday.'"

"I see," said Morten. "He had a fine figure, Uncle Fernand. And Aunt Adelaide, is she dead too?"

"Yes, she died even before he did," said Fanny. She meant to tell him something of the death of Madame Adelaide De Coninck, but did not go on. She felt depressed. These people were dead; he ought to have known of them. The loneliness of her dead brother made her a little sick at heart.

"How she used to preach to us, Aunt Adelaide," he said. "How many times did she say to me: 'This melancholy of yours, Morten, this dissatisfaction with life which you and the girls allow yourselves, makes me furious. What is good enough for me is good enough for you. You all ought to be married and have large families to look after; that would cure you.' And you, Fanny, said to her: 'Yes, little Aunt, that was the advice, from an auntie of his, which our Papa did follow.'"

"Toward the end," Eliza broke in, "she would not hear or think of anything that had happened since the time when she was thirty years old and her husband died. Of her grandchildren she said: 'These are some of the new-fangled devices of my young children. They will soon find out how little there is to them.' But she could remember all the religious scruples of Uncle Theodore, her husband, and how he had kept her awake at night with meditations upon the fall of man and original sin. Of those she was still proud."

"You must think me very ignorant," Morten said. "You know so many things of which I know nothing."

"Oh, dear Morten," said Fanny, "you surely know of a lot of things of which we know nothing at all."

"Not many, Fanny," said Morten. "One or two, perhaps."

"Tell us one or two," said Eliza.

Morten thought over her demand for a little while.

"I have come to know of one thing," he said, "of which I myself had no idea once. *C'est une invention très fine, très spirituelle, de la part de Dieu,* as Uncle Fernand said of love. It is this: that you cannot eat your cake and have it. I should never have hit upon that on my own. It is indeed an original idea. But then, you see, he is really *très fin, très spirituel,* the Lord."

The two sisters drew themselves up slightly, as if they had received a compliment. They were, as already said, keen church-goers, and their brother's words had ever carried great weight with them.

"But do you know," said Morten suddenly, "that little snappy pug of Aunt Adelaide's, Fingal—him I have seen."

"How was that?" Fanny asked. "Tell us about that."

"That was when I was all alone," said Morten, "when my ship had foundered at the Cay Sal bank. We were three who got away in a boat, but we had no water. The others died, and in the end I was alone."

"What did you think of then?" Fanny asked.

"Do you know, I thought of you," said Morten.

"What did you think of us?" Fanny asked again in a low voice.

Morten said, "I thought: we have been amateurs in saying no, little sisters. But God can say no. Good God, how he can say no. We think that he can go on no longer, not even he. But he goes on, and says no once more.

"I had thought of that before, quite a good deal," Morten said, "at Elsinore, during the time before my wedding. And now I kept on thinking upon it. I thought of those great, pure, and beautiful things which say no to us. For why should they say yes to us, and tolerate our insipid caresses? Those who say yes, we get them under us, and we ruin them and leave them, and find when we have left them that they have made us sick. The earth says yes to our schemes and our work, but the sea says no; and we, we love the sea ever. And to hear God say no, in the stillness, in his own voice, that to us is very good. The starry sky came up, there, and said no to me as well. Like a noble, proud woman."

"And did you see Fingal then?" Eliza asked.

"Yes," said Morten. "Just then. As I turned my head a little, Fingal was sitting with me in the boat. You know, he was an ill-tempered little dog always, and he never liked me because I teased him. He used to bite me every time he saw me. I dared not touch him there in the boat. I was afraid that he would snap at me again. Still, there he sat, and stayed with me all night."

"And did he go away then?" Fanny asked.

"I do not know, my dear," Morten said. "An American schooner, bound for Jamaica, picked me up in the early morning. There on board was a man who had bid against me at the sale in Philippsburg. In this way it came to pass that I was hanged—in the end, as you say—at Havana."

"Was that bad?" asked Fanny in a whisper.

"No, my poor Fanny," said Morten.

"Was there anyone with you there?" Fanny whispered.

"Yes, there was a fat young priest there," said Morten. "He was afraid of me. They probably told him some bad things about me. But still he did his best. I asked him: 'Can you obtain for me, now, one minute more to live in?' He said, 'What will you do with one minute of life, my poor son?' I said, 'I will think, with the halter around my neck, for one minute of *La Belle Eliza*.' "

While they now sat in silence for a little while, they heard some people pass in the street below the window, and talk together. Through the shutters they could follow the passing flash of their lanterns.

Morten leaned back in his chair, and he looked now to his sisters older and more worn than before. He was indeed much like their father, when the Papa De Coninck had come in from his office tired, and had taken pleasure in sitting down quietly in the company of his daughters.

"It is very pleasant in here, in this room," he said, "it is just like old days—do you not think so? With Papa and Mamma below. We three are not very old yet. We are good-looking people still."

"The circle is complete again," said Eliza gently, using one of their old expressions.

"Is completed, Lizzie," said Morten, smiling back at her.

"The vicious circle," said Fanny automatically, quoting another of their old familiar terms.

"You were always," said Morten, "such a clever lass."

At these kind direct words Fanny impetuously caught at her breath.

"And, oh, my girls," Morten exclaimed, "how we did long then, with the very entrails of us, to get away from Elsinore!"

His elder sister suddenly turned her old body all around in the chair, and faced him straight. Her face was changed and drawn with pain. The long wake and the strain began to tell on her, and she spoke to him in a hoarse and cracked voice, as if she were heaving it up from the innermost part of her chest.

"Yes," she cried, "yes, you may talk. But you mean to go away again and leave me. You! You have been to these great warm seas of which you talk, to a hundred countries. You have been married to five people— Oh, I do not know of it all! It is easy for you to speak quietly, to sit still. You have never needed to beat your arms to keep warm. You do not need to now!"

Her voice failed her. She stuttered in her speech and clasped the edge of the table. "And here," she groaned out, "I am—cold. The world is bitterly cold around me. I am so cold at night, in my bed, that my warming-pans are no good to me!"

At this moment the tall grandfather's clock started to strike, for Fanny had herself wound it up in the afternoon. It struck midnight in a grave and slow measure, and Morten looked quickly up at it.

Fanny meant to go on speaking, and to lift at last all the deadly weight of her whole life off her, but she felt her chest pressed together. She could not out-talk the clock, and her mouth opened and shut twice without a sound.

"Oh, hell," she cried out, "to hell!"

Since she could not speak she stretched out her arms to him, trembling. With the strokes of the clock his face became gray and blurred to her eyes, and a terrible panic came upon her. Was it for this that she had wound up the clock! She threw herself toward him, across the table.

"Morten!" she cried in a long wail. "Brother! Stay! Listen! Take me with you!"

As the last stroke fell, and the clock took up its ticking again, as if it meant to go on doing something, in any case, through all eternity, the chair between the sisters was empty, and at the sight Fanny's head fell down on the table.

She lay like that for a long time, without stirring. From the winter night outside, from far away to the north, came a resounding tone, like the echo of a cannon shot. The children of Elsinore knew well what it meant: it was the ice breaking up somewhere, in a long crack.

Fanny thought, dully, after a long while, What is Eliza thinking? and laboriously lifted her head, looked up, and dried her mouth with her little handkerchief. Eliza sat very still opposite her, where she had been all the time. She dragged the streamers of her cap downward and together, as if she were pulling a rope, and Fanny remembered seeing her, long, long ago, when angry or in great pain or joy, pulling in the same way at her long golden tresses. Eliza lifted her pale eyes and stared straight at her sister's face.

"To think," said she, " 'to think, with the halter around my neck, for one minute of *La Belle Eliza.'* "

The Dreamers

O N a full-moon night of 1863 a dhow was on its way from Lamu to Zanzibar, following the coast about a mile out.

She carried full sails before the monsoon, and had in her a freight of ivory and rhino-horn. This last is highly valued as an aphrodisiac, and traders come for it to Zanzibar from as far as China. But besides these cargoes the dhow also held a secret load, which was about to stir and raise great forces, and of which the slumbering countries which she passed did not dream.

This still night was bewildering in its deep silence and peace, as if something had happened to the world; as if the soul of it had been, by some magic, turned upside down. The free monsoon came from far places, and the sea wandered on under its sway, on her long journey, in the face of the dim luminous moon. But the brightness of the moon upon the water was so clear that it seemed as if all the light in the world were in reality radiating from the sea, to be reflected in the skies. The waves looked solid, as if one might safely have walked upon them, while it was into the vertiginous sky that one might sink and fall, into the turbulent and unfathomable depths of silvery worlds, of bright silver or dull and tarnished silver, forever silver reflected within silver, moving and changing, towering up, slowly and weightless.

The two slaves in the prow were still like statues, their bodies, naked to the waist in the hot night, iron-gray like the sea where the moon was not shining on it, so that only the clear dark shades running along their backs and limbs marked out their forms against the vast plane. The red cap of one of them glowed dull, like a plum, in the moonlight. But one corner of the sail, catching the light, glinted like the while belly of a dead fish. The air was like that of a hothouse, and so damp that all the planks and ropes of the boat were sweating a salt dew. The heavy waters sang and murmured along the bow and stern.

On the after deck a small lantern was hung up, and three people were grouped round it.

The first of them was young Said Ben Ahamed, the son of

Tippo Tip's sister, and himself deeply beloved by the great man. He had been, through the treachery of his rivals, for two years a prisoner in the North, and had escaped and got to Lamu by many strange ways. Now he was here, unknown to the world, on his way home to take revenge upon his enemies. It was the hope of revenge within Said's heart which, more powerful than the monsoon, was in reality forcing the boat on. It was both sail and ballast to the dhow. Had they now been aware that Said was in a ship on his way to Zanzibar tonight, many great people would have been hurriedly packing up their property and their harems, to get away before it should be too late. Of Said's revenge, in the end, other tales have told.

He sat on the deck crosslegged, bent forward, his hands loosely folded and resting on the planks before him, in deep thought.

The second, and eldest, of the party was a person of great fame, the much-renowned story-teller Mira Jama himself, the inventions of whose mind have been loved by a hundred tribes. He sat with his legs crossed, like Said, and with his back to the moon, but the night was clear enough to show that he had, at some rencounter with his destiny, had the nose and ears of his dark head cut clear off. He was poorly dressed, but still had kept a regard for his appearance. Around his thin body he had a faded, thick, crimson silk scarf, which sometimes, at a movement of his, flamed up and burned like fire or pure rubies in the light of the small lantern.

The third in the company was a red-haired Englishman whose name was Lincoln Forsner, and whom the natives of the coast called Tembu, which may mean either ivory or alcohol, as it pleases you. Lincoln was the child of a rich family in his own country, and had been blown about by many winds to lie tonight flat on his stomach on the deck of the dhow, dressed in an Arab shirt and loose Indian trousers, but still shaved and whiskered like a gentleman. He was chewing the dried leaves which the Swaheli call *murungu*, which keep you awake and in a pleasant mood, and from time to time spitting at a long distance. This made him communicative. He was joining Said's expedition out of his love for the young man, and also to see what would happen, as he had before seen things happen in various countries. His heart was light. He was very fond of a boat, and pleased with the speed, the warm night, and the full moon.

"How is it, Mira," he said, "that you cannot tell us a story as we are sailing on here tonight? You used to have many tales, such as make the blood run cold and make you afraid to trust your oldest friend, tales good on a hot night and for people out on great undertakings. Have you no more?"

"No, I have no more, Tembu," said Mira, "and that in itself makes a sad tale, good for people out on great undertakings. I was once a great story-teller, and I specialized in such tales as make the blood run cold. Devils, poison, treachery, torture, darkness, and lunacy: these were Mira's stock in trade."

"I remember one of your tales now," said Lincoln. "You frightened me by it, and two young dancers of Lamu, who really need not have been afraid of it, so that we did not sleep all night. The Sultan wanted a true virgin, and after much trouble she was fetched for him from the mountains. But he found her——"

"Yes, yes," Mira took up the tale, his whole countenance suddenly changing, his dark eyes brightening and his hands coming to life in the old telltale manner, like two aged dancing snakes called out from their basket by the flute, "the Sultan wanted a true virgin, such as had never heard of men. With great trouble she was fetched for him from the Amazon kingdom in the mountains, where all male children had been killed off by the women, who made wild wars on their own. But when the Sultan went in to her, between the hangings of the door he saw her looking out at a young water-carrier, who was walking to and fro in the palace, and heard her speak to herself· 'Oh, I have come to a good place,' she said, 'and that creature there must be God, or a strong angel, the one who hurls the lightning. I do not mind dying now, for I have seen what no one has ever seen.' And at that the young water-carrier looked up at the window too, and kept standing there, gazing at the maiden. So the Sultan became very sad, and he had the virgin and the young man buried alive together, in a marble chest broad enough to make a marriage bed, under a palm tree of his garden, and seating himself below the same tree he wondered at many things, and at how he was never to have his heart's desire, and he had a young boy to play the flute to him. That was the tale you heard once."

"Yes, but better told then," said Lincoln.

"It was that," said Mira, "and the world could not do without Mira then. People love to be frightened. The great princes, fed up with the sweets of life, wished to have their blood stirred again. The honest ladies, to whom nothing ever happened, longed to tremble in their beds just for once. The dancers were inspired to a lighter pace by tales of flight and pursuit. Ah, how the world loved me in those days! Then I was handsome, round-cheeked. I drank noble wine, wore gold-embroidered clothes and amber, and had incense burned in my rooms."

"But how has this change come upon you?" asked Lincoln.

"Alas!" said Mira, sinking back into his former quiet manner, "as I have lived I have lost the capacity of fear. When you know what things are really like, you can make no poems about them. When you have had talk with ghosts and connections with the devils you are, in the end, more afraid of your creditors than of them; and when you have been made a cuckold you are no longer nervous about cuckoldry. I have become too familiar with life; it can no longer delude me into believing that one thing is much worse than the other. The day and the dark, an enemy and a friend—I know them to be about the same. How can you make others afraid when you have forgotten fear yourself? I once had a really tragic tale, a great tale, full of agony, immensely popular, of a young man who in the end had his nose and his ears cut off. Now I could frighten no one with it, if I wanted to, for now I know that to be without them is not so very much worse than to have them. This is why you see me here, skin and bone, and dressed in old rags, the follower of Said in prison and poverty, instead of keeping near the thrones of the mighty, flourishing and flattered, as was young Mira Jama."

"But could you not, Mira," Lincoln asked, "make a terrible tale about poverty and unpopularity?"

"No," said the story-teller proudly, "that is not the sort of story which Mira Jama tells."

"Well, yes, alas," said Lincoln, turning around on his side, "what is life, Mira, when you come to think upon it, but a most excellent, accurately set, infinitely complicated machine for turning fat playful puppies into old mangy blind dogs, and proud war horses into skinny nags, and succulent young boys, to whom the world holds great delights and terrors, into old weak men, with running eyes, who drink ground rhino-horn?"

"Oh, Lincoln Forsner," said the noseless story-teller, "what is man, when you come to think upon him, but a minutely set, ingenious machine for turning, with infinite artfulness, the red wine of Shiraz into urine? You may even ask which is the more intense craving and pleasure: to drink or to make water. But in the meantime, what has been done? A song has been composed, a kiss taken, a slanderer slain, a prophet begotten, a righteous judgment given, a joke made. The world drank in the young story-teller Mira. He went to its head, he ran in its veins, he made it glow with warmth and color. Now I am on my way down a little; the effect has worn off. The world will soon be equally pleased to piss me out again, and I do not know but that I am pressing on a little myself. But the tales which I made—they shall last."

"What do you do in the meantime to keep so good a face toward it, in this urgency of life to rid itself of you?" Lincoln asked.

"I dream," said Mira.

"Dream?" said Lincoln.

"Yes, by the grace of God," said Mira, "every night, as soon as I sleep I dream. And in my dreams I still know fear. Things are terrible to me there. In my dreams I sometimes carry with me something infinitely dear and precious, such as I know well enough that no real things be, and there it seems to me that I must keep this thing against some dreadful danger, such as there are none in the real world. And it also seems to me that I shall be struck down and annihilated if I lose it, though I know well that you are not, in the world of the daytime, struck down and annihilated, whatever you lose. In my dreams the dark is filled with indescribable horrors, but there are also sometimes flights and pursuits of a heavenly delight."

He sat for a while in silence.

"But what particularly pleases me about dreams," he went on, "is this: that there the world creates itself around me without any effort on my part. Here, now, if I want to go to Gazi, I have to bargain for a boat, and to buy and pack my provisions, to tack up against the wind, and even to make my hands sore by rowing. And then, when I get to Gazi, what am I to do there? Of that also I must think. But in my dreams I find myself walking up a long row of stone steps which lead from the sea. These steps I have not seen before, yet I feel that to climb them is a great happiness, and that they will take me to something highly enjoyable. Or I find myself hunting in a long row of low hills, and I have got people with me with bows and arrows, and dogs in leads. But what I am to hunt, or why I have gone there, I do not know. One time I came into a room from a balcony, in the very early morning, and upon the stone floor stood a woman's two little sandals, and at the same moment I thought: they are hers. And at that my heart overflowed with pleasure, rocked in ease. But I had taken no trouble. I had had no expense to get the woman. And at other times I have been aware that outside the door was a big black man, very black, who meant to kill me; but still I had done nothing to make him my enemy, and I shall just wait for the dream itself to inform me how to escape from him, for in myself I cannot find out how to do it. The air in my dreams, and particularly since I have been in prison with Said, is always very high, and I generally see myself as a very small figure in a great landscape, or in a big house. In all this a young man would not take any pleasure at all; but to me, now, it holds such delight as does making water when you have finished with wine."

"I do not know about it, Mira; I hardly ever dream," said Lincoln.

"Oh, Lincoln, live forever," said old Mira. "You dream indeed more than I do myself. Do I not know the dreamers when I meet them? You dream awake and walking about. You will do nothing yourself to choose your own ways: you let the world form itself around you, and then you open your eyes to see where you will find yourself. This journey of yours, tonight, is a dream of yours. You let the waves of fate wash you about, and then you will open your eyes tomorrow to find out where you are."

"To see your pretty face," said Lincoln.

"You know, Tembu," said Mira suddenly, after a pause, "that if, in planting a coffee tree, you bend the taproot, that tree will start, after a little time, to put out a multitude of small delicate roots near the surface. That tree will never thrive, nor bear fruit, but it will flower more richly than the others.

"Those fine roots are the dreams of the tree. As it puts them out, it need no longer think of its bent taproot. It keeps alive by them—a little, not very long. Or you can say that it dies by them, if you like. For really, dreaming is the well-mannered people's way of committing suicide.

"If you want to go to sleep at night, Lincoln, you must not think, as people tell you, of a long row of sheep or camels passing through a gate, for they go in one direction, and your thoughts will go along with them. You should think instead of a deep well. In the bottom of that well, just in the middle of it, there comes up a spring of water, which runs out in little streamlets to all possible sides, like the rays of a star. If you can make your thoughts run out with that water, not in one direction, but equally to all sides, you will fall asleep. If you can make your heart do it thoroughly enough, as the coffee tree does it with the little surface roots, you will die."

"So that is the matter with me, you think: that I want to forget my taproot?" asked Lincoln.

"Yes," said Mira, "it must be that. Unless it be that, like many of your countrymen, you never had much of it."

"Unless it be that," said Lincoln.

They sailed on for a little while in silence. A slave took up a flute and played a few notes on it, to try it.

"Why does not Said speak a word to us?" Lincoln asked Mira.

Said lifted his eyes a little and smiled, but did not speak.

"Because he thinks," said Mira. "This conversation of ours seems to him very insipid."

"What is he thinking of?" asked Lincoln.

Mira thought for a little. "Well," he said, "there are only two courses of thought at all seemly to a person of any intelligence. The one is: What am I to do this next moment?—or tonight, or tomorrow? And the other: What did God mean by creating the world, the sea, and the desert, the horse, the winds, woman, amber, fishes, wine? Said thinks of the one or the other."

"Perhaps he is dreaming," said Lincoln.

"No," said Mira after a moment, "not Said. He does not know how to dream yet. The world is just drinking him in. He is going to its head and into its blood. He means to drive the pulsation of its heart. He is not dreaming, but perhaps he is praying to God. By the time when you have finished praying to God—that is when you put out your surface roots; that is when you begin to dream. Said tonight may be praying to God, throwing his prayer at the Lord with such energy as that with which the Angel shall, upon the last day, throw at the world the note of his trump, with such energy as that with which the elephant copulates. Said says to God: 'Let me be all the world.'

"He says," Mira went on after a minute, "I shall show no mercy, and I ask for none. But that is where Said is mistaken. He will be showing mercy before he has done with all of us."

"Do you ever dream of the same place twice?" asked Lincoln after a time.

"Yes, yes," said Mira. "That is a great favor of God's, a great delight to the soul of the dreamer. I come back, after a long time, in my dream, to the place of an old dream, and my heart melts with delight."

They sailed on for some time, and no one said anything. Then Lincoln suddenly changed his position, sat up, and made himself comfortable. He spat out on the deck the last of his *Morungu*, dived into a pocket, and rolled himself a cigarette.

"I will tell you a tale tonight, Mira," he said, "since you have none. You have reminded me of long-gone things. Many good stories have come from your part of the world to ours, and when I was a child I enjoyed them very much. Now I will tell this one, for the pleasure of your ears, Mira, and for the heart of Said, to whom my tale may prove useful. It all goes to teach you how I was, twenty years ago, taught, as you say, Mira, to dream, and of the woman who taught me. It happened just as I tell it to you. But as to names and places, and conditions in the countries in which it all took place, and which may seem very strange to you, I will give you no explanation. You must take in whatever you can, and leave the rest outside. It is not a bad thing in a tale that you understand only half of it."

Twenty years ago, when I was a young man of twenty-three, I sat one winter night in the room of a hotel, amongst mountains, with snow, storm, great clouds and a wild moon outside.

Now the continent of Europe, of which you have heard, consists of two parts, the one of which is more pleasant than the other, and these two are separated by a high and steep mountain chain. You cannot cross it except in a few places where the formation of the mountains is a little less hostile than elsewhere, and where roads have been made, with much trouble, to take you over them. Such a place there was near the hotel where I was staying. A road that would admit pedestrians, horses and mules, and even coaches had been cut in the rocks, and on the top of the pass, where, from laboriously climbing upwards, cursing your fate, you begin to descend, soon to feel the sweet air caressing your face and lungs, a brotherhood of holy men have built a great house for the refreshment of travelers. I was on my way from the North, where things were cold and dead, to the blue and voluptuous South. The hotel was my last station before the steep journey to the top of the pass, which I meant to undertake on the next day. It was a little early in the season yet to travel this way at all. There were only a few people on the road as yet, and higher up in the mountains the snow was lying deep.

To the world I looked a pretty, rich, and gay young man, on his way from one pleasure to another, and providing himself, on the way, with the best of everything. But in truth I was just being whirled about, forward and backward, by my aching heart, a poor fool out on a wild-goose chase after a woman.

Yes, after a woman, Mira, if you believe it or not. I had already been searching for her in a variety of places. In fact, so hopeless was my pursuit of her that I should most certainly have given it up if it had been at all within my power to do so. But my own soul, Mira, my dear, was in the breast of this woman.

And she was not a girl of my own age. She was many years older than I. Of her life I knew nothing except what was painful to me to swallow, and, what was the worst of the business, I had no reason to believe that she would be at all pleased should I ever contrive to find her.

The whole thing had come about like this: My father was a very rich man in England, the owner of large factories and of a pleasant estate in the country, a man with a big family and an enormous working capacity. He read the Bible much—our Holy Book—and had come to feel himself God's one substitute on earth. Indeed, I do not know if he was capable of making any distinction between his fear of God and his self-esteem. It was his duty, he thought, to turn the chaotic world into a universe of order, and to see that all things were made useful—which, to him, meant making them useful to him himself. Within his own nature I know of two things only which he could not control: he had, against his own principles, a strong love of music, particularly of Italian opera music; and he sometimes could not sleep at night. Later on I was told by my aunt, his sister, who much disliked him, that he had, as a young man in the West Indies, driven to suicide, or actually killed, a man. Perhaps this was what kept him awake. I and my twin sister were much younger than our other brothers and sisters. What flea had bitten my father that he should beget two more children when he had got through most of his trouble with the rest of us, I do not know. At the day of judgment I shall ask him for an explanation. I have sometimes thought that it was really the ghost of the West Indian gentleman which had been after him.

My father was not pleased with anything which I did. In the end I think that I became a carking care to him, for had I not been of his own manufacture he would have been pleased to see me come to a bad end. Now I felt that I was ever, as My Son Lincoln, being drawn, hammered and battered into all sorts of shapes, in order to be made useful, between one o'clock and three of the night. During these hours I myself generally had a pretty heated and noisy time, for I had become an officer in a smart regiment of the army, and there, to keep up my prestige amongst the sons of the oldest families of the land, spent much of the money, time, and wit which my father reckoned to be really and rightly his.

At about this time a neighbor of ours died, and left a young widow. She was pretty and rich, and had been unhappily married, and in her trials had consoled herself with a sentimental friendship with my twin sister, who was so like me that if I dressed up in her clothes nobody would know the one of us from the other. Therefore my father now thought that this lady might consent to marry me, and lift the burden of me from his shoulders onto hers. This prospect suited me as well as anything that I at that time expected from life. The only thing for which I asked my father was his consent to let me travel on the continent of Europe during the lady's year of mourning. In those days I had various strong inclinations, for wine, gambling and cockfighting, and the society of gypsies, together with a passion for theological discussion which I had inherited from my father himself—all of which my father thought I had better rid myself of before I married the widow, or, at least, which I had better not let her contemplate at too close quarters while she could still change her mind. As my father knew me to be quick and ardent in love affairs, I think that he also feared that I might seduce my fiancée into too close a relation, profiting by our neighborhood in the country, and, perhaps, by my likeness to my sister. For all these reasons the old man agreed that I should go traveling for nine months, in the company of an old schoolfellow of his, who had lived on his charity and whom he was pleased to turn in this way to some sort of use.

This man, however, I soon managed to rid myself of, for when we came to Rome he took up the study of the mysteries of the ancient Priapean cult of Lampsacus and I enjoyed myself very well.

But in the fourth month of my year of grace, it happened to me that I fell in love with a woman within a brothel of Rome. I had gone there, on an evening, with a party of theologians. It was thus not a dashing place where people with lots of money went to amuse themselves, neither was it a murky house frequented by artists or robbers. It was just a middling respectable establishment. I remember the narrow street in which it stood, and the many smells which met therein. If ever I were to smell them again, I should feel that I had come home. To this woman I owe it that I have ever understood, and still remember, the meaning of such words as tears, heart, longing, stars, which you poets make use of. Yes, as to stars in particular, Mira, there was much about her that reminded one of a star. There was the difference between her and other women that there is between an overcast and a starry sky. Perhaps you too have met in the course of your life women of that sort, who are self-luminous and shine in the dark, who are phosphorescent, like touchwood.

As, upon the next day, I woke up in my hotel in Rome, I remember that I had a great fright. I thought: I was drunk last night; my head has played a trick on me. There are no such women. At this I grew hot and cold all over. But again I thought, lying in my bed: I could not possibly, all on my own, have invented such a person as this woman. Why, only our greatest poet could have done that. I could never have imagined a woman with so much life in her, and that great strength. I got up and went straight back to her house, and there I found her again, such indeed as I remembered her.

Later on I learned that the extraordinary impression of great strength which she gave me was somehow false after all; she had not all the strength that she showed. I will tell you what it was like:

If all your life you had been tacking up against the winds and the currents, and suddenly, for once, you were taken on board a ship which went, as we do tonight, with a strong tide and before a following wind, you would undoubtedly be much impressed with the power of that ship. You would be wrong; and yet in a way you would also be right, for the power of the waters and the winds might be said rightly to belong to the ship, since she had managed, alone amongst all vessels, to ally herself with them. Thus had I, all my life, under my father's ægis, been taught to tack up against all the winds and currents of life. In the arms of this woman I felt myself in accord with them all, lifted and borne on by life itself. This, to my mind then, was due to her great strength. And still, at that time I did not know at all to what extent she had allied herself with all the currents and winds of life.

After this first night we were always together. I have never been able to get anything out of the orthodox love affairs of my country, which begin in the drawing-room with banalities, flatteries and giggles, and go through touches of hands and feet, to finish up in what is generally held to be a climax, in the bed. This love affair of mine in Rome, which began in the bed, helped on by wine and much noisy music, and which grew into a kind of courtship and friendship hitherto unknown to me, was the only one that I have ever liked. After a while I often took her out with me for the whole day, or for a whole day and night. I bought a small carriage and a horse, with which we went about in Rome and in the *Campagna,* as far as Frascati and Nemi. We supped in the little inns, and in the early mornings we often stopped on the road and let the horse graze on the roadside, while we ourselves sat on the ground, drank a bottle of fresh, sour, red wine, ate raisins and almonds, and looked up at the many birds of prey which circled over the great plain, and whose shadows, upon the short grass, would run alongside our carriage. Once in a village there was a festival, with Chinese lamps around a fountain in the clear evening. We watched it from a balcony. Several times, also, we went as far as the seaside. It was all in the month of September, a good month in Rome. The world begins to be brown, but the air is as clear as hill water, and it is strange that it is full of larks, and that here they sing at that time of the year.

Olalla was very pleased with all this. She had a great love for Italy, and much knowledge of good food and wine. At times she would dress up, as gay as a rainbow in cashmeres and plumes, as a prince's mistress, and there never was a lady in England to beat her then; but at other times she would wear the linen hood of the Italian women, and dance in the villages in the manner of the country. Then a stronger or more graceful dancer was not to be found, although she liked even better to sit with me and watch them dance. She was extraordinarily alive to all impressions. Wherever we went together she would observe many more things than I did, though I have been a good sportsman all my life. But at the same time there never seemed to be to her much difference between joy and pain, or between sad and pleasant things. They were all equally welcome to her, as if in her heart she knew them to be the same.

One afternoon we were on our way back to Rome, about sunset, and Olalla, bareheaded, was driving the horse and whipping him into a gallop. The breeze then blew her long dark curls away from her face, and showed me again a long scar from a burn, which, like a little white snake, ran from her left ear to her collar bone. I asked her, as I had done before, how she had come to be so badly burned. She would not answer, but instead began to talk of all the great prelates and merchants of Rome who were in love with her, until I said, laughing, that she had no heart. Over this she was silent for a little while, still going at full speed, the strong sunlight straight in our faces.

"Oh, yes," she said at last, "I have a heart. But it is buried in the garden of a little white villa near Milan."

"Forever?" I asked.

"Yes, forever," she said, "for it is the most lovely place."

"What is there," I asked her, oppressed by jealousy, "in a little white villa of Milan to keep your heart there forever?"

"I do not know," she said. "There will not be much now, since nobody is weeding the garden or tuning the piano. There may be strangers living there now. But there is moonlight there, when the moon is up, and the souls of dead people."

She often spoke in this vague whimsical way, and she was so graceful, gentle, and somehow humble in it that it always charmed me. She was very keen to please, and would take much trouble about it, though not as a servant who becomes rigid by his fear of displeasing, but like somebody very rich, heaping benefactions upon you out of a horn of plenty. Like a tame lioness, strong of tooth and claw, insinuating herself into your favor. Sometimes she seemed to me like a child, and then again old, like those aqueducts, built a thousand years ago, which stand over the *Campagna* and throw their long shadows on the ground, their majestic, ancient, and cracked walls shining like amber in the sun. I felt like a new, dull thing in the world, a silly little boy beside her then. And always there was that about her which made me feel her so much stronger than myself. Had I known for certain that she could fly, and might have flown away from me and from the earth whenever she choose to, it would have given me the same feeling, I believe.

It was not till the end of September that I began to think of the future. I saw then that I could not possibly live without Olalla. If I tried to go away from her, my heart, I thought, would run back to her as water will run downhill. So I thought that I must marry her, and make her come to England with me.

If when I asked her she had made the slightest objection, I should not have been so much upset by her behavior later on. But she said at once that she would come. She was more caressing, more full of sweetness toward me from that time than she had ever been before, and we would talk of our life in England, and of everything there, and laugh over it together. I told her of my father, and how he had always been an enthusiast about the Italian opera, which was the best thing that I could find to say of him. I knew, in talking to her about all this, that I should never again be bored in England.

It was about then that I was for the first time struck by the appearance, whenever I went near Olalla, of a figure of a man that I had never seen before. The first few times I did not think of it, but after our sixth or seventh meeting he began to occupy my thoughts and to make me curiously ill at ease. He was a Jew of fifty or sixty years, slightly built, very richly dressed, with diamonds on his hands, and with the manners of a fine old man of the world. He was of a pale complexion and had very dark eyes.

I never saw him with her, or in the house, but I ran into him when I went there, or came away, so that he seemed to me to circle around her, like the moon around the earth. There must have been something extraordinary about him from the beginning, or I should not have had the idea, which now filled my head, that he had some power over Olalla and was an evil spirit in her life. In the end I took so much interest in him that I made my Italian valet inquire about him at the hotel where he was living, and so learned that he was a fabulously rich Jew of Holland, and that his name was Marcus Cocoza.

I came to wonder so much about what such a man could have to do in the street of Olalla's house, and why he thus appeared and again disappeared, that in the end, half against my will—for I was afraid of what she might tell me—I asked her if she knew him. She put two fingers under my chin and lifted it up. "Have you not noted about me, *Carissime*," she asked me, "that I have no shadow? Once upon a time I sold my shadow to the devil, for a little heart-ease, a little fun. That man whom you have seen outside—with your usual penetration you will easily guess him to be no other than this shadow of mine, with which I have no longer anything to do. The devil sometimes allows it to walk about. It then naturally tries to come back and lay itself at my feet, as it used to do. But I will on no account allow it to do so. Why, the devil might reclaim the whole bargain, did I permit it! Be you at ease about him, my little star."

She was, I thought, in her own way obviously speaking the truth for once. As she spoke I realized it: she had no shadow. There was nothing black or sad in her nearness, and the dark shades of care, regret, ambition, or fear, which seem to be inseparable from all human beings—even from me myself, although in those days I was a fairly careless boy—had been exiled from her presence. So I just kissed her, saying that we would leave her shadow in the street and pull down the blind.

It was about this time, too, that I began to have a strange feel ing, that I have come to know since, and which I then innocently mistook for happiness. It seemed to me, wherever I went, that the world around me was losing its weight and was slowly beginning to flow upwards, a world of light only, of no solidity whatever. Nothing seemed massive any longer. The Castel San Angelo was entirely a castle in the air, and I felt that I might lift the very Basilica of St. Peter between my two fingers. Nor was I afraid of being run over by a carriage in the streets, so conscious was I that the coach and the horses would have no more weight in them than if they had been cut out of paper. I felt extremely happy, if slightly light-headed, under the faith, and took it as a foreboding of a greater happiness to come, a sort of apotheosis. The universe, and I myself with it, I thought, was on the wing, on the way to the seventh heaven. Now I know well enough what it means: it is the beginning of a final farewell; it is the cock crowing. Since then, on my travels, I have known a country or a circle of people to have taken on that same weightless aspect. In one way I was right. The world around me was indeed on the wing, going upwards. It was only me myself, who, being too heavy for the flight, was to be left behind, in complete desolation.

I was occupied with the thought of a letter that I must write to my father, to tell him that I could not marry the widow. when I was informed that one of my brothers, who was an officer in the navy, was at Naples with his ship. I reflected that it might be better to give him the letter to carry, and told Olalla that I should have to go to Naples for a couple of days. I asked her if she would be likely to see the old Jew while I was away, but she assured me that she would neither see him nor speak to him.

I did not get on quite well with my brother. When I talked to him, I saw for the first time how my plans for the future would appear to the eyes of others, and it made me feel very ill at ease. For while I still held their views to be idiotic and inhuman, I was yet, for the first time since I had met Olalla, reminded of the dead and clammy atmosphere of my former world and my home.

However, I gave my letter to my brother, and asked him to plead my cause with my father as well as he could, and I hastened to return to Rome.

When I came back there I found that Olalla had gone. At first they told me, in the house where she had been, that she had died suddenly from fever. This made me deadly ill and nearly drove me mad for three days. But I soon found out that it could not possibly be so, and then I went to every inhabitant of the house, imploring and threatening them to tell me all. I now realized that I ought to have taken her away from the place before I went to Naples—although what would it have helped me if she herself had meant to leave me? A strange superstition made me connect her disappearance with the Jew, and in a last interview with the *madama* of the house I seized her by the throat, told her that I knew all, and promised her that I would strangle her if she did not tell me the truth. In her terror the old woman confessed: Yes, it had been he. Olalla had left the house one day and had not come back. The next day a pale old Jewish gentleman with very dark eyes had appeared at the house, had settled Olalla's debts and paid a sum to the *madama* to raise no trouble. She had not seen the two together. "And where have they gone?" I cried, sick because I had not had an outlet for my despair in killing off the old yellow female. That she could not tell me, but on second thought she believed that she had heard the Jew mention to his servant the name of a town called Basel.

To Basel I then proceeded, but people who have not themselves tried it can have no idea of the difficulties you have in trying to find, in a strange town, a person whose name you do not know.

My search was made more difficult by the fact that I did not know at all in what station of life I was to seek Olalla. If she had gone with the Jew she might be a great lady by now, whom I should meet in her own carriage. But why had the Jew left her in the house where I had found her in Rome? He might do the same thing now, for some reason unknown to me. I therefore searched all the houses of ill renown in Basel, of which there are more than one would think, for Basel is the town in Europe which stands up most severely for the sanctity of marriage. But I found no trace of her. I then bethought me of Amsterdam, where I should have, at least, the name of Cocoza to go by. I did indeed find, in Amsterdam, the fine old house of the Jew, and learned about him that he was the richest man of the place, and that his family had traded in diamonds for three hundred years. But he himself, I was told, was always traveling. It was thought that he was now in Jerusalem. I ran, from Amsterdam, upon various false tracks which took me to many countries. This maddening journey of mine went on for five months. In the end I made up my mind to go to Jerusalem, and I was on my way back to Italy, to take ship at Genoa, and these things were all running through my mind when I was sitting, as I have told you, at the Hotel of Andermatt, waiting to cross the pass upon the following day.

On the previous day I had found a letter from my father, which had been following at my heels for some months, being sent after me from one place to another. My father wrote to me:

"I am now able to look upon your conduct with calm and understanding. This I owe to the perusal of a collection of family papers, to which I have during the three last months given much of my time and attention. From the study of these papers it has become clear to me that a highly remarkable fate lies, and for the last two hundred years has lain, upon our family.

"We are, as a family, only so much better than others because we have always had amongst us one individual who has carried all the weakness and vice of his generation. The faults which normally would have been divided up among a whole lot of people have been gathered together upon the head of one of them only, and we others have in this way come to be what we have been, and are.

"In going through our papers I can no longer have any doubt of this fact. I have been able to trace the one particular chosen delinquent through seven generations, beginning with our great-aunt Elizabeth, into whose behavior I do not want here to go. I shall only quote the examples of my uncles Henry and Ambrose, who in their days without any doubt . . ."

Here followed various names and facts for the support of my father's theory. He then continued:

"I do not know whether it would not be more of a fatal blow than of a blessing to our name and family should this strange condition ever cease to be. It might do away with much trouble and anxiety, but it might also lead to the family becoming no better than other people.·

"As to you, you have so perseveringly declined to follow my command or advice that I feel I have reason to believe you the chosen victim of your generation. You have refused to make, by your example, virtue attractive and the reward of good conduct obvious. I have now reached, in my relation to you, a sufficiently philosophical outlook to give you my blessing in the completion of a career which may make filial disobedience, weakness, and vice a usefully repugnant and deterring example to your generation of our family."

I never saw my father again. But from my former tutor, whom, many years later, I happened to meet again in Smyrna, in melancholy circumstances, I heard of him. My father had so far reconciled himself to the situation as to marry my young widow himself. They had a son, and him he christened Lincoln. But whether he did so because after all he had liked me better than I had known, or with the purpose of removing any unpleasant sensations which might present themselves to him between one and three o'clock of a night, in connection with the thought of his son Lincoln, I cannot tell.

I had read his letter twice, and was taking it from my pocket to read it again to pass the time, when, looking up, I saw two young men come into the dining-room of the hotel from the cold night outside. One of them I knew, and I thought that if he caught sight of me he would come and sit down with me, which he did, so that the three of us spent the rest of the night together.

The first of these two nicely dressed and well-mannered young gentlemen was a boy of a noble family of Coburg, whom, a year before, I had known in England, where he was sent to study parliamentary procedure, since he meant to become a diplomat, and also to study horse-breeding, which was the livelihood of his people. His name was Friederich Hohenemser, but he was, in looks and manners, so like a dog I had once owned and which was named Pilot, that I used to call him that. He was a tall and fair, handsome, young man.

But since it will please you, Mira, to hear your own ingenious parable made use of, I am going to tell you of him that he was a person whom life would on no account consent to gulp down. He had himself a burning craving to be swallowed by life, and on every occasion would try to force himself down her throat, but she just as stubbornly refused him. She might, from time to time, just to imbue him with an illusion, sip in a little of him, though never a good full draught; but even on these occasions she would vomit him up again. What it was about him which thus made her stomach rise, I cannot quite tell you; only I know this: that all people who came near him had, somehow, the same feeling about him, that, while they had nothing against him, here was a fellow with whom they could do nothing at all. In this way he was, mentally, in the state of a very young embryo.

It probably takes a certain amount of cunning, or luck, in a man to get himself established as an embryo. My friend Pilot had never got beyond that. His condition was often felt by himself, I believe, as very alarming; and so indeed it was. His blue eyes at times gave out a most painful reflection of the hopeless struggle for existence which went on inside him. If he ever found in himself any original taste at all, he made the most of it. Thus he would go on talking of his preference for one wine over another, as if he meant to impress such a precious finding deeply upon you. A philosopher, about whom I was taught in school and whom you would have liked, Mira, has said: "I think; consequently I am." In this way did my friend Pilot repeat to himself and to the world: "I prefer Moselle to Rhenish wine; consequently I exist." Or, if he enjoyed a show or a game, he would dwell upon it the whole evening, telling you: "That sort of thing amuses me." But he had no imagination, and was, besides, very honest. He could invent nothing for himself, but was left to describe such preferences as he really found in his own mind, which were always preciously few. Probably it was, altogether, his lack of imagination which prevented him from existing. For if you will create, as you know, Mira, you must first imagine, and as he could not imagine what Friederich Hohenemser was to be like, he failed to produce any Friederich Hohenemser at all.

I had named him, I have told you, after a dog of mine, which had so much the same sort of disposition—never having the slightest idea of what he wanted to do, or had to do—that I finished up by shooting him. The God of Friederich Hohenemser was more forbearing to him in the end.

With all this, Pilot did not get on badly in society, which, I suppose, demands but a minimum of existence from its members, on the continent of Europe. He was, besides, a rich young man, pink and white, with a pair of vigorous calves—about all of which he was not a little vain—and he was even thought by elderly ladies to be a very model of a youth. He liked me, and was pleased at having made such a definite impression on me that I had given him a nickname. A person, he thought, has given me a nickname. Consequently I exist.

As he now came up to me I noticed that a change had come upon him. He had come to life; there was a shine about him. Thus did the dog Pilot shine and wag his tail upon the rare occasions on which he hoped to have proved that he did really exist. It might have been, in the boy, the effect of his new friendship with the young gentleman who accompanied him. In any case he would be sure, I felt, to play out his ace to me in the course of the evening. I sighed. I would have given much, on that night, for the company of a really good dog. I thought regretfully of my old dogs in England.

He presented his friend to me as Baron Guildenstern of Sweden. I had not had the pleasure of their company for ten minutes before I had been informed by both of them that the Baron in his own country held the reputation of a great seducer of women. This made me meditate—although all the time my intercourse with other people was carried on only upon the surface of my mind—on what kind of women they have in Sweden. The ladies who have done me the honor of letting me seduce them have, all of them, insisted upon deciding themselves which was to be the central point in the picture. I have liked them for it, for therein lay what was to me the variety of an otherwise monotonous performance. But in the case of the Baron it was clear that the point of gravity had always been entirely with him. You would suppose him to be of an unenthusiastic nature, even while he was talking of the beauties whom he had pursued, but you would not find him lacking in enthusiasm when he had once turned your eyes toward what he wanted you really to admire. It appeared from his talk that all his ladies had been of exactly the same kind, and that kind of woman I have never met. With himself so absolutely the hero of each single exploit, I wondered why he should have taken so much trouble—and he was obviously prepared to go to any length of trouble in these affairs—to obtain, time after time, a repetition of exactly the same trick. To begin with I was, being a young man myself, highly impressed by such a superabundance of appetite.

Still I got, after a while, from his conversation, which was very lively and became more so after we had emptied a few bottles together, the key to the existence of the young Swede, which lay in the single word "competition." Life, to him, was a competition in which he must needs shine beyond the other entrants. I had myself been fairly keen for competition as a boy, but even while I had been still at school I had lost my sense of it, and by this time, unless a thing was in itself to my taste, I thought it silly to exert myself about it just because it happened to be to the taste of others. Not so this Swedish Baron. Nothing in the whole world was in itself good or bad to him. He was waiting for a cue, and a scent to follow, from other people, and to find out from them what things they held precious, in order to outshine them in the pursuit of such things, or to bereave them of them. When he was left alone he was lost. In this way he became more dependent upon others than Pilot himself, and probably he shunned solitude as the very devil. His past life, I found from his talk, he saw as a row of triumphs over a row of rivals, and as nothing else whatever, although he was a little older than I. Neither in his rivals nor in his victims had he any interest at all. He had in him neither admiration nor pity, no feeling that was not either envy or contempt.

Yet he was no fool. On the contrary, I should say that he was a very shrewd person. He had adopted in life the manner of a good, plain, outspoken fellow who is a little unpolished but easily forgiven on account of his open, simple mind. With that he had an attentive, lurking glance, and spied on you, when you least expected it, in order to get from you a valuation of things, so as to be able to defraud you of them. As he was without the nerves which make ordinary people feel the strain of things, he had without doubt an extraordinary strength and stamina, and was held by himself and by others to be a giant in comparison with those who have imagination or compassion in them.

The two got on very well together, Pilot being flattered into existence by the cute young Swede—I have got, Pilot thought, a friend who is a terrible seducer of women; consequently I exist—

and the Baron quite pleased to have outshone all former friends of the rich young German, and to be admired by him. They would really rather have been without me. But they were drawn magnetically toward me, Pilot to show off his friend to me, and the Baron hot on the track of something which I might value or want, and which he might win or trick from me.

I was so bored, after a while, with the conversation of the Baron that I turned my attention to Pilot—a thing rarely done by anyone —and as soon as he got the chance he began to reveal to me the great happenings in his life.

"You might not care to be seen in my company, Lincoln," he said, "if you knew all. I shall not be out of danger till I am out of Switzerland. The walls have ears in a country of so much political unrest." He waited to watch the effect of his words, then went on: "I come from Lucerne."

Now I knew that there had been a fight in that town, but it had never occurred to me-that Pilot might have been in it.

"It was hot there," he said. Poor Pilot! In his little, bashfully smiling mouth the very truth sounded badly invented. The Baron, I am sure, would have made a whole chain of lies come out with such aplomb that his audience would not for a moment have doubted them. "I shot a man in the barricade fight on the third of March," said Pilot.

I knew that there had been a fight in the streets between, on the one side, the parties in power, and particularly the partisans of the priests, and on the other, the common people in rebellion. "You did?" I asked, with a deep pang of envy because he had been in a fight. "You shot a rebel?" For Pilot had always been to me a figure of high respectability and small intellect. I took it for granted that he had sided with the priests, and this at least I did not envy him.

Pilot shook his head proudly and secretively. After a moment he said, "I shot the chaplain of the Bishop of St. Gallen."

The newspapers had been full of this murder, and the murderer had been searched for everywhere. I naturally became interested to know how the great deed had fallen to Pilot, and made him tell me his tale from the beginning. The Baron, bored by the recount of somebody else's martial exploits, sat without listening, drinking and watching the people as they went in and out.

"When I went away from Coburg," said Pilot, "I meant to stay in Lucerne for three weeks with my uncle De Watteville. As I was about to depart, all the elegant ladies of the place, one after the other, begged me to bring her back from Lucerne a bonnet from a milliner whom they called Madame Lola. This woman, they assured me, was famous from one end of Europe to the other. Ladies from the great courts and capitals came to her for their bonnets, and never in the history of millinery had there been such a genius. I was naturally not averse to doing the ladies of my native town a service, so I went off, my pockets bulging with little silk patterns, and even, will you believe it, with little locks of hair for Madame Lola to match her bonnets to. Still, in Lucerne, where the air was filled with political discussions, I forgot all about Madame Lola until one night, when I was dining with a party of high officials and politicians, I suddenly drew out, with my handkerchief, a little slip of rose-colored satin, and had to furnish my explanation. To my surprise the whole conversation immediately turned to the milliner. The married men, at least, and all the clericals, all knew about her. It was true, said the Bishop of St. Gallen, who was present, that the woman was a genius. The slightest touch of her hand, like a magic wand, created miracles of art and elegance, and the great ladies of St Petersburg and Madrid, and of Rome itself, made pilgrimages to the milliner's shop. But she was more than that. She was suspected of being a conspirator of the first water, who made use of her *atelier* as a meeting place for the most dangerous revolutionists. And in this capacity, also, she was a genius, a Circe, moving and organizing things with her little hands, and the roughest of her partisans would have died for her.

"They all warned me so strongly against her that naturally the first thing which I did on the following day was to go to her house, in the street which had been pointed out to me. On that occasion I found her only a highly intelligent and agreeable woman. She took all my orders, and talked to me of my journey and even of my character and career. A red-haired young man came in while I was there, and went out again, who looked much like a revolutionist, but to whom she paid but little attention.

"While she was completing all these bonnets for me, the atmosphere of Lucerne was darkening more and more; a thunderstorm hung over the town. My uncle, who held a high position in the town council, foresaw disaster. He sent my aunt and his daughters away to his château, and advised me to go with them. But I felt that I could not go away without having seen Madame Lola again, and having collected my goods from her.

"On the day on which I went to her at last, the disturbance in the streets was so great that I had to approach her abode by a network of little side streets, and even that was extremely difficult. But upon entering the house I found it, from doorway to garret, one seething mass of armed people streaming in and out, the whole place indeed like a witch's cauldron. There was no time to talk of bonnets. She herself, standing on the counter, discoursing and directing the people, at the sight of me jumped straight into my arms. 'Ah,' she cried, 'your heart has driven you the right way at last!' And the whole crowd, she with it, at this moment advanced out of the house and down the street. It dragged me with it, or I was so filled with the very enthusiasm of the woman that I went freely. In this way, in a second, I was whirled into a barricade fight, and on to the barricades, always at the side of Madame Lola.

"She was loading the guns and handing them to the combatants, and she was using for the terrible task all the verve and adroitness which she had used in trimming her bonnets. Now all the people around her, although they were brave, were afraid, and had reason to be so; but she was not in the least afraid. As she handed the rifles to the men on the barricade, she handed them with the weapons some of her own fearlessness. I saw this on their faces. And it was strange that I myself was at the time convinced that nothing could harm her, or could harm me as long as I was with her. I remembered our old cook at Coburg telling me that a cat has nine lives. Madame Lola, I thought, must have in her the life of nine cats. At that moment I really saw her as something more than human, although she was, as I think I told you, no lady of noble birth, but only a milliner of Lucerne, not young.

"It was then that I myself, carried away by the rage around me, seized a rifle and fired into the crowd of soldiers and town militia which was slowly advancing up the street against us. My own uncle De Watteville, for all I knew, might be leading them, but I had no thought for him. At the same moment I was struck down, I know not how, and dropped like dead.

"When I woke up I was in a small room, in bed, and Madame Lola was in the room with me. As I tried to move I found that my right leg was all done up in bandages. She gave a great exclamation of joy at seeing me awake, but then approached with her finger on her lips. In the darkened room she told me of how the fight was over, and how I had killed the chaplain of the Bishop of St. Gallen. She begged me to be very still, first because my leg had been broken by a shot, and secondly, because things were still upset in Lucerne. I was in great danger and must be kept a secret in her house.

"I was there in the garret of her house, for three weeks, being nursed by her. The fighting was still going on, and I heard shots. But of this, of my wound, of what I had done and what my people would say, even of my dangerous position, I hardly thought. It seemed to me that I had, somehow, got up very high outside the world in which I used to live, and that I was now quite alone there, with her. A doctor came to see me from time to time.

Nobody else came, but Lola would put on her shawl and leave me for a while, begging me to keep very quiet till she came back. These hours when she was away were to me infinitely long.

"But while I was with her we talked together much. When I have since thought of it, I remember that she did not say a great deal, but that I myself talked as well as I have always wished to do. Altogether, I understood life and the world, myself and God even, while I was in the garret. In particular we talked of the great things which I was to do in life. I had, you understand, already done enough to be known amongst people, but both of us felt that this was only the beginning.

"I understood that many of her friends had left Lucerne, and that she was exposing herself to dangers for my sake, and I begged her to go away. No, she said, she would not leave me for anything in the world. First of all, after what I had done, the revolutionists of Lucerne looked upon me as a brother, and would all be ready to die for my sake. But more than that, she explained, blushing deeply, in case we were found by the tyrants of the town or their militia, she and I must both insist that we had taken no part in the fight, but were here together because of a love affair. She would have to pose as my mistress, and I as her lover, while my wound would be said to have been given me by a jealous rival. These words of hers, although the whole thing was only a comedy, again made me feel extraordinarily happy, and made me dream of what I would do when I got well again. Yes, I do not know if any real love affair could possibly have made me as happy.

"At last one evening she told me that the doctor had declared me to be out of danger, and that we must part. She was leaving Lucerne herself that night. I was to go away, secretly, in the early morning. A friend, she said, would place his carriage at my disposal, and himself escort me out of town. A sort of terror came over me at her words. But I was too slow. I did not know what was the matter with me till it was too late. Madame Lola went on talking gently to me. I was, she said, to have something for my trouble, and she would give me all the bonnets that she had in her shop. 'For I myself,' she said, 'am not coming back to Lucerne.' So with the assistance of her little maid she made the journey up and down the stairs twelve times, each time loaded with bandboxes, which she placed around me. I began to laugh, and in the end could not stop again, for I found myself nearly drowned in bonnets of all the colors of the rainbow, trimmed with flowers, ribbons, and plumes. The floor, the bed, chair, and table were covered with them, probably the prettiest bonnets in all the world. 'Now,' she said, when she had filled the room with them, 'here you have the wherewithal to conquer the hearts of women.' She herself put on a plain bonnet and shawl, and took my hand. 'Do not ever,' said she, bear me any grudge. I have tried to do you good.' She put her arms around my neck, kissed me, and was gone. 'Lola!' I cried, and sank back in my chair in a faint. I passed, when I woke up, a terrible night. There was not a single pleasant thing for me to think of. The image of the curate of the Bishop of St. Gallen also began to worry me, and it seemed to me that I had nothing to turn to in all the world.

"Lola was as good as her word. The next morning an elderly Jewish gentleman, of great elegance, presented himself in my garret, and at the foot of the stair I found his handsome carriage waiting for me. He drove me through the town, where here and there I still saw traces of the fighting, and entertained me pleasantly on the way. As we were nearing the outskirts of the city he said to me: 'The Baron de Watteville's carriage will meet us at such and such a park. But the feelings of Monsieur your Uncle have been hurt by your behavior, and he has charged me to say that he prefers you to continue your journey straight on, so that he and you should not meet until later.'

"'But does my uncle,' I exclaimed in great surprise, 'know of what has happened to me?'

"'Yes,' said the old Jew, 'he has indeed known all the time. The Baron has much influence with the clergy of Lucerne, and it is doubtful whether we could have done without him.' He said no more, so we drove on in silence, I in a disturbed mind.

"My uncle's carriage was indeed waiting near a park, as the Jew had said. As we stopped, a man got out of it and slowly came up to meet us, and I recognized the red-haired young man whom I had seen in Lola's house on my first visit there, and later, I now remembered, on the barricade. He now looked as if he had gone through much. He limped when he walked, and his face was very pale and stern as he bowed to my companion. Still, as he looked around at me, he suddenly smiled. 'So this,' I heard him say, 'is Madame Lola's little caged goldfinch?'

"'Yes,' said the old Jew, smiling, 'that is her golem.'

"Then I did not know what I found out later, that the word *golem,* in the Jewish language, means a big figure of clay, into which life is magically blown, most frequently for the accomplishment of some crime which the magician dares not undertake himself. These golems are imagined to be very big and strong.

"The two saw me into my uncle's carriage, and we took leave of one another. I drove on, but I had too much to think of now, and I did not know where to find myself again. The smell of gunpowder of the barricades, our talks of God and Lola's kiss in the attic, together with all these bonnets which she had given me, all ran before my eyes, like the colored spots which you see before your eyes when you have for a long time been looking at the sun. I have not been able, since then, to think much of those great deeds which I was to perform. I cannot even remember what they were. But still, I have killed the curate of the Bishop of St. Gallen, and I must be careful until I get out of this country. I have seen a doctor, who tells me that my leg has been so skillfully put together that it is as if it had never been broken."

"And so you are," I said, "trying to find this woman, and searching for her everywhere, lying awake at night?"

"You guess that?" said Pilot. "Yes, I am looking for her. I do not know what to think or feel about anything until I shall see her again. Still she was not young, you know, and no woman of noble birth, but only a milliner of Lucerne."

Now I had heard Pilot's tale. And while I had been listening to it, I had been frightened more than once. There were many things in it alarming to my ears. I thought, I have not been drunk a single time since I lost Olalla, till tonight. It is obvious that when I drink now, even as much as two bottles of this Swiss wine, my head betrays me. That comes from thinking, for a long time, of one single thing only. This tale of my friend's is too much like a dream of my own. There is much in his woman of the barricades which recalls to me the manner of my courtesan of Rome, and when, in the middle of his story, an old Jew appears like a djinn of the lamp, it is quite clear that I am a little off my head. How far can I be, I wonder, from plain lunacy?

To clear up this question I went on drinking.

The Baron Guildenstern, during the course of Pilot's narration, had from time to time looked at me with a smile, and sometimes winked at me. But as it drew on he had lost his interest in it, and had had a new bottle brought in. Now he opened it, and refilled the glasses.

"My good Fritz," he said, laughing, "I know that ladies love their bonnets. A husband to them means a person who will buy them bonnets of all possible shapes and colors, God bless him. But it is a poor article of dress to get off a woman. I have let them keep the bonnet on after everything else had gone; and as to having it flung at your head, I prefer the chemise."

"Have you never, then, paid your court to a woman without getting the chemise?" Pilot asked, a little nervously, looking straight in front of him at things far away.

The Baron watched him attentively, as if he were on the point of finding out that a failure and an unsatisfied appetite might have a value for some kinds of people. "My dear friend," he said,

"I will tell you an adventure of mine in return for your confession":

"Seven years ago I was sent by the colonel of my regiment in Stockholm, the Prince Oscar, to the riding school of Saumur. I did not stay my term out there, as I got into some sort of trouble at Saumur, but while I was there I had some pleasant hours in the company of two rich young friends of mine, one of whom was Waldemar Nat-og-Dag, who had come with me from Sweden. The other was the Belgian Baron Clootz, who belonged to the new nobility, and possessed a large fortune.

"Through letters of introduction of old aunts of ours, my Swedish friend and I dropped for a time into a curious community of old ruined Legitimists of the highest aristocracy, who had lost all that they had in the French Revolution, and who lived in a small provincial town near Saumur.

"They were all of them very aged, for when they had been young the ladies had had no dowries to marry on, and the gentlemen no money to maintain a family in the style of their old names, so there had been no younger generation produced. They could thus foresee the near end of all their world, and with them to be young was synonymous with being of the second-best circles. The ladies held their heads together over my aunts' letters, wondering at the strangeness of conditions in Sweden, where the nobility still had the courage to breed.

"It all bored me to death. It was like being put on a shelf with a lot of bottles of old wine and old pickle pots, sealed and bound with parchment.

"In these circles there was much talk of a rich young woman who had for a year been renting a pretty country house outside the town. I had seen it myself, within its walled gardens, on my morning rides. In the beginning she interested me as little as possible. I thought her only one more of the company of Beguines. I wondered, though, how it was that the qualities of youth and prosperity were in her no faults, but on the contrary seemed to endear her to all the dry old hearts of the town.

"They themselves eagerly furnished me the explanation, informing me that this lady had consecrated her life to the memory of General Zumala Carregui, who had been, I believe, a hero and a martyr to the cause of the rightful king of Spain, and had been killed by the rebels. In his honor she dressed forever in white, lived on lenten food and water, and every year undertook a pilgrim's voyage to his tomb in Spain. She gave much charity to the poor, and kept a school for the children of the village, and a hospital. From time to time she also had visions and heard voices, probably the sweet and martial voice of General Zumala. For all this she was highly thought of. That she had, before his death, stood in a more earthly relation to the martyr in no way damaged her reputation. The collection of old maids of both sexes were on the contrary much intrigued by the idea of experience in this holy person, as were, very likely, the eleven thousand martyrized virgins of Cologne when they were, in paradise, introduced to the highly ranking saint of heaven, St. Mary of Magdala.

"But the heart of my friend Waldemar, when he met her, melted as quickly as a lump of sugar in a cup of hot coffee.

"'Arvid,' he said to me, 'I have never met such a woman, and I know that it was the will of fate that I should meet her. For as you know my name is Night-and-Day, and my arms two-parted in black and white. Therefore she is meant for me—or I for her. For this Madame Rosalba has in her more life than any person I have ever met. She is a saint of the first magnitude, and she uses in being a saint as much vigor as a commander in storming a citadel. She sits like a fresh, full flower in the circle of old dry perisperms. She is a swan in the lake of life everlasting. That is the white half of my shield. And at the same time there is death about her somewhere, and that is the black half of the Nat-og-Dag arms. This I can only explain to you by a metaphor, which presented itself to me as I was looking at her.

" 'We have heard much of wine growing since we came here, and have learned, too, how, to obtain perfection in the special white wine of this district, they leave the grapes on the vines longer than for other wines. In this way they dry up a little, become over-ripe and very sweet. Furthermore, they develop a peculiar condition which is called in French *pourriture noble,* and in German, *Edelfaule,* and which gives the flavor to the wine. In the atmosphere of Rosalba, Arvid, there is a flavor which there is about no other woman. It may be the true odor of sanctity, or it may be the noble putrefaction, the royal corrodent rust of a strong and rare wine. Or, Arvid, my friend, it may be both, in a soul two-parted white and black, a Nat-og-Dag soul.'

"On the following Sunday—in May, it was—I managed to be introduced to Madame Rosalba, after mass, at dinner in the house of an old friend of mine.

"These old aristocrats, in the midst of their ruin, kept a fairly good table, and did not despise a bottle of wine. But the younger woman ate lentils and dry bread, with a glass of water, and did this with such a sweet and frank demureness that the diet seemed very noble, and nobody would have thought of offering her anything else. After dinner, in the fresh, darkened salon, she entertained the company, with the same frankness and modesty, by describing a vision which she had lately had. She had found herself, she said, in a vast flowery meadow, with a great flock of young children, each of whom had around its head a small halo, as clear as the flame of a little candle. St. Joseph himself had come to her there, to inform her that this was paradise, and that she was to act as nurse to the children. These, he explained, were none other than those first of all martyrs, the babes of Bethlehem murdered by Herod. He pointed out to her what a sweet task was hers, inasmuch as, just as the Lord had suffered and died in the stead of humanity, so had these children suffered and died in the stead of the Lord. A great felicity had at his words come upon her, she said, and sighing with bliss she had declared that she should never want anything of all eternity but to look after and play with the martyrized children.

"I am not a great believer in visions or in paradise, but as this young woman told her tale I had no doubt that she had really seen with her own eyes what she described, or that she had been chosen for paradise. She had so much life in her that she made one feel how well the choice had been made; the little martyrs would have a great deal of fun.

"Once, while she was talking, she lifted her eyes. Good God, what a pair of eyes to have! They were, indeed, of the greatest power; and when she gave you one of her thirty-pound glances— puff!

"Now, as I was listening demurely myself and looking around at her happy circle of old disciples, I became convinced that some- where in all this stuff there was a very bold piece of deceit. Rosalba might very well be a saint of the first water. She might also be heaping benefactions on rich and poor, out of a horn of plenty. And she might have loved the General Zumala Carregui, in which case the general was to be envied. But she had not loved him only in all the world, and she was not living now for his memory alone. Monogamy—for it does exist, and I have myself been loved by women of a monogamous disposition—shows in a woman. You may confound the nun and the whore, but those ladies who in India, I am told, beg to be committed to the flames of their husbands' funeral pyres, you know when you see them. Either, I thought, this white swan Rosalba can count the names of her lovers with the beads of her rosary, or she is some perverse old maid—for as a maid she was not young; she had passed her thirtieth year—who, out of desperation, poses to my Legitimists as the mistress of a general.

"Rosalba had not looked at me more than once, but she was aware of me. She and I, for all that we were placed far apart, were as much in contact as if we had been performing a *pas-de-deux* upon the center of a stage, with the aged *corps du ballet* grouped around us. When she went to the window to look for her carriage, the folds of her white dress and the tresses of her dark hair moved and floated all for my benefit.

"I thought: I have never in my life had a dead rival. Let us see now what the General Zumala is capable of. At Easter I had to listen to a sermon on St. Mary Magdalen—this holy Mary, would she have been more difficult to seduce than any of the others of the name; or easier? The old war horse, we are told, raises its head to the war trumpet.

"I soon became a frequent visitor at Madame Rosalba's château. I do not know whether the old aristocratic community of the town had any idea of the peril of its saint. I was accepted as her companion on her visits to the poor and the sick. In the beginning I consulted her much upon my soul. I confessed to her many of my sins, and none of them seemed to impress her much. They might well have appeared familiar to her. I think that she really gave me good advice, and that if I had meant to reform I should have done well to follow it. She had the same earnest and sweet manner, and seemed to like me, but in our amorous *pas-de-deux* she was slow of movement. I, on my side, was patient. I had to keep my young friend Waldemar in view, and I knew that I had a pleasant surprise for her at the end of the dance.

"One thing was strange to me in that house. I have been brought up a Lutheran, and taken to church on Christmas Day by my good grandmother. I have heard many sermons, and I know the difference between saintliness and sin as well as old Pastor Methodius himself, even if we disagreed a little as to our personal tastes in the matter. But upon my honor as a guardsman, with her it was difficult to know which was which. She preached theology with as much voluptuousness as if the table of the Lord was the one real treat to a gourmet, and when we talked about love she would make it look like a pastime in a kindergarten. This I did not like. I had a nurse who believed in witches, and at times, in Rosalba's society, I remembered the dark tales of old Maja-Lisa. Even so, such a holy witch and wanton saint I had not come across before.

"In the end, however, I obtained from Rosalba the promise of a rendezvous in her house late on a Friday afternoon. On that day all the people were going to the funeral of a maréchal's widow, who had been a hundred years old. This was late in June. By then I was bored with her dallying, and I thought, It is to be on Friday, or I will never make love to a woman again.

"All this, I can tell you, might have ended up in a different way, had not something else happened in Saumur. But it came to pass that a very rich old Jewish gentleman—in the style of the Jew of your tale, Fritz—stopped there for a week on his way from Spain. He had everything of the best. His coach, his servants, and his diamonds were much talked of. But what struck our riding school to the heart was a pair of Andalusian horses which he brought with him. They were, particularly the one of them, the finest that had been seen in France. Even at my regiment in Sweden there were hardly any like that. Moreover they had been trained in the royal *manège* at Madrid, and it was a shame that they should be in the hands of a Jew, and a civilian.

"Because of these horses I neglected Madame Rosalba for a few days, so much talk was there about them. Few of us would have been rich enough to buy them, and still we thought it a point of honor with us that they should not leave Saumur. In the end Baron Clootz, who was a millionaire and a young nobleman of much wit, one evening after dinner made a proposition to five of us who had been for a long time his closest friends and associates. He promised that he would buy the horse of the Jew, and put it up as the prize in a competition in which we were to show what we were worth. The rule of this competition was that we were to ride, within one day, three French miles, drink three bottles of the wine of the district, and make love to three ladies in the course. In what order we would take the events it was for our own judgment to decide, but the Jew's horse was to belong to that one of us who arrived first at Baron Clootz's house after having fulfilled the conditions.

"His proposition was a great success, and I was already in my mind arranging the consecutive order of the items, and going through my circle of acquaintances amongst the pretty women of the district, when I found that the day chosen for the contest was the day of my rendezvous with Madame Rosalba. The day had been chosen for both purposes from the same reason: because the élite of the town would be occupied, and not able to poke their noses into our affairs.

"I had, however, confidence in myself, and as I walked away arm in arm with young Waldemar I thought it a good joke. He was still worshiping Rosalba from the footstep of her pedestal, so much so as to want to change his religion for her sake, even, I believe, and become a monk. I often had to listen to his panegyrics upon her. Still after some argument we had persuaded him to come into our contest. I think that he meant to show himself to Rosalba on the Spanish horse, for he was a tolerably good horseman.

"I was, without vanity, punctual at my rendezvous at the white château of Rosalba on that Friday afternoon. By her own maid—for there was not another soul in the house; they had all gone to the funeral—I was taken to her boudoir in the tower, and at the top of a long stone stair. The shutters were closed, the room was half dark, and, when you came from outside, as cool as a church. There were a great many white lilies, so that the air was heavy with their scent. Upon a table were glasses, and a bottle of the best wine that I have ever tasted, a dry Château Yquem. This made my third bottle of the day.

"Rosalba also was there. She was as ever very plainly attired, but she had shaken herself, with one shake, into very great beauty.

"If what happened to me in this tower seems somehow wild and fantastical, and more like a fairy tale or a ghost story than a romance, the fault is not mine. It is true that the day was hot; a thunderstorm followed it in the night; and that as I came in from the white road, heavy in my riding boots, I was not too sure of my head. I may even have been more in love with her than I myself knew, for everything seemed to me to turn on her, and my bottles and my wildly galloped races to be only the reasonably fit initiatory ceremonies to this great moment of love-making. But I remember well all that happened.

"I had not much time to give away. Light-headed as I was, with the room swinging up and down before my eyes, my words came easily to me, and I had her in my arms pretty soon, her clothes disheveled. She was like a lily in a thunderstorm herself, white and swaying, her face wet. But she held me back with her outstretched arms. 'Listen for one moment,' she said. 'Here we are all alone. There is no one in the house but we and my maid who brought you here, that pretty girl. Are you not afraid?

"'Arvid,' she said, 'have you ever heard the story of Don Giovanni?' She looked at me so intently that I had to answer that I had even heard that opera about him. 'Do you remember, then,' she said, 'the scene in which the statue of the Commandante comes for him? Such a statue there is on the tomb of the General Zumala, in Spain.' I said, 'Oh, let it keep him down in it, then.'

"'Wait,' said Rosalba. 'Rosalba belonged to General Zumala Carregui. When she betrays him, poor Rosalba must disappear. But then, an opera must have a fifth act to it sooner or later. And you, my star of the north, are to be the hero of it. You have your honor in the matter, as if you were a woman. You would have no mercy on St. Mary of Magdala. Rosalba was such a shining bubble, and when you break her, a little bit of wet will be all that you get out of it. But it was time that she went. The people, and her creator even, were becoming too fond of her. You give her her great tragic end. No other man in the world, I think, could have done that so well. You are well worthy of coming in.'

"'Let me come in, then,' I gasped.

"'You have no pity on poor Rosalba at all?' she asked. 'That

she should lose her last refuge, and be haunted and doomed forever—that means nothing to you?'

" 'You yourself have no pity on me,' I cried.

" 'Ah, how much you are mistaken,' she exclaimed. 'For you,
Arvid, I am worried, I am terribly sorry. An awful future awaits
you—waste, a desert—oh, tortures! If I could help you, I would;
but that is impossible to me. The thought of Rosalba will never
be any good to you; her example cannot help you. The thought of
this hour might, afterward, do you some good, but even that is
not certain. Oh, my lover, if to save you I made you a present of
a lovely horse, all saddled within my stable, fiery enough to carry
you away in a gallop from this terrible fall and the perdition of
us both, and if I sent my maid, that pretty girl who showed you
up here, with you to find him, would you not go?

" 'For soon,' she said, drawing herself up to her full height, her
hand still on my breast, as mine in hers, and speaking in the
manner of a sibyl, 'it may be too late, and we shall hear the fatal
step on the stair, marble upon marble.'

"In our agitation her dark hair, which used to hang down in
ringlets on both sides of her face, was flung back, and I saw that
she had indeed the brand of the witch upon her. From her left
ear to her collar bone a deep scar ran, like a little white snake——"

At these words of the Baron, Pilot cried out: "What! What are
you saying?"

"I said," said the Baron patiently, pleased with the impression
made by his tale," that from her left ear to the collar bone ran a
scar, like a snake."

"I heard it," cried Pilot. "Why are you repeating my words?
The milliner of Lucerne, Madame Lola, had on her neck just
such a scar, and I have this hour described it to you."

"You have not said one word of it," said the Baron.

"Have I not?" cried Pilot to me.

I said nothing at all. I thought: I am dreaming. By now I am
quite sure that I am dreaming. This hotel, Pilot, and the Swedish

Baron are all parts of a dream. Good God, what a nightmare! I have at last lost my reason for good and all, and the next thing that will happen will be that Olalla will walk in through that door, swiftly, as she always comes in dreams. With that thought I kept my eyes on the door.

From time to time, while we had been talking, new guests had come in from the outside, to sit down or to walk through the room to the inner apartments of the hotel. Now a lady and her maid came in, and passed us quickly and quietly. The lady wore a black cloak, which disguised her face and figure. The maid had her hair wrapped around her head in the Swiss way, and carried the shawls. Both looked so demure that not even the Baron gave them more than one glance. It was not till they were already gone that Pilot, suddenly stopping in his heated debate with the Baron, stood up like a statue, staring in their direction. When we asked him, laughing—for we had drunk enough to think one another ridiculous—what was the matter with him, he turned his big face toward us. "That," he cried, deeply moved, and even more so by the sound of his own voice, "was she. That was Madame Lola of Lucerne."

The lightning of madness had struck, then, but it had hit Pilot and not me. Still no one could tell what would happen next; and indeed at his words it seemed to me that there had been something familiar about the lady. Pilot began to pull his hair. "Come, my boy," I said, taking hold of his arm. "It is not necessary to be mad. We will go together and ask the porter, who will know her, if this lady be not the midwife of Andermatt, who will be found to have nothing whatever in common with the Maid of Orléans." Still laughing, I dragged him to the porter's *loge* and began to question the bald old Swiss about the newcomers. The porter was at first busy counting up various pieces of elegant luggage, and did not pay much attention to us.

"Come," I said to him, "here is a handsome reward for a little favor. Is that lady, in the black *juste-au-corps,* a revolutionist, who inspired the murder of the Bishop of St. Gallen's curate? Or is she a mystic who has dedicated her life to the memory of General Zumala Carregui? Or is she a prostitute of Rome?" The old man dropped his pencil and stared at me.

"God help me, Sir, of what are you talking?" he exclaimed. "The lady who has just gone through the dining room, and who is occupying our number nine, is no other than the wife of Herr Councilor Heerbrand, of Altdorf. The Councilor is the greatest man of the town, and was a widower with a large family. The present Frau Councilor Heerbrand is the widow of an Italian wine-grower, and owns a property in Tuscany, which obliges her to travel back and forth in this way. At Altdorf, where my own three granddaughters are in service, she is highly respected. She gives tone to all the town, and is known as a very fine card player."

"Well, Pilot," I said, as I guided him back, for he was so stupefied that he would have stood where he was left had I let go my hold, "this is a prosaic solution to our enigma. We may sleep calmly tonight in rooms eight and ten with the Frau Councilor in the bed next to the other side of the wall."

I did not look much where I was going, and knocked into a person who, with a little stick in his hand, was walking slowly through the dining room, in our own direction. As I apologized he lifted his tall hat a little to me, and I saw that it was the old Jew of Rome, Marcus Cocoza. At the same second he went on, and passed through the same door as had the lady.

"After my first moment of sheer terror at looking into his pale face and deep dark eyes I was seized with a fury which shook me from head to foot. I am slow to get angry, as you know, Mira, and was so even as a young man. When I really become so, it is a great relief to me. I had been depressed, disappointed, and made a fool of, and inactive for a very long time, and my despair had reached its climax in my meeting with the two friends at the hotel. Now, I thought, if all things in the world were really against me, and all of them equally damnable, the moment had come for a fight.

At least that was how I felt it at the time. Later on I reflected that it was nothing in myself which worked the change, but just the nearness of the woman. She had passed within six feet of me, and had liberated my heart by the waft of her petticoat, and I had once more the winds of life in my sails, and its currents under my keel.

I looked at my two companions and saw that they had both recognized the Jew. In their amazement they looked like two lay figures. Whatever magic I had encountered was encircling them as well as me, or else they were themselves creatures of my imagination. It mattered little to me. I was determined by now to drive fate into a corner. I took out my card, wrote on it the name of the old Jew, and a regular challenge in the best style, asking him to see me at once, and sent the waiter of the hotel to his room with it. I was not a little frightened of the old man whom Ollala had called her shadow. I truly believed that he belonged to the devil, but I had to see him. But the waiter returned to say that it was out of the question. The old gentleman had gone to bed, had had a hot drink brought him by his valet, and now had locked his door and would not be disturbed. I told the man that it was a matter of great importance, but he declined to do anything for me. He knew their guest, who went in his own splendid coach with his own servants, and was a man of unfathomable wealth.

"Has he traveled this way," I asked the waiter, "in the company of Madame Heerbrand?"

"No, never," declared the poor fellow, scared, I think, by my looks. He did not think that the lady and the gentleman knew each other at all, he said.

It was a loathsome thought to me that I should have to wait all night before I could do anything in the matter. Still, it could not be helped, and I therefore dragged a chair to the fireplace and stirred up the fire, not daring to go to sleep. I was afraid that the woman might leave the hotel early, so I called the waiter back, gave him money, and enjoined him to let me know when the

lady of number nine should be about to leave the hotel in the
morning.

"But, Sir," said the young man, "the lady has gone."

"Gone?" I cried, with Pilot and the Baron repeating my exclamation like a double echo. Yes, she had gone. No sooner had she
left the room by one door than she had come back to the porter's
loge by another, in great distress, and had ordered a coach at once
to take her to the monastery even tonight. She had, she told the
porter, found a letter for her at the hotel, informing her that her
sister lay dying in Italy. It was a matter of life and death to her
to get on.

"But is it possible," I asked, "to go up that road tonight, and in
this storm?" The waiter agreed that it would be difficult, but she
had insisted, offered to double and triple the fare, and had wrung
her hands in such grief that she had moved the heart of the
coachman. Besides, it was not easy to disobey Frau Heerbrand.
She was no ordinary lady. She had gone. We must ourselves have
heard the wheels of her coach. That was true. We had indeed just
heard wheels.

There we stood, like three hounds around a fox hole.

I did not doubt but that it was the sight of the old Jew which
had driven away the woman. He was, indeed, a conjurer and a
devil, the djinn who had somehow got the fair lady into his power.
For a moment it threw me into the most terrible distress that I
could not get at him and kill him. But it would cause too much
stir, and they would prevent it. Now there was nothing to do but
to follow her and protect her against him. At this idea my heart
flew up like a lark.

We had some trouble in getting a coach, but this in the end was
overcome by the Baron, who showed much energy and efficiency
in the matter. I understood that my two companions, who were
unaware of any personal interest of mine in the matter, felt surprised at my zeal. The Baron, holding me to be very drunk, was
still not averse to one more spectator for his exploits. Pilot took

my eagerness as a proof of my friendship for him. He even, although he seemed the whole time to have been struck dumb, tried to give words to his gratitude. "Go to hell, Pilot," I said to him. He thereupon contented himself with pressing my hand.

At last, at great cost, a coach was produced, and the three of us set off together for the monastery.

The wind was terrible, and the snow was thick on the road. Our coach, in consequence, went very irregularly in bumps and starts, and at times stood quite still. We sat inside it, each in his corner. From the time when we got into the stifling atmosphere of the closed carriage, behind the panes which were swiftly blinded by the snow beating in upon them, we did not talk together. Each of us would, I am sure, willingly have had his two fellow passengers perish on the journey. I myself, however, was soon so entirely swallowed up by the idea of seeing Olalla again that the outside world sank away and disappeared for me. We were going upwards all the time. We might, for all I knew, be driving into heaven. My heaven, had I been free to choose it then, must also have been turbulent, filled with wild galloping air.

As we drove on, the road became steeper and the snow more fierce. Our coachman and groom were unable to see six feet in front of them. Suddenly the coach gave a particularly bad jump, and stopped altogether. The coachman, descending from his box, tore open the carriage door to a great gust of wind and snow, and, himself all covered with snow, roared in, infuriated, that it was impossible to get out of the drift in which the coach was stuck.

We held a short consultation inside, which meant nothing to any of us, as no one would give up the journey. We tumbled out, buttoning our coats and turning up the collars, and, doubling over like old men, we took up the pursuit.

It had stopped snowing. The sky was almost clear. The moon, running along behind thin clouds, showed us the way. But the wind was terrible here. I remembered, just as I got out of the coach, a fairy tale, which I had been told as a child, in which an old witch keeps all the winds of heaven imprisoned in a sack. This pass, I thought, must be the sack. The locked-up winds were raging wildly in it, jumping down straight, like fighting dogs chained by their collars. Sometimes they seemed to beat down vertically upon our heads, again they rose from the ground, whirling the snow sky-high. In the carriage it had been cold, but here, as we were already high up in the mountains, the air felt as frigid as if someone had emptied a bucket of iced water over our heads. We could hardly breathe in it. But all this wildness of the elements did me good. In such a world and night I should find her, and she would need me.

The figures of my fellow travelers, even at arm's length dim and vague like shadows on the snowy road, were insignificant to me. This search I felt to be mine alone, and soon I was a good bit in front of them. Pilot dropped out of sight. The Baron kept fairly close to me, but did not reach me.

Suddenly, after perhaps an hour's walk, as the road turned around a rock, a large square object, slanting on the edge of the track, loomed like a large tower in front of me. It was Olalla's carriage. It was standing there, stuck like our own and half upset, and there were neither horses nor coachman with it. I jerked open the door, and a woman inside gave a terrible shriek. It was the maid whom I had seen in the hotel. She was crouching on the carriage floor with shawls pulled over her. She was alone, and when she saw that I did not mean to kill or rob her, she cried to me that the coachman had unhitched the horses to get them into a shelter, after he had had to give up, like our own coachman, the hope of getting any farther. But where, I cried back to her, was her mistress? She had, the maid told me, gone ahead on foot. The girl was horribly scared, and in describing her lady's flight and danger she sobbed and cried, and could hardly get her words out. I tore myself loose from her, for she did not want to let me go, and banged the door upon her. What terror, what danger, I thought, had there been in that coach to drive a woman out of it, alone, in the dead of the night and amongst wild mountains? What could it be that threatened her at the hands of the old Jew of Amsterdam?

I had stopped beside the coach for a quarter of an hour, perhaps, and this had enabled the Baron to catch up with me. The two lanterns on the coach were still burning, and as he came up behind me and spoke to me it was curious to see, in the moon-cold night, his face appear, flaming scarlet in the light of them. In the shelter of the coach we exchanged a few words. We started again, going for a while side by side.

At a place where the road got steeper, through the mist of the loose whirling snow which was driven along the ground like the smoke from a cannon, I caught sight of a dark shadow in front of me, not a hundred yards away, which might be a human figure. At first it seemed to disappear and to appear again, and it was difficult in the night and in the storm to keep your eyes fixed upon it. But after a time, although I got no nearer, my eyes became used to their task, and I could follow her steadily. She walked, on this steep and heavy road, as quickly as I myself did, and my old fancy about her, that she could fly if she would, came back. The wind whirled her clothes about. Sometimes it filled them and stretched them out, so that she looked like an angry owl on a branch, her wings spread out. At other times it screwed them up all around her, so that on her long legs she was like a crane when it runs along the ground to catch the wind and get on the wing.

At the sight of her I felt the Baron's nearness intolerable. If I had chased Olalla for six months, to run her down in this mountain pass, I must have her alone to myself. It would be of no use to try to explain this to him. I stopped, and as he stopped with me, I seized him by the front of his cloak and threw him back. He was tired by our climb. He was breathing heavily, and had stopped a couple of times. But he came to life at my grip and on seeing the expression of my face. Now he would by no means let me go on alone. His eyes and teeth glinted at me. We had a few minutes' fight on the stony road, and he knocked off my hat, which rolled away. But, still gripping his clothes with my left hand, I struck him a strong blow in the face, which made him lose his balance. The road was slippery, and he fell and rolled backwards. As he fell he had taken hold of a muffler around my neck, and had nearly strangled me. Cursing the delay, I sprang on, hot and shaking from the effort.

Alone again, and certain now to catch Olalla in the end here in the high hills, I was filled both with great happiness and with that fear which had first taken hold of me beside the coach. Both drove me forth with equal strength. I thought again, as I ran along down here on the dark ground, like the moon up in the sky, that I was very likely mad. It was indeed a maddening situation, suitable for an extravaganza for the theaters of Rome. Here was I, out after a woman whom I loved, and she fleeing before me in the night as fast as her legs would take her, in the belief that I was that same old enemy of hers and mine who had first parted us, and whom I longed to kill. She did not turn her head a single time, and it would have been quite hopeless to shout to her against the wind. Also, we were, both of us, exerting ourselves to our utmost strength in the flight and pursuit; and even at that, going along, as we were, bent double like old people, we could cover only about two miles to the hour. But the strangest thing of all, and the one which worried me most, was how she could possibly take me to be the old Jew. In the streets of Rome and in the room of Andermatt he had been walking very slowly on a stick. I was a young man and a good athlete, and yet she could mistake me for him. He must be, in reality, a devil, or he must have it in his power to dispatch devils on his errands. I began to feel myself as his messenger, sent on by him. Was I, perhaps, without knowing it, already in his power, and was I, against my will, the familiar of the old wizard of Amsterdam?

While all this had been running through my head I had been

gaining on her. And then, spurred on by her nearness, quite mad to catch and hold her, I made a few last long leaps. Suddenly her long cloak, swept backwards, blew against my face, and in the next moment I was at her side, I leaped past her, and, spinning around, stopped her. She ran on straight into my arms and would have fallen had I not caught her. In a moment we were under the wild winter moon, in a tight embrace. Pressed to each other by the elements themselves, we both panted for breath.

Do you know, Mira, it is a great thing, the foolishness of human beings. I had run for my life, sure that the moment I caught her up, my happiness of Rome should be caught again. I do not remember now what I had meant to do—to lift her up, make love to her there, or kill her, perhaps, so that she should not make me unhappy again. I did have one moment of it, too, just as I held her in my arms and felt her breath on my face, and her long-missed form on my own body. That was a very short time to have, surely. Her bonnet, like my hat, had blown off and away. Her upturned face, white as bone, with its big eyes like two pools, was quite close to me. I saw now that she was terrified of me. It was not from the Jew that she had run—it was from me.

Many years later, on crossing the Mediterranean in a storm, I looked, for one moment, into the face of a falcon which had tried many times in vain to hook itself to the rigging of my ship, before it was blown off and down into the sea for good. That was again the face of Olalla in the mountain pass. That bird, too, was wild and mad with fear, broken by overstrain, without hope.

I suppose that I stared at her, just as terrified as she was herself, when I understood, and cried her name into her face two or three times. She herself had no breath left to speak, and I do not know if she heard me.

Now that I was sheltering her from the wind her long dark hair and dark clothes sank down all around her. She seemed to change her form, and to be transformed into a pillar in my arms. After we had stood there for a little while I said to her: "Why do you run away from me?" She looked at me. "Who are you?" she said at last. I held her closer to me and kissed her twice. Her face was quite cold and fresh. She stood still and let me kiss her. It might as well have been the snowflakes and the wild air pressing themselves upon her lips as my face and mouth. "Olalla," I said, "I have sought you all over this world my whole life. Can we not be together here now?"

"I am all alone here," she said after a little time. "You frightened me. Who are you?"

By this time I had been chased all around the compass, and thought that it might be enough just for the present. So I stood still to think the situation over. I could not leave her alone in the night and wind. I released her a little, still supporting her with my right arm.

"Madame," I said, "I am an Englishman, traveling in these cursed mountains. My name is Lincoln Forsner. It is not right that a lady should be out alone on this bad road, at this time of the night. If you will therefore allow me to escort you to the monastery I shall feel much honored."

This she thought over, and she seemed to lean with a good grace on my arm. But she said: "I cannot possibly walk any farther."

It was clear that she could not. If I had not held her she would have fallen. What were we to do? She herself looked all around her, and up at the moon. When she had regained her balance a little, she said: "Let me rest a little. Let us sit down here and rest ourselves; then I can go with you to the monastery."

I looked around for a place of shelter, and saw one that was not too bad, close to where we stood, under a great rock which projected over the road. The snow had been whirled in there, but into the hook of it the wind could not quite get. It was perhaps ten yards away. I led or carried her to that place. I took off my cloak, and the muffler with which the Baron had come near to strangling me, and made her as comfortable as I could. The night grew clearer at the same time. The whole great landscape was quite white and bright, except when from time to time a cloud passed over the moon. I sat beside her, and hoped that we might be left in peace for a little, up here.

Olalla sat close to me, her shoulder even touching mine, calm and perfectly friendly. I felt again the same thing about her that I have talked of before: that pain and suffering did not affect her, but that all things were in some way the same to her. She sat in the cold, waste, mountain pass as a little girl would sit in a flower meadow, her skirt filled with the flowers she had picked.

After a time I said to her: "What brings you up in these mountains, Madame? I am traveling myself in search of something, but I have no luck. I wanted, also, to assist you, and am sorry that I frightened you, because it makes it more difficult for me to be of any help."

"Yes," she said, after a silence, "it is not easy to live, for any of you. That was so, too, with Madame Nanine. She wanted to keep her girls well disciplined, and at the same time she did not like to crush our spirits, for then we should have been no good to the house."

"Madame Nanine was the woman who ran the house in Rome of which I have spoken. This she said to me in a friendly way, as if to show me a courtesy. She evidently thought that since I had been kind enough to admit that she was a perfect stranger to me, she would make me a return by admitting that we had known each other long ago.

I said to her: "It is only here that it is so cold. Tomorrow, when you descend the pass, you will meet the spring winds. In Italy it is spring now, and in Rome, I think, the swallows are back."

"Is it spring there?" she said. "No, not yet. But it will be soon, and that will be very pleasant to you, who are so young."

"Do you know, Mira," Lincoln said, interrupting himself in his tale, "that this is the first time that I have thought at all of that hour up there? I only remember it now step by step, so to say, as

I tell you of it. I do not know why I have not thought of it before. Does this moon remember it perhaps? She was there, too."

"Madame," I said to her, "if we were now in my own country I should prepare for you a drink, when we arrive at a house, which would revive you—yes, and ginger should be hot in the mouth, too." I described to her our strong spirits and how one comes home on a winter day, with fingers and toes frozen, and drinks them in front of the fire. We came to talk about drinks and food, and of how we should manage if we were left up here forever. It was pleasant that here one could speak and be heard without shouting. Altogether, this cave under the rock was very much like a house to her and me, such as we had never before owned between us. It seemed to me that everything would fit in well here, that even my father, could I have conjured forth his ghost, would have joined us with pleasure and pride. She did not say much, but laughed a little at me. Neither did I speak all the time. We sat there, I believe, for three-quarters of an hour or so. I knew that it would be dangerous to go to sleep.

Just then I caught sight of a light on the road, and of two doleful figures advancing in it, pausing from time to time. It was Pilot, dead tired and sore from his climb, with the Baron leaning on his arm and limping along the heavy road in the moonlight. I learned afterward that the Swede had sprained his ankle in his fall, and that Pilot, coming up behind him, had helped him up and assisted him. The Baron had sent the other back to take off the one lantern which was then still burning on Olalla's coach. This they carried with them, with much trouble, and they were both benumbed with the cold.

My bad luck had it that they stopped to gather up strength to go on with their journey, and put down their lantern on the ground just beside our refuge. Pilot did not see us; he never saw anything of the world around him. But the Baron, even limping, his face white with pain, was watchful and quick of eye as a lynx.

He turned around, pulling Pilot with him. I had got up at the sight of them. I thought that it might perhaps be as well that they had come; they might help me to bring Olalla to the house.

I do not think that the Baron wanted to fight me once more, but he was in a rage against me. It was probably always difficult to get him out in a fight with anyone as strong as himself. But here he felt, I think, that he had got Pilot with him. He must have described our encounter to him, and made me out a madman or dead drunk.

"Hullo," he cried, "the chase is up and the Englishman has won. He has improved the occasion at once, and that at ten degrees of frost. We ought not to have told him of so many attractions. He has seen only the women of his own country till now, and we drove him mad straight away. Let us have a look at the lady now ourselves, Fritz."

They looked like two big birds of ill omen as they came upon us. Pilot had turned the lantern around, so that the light fell upon Olalla. She had got up, and stood by my side, but she did not lean upon me at all now.

The Baron stared at her. So did Pilot. "So it is you, indeed, my sainted Rosalba," said the former, "pausing a moment on your way to heaven. I wish you luck in the more pleasant career."

I could see that at his words Olalla could with difficulty keep from laughing. In fact every time she looked at the Swede she was tempted to laugh. But she was very pale, and with every minute she grew paler.

Now Pilot, who had been holding the lantern, and had stood as if he was himself blinded by the light, made a step nearer to us and stared into her face. "Madame Lola," he cried, "is it you?"

"No, that is not I," said she. "You are making a mistake."

This confused Pilot terribly. He pulled his hair. I believed that he would go mad then and there. "Do not deceive me, I beg you," he said, "tell me who you are, then."

"That would not mean anything to you," she said. "I do not know you at all."

"I know that you are angry with me," he cried, "for having told our story to other people. But I did not know what to do. Indeed, since I saw you last, I have not known what to do at all. I am unhappy, Madame Lola. Tell me who you are."

By the light of the lantern I saw that Olalla's clothes were stiff and shining with frozen snow, her shoes thickly covered with it. But still I did not drag her away, but stood on and listened.

Suddenly Pilot dropped on his knees, in the snow, before her. "Madame Lola," he cried, "save me. You are the only person in the world who can do it. Those weeks of Lucerne were the only time of my life that I have been happy. And all the things which I was to do! I myself have forgotten what they were. Tell me who you are!"

The Baron snatched the lantern, which Pilot had dropped, and held it high. I think that he was upset at seeing his partner brought so low. "That Madame Rosalba," he cried, *"elle se moque des gens!* I was told that from the first. But not for a long time of little Arvid Guildenstern. That holy lady has on her back a little brown mole. We can find out quickly enough about that, between us, to know who she is."

Again I saw Olalla restrain herself from laughing at him. But she spoke to Pilot gently. "If I had ever known you," she said to him, "I should have done you no harm. I should have tried to give you a little pleasure. But I do not know you. Now let me go."

She turned to me, slowly, and looked at me, as if she were confident that I would be on her side. So I should have been, against all the world, ten minutes before, but it is extraordinary how quickly one is corrupted in bad company. When I heard these other people talking of their old acquaintance with her, I myself, who stood so much closer than the others, turned toward her, staring into her face. "Tell them," I cried. "Tell them who you are!"

She gave me a great dark and radiant look, then turned her eyes off me and looked up at the moon. A long shiver ran through her body.

"We shall put an end to the mystery," cried the Baron, "when we get hold of your old Jew. He seems to have held the paint-cup to all your disguises."

"Of whom are you talking?" said Olalla, laughing a little, "there is no old Jew here."

"But not far off," said the Baron, "we shall all be together at the monastery."

At this she stood quite still, like a statue. And this stillness of hers, toward the others, was intolerable to me. "I will chase these two away for you," I said to her, "but this once tell me only the truth— Who are you?"

She did not turn, or look at me. But the next moment she did what I had always feared that she might do: she spread out her wings and flew away. Below the round white moon she made one great movement, throwing herself away from us all, and the wind caught her and spread out her clothes. I have said already that on her flight from me up the hill she had looked like some big bird which runs to catch the wind and get on the wing. Now again she behaved exactly like a black martin when you see it throw itself out from a slope or a roof to get off the ground and take flight. For one second she seemed to lift herself up with the wind, then, running straight across the road, with all her might she threw herself from the earth clear into the abyss, and disappeared from our sight.

I had had no time to try to stop her, and for a moment I meant to follow her. But standing on the brink of the precipice I saw that she had not fallen far, but onto a sort of projection about twenty feet down. She seemed in the dim light to be lying on her face, all covered by her large cloak.

I found Pilot weeping aloud at my side, and together the three of us worked for an hour or more to bring her up. We cut our cloaks by the light of the lantern, knotting the strips together. When we had finished we hung the lantern out over the edge of the road. Our task was made more difficult for us, first by the lantern suddenly going out, as the candle within it burnt down, and then by the snow, which started to fall again.

The first time that they lowered me down, I missed the terrace and kept hanging in the air. Finally I found my foothold on it, and touched her. She seemed quite without life. Her head fell back as I lifted it, like the head of a dead flower, but still her body was not quite cold. I tried to make fast the rope around her, but it would not do. As they dragged her up, her body beat against the rocks in a dreadful manner. I had to shout to the others and to lift her back into my arms. The terrace on which we stood was narrow and covered with thick snow. It was not easy to move about on it. The great gulf was below us, and once or twice I despaired of getting her up. I thought then of how it had been my question to her which had driven her into this great white full-moon death, in the end.

At last I managed to make a sort of noose in which to place my one foot, and to make fast her body to mine somehow, and I cried to the others to draw us up. This they did more quickly and easily than I had thought they could do it. As they loosened her from me, and I fell down flat, unable to hold myself up, I heard many voices around us, crying out that she was not dead.

When again I could lift my head I saw, without surprise, the old Jew of Rome, Amsterdam and Andermatt, with our party. It seemed to me natural that he should have come up with us. His coach was standing on the road, and his coachman and valet had helped to draw up Olalla and me. How he had ever managed to get his heavy carriage along in the night, on that road, I do not know; only to a Jew anything is possible.

They lifted Olalla into the carriage, and the Jew made me come in with her, as I was bleeding at the hands and knees. I sat there with him, holding her feet, and remembering how I had first met him in the street of Rome. I was very thirsty and cold, for I had been wet with sweat, and the night air went to my bones. At last we got to the large square stone building of the monastery, from a couple of windows of which light was shining out. People came out to meet us.

Here I had some hot wine to drink, and my hands washed. When I then inquired about Olalla, they showed me into a large room, where on a table two candles were burning.

Olalla was lying, as immovable as before, upon a stretcher which they had placed on the floor. I think that they had meant to carry her somewhere, but had given it up. They had only loosened her clothes. A large fur rug, which belonged to the Jew, was spread over her. Her head was slightly turned upon the pillow, and a dark shadow covered the one side of her face.

The old Jew sat on a chair near her, still in his furred cloak and with his tall hat on his head, his chin resting on the button of his walking stick. He did not take his dark eyes off her face, and hardly moved. I was surprised, on looking at a big clock in the room, to find that it was only three hours after midnight.

I sat down myself, for a long time without speaking. As then the clock struck, I made up my mind to speak to the Jew. If I had killed Olalla by my question, I might as well get an answer now, and he would know. I talked to him a little, and he answered me very civilly. I then told him all that I knew about her, and asked him, while we were waiting here, to tell me of her. For a time he did not seem to want to speak. Then in the end he spoke with much energy. Pilot and the Baron were in there too. Pilot came up from his chair at the other end of the room to look at her, and went back again. The Baron had fallen asleep in his chair. Later on, however, he woke up and joined us.

"I have indeed," said the Jew, "known this woman at a time when all the world knew her and worshiped her by her real name. She was the opera singer, Pellegrina Leoni."

At first these words meant nothing to me, so that there was a silence. But then my memory woke up, and recalled to me my childhood.

"Why," I cried, "that is not possible. That great singer was the star of whom my father and mother used to rave. When they came back from Italy they would talk of nothing else. And I well remember their tears when she was hurt at the theater fire of Milan, and died. But all this must have been when I was ten years old, thirteen years ago."

"No," said the Jew. "Yes, she died. The great opera singer died. Thirteen years ago, as you rightly say. But the woman lived on, for these thirteen years."

"Explain yourself," I said to him.

"Explain myself?" he repeated. "Young Sir, you are asking much. You might say: 'Disguise your meaning into such phrases as I am used to hear, which mean nothing.' Pellegrina was, at the theater fire of Milan, badly hurt. From the injuries and the shock she lost her voice. She never sang a note again as long as she lived."

It was clear to me, as he spoke, that this was the first time that he had ever given words to this story. I was so much impressed by his suffering and terror at his own words that I could find nothing to say, even though I wanted to hear more, for I found no explanation in his statement. But Pilot asked him: "Did she, then, not die?"

"Die, live. Live, die," said the Jew. "She lived as much as any of you, or more."

"Still," Pilot said, "all the world believed her to be dead."

"She made it believe that," said the Jew. "We—she and I—took much trouble to make it believe so. I saw her grave filled. I erected a monument upon it."

"Were you her lover?" the Baron asked.

"No," said the old Jew with great pride and contempt. "No, I have seen her lovers running about, yapping around her, flattering and fighting. No. I was her friend. When at the gate of paradise the keeper shall ask me: 'Who are you?' I shall give that great angel no name, no position or deed of mine in the world to be recognized by, but I shall answer him: 'I am the friend of Pellegrina Leoni.' You, who killed her now, as you have told me, by asking her who she was—when in your time you are asked, on the other side of the grave, 'Who are you?'—what will you have to answer? You will have, before the face of God, to give your names, as at the Hotel of Andermatt."

Pilot, at these words, seemed ill at ease; he wanted to speak, but thought better of it.

"Now, young gentlemen," said the old Jew, "leave me to tell this tale at my pleasure. Listen well, for there will be no such tale again.

"All my life I have been a very rich man. I inherited great fortunes from my father and mother, and from their people, who were all great traders. Also, for the first forty years of my life I was a very unhappy man, such as you yourselves are. I traveled much. I had always been fond of music. I was even a composer, and composed and arranged ballets, for which I had a liking. For twenty years I kept my own *corps du ballet,* to perform my works before me and my friends, or before me alone. I had a staff of thirty young girls, none more than seventeen, whom my own ballet master taught, and who used to dance naked before me."

The Baron woke up to attention, and grinned kindly at the old man. "You were not bored," he said.

"Why not?" asked the old Jew. "I was, on the contrary terribly bored, bored to death. I might very well then have died from boredom, had I not happened to hear, upon a small theater stage of Venice, Pellegrina Leoni, who was then sixteen years old. Then I understood the meaning of heaven and earth, of the stars, life and death, and eternity. She took you out to walk in a rose garden, filled with nightingales, and then, the moment she wanted·to, she rose and lifted you with her, higher than the moon. Had you ever been frightened of anything, miserable creature that you were,

she made you feel as safe, above the abyss, as in your own chair.
Like a young shark in the sea, mastering the strong green waters
by a strike of her fins, thus did she swim along within the depths
and mysteries of the great world. Your heart would melt at the
sound of her voice, till you thought: This is too much; the sweetness is killing me, and I cannot stand it. And then you found yourself on your knees, weeping over the unbelievable love and generosity of the Lord God, who had given you such a world as this.
It was all a great miracle."

I felt a great compassion for this old Jew, who had to pour out
his heart to us. He had not talked of these things till now; and
now that he had begun he could not stop himself. His long delicate nose threw a sad shadow upon the whitewashed wall.

"I had the honor, as I have said," he went on, "to become her
friend. I bought for her a villa near Milan. When she was not
traveling, she stayed there, and had many friends around her, and
sometimes also we were alone together, and then used to laugh
much at the world, and to walk arm in arm in the gardens in the
afternoons and evenings.

"She turned to me as a child to its mother. She gave me many
pet names, and she used to take my fingers and play with them,
telling me that I had the finest hands in the world, hands made to
handle only diamonds. As we had first met in Venice, and as my
name was Marcus, she used to call herself my lioness. That was
what she was: a winged lioness. I alone, of all people, knew her.

"She had in her life two great, devouring passions, which meant
everything to her proud heart.

"The first was her passion for the great soprano, Pellegrina
Leoni. This was a zealous, a terribly jealous love, such as that of
one of your priests for the miracle-working image of the Virgin,
which he attends, or of a woman for her husband, who is a hero,
or of a diamond-cutter for the purest diamond that has ever been
found. In her relation to this idol she had no forbearance and
no rest. She gave no mercy, and she asked for none. She worked

in the service of Pellegrina Leoni like a slave under the whip, weeping, dying at times, when it was demanded of her.

"She was a devil to the other women of the opera, for she needs must have all the parts for Pellegrina. She was indignant because it was impossible for her to perform two rôles within the same opera. They called her Lucifera there. More than one time she boxed the ears of a rival on the stage. Both old and young singers were constantly in tears when acting with her. And for all this she had no cause whatever, she was so absolutely the star of all the heavens of music. It was not only, either, in regard to her voice that she was jealous of Pellegrina Leoni's honor. She meant Pellegrina to be, likewise, the most beautiful, elegant, and fashionable of women, and in this connection she was fairly ridiculous in her vanity. On the stage she would wear none but real jewels, and the most magnificent attire. She would appear in the rôle of Agatha, a village maiden, all covered with diamonds and with a train three yards long. She drank nothing but water for fear of spoiling the complexion of Pellegrina. And were a prince or a cardinal or the pope himself to call on her before noon, she would meet him with her hair done up in curling pins, and her face covered with zinc cream, so that in the evening she might sweep the floor with all the other women, not only of the stage but of the parquet and boxes as well—and she had the most brilliant audiences of all the world. It was the fashion to adore Pellegrina Leoni. The greatest people of Italy, Austria, Russia, and Germany thronged to her *salons*. And she was pleased about it; she liked to see them all at Pellegrina's feet. But she would be rude to the Czar of Russia himself, and risk a sojourn in Siberia, before she would give up her own repertoire or her regular hours of practice.

"And the other great passion, young gentlemen, of this great heart was her love for her audience. And that was not for the great people, the proud princes and magnates and the lovely ladies, all in jewels; not even for the famous composers, musicians, critics, and men of letters, but for her galleries. Those poor people of the back streets and market places, who would give up a meal or a pair of shoes, the wages of hard labor, to crowd high up in the hot house and hear Pellegrina sing, and who stamped the floor, shrieked and wept over her—she loved them beyond everything in the world. This second passion of hers was as mighty as the first, but it was as gentle as the love of God, or of your Virgin, for the world. You people of the North, you do not know the women of the South and the East when they love. When they embrace their children, and weep over their dead, they are like holy flames When, after the first performance of *Medée,* the people of the town outspanned the horses of my carriage, in which she was driving, to draw it themselves, she did not look at the Ducas who put their noble shoulders to the task. No, she wept a rain of warm tears, more precious than diamonds, she lifted a rainbow of sweet smiles, over the streetsweepers, the carriers, the fruitsellers and watermen of Milan. She would have died for them. I was with her in the carriage, and she held my hand. She was not herself the child of very poor people. She was a baker's daughter, and her mother, the child of a Spanish farmer. I do not know where she had caught her passion for those lowest in the world. It was not exactly for them alone that she sang, for she wanted the applause of the great connoisseurs as well; but she wanted that for the sake of her galleries. She grieved for them when times were hard and they were suppressed. She would give them all her money and sell her clothes for them. It was curious that they never begged much of her, as if they had realized that she had given them the best she had to give when she sang to them. Had they asked her, they should have had all. Her gardens and her house were open to them, and she would sit with the children of the poor under the oleander trees of her terraces when she refused to receive great lords of England, who had crossed the sea to see her.

"In the relation between these two great passions of hers lay all her happiness. During the years of her triumphs it was perfect. Her voice and her art grew more wonderful every day. It was an incredible thing. I myself do not hold that she had, at the time of her fall, reached the fulfillment of her possibilities. The world rang with her name. She held in her little hand the philosopher's stone of music, which turned everything that she touched into gold. You, Sir," he said, turning to me, "have told me how, in far countries, people wept at the remembrance of that deep river of gold, of those tall cascades of diamonds, sapphires, and pigeon-blood rubies. And she was adored by the people. They felt that as long as Pellegrina was singing to them, on the stage, the earth had not been abandoned by the angels.

"This, then—that Pellegrina should sing like an angel to her galleries, to melt their hearts and make them shed tears of heavenly joy, and to make them forget all the hardships of their existence, and remember the lost paradise; that she should scatter her soul over them, like a swarm of stars, and that they, on their side, should worship Pellegrina as a Madonna of their own, and the manifestation upon earth of God in his heaven, and to them all that was lovely, great, elegant, and brilliant—in this was her happiness.

"Even when she played, as I have told you, the village maidens of the opera, all in brocades and plumes, it was not from personal vanity either. It was as much from a feeling of duty to her galleries, just as the priests of your churches will deck out the image of the Virgin in the most elegant clothes that they can find. Within the pictures of the Nativity themselves, where all are moved by the sight of the Mother and child of God in the stables, on straw, and with a crib for a cradle, the priest cannot bear to see the Virgin poorly dressed, but adorns her in silks, and hangs gold chains on her.

"I myself smiled at this passion of hers for the poor, for to me the common people have always smelled badly, and I have no conviction of their virtue. 'Oh, must we all be cut to the same pattern,' she asked me then, 'and be sinners worshiping the divinities?

Come, let me be what I am, Marcus, and choose to be. Let me be a divinity worshiping the sinners.'

"As to her lovers, I knew most of them, and they meant very little either to her or me. In fact, until she got used to them, they caused her more grief than pleasure.

"For she was ever in life, in spite of her excellent good sense, a Donna Quixotta de la Mancha. The phenomena of life were not great enough for her; they were not in proportion with her own heart. She was like a man who has been given an elephant gun and is asked to shoot little birds. Or like a great bird, an albatross, asked to hop and twitter with the little birds within an aviary. When she was hurt in her love affairs, it was not her vanity which was wounded. For outside of the stage she had none of it, and she knew well herself that the young men were not making love to the great soprano, but to the lovely woman of fashion, with eyes like two stars, and the grace of those gentle and wise gazelles of which a countryman of mine has written poems. On that account she took their shallowness and falsity lightly. But she was badly hurt and disappointed because the world was not a much greater place than it is, and because nothing more colossal, more like the dramas of the stage, took place in it, not even when she herself went into the show with all her might.

"She came back from these first love affairs of hers, when she was still a very young girl, even a little ashamed of herself. She would then, I think, have liked to become a man, and saw no sense in being a woman. For in all this splendor of woman's beauty, the magnificence of bosom and limb, and radiance of eye, of lip, and flesh, she was like a lady who has put on her richest attire to meet the prince at a great ball, only to find that what she has been invited to is a homely gathering in honor of the police magistrate, at which everyday clothes are worn. Such ladies also feel a little ashamed, and drag their long trains and *rivières* of diamonds along with anger and bashfulness, feeling that they are likely, in this place, to put them to ridicule.

"I should think," said the old Jew, "that many women, in their love affairs, must feel like that.

"In these hours of trouble she would turn to me, sure of my understanding. The world would have laughed at her, had it been at all possible for the vulgar and the unimaginative to recognize in one so beautiful and rich the traits of the knight of the woeful countenance. But I could not help laughing at her, as it was. I said to her: 'To the world, and to your lovers as part of it, the whole doctrine of love, and in fact of all human intercourse, presents itself under the aspect of toxicology, the science of poisons and counterpoisons. They are all of them prepared for and adjusted to poisons. They are like little vipers or scorpions, proud of their bite, and proof against poison proportionate to their own virulence. To most of them love is a mutual distribution of poisons and counterpoisons, and in the course of a long career of love affairs they pride themselves on having become immune to all poisons, as natives of India are said to train themselves to become immune to the venom of all snakes. But you, Pellegrina, are no venomous snake, but a python. Very often, in your walk, you recall to me the dancing snakes which I was once shown by an Indian snake-charmer. But you have no poison whatever in you, and if you kill it is by the force of your embrace. This quality upsets your lovers, who are familiar with little vipers, and who have neither the strength to resist you, nor the wisdom to value the sort of death which they might obtain with you. And, in fact, the sight of you unfolding your great coils to revolve around, impress yourself upon, and finally crush a meadow mouse is enough to split one's side with laughter.' In this way I used to make her laugh, even through her tears.

"However, as she was so intelligent, and had been trained by my intelligence, it was she who learned from her lovers, and in the end these matters meant no more to her than to them. For this I owed the young men much thanks. For they had assisted her to achieve a lightness in such things which was not hers by birth.

From the time that she had taken their lessons to heart, she reached perfection, on the stage, in the part of the young innocent girl in love."

"And this," said Lincoln, interrupting the tale, "you will yourself know to be true, Mira. You remember the old immortal song of the young maiden who refuses all the gifts of the Sultan to be true to her lover, which begins: *Ah Rupia, kama na Majasee.* It is a very lovely song about true and pure love. Only a whore has ever sung it well, that I know of."

He then returned to the story told by the old Jew:

"Thus did we live," the old Jew went on, "in the white villa of Milan, until the day of her disaster.

"Young men, you remember your fathers weeping over this Tuesday. It happened during a performance of *Don Giovanni,* in the second act, where Donna Anna comes on the stage, with Ottavio's letter in her hand, and begins the recitative: *Crudele? Ah nò, mio bene! Troppo mi spiace allontanarti un ben che lungamente la nostr' alma desia.* Just as Pellegrina entered, two or three bits of flaming wood fell down from the ceiling in front of her. She had a brave heart; she just steadily went on, gazing up a little only, taking the high note as easily as she breathed. But a whole burning beam followed, and the entire theater rose up in a panic, the orchestra stopping in the middle of a measure. People rushed to the doors, and women fainted. Pellegrina took a step back and looked around until her eyes met mine, where I sat in the front row of the parquet. Yes, she looked for me in that moment of despair. And have I no cause to be proud? She was not at all frightened. She stood there quite calm, as if she meant to say: 'Here we are to die together now, you and I, Marcus.' But I, I was afraid. I dared not force my way up onto that flaming stage, where all the trees, and the houses of the streets, were cardboard only. At that same moment, as a great cloud of smoke wafted out from the one wing of the stage to the other, and the heat struck out like the breath of a great furnace, she was hidden from my eyes. I ran along with the crowd and got out somehow, and in the street, which was like a madhouse, the cold air met me again. My servant, who had been waiting for me in the hall, held me up. We were informed then that Pellegrina had been saved by the man who sang the part of Leporelle, and whom she had helped in his career. He had carried her with him all through the burning wing, and down the stairs, her hair and her clothes all aflame. The people, when they heard that she was saved, fell on their knees.

"I brought her to her house, and collected the doctors of Milan around her, and she lived. She had been struck by a falling beam, and had a deep burn, where the smoldering wood had hit her, from the ear to the collar bone. Otherwise her burns were not deep. She recovered from them quickly. But it was found that from the shock she had lost her voice. She would never sing one note again.

"When I think of her as she was this first week after her loss, it seems to me that she had in reality been burned up, and was lying on her side in the bed, immovable, black and charred like those bodies which they have dug up from the burned town of Pompeii. I sat with her for six days, and she did not speak a word. And it seemed to me the most cruel thing amongst them all that the grief of Pellegrina Leoni should be dumb.

"I did not speak to her, either. The carriages of all the world drove up and turned on the paved terrace outside her room, asking for news of her.

"I sat in the darkened room and thought of the case. This to her is, I thought, like what it would be to the priest to find the miracle-working image of the Virgin, which he has served, only a profane, an obscene, pagan idol, hollow and gnawed by rats. Like what it would be to the wife to find her heroic husband no hero, but a lunatic or a clown.

"No, I thought again, it is not like that. I knew the distress to which hers might be compared. The distress of the royal bride, who goes, with a kingdom for her dowry, adorned with the treasures of her father's house, her young bridegroom, a king's son, waiting for her, the city decorated for her welcome, and ringing with cymbals and songs of maidens and youths, and who is ravished by robbers on her way. Yes, it was like that, I thought.

"None of the great people arriving from all parts of the world to inquire about her ever obtained access to her house. From that fact grew the rumor that she lay dying. What would they have said had she let them come in, I wondered. That she was still young and beautiful, and beloved by them all?

"What would those people, I thought, have said to the ravished royal virgin to comfort her? That she was young and lovely still, and that her bridegroom would cherish her? They might have told her that she had no fault, and had done nothing wrong: 'There is no sin in her worthy of death, for he found her in the field, and the betrothed damsel cried, and there was none to save her.' But the consolations of the vulgar are bitter in the royal ear. Let physicians and confectioners and the servants in the great houses be judged by what they have done, and even by what they have meant to do; the great people themselves are judged by what they are. I have been told that lions, trapped and shut up in cages, grieve from shame more than from hunger.

"You must excuse me, gentlemen, if I am talking of things too wonderful for you, things which you understand not. For where do your women keep their honor, in these modern times? Do they know the word even, when they hear it?

"That I did not speak one word of comfort to her, and that no word in the world could have comforted me myself, this made my presence bearable to Pellegrina during this week of ours.

"She grieved for her great name, and the applause of the courts, and for the homage of princes, as that ravished royal virgin would have wept over her splendor, her bridal crown, and the balls and pageants of the wedding festivities. But at the thought of her galleries she wept such tears as the bride would have wept for her royal bridegroom. For how were they to bear the loss of Pellegrina

Leoni? Were they, from now, to live on, day after day, going to their hard work, oppressed and wronged by their masters and the authorities, ill paid, and the heavens never open to them again? And no Madonna in the skies to smile on them? Their one star had fallen; they were left in the dark of the night—the galleries which had laughed and wept with her.

"During that week I learned what a difference there may be, in the length of twenty-four hours, between one month and the next. Here at our house time used to fly lightly, like a May breeze, like butterflies, like a summer shower and rainbow. Now the day was long as a year; the night, as ten years.

"After that first week, Pellegrina asked me to give her some strong poison, with which to shorten her time for good. I had been in the habit, as a young man, of carrying such stuff with me, in case life should become unbearable to me. I was at this time living in Milan, and I used to drive out to her house every day. I handed her the poison at noon on a Wednesday, and she asked me to come back the next afternoon.

"When I came, I found her still very ill. She told me that she had taken the full dose of opium, which I had given her, but that it had had no effect. She could not die. This, although she believed it herself, I know was not the truth. What I had given her could not have failed to kill any human being. She may have taken enough to be ill, perhaps unconscious, and she thought that she had taken it all. Still, this makes no difference. The truth was that, as she had said, she could not die. In one way or another she had too much life in her.

"Afterward I thought that had I at the time killed myself, she might have had the strength to follow me. From what she had said to me from time to time I have it that she had always dreaded death, as a thing too foreign to her nature, and that it had been a comfort to her to think that I, being so much older than she, would be likely to die before she did, and to prepare the way for her, or to receive her in the other world, did such a world exist.

That was one of the reasons why she preferred me to younger and stronger men. But at the time I did not think of that.

"All the same, my powders had worked a change in her. She had done with death. Dead tired, she had risen, in a way, from the dead. On that afternoon, for the first time, she wanted me to talk to her.

"I told her then how, after the long hours of the previous night, just before daybreak, a nightingale had taken to singing, wildly, exuberantly, as if she meant to overtake time, outside my window, and how, listening, I had thought of a ballet which was to take its theme from all the things that had befallen us. Pellegrina listened to this attentively, and in the course of the next day came back to the idea of my ballet, and asked me about the scenario and tunes of it. I told her that I meant it to be called Philomela, and explained to her how the scenes and dances were to follow one another. While we were talking about it she took my hand and played with my fingers. This was the first time since her fall that she had touched any human being.

"A couple of days later she sent for me very early in the morning, before sunrise. I was surprised to find her in the pergola outside her house, up and dressed in a negligee.

"It was a beautiful morning. The acacias and the grass of the garden spread a delicate, fresh, and lovely scent in the clear, somber blue air.

"She looked as she had before her misfortune. Her flower-like face was white in the dim light. But when she began to speak to me her voice was very low, as if she were afraid of waking somebody.

"'I have sent for you so early, Marcus,' she said, 'so that we should have all the day to talk together, if it be necessary.' She took my arm and made me walk up and down with her. As we came to the end of the pergola she stopped and looked, before turning, out over the landscape. The air was very fresh. 'I have much to say to you,' she said. But she did not go on. Only as we came back once more to the same spot, she said the same thing again: 'I have much to say to you, Marcus.'

"At last we sat down on a seat in the pergola. She did not release my arm, so we sat there side by side, as in a carriage.

"'You think, Marcus,' she said, 'that I have not thought of anything all these days, but you are mistaken. Only it is not easy to tell you of it, for these little thoughts of mine, I have fetched them from far, far away. Be patient, we have all the day.

"'You see, Marcus,' she went on, still speaking very softly, 'I have come to see, now, that I have been very selfish. I have always thought of Pellegrina, Pellegrina. What has happened to her, that has seemed to me terribly important, the most important thing in all the world. The people who loved Pellegrina, those only, I thought, were the kind, good people of the world, and it seemed to me that the only sensible thing that any wise person could do was to go and hear Pellegrina Leoni sing.' Again she sat silent, pressing my arm a little.

"'Even this disaster of mine,' she said suddenly, 'had it happened to someone else—say now, Marcus, to a soprano of China, of the Imperial Opera of China, a hundred years ago—we might have heard of it, and not have thought much about it, or wept many tears over it. Still, it would have been as sad and as terrible. But because it happened to Pellegrina, it seemed to us too cruel to bear. This, my Marcus, it need not be, and it shall not be so for us again.

"'Wait,' she said. 'I shall explain everything better to you.

"'Pellegrina is dead,' she said. 'Was she not a great singer, a star? You remember the song:

"'*A light of glory is put out,*
High from the sky a star has fallen. . . .

"'It was so with her; her death was a great sorrow to the world. Oh, sad, sad. You must now help me to tell the world of her death; you must make the grave of Pellegrina, and have a monument erected upon it. Do not put up a very splendid statue, such as we should have chosen had I died and never lost my voice, but still a marble plate, to give the name and the dates of her birth and her death. Put a short inscription upon it as well. Put this, Marcus: *By the grace of God.* Yes, *By the grace of God,* Marcus.'

"'Pellegrina is dead,' she said once more. 'Nobody, nobody must ever be Pellegrina again. To have her once more upon the stage of life, of this hard world, and to have such awful things happen to her as do happen to people on the earth—no, that must not be thought of. No human being could stand the thought. Now, you will promise me that, first of all?' she asked me.

"I said that I would do as she wished.

"She rose again, and went to the end of the pergola. It was getting lighter now; the last pale stars had gone; all the world around us was wet with dew, and the grass, which had been dark until now, was shining like silver with it. There was a great clarity in the air, as if the sky were lifting itself high above the earth. Pellegrina stood close to me. Her clothes were moist with dew. She played with her long dark tresses, drawing one of them along between her lips, and she shivered a little in the morning air. From this end of the pergola the ground sloped down; a great landscape lay far beneath us; now we could distinguish the roads, the fields, and the trees within it. Below us, on the road, we saw some workmen and women going out into the fields.

"'Look,' she said. 'I have waited for them, to explain things to you. It is easier for you to understand when you can see. See, there is a woman going out to her work in the fields. Perhaps she is a peasant's wife; perhaps her name is Maria. She is happy this morning, because her husband is good to her and has given her a coral necklace. Or perhaps she is unhappy, because he worries her with his jealousy. Well, what do we think of that, Marcus, you and I? A woman named Maria is unhappy, we think. There will always be such women here and there around us, and we do not think very much of it. Look, there is another, going the other way. She is taking vegetables and fruit to Milan, on her donkey, and she is annoyed because that donkey is so old, and can walk only very slowly, so that she will be late at the market. Nor of that do we think much, Marcus. Oh, I will be that now. The time has come for me to be that: a woman called one name or another. And if she is unhappy we shall not think a great deal about it.'

"We stood there in silence, and I tried to follow her thoughts.

"'And if,' she said, 'I come to think very much of what happens to that one woman, why I shall go away, at once, and be someone else: a woman who makes lace in the town, or who teaches children to read, or a lady traveling to Jerusalem to pray at the Holy Sepulcher. There are many that I can be. If they are happy or unhappy, or if they are fools or wise people, those women, I shall not think a great deal about that. Neither will you, if you hear about it. I will not be one person again, Marcus, I will be always many persons from now. Never again will I have my heart and my whole life bound up with one woman, to suffer so much. It is terrible to me to think of it even. That, you see, I have done long enough. I cannot be asked to do it any more. It is all over.'

"'And you, Marcus,' she said, 'you have given me many things; now I shall give you this good advice. Be many people. Give up this game of being one and of being always Marcus Cocoza. You have worried too much about Marcus Cocoza, so that you have been really his slave and his prisoner. You have not done anything without first considering how it would affect Marcus Cocoza's happiness and prestige. You were always much afraid that Marcus might do a stupid thing, or be bored. What would it really have mattered? All over the world people are doing stupid things, and many people are bored, and we have always known about it. Give up being Marcus Cocoza now; then what difference does it make to the world if one more person, one old Jew, does a stupid thing, or is bored for a day or two? I should like you to be easy, your little heart to be light again. You must, from now, be more than one, many people, as many as you can think of. I feel, Marcus—I am sure—that all people in the world ought to be, each of them, more than one, and they would all, yes, all of them, be more easy at heart. They would have a little fun. Is it not strange that no philosopher has thought of this, and that I should hit upon it?'

"I thought over what she said, and wondered whether it would be likely to do me any good. But I knew that it would not be possible for me to follow this advice of hers while she was still alive. Were she dead I might find refuge in her whim. The moon must follow the earth, but if the earth were to split and evaporate, it might perhaps swing itself free of its dependency, and be, in an unfettered flight in the ether, for a short time the moon of Jupiter, and for another, that of Venus. I do not know enough about astronomy to tell. I leave it to you, who may have more insight into the science.

"'What a lovely morning,' said Pellegrina. 'One thinks that it is dark still, but really the air is as filled with light as a glassful of wine. How wet everything is. But soon all the world will be dry again, and it will be hot on the roads. It does not matter to us. We shall be here together all day.'

"'And what do you want me to do?' I asked her.

"She sat for a very long time in deep silence.

"'Yes, Marcus,' she said, 'we must part. Tonight I am going away.'

"'Shall we not meet again?' I asked.

"She put her finger on her lips. 'You must never speak to me,' she said, 'if we ever happen to meet. You once knew Pellegrina, you know.'

"'Let me,' I said, 'follow you, and be near you, so that you can send for me if ever you want a friend to help you.'

"'Yes, do that,' she said. 'Be near me, Marcus, so that if ever anyone should mistake me for Pellegrina Leoni, I can get hold of you, and you can help me to get away. Be never far off, so that you can always keep the name of Pellegrina away from me. But speak to me you must never, Marcus. I could not hear your voice without remembering the divine voice of Pellegrina, and her great triumphs, and this house, where we stand now, and the garden.' She looked around at the house as if it were a thing which no longer existed.

" 'Oh, the currents of life are cold, Pellegrina,' I said.

"She laughed a little in the morning air, then became again very still. 'The swallows are cruising about now,' she said. 'What,' she said after a moment, 'do you think of this paradise that they talk about? Is it anywhere, really? There we two shall walk again into this house, and the paradise-winds shall lift the curtains a little. There it is spring, and the swallows are back, and everything is forgiven.'

"She went away," said the old Jew, "as she had said, upon the evening of that day.

"I have never spoken to her since," he said, "but she has written to me from time to time, to make me help her when she wanted to get away and to change from one thing into another. In Rome, if you had not"—he turned to me—"told her that your father was an enthusiast for the Italian opera, she would have gone with you to England. But only for a year or two. She would have left you again. She would never let herself become tied up in any of her rôles."

Thus the old man finished his tale. He looked around at us, then quieted down again, rested his chin upon the golden button of his walking stick, and sank into deep thought, always watching the face of the dying woman on the stretcher.

We three, who had been listening to him, sat on in silence, feeling, I should say, a little sheepish, all of us.

Lincoln himself, here, fell into a reverie, and for some time said nothing.

And I ought to tell you here, now, Mira, that afterward in life my friend Pilot took the advice of Pellegrina Leoni.

It is like this: I do not now quite remember whether, many years later, I met, at the Cape of Good Hope, an elderly German clergyman, by the name of Pastor Rosenquist, who, while we were discussing the strangeness of human nature, recounted to me this tale of my friend, or whether I amused myself, many years later, by imagining that I had met, at the Cape of Good Hope, a German clergyman who told me all this about him.

But there it is, in any case. Pilot followed her advice, and took to being more than one person. From time to time he withdrew from the hard and hopeless task of being Friederich Hohenemser and took on the existence of a small landowner in a far district, by the name of Fridolin Emser. He surrounded this second existence of his with the greatest secrecy, and let nobody know what he was doing. He felt, when he got away, as if he were running for his life, and he cuddled up in Fridolin's little house, outside a village, like an animal safe in his den. Had anyone become suspicious of him and followed up the track which he took such pains to cover, to find out what, in the end, he did in his concealment, he would have found that Pilot as Emser did absolutely nothing. He looked after his little place with care, collected day by day a little money for Fridolin, and sat of an evening in the arbor of his garden, beneath a blackbird in a cage, smoking his long pipe; or sometimes he would go and drink beer in the inn, and discuss politics with friendly people. Here he was happy. For since he himself, from the beginning, knew Fridolin to be nonexistent, he was never worried by efforts to make him exist. The one thing which troubled him was that he dared not remain too long in his holiday existence for fear that it might put on too much weight, and tilt him over. He had to return to the country place of the Hohenemsers. But even Friederich Hohenemser was happier after he had begun to follow the plan of Pellegrina, for a secret in his life was an asset to him as well as to Fridolin.

I do not know if, in any of his existences, he married. The marriage of Friederich Hohenemser would have been bound to be miserably unhappy, and I would have pitied the woman who had to drag him along with her in it; but Fridolin might well have married and given his wife a peaceful and pleasant time. For he would not have been occupied all the time in proving to her that he really existed, which is the curse of many wives, but might have quietly enjoyed seeing her existing. I do not know why it should be so, but whenever I think of Pilot now, I picture him under an umbrella—he who was so exposed, once, to all weathers. Beneath this shelter the sun shall not smite him by day, nor the moon by night.

Shaking himself out of these reflections, Lincoln resumed his account of the old Jew's tale:

Suddenly a violent change came over the face of the old Jew. It was as if we, to whom he had just lately recounted the story of his life, had all at once been annihilated. Lowering his stick, he bent forward, his whole being concentrated on Pellegrina's face.

She stirred upon her couch. Her bosom heaved, and she moved her head slightly on the pillow. A tremor ran over her face; after a minute her brows lifted a little, and the fringes of her dark eyelids quivered, like the wings of a butterfly that sits on a flower. We had all got up. Again I looked at the Jew. It was obvious that he was terrified lest she should see him, in case she opened her eyes. He shrank back and took shelter behind me. The next second she slowly looked up. Her eyes seemed supernaturally large and somber.

In spite of the Jew's move to hide himself, her gaze fell straight upon him. He stood quite still under it, deadly pale as if he feared an outburst of abhorrence. But none came. She looked at him attentively, neither smiling nor frowning. At this I heard him drawing in his breath twice, deeply, in a sort of suspense. Then he timidly approached a little.

She tried to speak two or three times, without getting a sound out, and again closed her eyes. But once more she opened them, looking again straight at him. When she spoke it was in her ordinary low voice, a little slowly, but without any effort.

"Good evening, Marcus," she said.

I heard him strain his throat to speak, but he said nothing.

"You are late," she said, as if a little vexed.

"I have been delayed," said he, and I was surprised at his voice, so perfectly calm and pleasant was it, and nobly sonorous.

"How am I looking?" asked Pellegrina.

"You are looking well," he answered her.

At the moment when she had spoken to him, the face of the old Jew had undergone a strange and striking change. I have spoken before of his unusual pallor. While he was telling us his tale he had grown white, as if there were no blood in him. Now, as she spoke and he answered her, a deep, delicate blush, like that of a young boy, of a maiden surprised in her bath, spread all over his face.

"It was good that you came," she said. "I am a little nervous tonight."

"No, you have no reason to be," he reassured her. "It has gone very well up till now."

"Do you really mean that," she asked, scrutinizing his face. "You do not criticize? Nothing could have been improved? I have done well, and you are pleased with it all?"

"Yes," he answered, "I do not criticize; nothing could be improved. You have done well, and I am well content with the whole thing."

She was silent for perhaps two or three minutes. Then her dark eyes slid from his face to ours. "Who are these gentlemen?" she asked him.

"These," he said, "are three foreign young gentlemen, who have traveled a long way to have the honor of being introduced to you."

"Introduce them, then," she said. "But I am afraid that you

must be quick about it. I do not think that the *entr'act* can last much longer."

The Jew, advancing toward us, took us by the hand, one by one, and led us nearer to the stretcher. "My noble young Sirs," he said, "from beautiful, distant countries, I am pleased to have obtained for you an unforgettable moment in your lives. I introduce you herewith to Donna Pellegrina Leoni, the greatest singer in the world."

With this he gave her our names, which for each of us he remembered quite correctly.

She looked at us kindly. "I am very glad to see you here tonight," she said. "I shall sing to you now, and, I hope, to your satisfaction." We kissed her hand with deep bows, all three. I remembered the caresses which I had demanded of that noble hand. But immediately after she turned again to the Jew.

"Nay, but I am really a little nervous tonight," she said. "What scene is it, Marcus?"

"My little star," said he, "be not nervous at all. It is sure to go well with you tonight. It is the second act of *Don Giovanni;* it is the letter air. It begins now with your recitative, *Crudele? Ah nò, mio bene! Troppo mi spiace allontanarti un ben che lungamente la nostr' alma desia."*

She drew a deep sigh and repeated his words: *"Crudele? Ah nò, mio bene! Troppo mi spiace allontanarti un ben che lungamente la nostr' alma desia."*

As she spoke these words of the old opera a wave of deep dark color, like that of a bride, like that in the face of the old Jew, washed over her white and bruised face. It spread from her bosom to the roots of her hair. The three of us who were lookers-on were, I believe, pale faced; but those who, looking at each other, glowed in a mute, increasing ecstasy.

Suddenly her face broke, as the night-old ice on a pool was broken up when, as a boy, I threw a stone into it. It became like a constellation of stars, quivering in the universe. A rain of tears sprang from her eyes and bathed it all. Her whole body vibrated under her passion like the string of an instrument.

"Oh," she cried, "look, look here! It is Pellegrina Leoni—it is she, it is she herself again—she is back. Pellegrina, the greatest singer, poor Pellegrina, she is on the stage again. To the honor of God, as before. Oh, she is here, it is she—Pellegrina, Pellegrina herself!"

It was unbelievable that, half dead as she was, she could house this storm of woe and triumph. It was, of course, her swan song.

"Come unto her, now, all, again," she said. "Come back, my children, my friends. It is I—I forever, now." She wept with a rapture of relief, as if she had in her a river of tears, held back long.

The old Jew was in a terrible state of pain and strain. He also swayed for a moment where he stood. His eyelids swelled and heavy tears pressed themselves out under them and ran down his face. But he kept standing, and dared not give way to his emotion, although tried to his utmost. I believe that he held out against it so strongly for fear that he might otherwise, very weak as he was, die before her, and thus fail her in her last moments.

Of a sudden he took up his little walking stick and struck three short strokes on the side of the stretcher.

"Donna Pellegrina Leoni," he cried in a clear voice. *"En scène pour le deux."*

Like a soldier to the call, or a war horse to the blast of the trumpet, she collected herself at his words. Within the next minute she became quiet in a gallant and deadly calm. She gave him a glance from her enormous dark eyes. In one mighty movement, like that of a billow rising and sinking, she lifted the middle of her body. A strange sound, like the distant roar of a great animal, came from her breast. Slowly the flames in her face sank, and an ashen gray covered it instead. Her body fell back, stretched itself out and lay quite still, and she was dead.

The Jew pressed his tall hat on his head. *"Iisgadal rejiiskadisch schemel robo,"* he said.

We stood for a little while. Afterward we went into the refectory to sit there. Later, when it was nearly morning, it was announced to us that our two coaches had at last arrived. I went out to give orders to the coachmen. We wanted to go on as soon as it was quite light. That would be best, I thought, although I did not know at all where to go.

As I passed the long room the candles were still burning, but the daylight came in through the windows. The two were there: Pellegrina on her stretcher and the old Jew by her side, his chin resting on his stick. It seemed to me that I ought not to part from him yet. I went up to him.

"Then, Mr. Cocoza," I said, "you are this time burying, not the great artist, whose grave you made many years ago, but the woman, whose friend you were."

The old man looked up at me. *"Vous êtes trop bon, Monsieur,"* he said, which means: You are too good, Sir.

"This," Lincoln said, "is my tale, Mira."

Mira drew in his breath, blew it out again slowly, and whistled.

"I have thought," said Lincoln, "What would have happened to this woman if she had not died then? She might have been with us here tonight. She was good company and would have fitted in well. She might have become a dancer of Mombasa, like Thusmu, that tawny-eyed old bat, the mistress of his father and grandfather, for whose arms Said is even now longing. Or she might have gone with us into the highlands, on an expedition for ivory or slaves, and have made up her mind to stay there with a war-like tribe of the highland natives, and have been honored by them as a great witch.

"In the end, I have thought, she might perhaps have decided to become a pretty little jackal, and have made herself a den on the plain, or upon the slope of a hill. I have imagined that so vividly that on a moonlight night I have believed that I heard her voice amongst the hills. And I have seen her, then, running about, playing with her own small graceful shadow, having a little ease of heart, a little fun."

"Ah la la," said Mira, who, in his quality of a story-teller, was an excellent and imaginative listener, "I have heard that little jackal too. I have heard her. She barks: 'I am not one little jackal, not one; I am many little jackals.' And pat! in a second she really is another, barking just behind you: 'I am not one little jackal. Now I am another.' Wait, Lincoln, till I have heard her once more. Then I shall make you a tale about her, to go with yours."

"Well," said Lincoln, "this is my tale. The lesson for Said."

"I know all your tale," said Mira. "I have heard it before. Now I believe that I made it myself."

"The Sultan Sabour of Khorassan was a great hero, and not that only, but a man of God, who had visions and heard voices which instructed him in the will of the Lord. So he meant to teach this to all the world, with fire and sword. But alas, he was betrayed by a woman, a dancer, just at the zenith of his orbit; it is a long story. His great army was wiped out. The sand of the desert drank their blood; the vultures fed on it. The wails of the widows and orphans rose to heaven. His harem was scattered amongst his enemies. He himself was wounded, and only dragged away and saved by a slave. For the sake of his soldiers, then, he will not show himself or let himself be known in his beggar's state. He has become, like your woman, many persons, and gives up, like her, to be one. Sometimes he is a water carrier, again a Khadi's servant, again a fisherman by the sea, or a holy hermit. He is very wise. He knows many things and leaves deep footprints wherever he goes. He does all people whom he meets much good and some harm; he is a king still. But he will not remain the same for long. When he gains friends and women to love him, he flees the country from them, too much afraid of being again the Sultan Sabour, or any one person at all. Only his slave knows.

This slave, I now remember, has had his nose cut off for Sabour's sake."

"Alas, Mira, life is full of disagreeables," said Lincoln.

"Ah, as to me," said Mira, "I am safe wherever I go. You yourself have it written down in your Holy Book that all things work together for good to them that love God."

"Does that declaration of love," asked Lincoln, "come from the heart? Or from the lips of an old court poet?"

"Nay, I speak from my heart," said Mira. "I have been trying for a long time to understand God. Now I have made friends with him. To love him truly you must love change, and you must love a joke, these being the true inclinations of his own heart. Soon I shall take to loving a joke so well that I, who once turned the blood of all the world to ice, shall become a teller of funny tales, to make people laugh."

"Then, according to the law of the Prophet," said Lincoln, "you will be, with barbers and such people as kiss their wives in public, debarred from giving evidence before a court of law."

"Yes, that is so," Mira agreed. "I shall be debarred from giving evidence."

"What says Said?" asked Lincoln.

Said, who had sat silent and motionless all the time, laughed a little. He looked toward land. In the moonlight a dim white strip showed, and there was a murmur, like to the vibrating of a string, in the air.

"Those," said Said, "are the great breakers of Takaungu Creek. We shall be in Mombasa at dawn."

"At dawn?" said Mira. "Then I will go to sleep for an hour or two."

He crawled down on the deck, drew his cloak around him and over his head, and laid himself down to sleep, immovable as a corpse.

Lincoln sat for a little while, smoking a cigarette or two. Then he also lay down, turned himself over a couple of times, and went to sleep.

The Poet

AROUND the name of the little town of Hirschholm, in Denmark, there is much romance.

In the early years of the eighteenth century, Queen Sophia Magdalena—the consort of that pious monarch, King Christian VI, who went to chapel with his court three times a day and had all the theaters of Copenhagen shut up—one summer evening, after a long day's hunting, killed a stag on the bank of a tranquil lake in the midst of a forest. She was so much pleased with the spot that she resolved to have a palace built there, and she named it after the stag: Hirschholm. It was, like most teutonic architecture of the period, a pompous and finicky affair when it was finished, built up as it was in the middle of the lake, with long straight embarkments across the water, upon which the royal coaches could drive up in all their splendor, reflected, head down, in the clear surface, as had been the stag, surrounded by the Queen's hounds. Around the lake the little town, with its employees' houses, taverns and little modest shops grew up, red-tiled, around the huge royal stables and *manèges*. It was very quiet most of the year, but they had a great time when the magnificent court arrived for the hunting season.

Fifty years later, when Sophia Magdalena's grandson, King Christian VII, ruled over Denmark, the tragedy of his young English Queen, Carolina Mathilda, took place, or was prepared, at Hirschholm. This pathetic pink-and-white and full-bosomed young Princess sailed over the North Sea at the age of fifteen to marry a debauched and heartless little king, not much older than herself, but already far on his way toward that royal lunacy which swallowed him up some years later, a sort of Caligula in miniature, whose portrait gives you a strange impression of an entirely lonely and disillusioned mind. After a few unhappy years that were probably both dull and bewildering to the English maiden, she, by the time when the King took to playing at horses with his Negro page, met her fate. She fell deeply, desperately, in love with the doctor who had been summoned from Germany to heal, by means of his novel cold-water cures, the sickly little Crown

357

Prince. This doctor was a very brilliant man who was much in advance of his time. Her great passion for him first raised her lover to the highest places in the land, where he shone surprisingly as a star of the first magnitude, a reckless revolutionary tyrant, and then ruined them both. They had their short good time at Hirschholm, where Carolina Mathilda impressed her Danish subjects by riding to hounds in men's clothes—attire which one cannot imagine, from her portraits, to have been very becoming to her. Then the rancor of the indignant old Dowager Queen encircled the lovers and brought them down. The doctor had his head cut off for pilfering the regalia of the crown of Denmark, and the young Queen was sent in exile to a little town in Hanover, and died there. Virtue triumphed in its most dismal form, and the palace that had housed such blasphemy was itself left and finally pulled down, partly because the royal family did not like to see it, partly because it was said to be sinking, of itself, into the lake. The whole splendor disappeared, and a church, in the classical style of the dawning nineteenth century, was erected where the palace had stood, like a cross upon its grave. Many years later statues and carved and gilt furniture, with rose garlands and cupids, were to be found in the houses of the wealthy peasants around Hirschholm.

After the storm had passed over its head the little town gave for years the impression of someone benumbed by shock and lying very low. It had not been able to believe that such things could happen, in any case not in its very middle. It had perhaps still in its heart remnants of a loyal sympathy for the gay young Queen who had smiled at it. But to have one's head cut off is a serious business, and it had only to look toward the place where the palace had stood to have the wages of sin brought home to it. Hard times came upon the country: wars, the loss of the fleet, bankruptcy of the state, the spirit of virtue and severe economy. The frivolous days of the eighteenth century were gone forever.

Then, about fifty or sixty years after the tragedy of the young

Queen and her premier, the town had a pleasant little renaissance.

It could not go on forever being repentant of sins in which it had in reality no part, and it could, no more than the rest of the country, live forever upon the conviction of the excellency of prudence. When one is tied down heavily enough to an existence of care, it becomes pleasant to think of careless times and people. Also, though people do not like their mothers' virtue to be questioned, the frivolities of grandmothers may be charming things to smile at. By the time when men began to grow whiskers and ladies to wear sidecurls, the sins of people in powder began to look romantic, like passions and crimes on the stage. The time had come when poets would drive out in wagonettes from Copenhagen and board at Hirschholm to sing of the unhappy Queen Carolina Mathilda, and see her shadow, flighty on her flighty steed, galloping past them in the forest. The avenues of lime trees, planted upon the embankments in the unselfish spirit of the eighteenth century—which must have walked between sticks six feet high in order to give coming generations shade and foliage—had grown up and grown old, and within their green bowers old ladies and men who had seen, as children, the Queen ride clattering across the stone bridges with her hounds, or the King, like an elegant powdered and corseted little doll with a blank face, pass in his coach, were expanding upon the excitement of court life to pretty maidens, matrons, and youths of the town, who held their own hearts carefully in check.

At this time there lived in Hirschholm two men who distinguished themselves, in different ways, from the average burgher.

The first of these was, rightly, the prominent figure of the town, a citizen of great influence, and a man not only of property and prestige, but of the world and of great charm. His name was Mathiesen, and he had been made a *Kammerraad*, a chambercouncilor. Later a bust of him was erected, in remembrance of him, at the entrance to one of those long lime avenues in which he loved to walk.

He was at the time—that is, in the early 'thirties—between fifty-five and sixty years old, and lived quietly and contentedly in Hirschholm. But he had been younger, and had lived in other places. He had even traveled much and had been in both Germany and France during those fatal and restless times which preceded the idyll: in the days of the French Revolution and the wars of Napoleon. There he had seen, and probably himself played a part in, many things which the little town could not have dreamed of, and the people who had known him as a young man said of him that he had come back with other eyes—formerly they had been blue, but now they were light gray or green. If he had lost illusions out there, he was not likely now to think the loss very great, and he had surely won instead a talent for making life pleasant and himself comfortable. There is probably no better place for a sensible epicurean than a small provincial town. The councilor, who had been a widower for fifteen years, had an excellent housekeeper and a cellar which might have done honor to a Cardinal. It was said of him in Hirschholm that when alone of an evening he did needlework in cross-stitch; but then, there was no reason why, in his position, he should give up any pleasant pastime in life for the sake of conventionality.

Amongst the treasures which the Councilor had collected in the great world and brought home to Hirschholm, there was none that he valued as highly as his recollections of Weimar, where he had lived for two years, and his remembrance of having once lived in the atmosphere of the great Geheimerat Goethe. It is a great thing to have been face to face with the highest, and a law of life that one thing amongst all that we meet must impress itself deeper upon our souls than any other; and the image of that serene town and of the great poet were stamped forever on his being. Here was the ideal man—the superman, he might have thought, if the word had been invented—who combined in himself all the qualities which humanity envies and toward which it strives: the poet, philosopher, statesman, the friend and adviser of princes and the conqueror of women. The Councilor had many times met Goethe on his morning walks, and had heard him talk with friends who accompanied him. On one occasion he had even been introduced to the great man himself, had met the glance of those Olympian and yet human eyes, and had exchanged a few words with the Giant. The poet and Herr Eckermann had been discussing a question of Nordic archeology, and Herr Eckermann had called upon the young foreigner to give evidence in the argument. Goethe then questioned him upon the matter, and courteously asked him if he could possibly procure certain information. Mathiesen had made a deep bow and had answered:

Ich bin Eurer Excellenz ehrerbietigster Diener.

The Councilor was not an ordinary man, and had none of the ordinary man's ambitions. He had a high opinion of his position in Hirschholm—as indeed he had reason to have—and in his daily existence he had no wants which were not well satisfied. If he did, for the rest of his days, cherish, together with a picture of the Geheimerat, an ambition to feel himself, in his smaller surroundings, a superman in miniature, it was known only to himself, and in real life played the part of ideals in general—that of an unseen directive force, which makes for balance. But he was a man of broad outlook who took a long and wide view of things. He maintained an idea of paradise, for his generation had been brought up on the thought of life everlasting, and the idea of immortality came naturally to him. His paradise was to be a Weimar—an elysium of dignity, grace, and brilliancy. Still, his feelings about another world were not of vital importance to him; he might have given them up without too much pain. But he had a very firm faith in history, and in the immortality which it may grant you. He had seen it made around him and had felt its breath upon his cheek, and he knew the great Emperor and the heroes of the Revolution to be more alive than the functionaries and tradesmen of Hirschholm who lifted their hats to him in the roughly paved streets and with whom he exchanged little pleasant remarks every day. It was upon the arena, and in this high society of history, that he desired to live on.

It was either the deep impression which poetry had made upon him when it manifested itself with so much grandeur, or an inborn tendency in his own heart, which one might perhaps not have expected—but who can tell, seeing how little we know about hearts?—which made this art take such a great place in his scheme of things. Outside of poetry there was to him no real ideal in life, or, indeed, any satisfactory immortality. It was natural, then, that he should have tried to write poetry himself. On his return from Weimar he had produced a tragedy which took its theme from old Danish history, and later he wrote a few poems inspired by the romance of Hirschholm. But he was a judge of art, and realized, as quickly as anybody else could have done, that he was no poet. So he had been aware for some time that the poetry of his life would have to come from somewhere else, and had recognized his own part in connection with it to be that of a Mæcenas, a part for which he felt himself well fitted and which he thought would be becoming to him in that immortality toward which he was striving.

It so happened that what he was looking for had come to meet him, in the person of a young man who also lived at Hirschholm and who was at this time a district clerk and—although this was only known to the Councilor and himself—a great poet.

His name was Anders Kube, and he was twenty-four years old. He was considered not at all good-looking by the people who knew him, but at the same time an artist painting a sacred picture and looking for a model for a young angel's face might have found it in him. He had a broad face and dark blue eyes set wide apart. For his work he used spectacles, and when he took them off and looked directly at the world his eyes had a clear and deep gaze, such as Adam's eyes may have had when he first walked around the garden and looked at the beasts. Of a strange, slow and angular, unexpected gracefulness in all his movements, with thick dark red hair and very big hands, he was a nearly perfect specimen of a type of Danish peasant which was then to be found amongst parish clerks and fiddlers, but which has, now that peasants are sitting in parliament, disappeared.

Of the two worlds in which he lived, the one that gave him his daily bread was very limited, made up of the whitewashed office room of the district court, his own rooms—very neatly kept by his landlady, who was fond of him—at the top of a stair and behind a large lime tree, and the woods and fields around Hirschholm, where he roamed in his free hours. He was also received into the houses of a few kind and respectable burghers of Hirschholm, to play cards and listen to political arguments, and he had friends amongst the wagoners of the great road who outspanned and supped at the inn, as well as among members of the strange tribe of charcoal burners who carted their charcoal from the great woods near Elsinore to Copenhagen. The Councilor's house held a position of its own in his existence. Three years before, when he first came to the town, he had carried letters from a friend of the Councilor's, old Apothecary Lerche, who had recommended him as a talented and industrious young man, and on the strength of them he had received a standing invitation for supper with the Councilor on Saturday nights. These evenings were pleasant to him, and gave him many impressions. He had never before had the chance of listening to so much wordly wisdom, such rich stock of experience, as that with which he was here regaled. Probably the Councilor did indeed speak more openly to him than to anybody else, but the youth had no idea that he himself played such a part in the life of his protector.

Neither had he any notion of a theory which the Councilor had developed on his behalf, which came to this: that the young man had to be kept in a sort of cage or coop in order to bring out his best as a poet. Perhaps this theory was based upon experiences of the Councilor's own life; he may have felt that he himself had, in the course of events of the past, lost powers and ideals essential to a poet. Perhaps it was entirely a matter of instinct. In any case it was a deeply rooted conviction of his heart that he had to guard his protégé. As long as he could keep him quietly in Hirschholm, treading the pavement from his lodgings to his office, or the long avenues, the great forces within him would have to come out in poetry. But if the world and its wild and incalculable influences were to get hold of him, he might be lost to literature and to his Mæcenas; he might be dragged into uproars and rebellions against that law and order of which the Councilor was himself a staunch support, and come to finish his days upon a barricade. Seeing that nobody else would have imagined young Kube upon a barricade, the theory showed, if true, a deep insight into human nature on the part of the Councilor—except that perhaps the people found on barricades may generally be those least expected there. At any rate its effect was that the old man kept an untiring eye on the youth, like a sort of unselfish lover, like a mighty and dignified Kislar Aga toward a budding beauty of the seraglio for whom he has planned great things.

On his part the Councilor could have no knowledge that he himself was, in the eyes of his protégé, encircled by a poetic halo. It had been created, at the beginning of the youth's stay at Hirschholm, by a tale of his landlady's, the truth of which was doubtful, and which ran as follows:

The Councilor was, as already said, a widower, but before he came to this state he had gone through much. The late Madame Mathiesen had been an heiress in a modest way. She had come from Christiansfeld, which is the seat, in Denmark, of the Hernhuten, a severe puritan sect, like the Jansenites in France, and she was a woman with a highly developed conscience. But one summer evening, two years before her death, she had suddenly lost her mind in a fit of terror of the devil, and had wanted to kill her husband or herself with a pair of scissors. They sent for the old doctor, who tried all his arts on her without doing her any good, so, as there was no hospital for that kind of patient near by, they boarded her with the old palace gardener of Fredensborg—another royal palace at some distance from Hirschholm—and his wife, who were kind people and owed their appointment to the influence of the Councilor. There she lived, without regaining her reason, but in a happier state of mind, for she believed that she was dead and in heaven, waiting for her husband. Sometimes, though, she expressed a fear of his never getting there, for she said that he was a great sinner; but she trusted to the grace of God.

The narrator of the tale, who had at the time been a maid in Madame Mathiesen's house, was the only person, outside of the narrow family circle, who knew how this crisis had been brought on. On that July evening, after a thunderstorm, and while a double rainbow stood burning over the landscape, the Councilor and his wife, with a young girl who was the daughter of a functionary at Court, the Councilor's friend, and who had been sent to Hirschholm to recover from a disappointment in love, were going out for a walk. Madame Mathiesen was in her room putting on her bonnet, when, through the open window, she saw the girl pick a yellow pansy and fasten it upon the Councilor's coat. There may be, for the Hernhuten, some magic in a yellow pansy or in the air under a double rainbow. At any rate the sight had upon Madame Mathiesen an effect which nobody else could have foreseen.

Two years later, at about the same time of the year, the Councilor had news from Fredensborg that his wife's health had improved, she no longer thought that she was in heaven, and they believed that it would do her good to see him. So he had his gig brought out on a fine afternoon, got into the neat little carriage, and took the reins himself. Then he seemed to think better of it, got out again, and went into the garden, where he picked a yellow pansy and fastened it on his coat lapel. The meeting between the husband and the wife did not turn out as their friends had hoped, though she had been in her window all day waiting for him. She no sooner saw him than she was seized by her old confusion. She became so wild that they had to call for assistance. In fact, she fell back into madness altogether, from which she never recovered, for she died a year later.

Young Kube had not a judging mind, and would never, left to himself, approach any phenomena in life from a moral standpoint. He neither admired nor blamed the Councilor for his rôle in the drama. But he had a mind which strangely enlarged everything he met. Under the handling of his thoughts, things became gigantic, like those huge shadows of themselves upon the mist, which travelers in mountains meet and are terrified of, gigantic and somehow grotesque, like objects playing about, a little outside of human reason. So the Councilor began to swell and evaporate and to move in mystic serpentine windings, like the spirit which came out of Solomon's bottle and showed itself to the poor fisherman of Bagdad; and every Saturday night the young poet sat down to supper with Loki himself.

On most other nights he would be alone, and as he was a poorly paid clerk, by instinct very careful about his money, and encouraged therein by his landlady, he would sup on porridge and afterward let his big cat drink milk out of his plate. Then he would sit very still, looking at the fire, or, on summer nights, out of the window to where a slight milky mist upon the surface indicated the contour of the lake, and let all the world quietly open its heart to him, unfold and reveal itself in such wild forms as appeared natural to him. The young son of the soil, tied to a register, had the soul of the old Eddas, which created the world around them in terms of gods and demons, and filled it with heights and abysses unknown in their country; and also the playful mentality of those old mystics who populated it with centaurs, fauns, and water deities who did not always behave properly. Those Danish peasants, who were by nature their descendants, had, under a deep gravity like that of a child, more playfulness and shamelessness of mind than a clown. Generally they have not been much understood or appreciated except as they could turn this side of their being out, and in a craving for understanding they have often had to take to drink. Anders Kube still, because he thought it the right thing, would write little poems of a spider upon a branch of roses, but later on, when he came more into his own, his creations took quite different dimensions.

Some evenings he would go out not to come back till daylight, and his landlady could not get out of him where he had been.

A few miles out of Hirschholm there is a little property with a pleasant white manor house, surrounded by trees and pretty grounds, called La Liberté. For years nobody had been living there. The owner had been an old apothecary, the same man who had given Anders Kube his letters of introduction, who had his business in Copenhagen and had been making money all his life. At the age of seventy, after having borrowed some romantic narratives of travel at his club, he made up his mind to see the world, and started on a voyage to Italy. A halo of adventurousness had surrounded his enterprise from the beginning. It grew brighter when it was reported how he had experienced an earthquake at Naples, and had there made the acquaintance of a compatriot, a mysterious figure who was sometimes described as a merchant captain and sometimes as a theatrical director, and who died in the apothecary's arms, leaving a large family in distress. From Naples the old man had informed his friends that he had taken charge of the eldest daughter of this family, and was thinking of adopting her; but from Genoa, a fortnight later, he wrote that he had married her. "Now why did he do that?" asked his female acquaintances at home. He never did tell them. He died at Hamburg on the return journey, leaving his fortune to his relations, and La Liberté and a small pension to his young widow. Toward the end of the winter of 1836 she came and settled there.

The Councilor drove out to assist her and to see the adventuress of Naples who had ensnared—and, he suspected, killed off—his old friend. He found her demure, very ready to do everything that he told her. She was a short, slight young woman who looked like a doll; not like the dolls of the present day, which are imitations of the faces and forms of human babies, but like the dolls of old days which strove, parallel with humanity, toward an abstract ideal of female beauty. Her big eyes were clear as glass, and her long eyelashes and delicate eyebrows were as black as if they had been painted on her face. The most remarkable thing about her was the rare lightness of all her movements, which were like those of a bird. She had what the Councilor knew, in the technical language of the ballet, as *ballon*, a lightness that is not only the negation of weight, but which actually seems to carry upwards and make for flight, and which is rarely found in thin dancers—as if the matter itself had here become lighter than air, so that the more there is of it the better it works. Her mourning frocks and bonnets were somewhat more elegant than those commonly seen in Hirschholm; or perhaps it was that, having been bought in Hamburg, they appeared a little outlandish in the village. But she was either careful of her money or simple of taste. She altered nothing in the old house, and did not even move about any of the musty old furniture that had for so long led a forlorn existence in the painted rooms. In the garden-room there was a large and costly musical box which had been brought all the way from Russia. She seemed to like to walk about and to sit in the garden, but she let it remain overgrown, as it had been for years. Apparently she was bent on behaving with great correctness, for she drove about to call on the ladies of the neighborhood, who gave her good advice and recipes for making sausages and gingerbread, but she spoke little herself, and was perhaps shy because of a slight accent in speaking Danish. There was another characteristic which the Councilor noted in her: she was to the utmost shy of, or averse to, touch. She never kissed or caressed any of the other ladies, such as was the custom at Hirschholm, and evidently disliked being petted by them. There was something of a Psyche in the doll. The ladies of Hirschholm thought her harmless. She would be no rival either at making gingerbread or within the brilliant little school of scandal of the town. They wondered whether she was not a bit feebleminded. The Councilor agreed with them, and disagreed. There was something there, he thought.

On Easter day the Councilor and Anders went to church at Hirschholm. The sun was shining and the lake around the church was a bright blue, but still the day was cold with a sharp east wind, and there were showers from time to time. The daffodils, the crowns-imperial, and the Diclytra—which the Danes call "heart-of-a-lieutenant," because, when you open the blossom, you find inside a champagne bottle and a dancer—which were just out in the little gardens, were harshly treated and bowed down by the wind and rain. The peasant women, who came to take holy communion in their gold-embroidered caps, had to struggle with their heavy skirts and long silk ribbons at the church entrance.

Just as the Councilor and his protégé were about to go in, the young lady of La Liberté arrived in a landaulet drawn by two heavy bay horses, which amply allowed themselves everything in front of the church door. She had got out of her widow's weeds for the first time, it being now a year since her old husband had died, and was in a pale gray cloak and a blue bonnet. She felt as happy as a stock-dove within a green tree, and radiated a joy of life that was like a waltz played upon a violin with a sordine.

As the Councilor was exchanging ideas with the parson at the moment, it was young Kube who went to help her out of her carriage. In respect to the widow of his old patron he held his hat in his hand while they talked together for a moment. The Councilor was watching the scene from the porch and found himself strangely attracted by the sight. He did not take his eyes off them. Both the young people were exceedingly shy. Together with the slow and heavy grace of the young man's countenance and her extraordinary lightness of movement, this double shyness seemed to give the brief encounter a particular expressiveness, a pregnant quality, as if there were a secret in it, and something would come out of it. The Councilor did not know himself why it so struck and moved him. It was, he thought, like the opening bars of a piece of music, or the first chapter of a romance called "Anders and Fransine."

Geheimerat Goethe, he reflected, might—would indeed—have made something of it. He went into the church in a thoughtful mood.

All through the service the Councilor's mind was playing about with his recent impression. It had come to him at a seasonable moment, for he had lately been uneasy about his poet. This young slave of his had been singularly absent-minded, and even absent bodily from one or two of their Saturday suppers. There was in his whole manner an unconscious restlessness, and underneath it the sign of a melancholy about which the Councilor was anxious, for he knew well that he could find no remedy for it. From a talk with the landlady he had got the idea that the young clerk might be drinking too much. Many great poets had been drunkards, he knew, but it did not quite fit into the picture with his own figure as a Mæcenas. Under the influence of drink, which he knew to have played a part in the history of the boy's family, he might get out of hand, might run away to play the fiddle at the peasants' weddings. The Councilor had opposed a raise in the young clerk's salary at the district office, knowing that that would do him no good, but he should have liked a surer way of anchoring him. Now it occurred to him that marriage might be what was needed. The little widow with her small income, in the white house of La Liberté, might have been provided by providence as the ideal wife for his genius. She might prove to be, even, a Christiane Vulpius, the only woman, he had been informed, who had lain in the arms of the Geheimerat for whole nights without asking him questions about the meaning of life. These vague pictures pleased the Councilor.

From the men's section, to the right of the aisle, his eye turned once or twice toward the women's benches. The young woman kept very still. She was absorbed in the parson's words, but all the time her face had the expression of deep secret joy. Toward the end of the service, as she was kneeling, deeply moved, she held a small handkerchief to her face. The old man wondered whether she was really crying or laughing into it.

After the service the older and the young man walked together to the Councilor's house. As they passed the bridge a lashing, ice-cold shower was swept across the landscape. They had to put up their umbrellas, and they stopped on the little arched stone bridge to watch the hail beating down on the water, and the two swans of the lake rushing angrily under the arch through the gray waves. They kept standing there longer than they knew, both deep in thought.

Anders had had his mind filled, by the Easter sermon, with a row of shadows, which slowly took shape, like clouds banking up.

Mary Magdalena, he thought, came hurriedly on the dawn of Friday to the house of Caiaphas. She had seen in a vision how, upon the afternoon of the morrow, the veil of the temple was to be rent. She had seen the graves opening, and the saints coming forth. She had also beheld the angel of the Lord rolling back the stone of the grave and sitting upon it; and she hurled at the high priests reproaches for the monstrosity they were about to commit in crucifying God. Her words convinced the old men that Christ was in reality the only-begotten son of God, and the redeemer of all the world, and that what they were about to do would be the only true crime in all the history of mankind.

Thereupon they held a council within the dark room of the palace, in which a lamp shone upon their multicolored caftans and bearded, passionately pensive faces. Some of the priests were struck with terror and demanded that the prisoner be released at once; others went into ecstasy and prophesied in shrill voices. But Caiaphas and a few of the very old men discussed the matter with thoroughness, and agreed that they must carry through their prospect. If the world had really this one hope of salvation, they would have to fall in with the plan of God, however dreadful the deed.

Mary, in despair, talked to them of the sins and the misery of the earth, about which she knew so much, and of the holiness of Christ. The more they listened the more they shook their heads.

Caiaphas called forth Satan to talk the matter over with him. As his first impersonation, red-haired Judas came into the room and offered to.return his thirty pieces of silver. When the council refused, he laughingly depicted to them the long future misery of the chosen people, from now forever hunted down and spat upon by the world, with the pieces of silver forever in their hands. He even described to the high priests the Ghetto of Amsterdam, which the Councilor had himself, upon a Saturday evening, painted to his protégé. The head of the old priest fell down upon his heavy textbook.

The Councilor's own face was somewhere in the council of the high priests, although not yet quite distinctly placed. Mary Magdalena was kneeling, hiding her face.

The head of the young clerk swam a little. He had sat up late last night, playing cards with wayfaring people at the inn.

The rain had stopped. They put down their umbrellas and walked on.

The Councilor also, in spite of his matrimonial plans, had got stuff for thought from the sermon. He reflected how strange it is that St. Peter, who was the only person who knew of it, and who must have been in a position to suppress it, should ever have allowed the story of the cock to get about.

During the next three weeks the weather was very mild, but it rained. The soil was filled with growth, and the air with a fragrance that was only waiting for a clear day and sun to expand. Flowering plum trees floated like clouds of chalk around the farmhouses. Later the ground of the woods, underneath the beech trunks, was covered with windflowers, pink as shells, with digitate leaves and sweet and bitter scent. The nightingales arrived and turned all the world into a violin, still in sweetly dripping rain and mist.

Upon a Thursday toward the end of May the Councilor supped and played cards at Elsinore with a friend who was an officer in the service of the Sound duties. These parties were annual festivities where old friends met. They always drew out late, and it is thirteen miles from Elsinore to Hirschholm; but the Councilor did not mind, for the nights are light in Denmark at this season. He drove in his neat gig, lolling in his big gray riding cloak, while Kresten, his old coachman, drove the horse, and taking in a little sleepily the beauty of the May night and the smell from the fields and budding groves through which they were driving. A little way out of Hirschholm something in the harness broke. They had to stop, and Kresten concluded that they would have to borrow a piece of rope at the nearest farm to repair the damage. On looking around the Councilor found that they were just outside of La Liberté. Fearing that Kresten might make too much noise and disturb the sleep of the lady of the house, he decided to go himself. He knew the caretaker of the place; in fact, had himself got him the job, and could knock at his window without waking up anybody else. A little chilled, he got out of his carriage and walked up the drive. It was just before dawn.

The dim air was filled with the sweet and acid scent of fresh wet leafage. Upon the graveled drive there were still little pools of water; but the night was clear. He walked slowly, for here amongst the trees and bushes it was dark. An avenue of populus balsamifera led off the drive toward the farmyard, contributing the nectarous acrid breath of their shaggy flowers to the harmony of the atmosphere.

Suddenly, as he was walking on, he heard the sound of music. He stopped, hardly believing his ears—yes, there was no doubt: it was music. A dancing tune was being played, and it came from the house. He walked a little, then stopped again, wondering. Who was playing and dancing here before sunrise? He left the drive and walked across the wet grass of the lawn toward the front side of the house. As he came up toward the terrace the façade of the white house shone a dead white, and he saw a clear light between the lists of the closed shutters. The young widow might be having a ball in her garden-room tonight.

The wet lilac bushes on the terrace were full of unfolded flowers. The dark spiky clusters held a surprise in them; they would be so much lighter when they opened. A row of tulips kept their white and pink cups prudently closed to the night air. It was very still. The Councilor remembered two lines of an old poem:

> *The gentle zephyrs cease to rock*
> *Newly inslumbered Nature's cradle.*

It was that hour just before sunrise when the world seems absolutely colorless, when it gives indeed a sense of negation of color. The rich hues of night have withdrawn, oozed away like the waves from a shore, and all the colors of daytime lie dormant in the landscape like in the paints used for pottery, which are all alike gray clay until they come out in the furnace. And in this still world there is a tremendous promise.

The old man, gray in his gray cloak, would have been nearly invisible even to somebody looking for him. In fact he felt extremely lonely, as if he knew that he could not be seen. He dared not put his hand to the shutter for fear of making a noise. With his hands on his back he leaned forward and peeped in.

He had hardly ever been more surprised. The long garden-room with its three French windows opening on to the terrace was painted a sky blue, much faded with time. There was but little furniture in the room, and what was there had been pushed back against the walls. But from the ceiling in the middle of the room hung a fine old chandelier, and it was all ablaze, every candle in it being lighted. The big Russian musical box was open, placed upon the old dumb spinet, and was pouring forth in high clear notes the tune of a mazurka.

The young mistress of the house stood on the tips of her toes in the middle of the room. She had on the very short diaphanous frock of a ballet dancer, and her little heelless shoes were fastened with black ribbons laced around her delicate ankles and legs. She held her arms over her head, gracefully rounded, and stood quite still, watching the music, her face like the placid, happy face of a doll.

As her bar of music fell in, she suddenly came to life. She lifted her right leg slowly, slowly, the toe pointing straight at the Councilor, higher and higher, as if she were really rising from the ground and about to fly. Then she brought it down again, slowly, slowly, on the tip of the toe, with a little gentle pat, no more than a fingertap upon the table.

The spectator outside held his breath. As before, on watching the ballet at Vienna, he had the feeling that this was too much; it could not be done. And then it was done, lightly, as in jest. One begins to doubt the fall of man, and not to worry about it, when a young dancer can thus rise from it again.

Standing upon the tip of her right toe now, she lifted her left leg, slowly, high up, opened her arms in a swift audacious movement, whirled all around herself, and began to dance. The dance was more than a real mazurka, very fiery and light, lasting perhaps two minutes: a humming-top, a flower, a flame dancing, a play upon the law of gravitation, a piece of celestial drollery. It was also a bit of acting: love, sweet innocence, tears, a *sursum corda* expressed in music and movement. In the middle of it there was a little pause to frighten the audience, but it went on all the same, only even more admirably, as if transposed into a higher key. Just as the music box gave signs of running down, she looked straight at the Councilor and sank down upon the floor in a graceful heap, like a flower flung stem upward, exactly as if her legs had been cut off with a pair of scissors.

The Councilor knew enough about the art of the ballet to value this as a very high-class performance. He knew enough about the pretty things in life altogether to value this early morning apparition altogether as a vision worthy of the Czar Alexander himself, if it came to that.

At her direct clear glance, he took alarm and drew back a little. When he looked in again she had got up, but remained as if irresolute, and did not turn on the box again. There was a long mirror in the room. Pressing the palm of her hand gently upon the glass she bent forward and kissed her own silvery image within it. Then she took up a long extinguisher, and one by one she put out the candles of the chandelier. She opened the door and was gone.

In spite of his reluctance to be seen there by anybody, the Councilor stood still on the terrace for a minute or two. He was as astonished as if he had happened to surprise, upon this early May morning, Echo, practicing all on her own in the depths of the woods.

As he turned from the house he was struck by the greatness of the view from La Liberté. He had not noticed it before. From this terrace he looked out over all the surrounding country, verdant and undulating, even over the top of the forest. In the far distance the Sound shone like a strip of silver, and above the Sound the sun arose.

He walked back to his carriage in deep thought. Stupidly, a bit of a nursery rhyme, with a lovely little tune to it, came into his head:

> Oh, it is not the fault of the hen,
> That the cock be dead.
> It is the fault of the nightingale,
> Within the green garden.

He had forgotten all about the rope. On being informed by Kresten that he had managed to do the repair without it, he did not find a word to say to him.

During the rest of the drive he was very wide awake. It seemed to him that he had much to do, that he must rearrange all the chess men upon the board. The occupation carried in its train many ideas pleasantly refreshing to a man who in his daily life deals much with books and law, and who had been playing omber with three old bachelors only this last night.

The apothecary's widow was no Christiane Vulpius, that was clear. She was not a person to anchor anybody. She might on the contrary have it in her to lift the young man, whom he had decided for her, off the ground, and together those two might fly, nobody could tell where to, all away from his supremacy. That she had thus deceived him he did not mind. He liked her for it; he was so rarely surprised in life. But it was a lucky thing that he had found her out, for he would not lose his poet. Indeed, he thought, he should like to keep them both. He took off his hat for a moment, and the wind of the young morning played around his temples. He was not an old man; he was young, compared with what she was used to. He was a rich man, a man who valued and deserved the rarest things in life. Could he make her dance for him of an evening? That would make a different married life from what he had before experienced. The poet would remain his protégé, and the friend of the house.

His thoughts went a little further while the sun rose up higher. An unhappy love is an inspiring feeling. It has created the greatest works of history. A hopeless passion for his benefactor's wife might make a young poet immortal; it was a dramatic thing to have in the house. The two young people would remain loyal to him, however much they might suffer, and though love and youth are such strong things. And if they did not remain so?

The Councilor helped himself to a pinch of snuff, in the relish of which his delicate nose seemed to twist a little. His drive was nearly finished now. In the still limpid morning air the little town looked like a town at the bottom of the sea. The tiled roofs blossomed forth like a growth of bold or pale coral; the blue smoke arose like thin seaweeds rising to the surface. The bakers were taking their fresh bread from the ovens. The morning air made the Councilor feel a little sleepy, but very well. He came to think of that old saying which the peasants call the bachelors' prayer:

"I pray thee, good Lord, that I may not be married. But if I am to be married, that I may not be a cuckold. But if I am to be a cuckold, that I may not know. But if I am to know, that I may not mind."

These are the thoughts which only such a man can allow himself who has within the structure of his mind a perfectly swept room to which he is absolutely sure that no one but himself has the key.

The next evening, that being Saturday, Anders came to the Councilor's house for supper. Afterward he read to his host a poem about a young peasant who watches three wild swans at night transform themselves into three maidens, and bathe in the lake. He steals the wings of one of them, which she has laid off while bathing, and makes her his wife. She bears him children. But one day she recovers her wings from where he has hidden them, and puts them on. She circles above the house in ever larger rings, and at last disappears in the air.

How is it that he writes this, that he should write this? the Councilor thought. It is curious. He has not seen her dance.

Now the beech forests of the province unfolded themselves. The gray rain fell for a few days around all the world as the veil around a bride, and there came a morning when all the woods were green.

This happens in Denmark every year in May, but impresses you every year, and it impressed these people of a hundred years ago as something entirely surprising and inexplicable. Through all the long months of winter you have been, even within the deep of the woods, exposed to the winds and the bleak light of heaven. Then, all of a sudden, the month of May builds a dome over your head, and creates for you a refuge, a mysterious sanctuary for all human hearts. The young light foliage, soft as silk, springs out here and there like little tufts of down, little new wings which the forest is hanging out and trying on. But the next day, or the day after, you walk in a bower. All perpendicular lines may give the impression of either a fall or a rise. The beech trees' pewter-gray columns not only raise themselves, and reach forth from the ground toward infinity, the ether, the sun as the earth swings around it, but they lift and carry the lofty, the tremendous, roof of the airy hall. The light within, less bright than before, seems more powerful, filled with meaning, pregnant with secrets which are light in themselves, although unknowable to mortals. Here and there an old rugged oak, slow in putting out its leaves, opens a peephole in the ceiling. The fragrance and freshness encircle you as in an embrace. The branches, swaying down from above, seem to caress you or bless you, and as you walk onward you go under an incessant benediction.

Then all the country goes to the woods! to the woods! to make the most of a glory which does not last, for soon the leaves will darken and harden, and a shadow sink within. Driving and walking, the towns emigrate to the forest, sing and play amongst the tall trees, and bring bread and butter and make coffee upon the sward.

The Councilor also walked in the woods, and *Domine, non sum dignus,* he thought. Young Anders also confused the registers in the office, and left his bed untouched at night, and from La Liberté Fransine went out, her new straw bonnet upon her arm.

When the landscape was at its prettiest, the Councilor received a visit from his friend, Count Augustus von Schimmelmann. In spite of a difference in age of fifteen years, the two were real friends, united by many sympathies and common tastes. When the young Count was fifteen years old, the old Councilor had for a year filled the place of a friend of his, who had died, as tutor to the boy, and later they had met abroad, in Italy, and could talk together of books and religions, and of far people and places.

For some years they had not met, but this was due to no estrange-
ment between them, but to a development through which the
Count had been passing, during which he had been engaged in
making for himself a sort of *modus vivendi,* in which undertaking his old friend could have been of no use to him.

Count Augustus was by nature of a heavy and melancholy disposition. He wanted to be very happy but he had no talent for
happiness. He had suffered during his youth. Somewhere, somewhere in the world, he had thought, there must be a great, a
wonderful, happiness, the *fons et origo* of the power which mani-
fests itself in the delights of music, of flowers, and friendship. He
had collected flowers, studied music, and had many friends. He
had tried a life of pleasure and had been made happy many times.
But the road leading from it all into the heart of things he had
not found. As time went on a dreadful thing had happened to
him: one thing had become to him as good as another. Now, later
in life, he had accepted the happiness of life in a different way,
not as he really believed it to be, but, as in a reflection within a
mirror, such as others saw it.

This inner development had begun when he had unexpectedly
come into a very large fortune. Left to himself, he would have
thought very little of it, for he did not know what he was to do
with the money. But upon this occasion he was impressed by the
attitude of the world around him: the happening occupied it
much; the world thought it a great and splendid thing for him.
Count Augustus was by nature very envious himself, and had
housed this particular agony many times, mostly toward people
in books, so that he was in a position to value the weight of the
feeling. Next to painting a picture of which you yourself approve,
the most pleasant thing is perhaps to paint a picture about which
the whole world agrees to approve. Thus with the happiness of
Count Augustus. Slowly he took to living, so to say, upon the
envy of the outside world, and to accept his happiness according
to the quotation of the day. He never let himself be deceived into

believing that the world was right; he worked upon a system of bookkeeping by double entry. Under the entry of the world he had much to be proud or thankful for; he had hardly anything but assets in this account. He had an old name, one of the greatest estates and finest houses in Denmark, a beautiful wife, four pretty and industrious boys, the eldest twelve years old, a great fortune, a high prestige. He was an unusually handsome man, and became even more so with age, which went well with his type, and at this time of life he was a majestic figure. In the Consultation Chamber he had been called the Alcibiades of the North. He looked stronger than he was, like a man who enjoys his food and wine and sleeps well at night. He did not enjoy his food or wine much, and thought that he slept very badly, but to be envied by his neighbors for these goods of life became to him quite an acceptable substitute for the real goods.

Even the jealousy of his wife was, from this point of view, useful to him. The Countess had no reason to be jealous of her husband. Indeed it was doubtful whether, amongst all the women he had met, he did not like his wife best. But fifteen years of married life and four big sons had not cured her of her watchfulness and distrust, of the tears and long scenes, sometimes ending in her fainting away, which as a young man Count Augustus had thought a heavy cross. Now her jealousy took its place in his scheme of things, suggesting or proving to him the possibility, not of the ladies of the surrounding country seats and of the court falling in love with him—for that they unquestionably did—but of him himself falling in love with them, or with one of them. He came to depend upon her attitude, and had she reformed and done away with her jealousy, he would have missed it. Like to the Emperor in his new clothes, he was walking on, dignified, his life a continual procession, entirely successful in every respect except perhaps to himself. He did not think highly of his system, but it did not work badly, and during the last five years he had been happier than before.

While he had thus, like a coral polyp, been building up his moral world, the Councilor could have done him no good whatever. For he had not got it in him to be envious of anybody, and he might have shaken the whole building. But now that it was firmly fastened, and he himself safely encysted within it, with no soft parts exposed, even to the extent of taking the whole matter a bit in jest, he met his old friend again with great pleasure. The Councilor, for his part, would always have been pleased to meet him. So would probably Diogenes always have been pleased to meet Alexander. Alexander was pleased with the moment when he declared that had he not been Alexander he would have been Diogenes. But who knows whether the great conqueror, who was very likely to a certain extent dependent upon the opinion of the world, would at the time have liked to hear the philosopher of the tub declare that had he not been Diogenes he would have liked to be Alexander. Later on in his career he might have allowed himself the luxury of a second meeting, and a real discussion upon the nature of things, with the Cynic. So did Count Augustus.

The two friends might still have passed as Alexander and Diogenes of 1836 as they walked in the woods, along roads strewn with the silky fallen teguments of the young leaves. In their dark clothes they were like two sedate birds, rooks or magpies, out to enjoy the May afternoon with their gayer colleagues.

They sat down upon a rustic seat in the forest and talked.

"As we live," said Count Augustus, "we become aware of the humiliating fact that as we are dependent upon our subordinates —and without my barber I should be, within a week, socially, politically, and domestically a wreck—so are we, in the spiritual world, dependent upon people stupider than ourselves. I have, as you may know, some time since given up any artistic ambitions and have been occupying myself, within the sphere of the arts, with connoisseurship." (He was indeed a shrewd critic of all objects of art.) "Here I have learned that it is not possible to paint any definite object, say, a rose, so that I, or any other intelligent critic, shall not be able to decide, within twenty years, at what period it was painted, or, more or less, at what place on the earth. The artist has meant to create either a picture of a rose in the abstract, or the portrait of a particular rose; it is never in the least his intention to give us a Chinese, Persian, or Dutch, or, according to the period, a rococo or a pure Empire rose. If I told him that this was what he had done, he would not understand me. He might be angry with me. He would say: 'I have painted a rose.' Still he cannot help it. I am thus so far superior to the artist that I can mete him with a measure of which he himself knows nothing. At the same time I could not paint, and hardly see or conceive, a rose myself. I might imitate any of their creations. I might say: 'I will paint a rose in the Chinese or Dutch or in the rococo manner.' But I should never have the courage to paint a rose as it looks. For how does a rose look?"

He sat for a while in thought, his walking stick upon his knees.

"Thus," he said, "with the general human idea of virtue, justice, or, if you will, of God. If anybody were to ask me what was the truth about these things, I should answer: 'My friend, your question is without meaning. The Hebrews conceived their God like this; the Aztecs of America, about whom I have just read a book, like that; the Jansenites again, like that. If you want any details of the various views I shall be pleased to give them, having devoted a certain amount of my time to this study. But let me advise you not to repeat your question in intelligent company.' But at the same time I should be, for this superior view of mine, in debt to the naïve people who have believed in the possibility of obtaining a direct and absolutely truthful idea of God, and who were mistaken. For had they made it their object only to create a special Hebrew, Aztec or Christian idea of God, where would the presuppositions of the observer have been found? He would be in the position of the Israelites, who were to make bricks without straw. Indeed, my friend, while the fools could have done without us, we are dependent upon the fools for our better knowledge.

"When," he went on after a little pause, "you and I, on our morning walk, pass a pawnbroker's shop, and, pointing at a painted board in the window, on which is written 'Clothes mangled here,' you say to me: 'Look, clothes are mangled here—I shall go and bring my washing,' I smile at you, and inform you that you will find neither mangle nor mangler here, that the painted board is for sale.

"Most religions are like that board, and we smile at them.

"But I should have no opportunity of smiling, or of feeling or showing my superiority, and, in fact, the painted board would not be there at all, if, at some time or other, some people had not believed firmly in the possibility, in the wisdom, of mangling clothes, had not even been firmly convinced of the existence of their own mangle, with which clothes were indeed mangled."

The Councilor listened to him. Now that they were out here together in the green wood, he thought that he would like to talk of his marriage plans, of which he had not yet informed anyone, not even Madame Fransine.

"My friend," he said, "in all this foolishness of which you are speaking, I myself fit in harmoniously. *Alter schützt vor Thorheit nicht*. Under this venerable beaver hat of mine, I, while listening to you, have been harboring little thoughts which came out and fluttered like those two yellow butterflies"—he pointed at them with his stick—"little creeds, if you will forgive me, in absolute virtue, in beauty, even, perhaps, in God. I am seriously contemplating entry into the bonds of Hymen, and had you come to Hirschholm three months later, I might have had a Madame Mathiesen to do the honors to you."

Count Augustus was much surprised, but he had so much faith in the wisdom of his friend that before the eyes of his mind the image of a mature and pleasant beauty, witty and thrifty, with

an agreeable dowry, was instantly formed. Smiling, he hastened
to congratulate the Councilor.

"Yes, but I do not know yet if she will have me," said the old
man, "which is the worst of it. For she is not more than a third
of my age, and, to the best of my belief, a romantic little devil.
She can neither make a pancake nor darn a sock, and she will
not read the philosophy of Hegel. If I get her I shall have to buy
the French fashion papers, carry my wife's shawl at the balls of
Hirschholm, study the language of flowers, and take to narrating
ghost stories in the winter evenings."

Count Augustus at these words received quite a little shock, so
much was he reminded of old days. It was indeed as if he saw
young Augustus Schimmelmann playing chess with his tutor at
the open window of the library of Lindenburg. For this had always been a particular little trick of the Councilor's whenever you
brought out anything for his inspection. When you were most
confident in your aces and kings he would put down a tiny little
trump to knock them on the head, and that at a moment when
you had not been aware that there were any trumps in. He had
been the same as a little boy. When the other children had, in
the autumn, been playing under the trees, pretending that the
chestnuts were horses, he would come out with a little cage of
white mice, really alive and thus much more like horses; or, as
they were comparing their various treasures of knives, wooden
soldiers and fishing hooks, he would pull out of his pocket a bit
of gunpowder, which might blow up the whole lot in a very fine
flash. He did not run down his friends' acquisitions; there was
nothing negative in his argument. But he had a little familiar
devil which at the right moment put out its head and conjured
the weight out of your things, so that you would feel a little
flat about them. Those who have no taste for devils disliked
this quality in the man. The opposite type, the chess player for
one, was attracted by it. Here Count Augustus had been prome-
nading before him, serenely, his superiority to life, his secure and

unassailable relation to it, when pat! the Councilor took out of his pocket a little bright bit of risk and made it sparkle between his fingers like a jewel. The younger man had been uttering words of wisdom, and the old man produced a little flute and played three notes on it, just to remind him that there was such a thing as music, and also such a thing as folly, and alas for the heart of his old pupil.

The Councilor's eyes followed the dance of the butterflies as they disappeared between the trees. "But light," he said, "terrible as an army with banners."

Count Augustus took off his hat and put it on his knees. The calm sweet air of the May evening ran like caressing fingers through his locks. All this was so much like old days, this little gentle shock of envy, as if the wings of the yellow butterflies had touched his heart. Young Augustus was again walking, and meditating upon heroism and the fun of life, in the cool and sweet-smelling air, under a light and silky young foliage. He let his silver-headed walking stick describe circles on the ground. What was his reputation for enjoying his wine and sleeping well at night—what was even the genuine enjoyment of these things? he asked himself now as he remembered words that he had heard long ago: "Who never ate his bread with tears, and never through the sorrowful night sat weeping on his bed, he knows ye not, ye heavenly powers." Those heavenly powers—he had not thought of them for so long. His heart swelled a little at the remembrance of the way in which hearts do swell.

A figure came toward them down one of the forest paths, drew nearer, and was recognized by the Councilor as that of his protégé. The Councilor introduced him to his influential friend, and after a few remarks asked him to recite a poem for them.

Anders found it difficult to think of anything. His heart, in this particular spring, was moving in circles as large as those of the planets around the sun. Still he wanted to oblige this majestic, cold elderly gentleman. For he was not deceived by the Emperor's new clothes, but saw him at once as the center of a procession, shivering, in his shirt. In the end he found a little ballad to recite, a little gay drop of overflow from all that happiness and pain which had filled him lately. It was about a young man who goes to sleep in the forest and is taken into fairyland. The fairies love him and look after him with great concern, puzzling their little brains to make him happy. The delights of forest life were inspiredly painted, a long line running out at the end of each stanza giving it something of the babbling of a spring in the woods. But the fairies never sleep and have no knowledge of sleep. Whenever their young friend, fatigued by exquisite pleasure, dozes off, they lament "He dies, he dies!" and strain all their energy to keep him awake. So in the end, to their deep regret, the boy dies from lack of sleep.

Count Augustus praised the beauty of the poem and thought the beauty of the little fairy queen charmingly put into words. This boy, he thought, had in him a very strong streak of primitive sensuality which would have to be watched if the tastefulness of his production were not to suffer.

"Beware," he said smilingly to the Councilor, "of the delights of fairyland. To poor mortals the value of pleasure, surely, lies in its rarity. Did not the sages of old tell us: He is a fool who knows not the half to be more than the whole? Where pleasure goes on forever, we run the risk of becoming blasé, or, according to our young friend, of dying."

An idea occurred to the Councilor. This green wood, he thought, might do well as the setting for a bit of drama. "The Count," he said, smiling, to the boy, "smiles at a little secret into which I have taken him. I will make you my confidant as well, Anders; only you must not smile at your old friend. I hope to procure for you, before long, a young patroness to recite to, who may, in the beauty of your fairy queens, dryads and undines, see her own beauty reflected as in a mirror." As in a dim and silvery mirror, just before sunrise, he thought.

The young man, who was still standing up before the two dark figures on the sea, remained thus for a few moments in silence, as if in deep thought. Then he lifted his hat a little to the Councilor. "I wish you happiness, I am sure," he said, gravely, looking at him, "and thank you for telling me. When is this going to be?"

"Ah, I do not know. In the time of the roses, Anders," said the Councilor, taken somewhat aback by the youth's directness. Anders, after a moment, bade good-by to the Count and to his patron and went away. Count Schimmelmann, who was an observer of men, followed him with his eyes. What! he thought. Did the old conjurer of Hirschholm have at his disposal not only his old familiar spirit and evidently a dryad to make love to, but also a young slave of that tribe of Asra who die when they love?

He felt a little cold, as if left out, not only of life in the abstract, but of some fullness of this particular May evening. He rose from the rustic seat and began to walk back. As, in the conversation with his host, he looked at his face, he noted there a deep, a gently inspired and resolute, look. *"Das,"* thought the Count, who came of a military race, smiling, *"das ist nur die Freude eines Helden den schönen Tod eines Helden zu sehen."* Later on, however, he thought of these moments.

Now Count Augustus had one real talent and happiness, which other people might well have envied him, but of which he never spoke. He took hashish, and he took a little only, without ever overdoing the pleasure. Somewhere in the world he may have had brothers in hashish who would have given him half of their lives could he have sold them this capacity.

Walking at the Councilor's side, he thought: What shall I dream tonight? Opium, he reflected, is a brutal person who takes you by the collar. Hashish is an insinuating oriental servant who throws a veil over the world for you, and by experimenting you can arrive at the power of choosing the figures within the web of the veil. He had already been a rajah hunting tigers from the backs of elephants, and watching bayaderes dancing; he had been the director of the great opera of Paris; and he had been Shamyl, pushing onward with his rebellious freemen, through the towering, snow-clad mountain passes of the Caucasus. But tonight what would he choose to dream? Could he recall the dewy May nights within the festoons of boughs at Ingolstadt? If he choose to, could he?—If he could, would he?

After supper at the Councilor's house he ordered his magnificent landaulet and his much-envied English pair of horses, and drove away.

As Councilor Mathiesen was preparing to go to La Liberté, a-wooing, the next day, news was brought which proved to be a nut somewhat hard for him to crack. It was served him by his housekeeper, along with his new hat which he had asked her to take out of the box.

This woman, whose name was Abelone, had been in his house for more than fifteen years, but was still a young woman, tall, red-haired, and of an extraordinary physical strength. She had lived all her life at Hirschholm, and there was no particle of the life of the little town that she did not know. It was strange that there should be any mystery about herself, but there were people who told that she had been, as a girl of fifteen, suspected of concealment of birth and infanticide, and had had a narrow escape. The Councilor held her in respect. He had not met her match as an economist, not only in the keeping of his house, but in existence as a whole. To her, waste was probably the one deadly sin and abomination. Everything which came within the circle of her consciousness had to be made use of in one way or another, and nothing, as far as he could see, was ever thrown away by her. If she had had nothing but a rat to make a ragoût of, she would have made a good ragoût of it. In his own intercourse with her he always felt that every word and mood of his was somehow taken stock of, and kept, to be made use of sooner or later.

On this pleasant May day she proceeded to report to him the behavior, on the previous night, of his young clerk, whom she had until then taken into possession as an article of inventory of the household, and treated kindly.

This young man had been part of a company at the inn. As the beer had come to an end, he had promised his convives that he would give them something better, and being, as the Councilor knew, in possession of the keys to the church, where he had been going through the parochial registers, he had fetched from the sacristy four bottles of communion wine, with which he had regaled the party. He had not been in the least drunk, but quiet in his manner, as usual. He had, Abelone added, proposed the Councilor's health in this wine.

While she was narrating, the Councilor was looking at himself in the glass, for he had decided, with the slight nervousness suitable in a suitor, to put on another stock, and was now tying it with solicitude. It is not too much to say that Abelone's tale frightened him. This was, in a Hirschholm format, Lucifer storming heaven. In what words had his own toast been drunk?

He came to look at Abelone, behind him, in the mirror. Something in her manner, more than in her broad, stagnant face, which was ever like the locked door behind which was kept her rich store of material to be made use of, gave him the impression that she, too, was frightened, or deeply moved. There was more here, then, than met the eye. Abelone was by no means a gossip. Whatever she knew about other people she did not let out—she probably knew of a better recipe for making use of it—and four bottles of communion wine would be no more to her than four bottles. If she would not let the devil have the boy, was it that she wanted him herself? Was he the rat out of which she was to make her ragoût?

He turned back to his own face, and met the eyes of a good councilor. To be a spectator when Lucifer was storming heaven might be a highly interesting experience; more interesting still if one could succeed in putting a spoke in the wheel for him.

"My good Abelone," he said, smiling, "Hirschholm seems to

have a little talent for scandal. I myself instructed Mr. Anders to
take away the wine from the sacristy. I have reason to believe
that it was, by mistake, mixed with rum, which, not being made
from the grape, can hardly be suitable for the transubstantiation.
Mr. Anders will see to it that it is replaced."

Thereupon he drove off to La Liberté with much stuff for
thought, most of it, curiously enough, about his housekeeper. It
was not till he turned up the poplar avenue that his mind turned
again toward his future.

On his arrival he did not find the young lady in, and had to
wait for a little while in the garden-room. On a little console
table Fransine had put a large bunch of jessamine in a vase. The
sweet and bitter scent was strong, nearly stifling, in the cool room.
He was a little nervous about his own appearance in the rôle of
a suitor, not about her answer. For she would accept him. She
was pretty sure to do, in life, as she was told. He wondered
whether, when he should be driving away again from La Liberté
as her accepted wooer, she would occupy herself at all with the
thought of her future as his wife. That it would be he, who, later
in life, would be told how things were to turn out under her
hands, that was a different matter.

It seemed to him, while he was waiting, that he was coming
into a closer understanding with the furniture in the sky-blue
room. The spinet, the musical box, and the chairs had withdrawn
a little, with their backs to the wall, as if uneasy about him, like
the furniture of a doll's house, frightened at the intrusion of a
grown-up person. Would the time for games be over now? He
tried to set them at ease. "I have not come," he said to them all,
"to destroy, but to fulfill. The best games are to come."

At this, as if actually soothed into existence again, young Madame Lerche came into the room in a pink frock with flounces,
followed by her maid who carried the samovar and tea tablecloth for the guest. He could, after a bit of pleasant conversation,
begin his proposal.

Fransine always gave him the impression of being anxious, or pleased, to have done with what she had taken on. For what reason he knew not, for there was nothing else on which she seemed at all keen to get started. She did not, he thought, run the risk of Faust in asking the moment to stay because of its loveliness. She pushed all her moments on as quickly as a little nun of Italy, who counts her rosary, pushes on the beads. As he now talked to her of his love and audacious hopes, she grew a little paler and moved her slim figure slightly in the big chair. Her dark eyes met his and looked away again. She was pleased when it was over. She accepted him as he had thought, even with a little emotion, as a refuge in life. The Councilor kissed her hand, and she was pleased to have that over.

Afterward, as the betrothed couple were having tea together, Fransine presiding on the sofa behind the tall samovar, to affect a little importance the Councilor told her of Anders and the communion wine. Here he nearly got more than he had bargained for, for it made a terrible impression upon her. She looked as if she wanted to sink into the ground to get away from such abomination. When she could speak, she asked him, deadly pale, whether the pastor knew it. The Councilor had not expected such a profound awe of sacred things in her. It was an amiable quality, but there was more here, a fear of ghosts, or a ghost itself. He reassured her, and told her how he had decided to free the young clerk from the consequences of his folly. Upon this she gave him a great luminous glance, so languishing and alive in its deep dark sweetness that it filled all the room, like the perfume of the jessamine, and made him feel powerful and benevolent.

"I ought," said the Councilor, "to frighten the boy for his own sake. Why, if I had not helped him to this job, he would be starving." At this last word Fransine again grew pale. "And still you know, my dear," the Councilor went on, "he has a great career in front of him. This is a sad thing: to see a thoughtless boy, a vagabond, ruin the future of a great man. And to me it is somewhat my future too, as if he were my son. But I am afraid to awaken in him an obstinacy which I shall not be able to subdue. The gentle touch of a woman might appeal to his better feelings. He is, surely, the type of human who ought to have a guardian angel, and it would be noble in you if you would assist me in saving him by reading him a little sermon."

So it was arranged that Fransine should accompany the Councilor to Hirschholm to preach to Anders Kube. She quickly put on a pink bonnet through which the sun heightened the color of her face to the glow of a rose. It was a little unusual for a young woman to drive out alone with a gentleman. Even with Kresten on the back seat, the Councilor thought that the passers-by would conclude upon their engagement, and he enjoyed the drive. Fransine, by his side, looked at the trotting horse and seemed happy to be getting it over with.

The Councilor and his young bride, who was to act the part of a guardian angel, arm in arm ascended the narrow stair to Anders's small rooms behind the big, newly unfolded lime tree, and found his sister, who was the wife of a merchant captain of Elsinore, and her little boy with him. This made the young woman's errand more complicated, but eased her heart. She felt that she might pass a peaceful and pleasing hour in this company. The sister and brother were much alike, and when the child looked at her, the heart of Fransine ceased to beat, for here was a bambino such as she had known in the churches of Naples —a cherub with Anders's eyes, showing the poet's personality as might a little mirror in heaven.

Fransine had come, in her elegant shawl, as a patroness to the poor and erroneous. She stood now, dark-eyed and stock-still, with the face of Rachel as she said to Jacob: "Give me children or else I die." She wanted to kneel down to hold the child against her, but was doubtful about the correctness of such a move. Then it occurred to her that she might obtain the same result by lifting him to her level. She placed him upon a chair, first to look out of the window, then to play with her fingers in their black mittens. The child stared at her. He had never seen such ringlets as hers, and poked his little hand into them. To amuse him she took off her bonnet and shook the whole mass of dark tresses forward. They fell like clouds around her face, and the child laughed and pulled at them with both hands. She held him against her bosom, lightly, laughing, looking into his face, and felt for a moment his heart, like a small clock, beating against her own. As the others looked at them she blushed. Waves of deep color washed over her face, but still she could not help smiling.

The Councilor began to converse with the young mother, who sat down on the sofa, in her neat white fluted cap, with the little boy on her lap, and the two young people were left at the window in a tête-à-tête. Fransine felt that the time had come for her to enter upon her mission.

"Mr. Anders," she said, "the Councilor—my fiancé"—she corrected herself, "has told me with much regret that he has had reason to be disappointed, to be angry with you. It is not right; you must not let it be so. You do not know, perhaps, in Hirschholm, how much evil and misery there is in the world. But I pray you, Mr. Anders, do not do these things which bring people into perdition."

Although she was addressing him so solemnly, her face still wore a reflection of her smile of a moment ago. Even as she went on talking and was deeply moved, it remained there.

Anders did not hear a word of what she was saying. With that great talent for oblivion, which the Councilor did not always appreciate in his protégé, Anders had long since forgotten all about the matter to which she was referring. He smiled back at her with exactly her own expression. As her face changed, his changed. They took light and shade from each other like two mirrors hung opposite each other in a room.

Fransine felt that the situation was not developing quite as it ought to, but she did not know what to do.

"The Councilor," she said, "loves you as if you were his son, and if he had not helped you, you might have been starving. He is wise. He knows better than we do how to behave in the world. Look," she said, fumbling at a small object which was tied to the golden watch-chain around her neck. It was a little piece of coral, formed like a horn, such as the plain people of Italy use as a talisman. "This my grandmother gave me. It is said to protect you against evil eyes. But she thought that it would guard you also against smallpox, and your own dangerous thoughts. For this reason she gave it to me. You take it now, and let it remind you to be careful, to follow the Councilor's advice."

Anders took the little amulet from her. As their hands met, they both grew very pale.

From his place on the sofa, the Councilor could see with the corner of his eye that great forces were in play. And he saw plainly that his bride gave to the young clerk, as some sort of symbol, what looked like a little pair of horns. With this, were it more or less than he had expected, he had to be content, and he and Fransine walked down the stair, arm in arm, to where Kresten was waiting for them with the carriage.

As it was not considered by the social world of Hirschholm quite proper that an engaged couple, even though the bridegroom were a man of a certain age, and the bride a widow, should be much together by themselves, it became, during the summer months, the custom for Anders, in the capacity of a chaperon, to accompany the Councilor on his visits to La Liberté. Upon fine evenings the three of them would have tea on the terrace, and Fransine made them pretty little Italian dishes which reminded the Councilor of other days and things. Looking then, in the mild, glowing evening light, across the tea table at the two young people who were both so precious to him—although their order of precedence within his heart might have surprised them—the Councilor felt happy and in harmony with the universe as he very rarely had before. It was difficult, he thought, to imagine a more perfect idyll. "I, too," he said to himself, "have been in Arcadia."

At times the attitudes of his young shepherd and shepherdess surprised him and made him uneasy, and he was reminded of a tale which he had read in a book of travel. Therein a party of British explorers in a Negro village came upon a troop of prisoners who were being fattened, behind a palisade, for the table of their capturers. The indignant Britishers offered to buy their freedom, but the victims refused, for they thought that they were having a more pleasant time than they had ever had. Was it possible, the Councilor thought, that the young people had some plan of escape that they were skillfully concealing, or were they no more provident than the cannibals' captives? Both possibilities seemed to him equally unlikely.

Still he was not in his parable very far from the truth; or the truth, had he known it, would not have appeared to him any more probable.

To Anders the situation was simplified by his decision to kill himself on Fransine's wedding day, a decision which he had made when he heard of her engagement, and which seemed to him as inevitable as death itself. To the Danish peasant of his type the idea of flinging away your life comes very easily. Life never seems —or, indeed, is—to them any very great boon, and suicide in one way or another may be said to be the natural end of them.

Anders had not been spoiled by fate. If he had been spoiled at all, it had been done by other powers. He had felt the common lot of his kind, that is: to be, as if he had been made out of some stuff essentially different from the rest of the world, invisible to other people. When he had met Fransine, she had seen him. Without any effort, her clear eyes had taken him all in. This sort of human non-existence of which he had at times been tired had come to an end, and he had promised himself much from his newly gained reality. If she was marrying the Councilor, and turning away her eyes, it was only reasonable that he himself should turn elsewhere.

He was always very reserved about his own plans, and in this case felt that his decision concerned nobody but himself. Therefore he did not let it out in any manner. The Councilor, had he known of it, would not only have prevented it, but would also have disliked it. Few people would choose to sit down at their tea tables with a ghost of today a week. Fransine it might have made unhappy. Anders had no chivalry in his disposition, but he had a talent for friendliness, and he would not have liked to grieve any of them. To avoid it he had even planned to borrow a sailing boat from a friend of his amongst the fishermen of Rungsted and to capsize by accident. He was a skilled sailor and could manage that. From time to time he had a strange feeling toward Anders Kube, as toward some central figure in one of his own poems. Sometimes he felt a little guilty, and then again as a benefactor, for he was helping him to escape a lot of unpleasant things. Upon the whole he had, behind his palisade, as quiet eyes as those of the Negro prisoners in the tale.

Apart from this central idea of his, he had in his head a great poem, a swan song, which he was to finish before himself. Having written before of the forests and fields, and relying upon the sea for a last embrace, he had let all his thoughts wander toward her. Naiads and tritons danced in the waves within this last great epos of his; the whales passed over their heads like clouds; dolphins, swans, and fishes played in the powerful and pearly foam of long breakers, and the winds played at flutes and bassoons, and joined in great orchestras. That freedom in which people live, who can die, had got into it; and although it was not, as a drama, very long, there was no end to its many aspects. He read it to Fransine, in the afternoons at La Liberté, as it proceeded.

As to Fransine, it was natural for her to live like this, from hand to mouth. She had no real idea of time; indeed did not have it in her to distinguish between time and eternity. That was one of the traits of character which made the ladies of Hirschholm think her a little feebleminded. She had never before in her life been as happy as this, and could not feel sure whether the uncertainty about its duration and about the future might not be a peculiarity of happiness. For the rest her thoughts followed the moods of Anders. She read his last great poem, and as it was all about the sea, she had the frocks of her trousseau made in hues of sky and sea blue—rather heavenly the two men thought her.

As during these months the Councilor came to know his bride better, he was often surprised by her extreme disregard of truth. He was himself a rearranger of existence, and in many ways in sympathy with her; also in this he found her methods to fall in well with his own plans. But still more than once this talent of hers impressed him. It was, he reflected, an especially feminine trick, a *code de femme* of practical economy, proved by innumerable generations. Women, wanting to be happy, are up against a *force majeure*. Hence they may be justified in taking a short cut to happiness by declaring things to be, in fact, that which they want them to be. They have by practice made this household remedy indispensable in the housekeeping of life. In this way, because he was to be her husband, he was pronounced by his young bride *ipso facto* good, clever, and generous. He did not take it as a personal compliment; she had probably made use of the same formula in connection with the old apothecary Lerche. So were his presents to her always beautiful, so were the sermons of old Pastor Abel of Hirschholm highly moving, so was the weather nice when he took her out for a drive. An exception to the rule was formed by her frocks and bonnets, about which she took much genuine trouble; but then she had such a talent for wearing clothes that in this she could successfully strive toward an ideal. Whether she had come to take refuge in this woman's religion from personal need, or had been inaugurated into it by wise female Nestors, he did not know. Few women, he thought, come to know romance, married bliss, or success in life except by such an arrangement. The principle had some likeness to Count Schimmelmann's new clothes, but, invented by simple women, it was devoid of any masculine ambition to prove; it was plain dogma, indisputable.

Thus did the witches of old make up wax children, carry them for nine months under their clothes, and then have them christened, at midnight, with the name of someone of their acquaintance, and after that for all practical purposes the wax child served in place of its namesake. In the hands of an amiable witch this pretty white magic might work much good. But if ever a young witch conceives and carries for nine months a child of her own flesh and blood? Ah! it is then that there will be the devil and all to pay.

The Councilor, seeing his protégé so absorbed in his new work, asked him to read it to him. Anders saw no reason whatever why his old friend should not know of it, and recited bits of it to him from time to time. The old man was very much impressed, filled with an admiration which at times came near to idolatry. It seemed to him, too, that he had come out into a new sort of space and time, into the ether itself, until he was swimming and flying in the blue, and in a new kind of harmony and happiness. He thought it the beginning of great things. He discussed it much with the poet, and even advised him upon it, so that not a few of the Councilor's own ideas and reflections were, in one way or another, echoed within the epos, and he was, during these summer months, in a way making love, and writing poetry, to his bride by proxy—a piquant situation, which would last till his wedding day. For days and weeks the three of them, even while taking tea upon the terrace, would be living in the waters of great, heavenly seas.

Two days before the wedding the Councilor received from a friend in Germany a copy of the new novel, *Wally: Die Zwei-*

flerin, by young Gutzkow, about which the waves of indignation and discussion were at the time going high there.

As it will be remembered, Wally and Cæsar love each other, but they cannot marry, for Wally has promised to become the bride of the ambassador of Sardinia. Cæsar then demands of her that she shall, to symbolize the spiritual marriage between her and him, upon the very wedding morning, show herself to him naked, in her full beauty. There exists an old German poem in which Sigune in this way reveals herself to Tchionatulander.

The Councilor was so much interested in the novel that he brought it with him on his afternoon visit to La Liberté, and went on with his reading, seated under a tree on the terrace, while the young people went to look at a tame fox cub which Fransine kept in the kennel. He considered that he would not, in the coming week, have much time for reading, and that he had better finish his book today.

He read:

To his left appears a picture of enrapturing beauty: Sigune, who uncovers herself more bashfully than the Medician Venus covers her nudity. She stands there helpless, blinded by the divine madness of love. It has asked this grace of her, and she is no more free of will; she is all shame, innocence, and devotion. And as a sign that a pious initiation sanctifies the scene, no red rose flowers there; only a tall white lily, blooming close to her body, covers her as a symbol of chastity. A mute second—a breath—that was all. A sacrilege, but a sacrilege inspired by innocence and by ever faithful renunciation. . . .

The Councilor closed his book, and leaning back in his chair, as if he were looking toward heaven, he even closed his eyes. The air under the crown of the lime tree was filled with green and golden light, with the sweet scent of the linden blossoms, and the humming of innumerable bees.

This, he thought, is very pretty. Very pretty, let old Professor

Menzel thunder against it as he likes. A dream of a golden age, of an eternal innocence and sweetness came back to him. Let the critics say that such things do not happen; that does not really matter, for a new variety of flower has been forced in the frame of imagination. He could hear Fransine and Anders talking a little way off, but he could not hear what the talk was about.

From the kennel the two young people had walked down to the vegetable garden, south of the house, to pick some lettuce, peas, and young carrots for the supper table. Part of the low garden was already shaded by a row of old crooked birches which formed the boundary fence of the garden. Through an opening they could look out on the fields, where, in the mellow, golden, evening air two maids, walking out to milk the cows and carrying their tall milk pans on their heads, threw tremendously long blue shadows across the clover field.

Fransine asked Anders's advice about the fox cub. "In the autumn," she said, "if I let him out, will he be able to find his own food?"

"I should let him out," said Anders, "only he may be too familiar with your hen-coops, and come back in the night." He had a vision of the sharp-toothed, lonely fox, the ghost of the woolen playmate of their summer evenings, in a frosty, silvery, winter night, trotting on to La Liberté. "Then you must come and catch him again," said Fransine.

"But then I shall not be here," said Anders, without thinking.

"Oh," said she, "what high offices, in what state, are taking you away from us, Mr. Anders?" Anders was silent. What high offices, in what state?

"I have got to go away," he said at last. Fransine did not dispute the fact. Probably she knew enough of the hard necessity, mistress of men and gods. But after a moment she looked at him, as intently as if she had thrown her whole being at him in the glance. "But if you are not here," she said, "it will be—" she reflected for a second—"it will be too cold here!" she said. Anders understood her very well. An immense wave of pity lifted him up and hurled him at her feet. It would indeed be too cold for her. And his soul was rent between the despair of her feeling cold, and the despair of his being, by that time, too cold to comfort her. "What am I to do then?" she asked him. She was standing up before him. Except that she was clothed, and her two hands were therefore reposing lightly on the flounces of her dress, she was holding the exact pose of that Venus of Medici of which the Councilor was at the same moment reading. Looking at her, Anders remembered that he had before seen her as a child who would not lose, in him, her favorite doll. Now he saw her differently, as the doll which could not lose its child, the child who was to play with it, dress and undress it, and go into ecstasies over it—an ownerless doll, a stray doll, except in his hands.

"Mr. Anders," she said, "in those weeks after Easter, when we were much together in the Councilor's house, at that picnic in Rungsted—do you remember?—you told me that it would be your happiness to remain here, as my friend, all your life." He did not speak. Those weeks after Easter hurt when you thought of them, and they might kill if you spoke about them. "Are you such a faithless friend?" she asked.

"Listen, Madame Fransine," he said, "I dreamed of you two nights ago." At this she smiled, but was much interested. "I dreamed," he said, "that you and I were walking to a great seashore, where a strong wind was blowing. You said to me: 'This is to go on forever.' But I said that we were only dreaming. 'Oh, no, you must not think that,' you said. 'Now, if I take off my new bonnet and throw it into the sea, will you believe that it is no dream?' So you untied your bonnet and threw it from you, and the waves carried it far away. Still I thought that it was a dream. 'Oh, how ignorant you are,' you said, 'but if I take off my silk shawl and throw it away, you must see that all this is real.' You threw back your silk shawl, and from the sand the wind lifted it and carried it off. But I could not help thinking that it was a

dream. 'If I cut off my left hand,' you said, 'will you be convinced?' You had a pair of scissors in the pocket of your frock.
You held up your left hand, just as if it had been a rose, and cut
it off. And with that——" He stopped, very pale. "With that I
woke up," he said.

She stood quite still. She had much faith in dreams, and had
felt herself walking with him on the seashore of which he had
just told her. But now she was collecting all her arsenal to keep
him, for she really thought that if she were to lose him she would
die. She would cut off her left hand for him, if he wanted it, but
it were better that it should be under his head. In the clear and
sweet evening air she felt her own body strong and light as a
young birch tree, her slim waist pliant as a branch, her young
breasts resting lightly, like a pair of smooth, round eggs, in the
nest of warm and fresh lawn. Her flaming gaze was so deeply
sunk in his, and his in hers, that it would take a powerful crane to
lift them apart again.

She lifted the Venus's lower hand just a little and held it toward him, slowly, as if it had been a heavy weight. He stretched
out his hand and touched her finger tip. It was exactly the gesture
of the Creator of Michelangelo transmitting divine life to young
Adam. Such various reproductions of high classic art were moving about, in the evening, in the kitchen garden of La Liberté.

They heard the Councilor stirring in his seat, laying away his
book and gazing up into the crown of the tree. Slowly, without
a word, Fransine turned and walked along the terrace toward
him, and Anders followed her with the basket of lettuce and peas.

The Councilor still had a finger in the book, at the page where
he had last been reading. "Ah, Fransine," he said, "here I have
been smuggling into the academy of refinement of La Liberté
a little *sans-culotte* of literature. The young author has been put
into prison for it in Germany. That is right. Punish the flesh and
let the spirit fly. Since the professors of universities have con-
fiscated the poet, we may enjoy his poetry. I am speaking frivol-

ously, my dear," he went on, "but upon an evening like this, the moralist cuts a poor figure. And what really captivated me was a curious incident, a very minor matter. For it seems to me that Gutzkow gives, in the meeting place of the rash young lovers, an accurate description of your own little temple of friendship, at La Liberté, down in the beech wood."

With these words he got up, and went to have tea with his bride, leaving the book on the seat under the linden.

Upon the last day before his wedding the Councilor paid no visit to La Liberté. This is considered the correct thing in Denmark. The bride is given the last day to meditate in peace upon the past and the future; and the bridal couple meet again only in church. The Councilor also had much to do, and spent his day going through papers and making arrangements with his subordinates, so as not to have the first days of his honeymoon disturbed by prosaic matters. But he sent over young Anders with a large bouquet of roses. It was a fine summer day.

In the evening, after sunset, Anders took his gun and went out to shoot duck. The Councilor, also, found no rest in his rooms, and started for a long walk, as may a bridegroom, filled with sentiments. He took the road across the fields to La Liberté, to roam, unnoticed by the world and by her, in the nearness of his bride.

The sky of that summer night was a clear candid blue, like the petal of a periwinkle. Large silvery clouds were towered up all around the horizon; the big trees were holding up their severe dark crowns against them. The long wet grass was of a luminous green. All the colors of the day were within the landscape, no less bright than in daytime, but changed, as if revealing a new side of their being, as if the whole world of color had been transposed from a major to a minor key. The stillness and silence of the night was filled with a deep life, as if within a moment the universe would give up its secret. As the old Councilor looked up, he was surprised to see the full summer moon standing in the middle of the sky. Its shining disc threw a narrow bridge of gold across the iron-gray plane of the sea, as if a shoal of many hundred little fishes were playing in the surface; and still it did not seem to spread much light, as if no more light were needed.

Now that he knew them to be there, however, he began to distinguish the transparent pools of shadow under the trees, which the moon was making, and the narrow little puddles along the road, just at the edge of the long, wet, and fragrant grass.

The Councilor found that he had been standing for some time, looking at the moon. She was a long way off, he knew, but there was nothing between her and him but the diaphanous air, thinner, he had been told, the higher you got up. How was it that he had never been able to write a poem to the moon? He had much to say to her. She was so white and round, and the white and round things he had always loved.

Suddenly it seemed to him that the moon had as much to say to him as he to her. More, or at least she expressed it with more power. Old, yes, he was old; so was she, older than he. It is not a bad thing to be old, he thought; you see and enjoy things better than when you are young. It is not only in the old wine that the bouquet lies; it wants an old palate as well.

But was this powerful communication from the moon a warning? He remembered the nursery tale of the thief who has stolen a fat sheep and is eating it in the moonlight. Mockingly he holds up a bit of fat mutton to the moon, crying:

> *See, my dear,*
> *What I here*
> *Can with pleasure offer.*

And the moon replies:

> *Thief! beware!*
> *Key, with care,*
> *Burn that stupid scoffer.*

Whereupon a red-hot key comes flying through the air and brands the face of the thief. That story must have been told him by his old nurse fifty years ago. Everything was in the night. Life, yes, and death, a *memento mori* somewhere. "Take care, death is here!" the moon said. Must he let himself be warned?

Or was it a promise? Was his old self to be lifted now, like to Endymion, to be rewarded for the trouble of life by an everlasting sleep, sweet as this night? Would the world then have a statue erected to him, here in the hayfield of La Liberté, in memory of his apotheosis?

What strange fancies were these? The dripping-wet, heavy-headed, honey-sweet clover brushed against his shins. He had a curious sensation of walking a little above the ground. There were cows lying or walking in it somewhere; he could not distinguish them in the moonlight, but their deep sweet fragrance was in the air.

Suddenly he remembered something that had happened more than forty years before. Young Peter Mathiesen, a reserved, speculative boy then, had been staying with his uncle, the parson at Mols, and in the same house a little girl, a farmer's daughter, was being prepared for her confirmation. His uncle had been a well-read man who talked about everything—God, love, life everlasting—and who was an enthusiast about the new romantic literature. They used to read poetry in the evening at the parsonage, and one night, because the little girl's name was Nanna, it had amused the pastor to make the children take part in the recital of the tragedy *Death of Baldur*, and to address to each other the burning, passion-sick verses of Baldur and Nanna. With his glasses pushed back the old parson had listened, transported, with that kind of shamelessness which also makes old maids grow hyacinths in tall glasses so that they may watch the roots, and had not known that the country children were burning and turning pale under the sound of their own voices. When bed time came the boy had not been able to go to bed. Hot and bewildered, he had wandered about the farm buildings, seeking for something which might wash off this touch, and he had come down to the stables. It was a moonlight, misty night in early spring. Leaning against the wall, he had felt terribly lonely, and not only lonely, but betrayed, as if something were lying in wait for him. Then he had come to think of the cows inside, and of their imperturbability in the darkness. There was one big white cow, by the name of Rosa, which had been a favorite with the children. He had felt that she might give him comfort. Within her stall, his chest against the side of the reposing, gently chewing animal, a sweetly penetrating calm and balance had come upon him, and he had made up his mind to sleep with her all night. But hardly had he lain down in the straw when the stable door was opened gently, and a soft step approached. As he peeped over Rosa's back he saw the little girl come in, dim and light in the dim moonlight. She had been unhappy like him, he thought, and had felt that only a cud-chewing animal would have power to give her back her peace of heart. The moon shone in through the little stable window—that same moon —turning the white-washed wall milk white where it struck it. The girl's fair hair glittered under its touch, but he was in the dark, and he kept very still, like a fugitive in danger of discovery. He watched her kneeling down in the straw, so close to him, breathing so hard. He was not sure that she was not sobbing a little to herself. They had lain there for several hours of the short spring night, sometimes sleeping, sometimes awake, with the tranquil, sweet-smelling Rosa between them like the two-edged sword in the poem of chivalry. Many thoughts, many pretty and strong pictures had run through the boy's head. When he had slept he had dreamed of Nanna, and when he had woke up and had raised himself to look at her, she was still there, unaware of his presence. Very early in the morning she got up, brushed the straw from her skirt, and was gone, and he had never told her that he had been there with her.

The Councilor walked on, pleased. He thought of Count

Schimmelmann's quotation: "He is the fool who knows not the half to be more than the whole." This long-forgotten incident was a little flower in his life, in the garland of his life, a field flower, a wild forget-me-not. There were not a few flowers, violets, pansies, in his life. Would this night put a rose into the garland?

A little way from the garden of La Liberté, in the hayfield, there was a beech grove. In the corner of it, upon a mound, a lady of the manor who had, a hundred years before, been partial to the quiet and sweet solemnity of the spot, had had a little summer house erected, a temple to friendship. There were five wooden pillars which carried a domed roof. Two steps led up to it, and a seat ran along the inner side of the columns, in a half circle. From here you could see the sea. Later on, since the climate of Denmark is not always in harmony with Greek architecture, the one side of the building had been thatched to give shelter to the meditator. The whole place was now dilapidated, and in the daytime a little tristful, but below the full moon it looked romantic.

He turned his steps toward the little temple as a harmonious spot for the dreams of a bridegroom, but he walked slowly and with prudence, for his young bride might have had the same fancy, and if so he would not frighten or disturb her. As he came nearer, however, voices coming from the mound made him first stand stock-still, then move along quietly, following the sound. For the second time a lurker in the grounds of La Liberté, he took care to approach without a sound, behind the thatched wall.

Anders and Fransine were together in the temple, speaking softly. The young man sat on the seat, immobile. The young woman stood up opposite him, her back against a pillar. The moon was shining on them; the whole world around them was light, like a landscape under snow. But the old Councilor was in the deep shade of his hiding place. Indeed, he was like that statue of himself about which he had recently been dreaming. Statues also, sometimes, see a lot.

The young woman had on an outlandish garment, a sort of

black domino or opera cloak, which he had never seen in her possession, and which she was holding closely together about her. Her dark hair hung down, a live, odorous mantle, and her face within it was like a white rose, dew-cool, in the night air. He had never seen her look so lovely. He had indeed never seen any human being look so lovely before. It was as if the whole summer night had brought forth one flower, the epitome of its beauty. She seemed to sway a little, like a flexible branch, too heavy with the weight of its white roses.

There was a long silence. Then Fransine gave a low laugh of happiness, as soft and sweet as a dove's cooing.

"They are all lying down," she said, "like dead people in a churchyard. Only you and I are afoot. Is it not stupid to lie down?" She twisted a little in her cloak. "Oh, I am tired of them," she exclaimed, passionately, "talking, talking always. I wish to God they would lie forever, so that we could be left alone in the world a little." The sweetness of the thought seemed to overwhelm her. She drew in her breath. She stood still, waiting for him to move or answer her. After a while she asked him, her voice still filled with laughter and tenderness: "Anders, what is the matter?"

Anders was a long time in answering her, then he spoke very slowly: "Yes," he said, "you may well ask, Fransine. It is important. The spirit we need not talk about; it is not dangerous. But what is the matter? It has many strange things about it. It is the phlogiston of our bodies, being of negative weight, you might say. That is easy to understand, of course, but it gives you such great pain when it is demonstrated upon you. First we are treated by fire—burned, or roasted slowly, that comes to the same thing—and even then we cannot fly."

Now the cause of the lover's immobility became clear to the old listener. This young man was dead drunk. He could just manage to keep himself, seated, in balance, but could make no further movement. He was pale as a corpse; the sweat kept pouring down his face; and he kept his eyes on the face of the girl as if it would have caused him infinite pain to move them away from it. The Councilor, who had been repeating to himself his little aphorism, "the half to be more than the whole," here had the theory proved straight in his face.

Fransine smiled at the young man. Like many women, she did not recognize the symptoms of drunkenness in a man. "Oh, Anders," she said, "you do not know it, so I will tell you: I can fly. Or nearly. Old ballet-master Basso said to me: 'The other girls I have to whip up, but I shall have to tie two stones to your legs soon, or you will fly away from me.' These old men are mad, and they want strange things of you. I do not mind now. I will show you soon that I can fly, like the flying fishes with which the sea children made ducks and drakes."

"You see, my girl," said Anders, "you are like a cook who kills a whole, good, live duck just for making a giblet soup. You may use me for a giblet soup if you like, but you must come and cut out the bits you want yourself. The birds do not themselves know the places of their liver and heart. That is woman's work, Fransine."

Fransine thought this over for a little while. She was sure that every one of his words was wise, and kind to her. "My mother," she said, "came from the ghetto of Rome. You did not know that. Nobody knows that. There I saw her kill the birds in the right way, so that no blood was left in them. That ghetto, Anders, that is the place, you can be sure, where people suffer, where you have to be careful, or else you are robbed and hurt. Hanged, even. I have seen people hanged. My grandfather was hanged there. The world has been hard to me, Anders, and to you as well. But then it is even sweeter still to be happy." She paused a moment. "To be happy," she said. "Do you not think so?"

"But it is too late," Anders said. "Things happen, even when you are not there. That is the trouble. That is what you do not know. The cocks are crowing, though we cannot hear them here." Quoting an old ditty of the charcoal burners, he said, slowly and gently:

Early at midsummer-dawn the cock was crowing,
Twenty-nine cradles had I set a-going.

"No, they are not crowing," she said. "It is not daylight, Anders. It is not even midnight." She stood still before him.

"There are two," said Anders, "who will take me whole, as I sit here. Abelone will take me whole. She wants to keep a public house at Elsinore, and me to marry her and be landlord to the seamen. The sea, also, will take me whole. When one of the two has been at you, you will have had your bones well picked."

The Councilor, even though absorbed in their talk, here got a small shock. Had his housekeeper been entertaining such prospects, and not said a word to him? Had she, perhaps, even, perceived in Fransine a rival of her own dignities, and in this shown more insight than he himself had?

Fransine stood staring at Anders, bewildered. "Anders," she said, "do not speak like that. Listen. At the fairs, when I danced to them, they cried: 'Again! Again!' They said: 'It is like seeing the stars dancing, the hearts burning.' Do you not believe that I can make you happy?"

"Oh, my lass," said he, "let us be good. Let us behave like good people. Let me pay you what the seamen pay the girls at Elsinore. I have not much to give you, and that is a great pity. The other night I spent a lot of my savings on beer for the people at the inn, and that was bad of me. But fifty specie-dollars I have still laid aside. Do take them now, for God's sake. I do not ask you this for my own sake, I swear to you, for I am going to die sooner or later in any case, but for yours, you poor, pretty girl. It is always a good thing for a girl to have fifty specie-dollars. Go buy yourself a shift, and do not run about naked in the cold nights."

There was much strength in Fransine. Upon this she made a movement towards him. Her tightly drawn cloak and long hair followed it. Within her self-luminous face her two big dark eyes were fixed upon his face. She looked like a young witch under the moon. "Anders, Anders!" she said, "do you not love me?"

"Oh, God!" he said. "That was coming, I knew. I can answer that, from practice, quite well. I love you, my pretty vixen. Your hair, now, is like a little red flame in the dark, a cloven tongue of fire, a little marsh fire to show people the wrong way, the way to hell."

The young woman was trembling from her head to her feet. "Did you not," she said, wringing her hands, "want me to come, here, to you, tonight?"

He sat silent for a moment. "Well," he said, "if you are asking me my honest opinion, Madame Fransine, No. I should like to be by myself."

Fransine turned and ran away. Her long cloak of Naples, trailing in her wake, hindered her. Still she held it closely wrapped about her. Thus fled Arethusa, when, long ago, she was changed into a river, and loudly lamenting, hurled herself through the myrtle groves.

Anders sat for a long time like a dead man. Then, with the slow and uncertain movement of drunken people, he took up his gun and got onto his feet. He turned around, and in so doing was brought face to face with the Councilor.

He did not seem at all surprised to see him. Perhaps he had thought of him, or had felt his presence, somehow, in the atmosphere of his rendezvous. He only grinned, when he set eyes on him, as if he had been shown the solution of a crafty riddle. The Councilor felt the moment more awkward. For a few seconds the two stared at each other. Then, with a smile such as a boy might show in playing a bad prank on somebody, Anders half lifted his gun, and without taking aim fired it off straight into the body of the old man. The retort boomed and echoed far away in the summer night.

The roar and the sudden, overwhelming pain struck the old man as one thing, as the end or the beginning of the world. He fell, and in falling saw his murderer, with an agility surprising in a dead-drunk man, swing himself over the low wall of the little temple and disappear.

The Councilor found himself, after a long stay in a strange world, lying on his back in the clover, in a pool of something warm and sticky: his own blood, which was blending with the moisture of the field.

He had the feeling that he had been terribly angry. He was not sure whether the din and the darkness were not the effects of his wrath, an anathema flung at the head of his ungrateful protégé. Slowly returning to consciousness, he was still suffering from the pain and exhaustion which a great anger leaves in the breast, but he no longer hated or condemned. He was past all that.

He had lost a lot of blood. He thought that he must have had the full barrel fired into his right side. He could not move his right leg, either. It was strange that you could change things so completely just by lying down where you had been standing up. He had never known that the scent of the flowering clover could be so strong, but that was because he had not before been lying down, buried, bathed in it, as now.

He was going to die. The young man, whom he loved, had meant him to die. The world had thrown him out. His will, he remembered, was in order. He was leaving his money to his bride. His old servants were provided for, and his cellar was going to Count Schimmelmann, who took such pleasure in wine. In making this will he had been wondering whether the thought of a well-made will might be any comfort to a dying man. Now he knew it to be so.

After a little while he tried to realize whereto he had been thrown, out of the world. As he recognized the place, it occurred to him that he might still save himself. He might control his world once more.

He must be about a mile from La Liberté. If he could manage to turn, and shift his weight onto his sound arm, he might be able to move. Could he get as far as the long avenue which led to the house, he might crawl along the stone fence, and rest against it.

He was in great pain as soon as he started to move, and he wondered whether it would be worth while. "Now, my dear friend," he said to himself, feeling that it was time for a kind word, "try. You will be all right." He could draw himself along in this way, like an old snake which has been run over on the road, but still wriggles on.

His arm gave way; he fell straight upon his face, and his mouth, open in the struggle for breath, was filled with dust.

As he raised himself again he saw that he had been mistaken about the place; he was not in Denmark, but at Weimar.

The sweetness of this discovery nearly overwhelmed him. Weimar, then, was so easy to get to. A road led there from the hayfield of La Liberté. This place—he saw it clearly now—was the terrace; the view over the town was as fine as ever; it was the sacred garden itself, and the solemn lime trees were guarding the sanctuary; he felt their full, balsamic scent. The moon was shining serenely on it all, and from a shining window the great poet might at this moment be watching her, forming divine lines to her divinity.

He remembered now: he himself was writing a tragedy. He had, upon a time, considered this undertaking the greatest of his life, and he did not know how it was that he had for some time not thought about it. He had even had a plan for maneuvering it into the hands of the Geheimerat, to get his opinion on it. Perhaps this night would be the right moment. It had been called *The Wandering Jew*. It might not be worth very much. There were reminiscences of the Geheimerat's own *Faust* in it; still, there was also some imagination. The imaginary cross, which his Ahasuerus had been carrying through the world on his long weary road, that was not without effective power.

He thought: Would the great poet let his own people—Wilhelm Meister, Werther, Dorothea—associate with the creations of his, the Councilor's, mind? Undoubtedly there would be a social order

in the world of fiction as there was everywhere, even in the world
of Hirschholm. Indeed, it might be the criterion of a work of art
that you should be able to imagine its characters keeping company
with the people, or frequenting the places, of the works of the
great masters. Would not Elmire and Tartuffe land at Cyprus, and
be received there, on his master's behalf, by young Cassio, having
passed on the way a ship with brown sails, a-sail for Scheria?

He fell again, and rolled over on his back. This was a more difficult position from which to raise himself, and while he was lying
thus, gasping for breath, a dog barked some way off.

"The little dogs and all—Tray, Blanch, and Sweetheart—see, they
bark at me."

Yes, they might have reason to do so. He saw his own clothes
in the light of the summer moon, stiff with blood and dust. No
beggar could look worse.

King Lear, also, had at a time been in a bad position. Murderers
had been after him, too. He had been alone upon a heath and had
struggled and fallen. The night that he had been out in had been
much worse than this. But all the same the old King had somehow been so safe, so unshakenly secure. Still lying flat upon the
ground, panting, the Councilor tried to remember what it had
been that had made King Lear so exceptionally safe, so that even
the storm on the heath, and even all the wickedness in the world,
could not harm him in the least. He had been in the hands of two
ungrateful daughters; they had treated him with dreadful cruelty;
there was nothing safe in the situation there. It was something
else. The old King had been in the hands, whatever happened to
him, of the great British poet, of William Shakespeare. That
was it.

The Councilor had reached the stone fence of the garden. With
a very great effort he sat himself up against it. It gave him rest.
And suddenly, with the face of the moon looking into his own
blood-stained and smirched face, the old Councilor understood
everything in the world.

He was not only at Weimar. No, it was more than that. He had
got inside the magic circle of poetry. He was in the world of the
mind of the great Geheimerat. All this still landscape around him,
also this great pain which washed over him from time to time,
they were the accomplishments of the poet of Weimar. He himself had got into these works of harmony, deep thought, and order
undestroyable. He was free, if he liked, to be Mephistopheles, or
the silly student who comes to ask advice about life. In fact he
might be anything without ever running any risk, for whatever
he did the author would see to it that things would somehow come
out all right, that high and divine law and order would be maintained. How was it that he had ever in his life been afraid? Had
he believed that Goethe might fail?

> *Make ten of one,*
> *and two let be.*
> *Make even three.*
> *And nine is one,*
> *and ten is none. . . .*

The words gave him an extraordinary comfort. What a fool,
what a fool he had been! What could anything matter? He was in
the hands of Goethe.

The old man looked, as if for the first time in his life, up toward
the sky. His lips moved. He said:

Ich bin Eurer Excellenz ehrerbietigster Diener.

At this moment of his apotheosis he became aware of somebody
crying a little way off. The sound came nearer, then suddenly
turned off and withdrew. Was this, he thought, Margaret weeping in her desertion?

> *My mother, the harlot,*
> *who put me to death,*
> *My father, the varlet,*
> *who eaten me hath. . . .*

No, he thought, it must be the young lady of La Liberté, his bride of the same day, poor Fransine. From the sound he judged her to be walking up and down near him. She had gone to the farthest end of the terrace, so as not to be heard from the house. If he could get a few yards farther, he would be within earshot, and he would be saved.

With this certainty also a great feeling of pity came upon the Councilor. Fransine must have heard the shot, he thought, and be beside herself with fear. Her sobbing sounded wild and without hope, and there she was, all alone in the night. This was rather cruel of the Geheimerat. Still, he had done worse when he had made Margaret kill her child; and yet that had also been right, had been in good order, somehow.

He leaned against the fence, his paralyzed legs trailing in the dust, and tried to collect and control all these thoughts. Out of his richer knowledge he would have to console the unhappy young woman, and make things right for her. She was young and simple; it would be no use to try to make her see how it was that everything was in order. But that did not matter; it was really better so. Children, who cannot digest the full produce of the earth, are made happy with a stick of barley sugar. He would arrange to get for Fransine that which is generally called happiness. This, he felt, was in the plan of the author, of the Geheimerat.

In the sky the moon had changed position and color. The dawn was approaching. The summer sky was slowly rusting; the stars hung in it like clear drops, ready to fall. Balsamic winds ran along, close to the earth.

The Councilor thought that he must look like a ghost, and with great difficulty he got out his handkerchief and wiped his face. The effort nearly killed him, and he succeeded only in smearing blood and dust all over his face. He felt that it would be no use to try to call to her; his voice was too faint. He must try to get nearer. There were two stone steps leading from the road to the end of the terrace, through the fence, and if he could get there he would be seen by her. With his last strength he moved forward, on elbow and knee, another ten yards, and this, he knew, was the end; he could do no more. He got up onto the lower stone and leaned against the top step. He had meant to call, but could not make a sound. Just then she turned and caught sight of him.

If he looked like a ghost, which he did—so much so that she took him for one—she herself looked, she was indeed, the ghost of that young beauty of La Liberté, of lovely Fransine Lerche. She had on a plain nightgown only, put on in a hurry, for she had done with her body. When she had flung away the domino of Naples, she had thrown away with it that delicate, fragrant garland of roses and lilies of her beauty, which had meant everything to her. Her rounded bosom and hips had shrunk; there seemed to be nothing inside her white garment but a stick. Even her long hair was hanging down, lifeless, like her arms. Her fresh and gentle doll's face was dissolved and ruined by tears; the doll had been broken; its starry eyes and rosebud mouth were now no more than black holes in a white plane. Dead-tired, she could not sit or lie down. Her despair kept her upright, like the lead in the little wooden figures which children play with, like the weight tied to dead seamen's feet, which keeps them standing up, swaying, at the bottom of the sea.

The two stared at each other. At last the old man gathered enough strength to whisper, "Help me. I cannot move any more."

She stood stock-still. The idea occurred to him that he must tranquillize her, for she was mad with horror. He said: "I have been shot, as you see. But it does not matter." He did not know whether she had heard him. He hardly knew whether he had spoken.

At last the girl understood. Her lover had shot this old man. In a short moment, as in a great, white, flash of light, a vision was shown her: Anders with the halter around his neck. And instantly a ghost of her old strength came back to her, as a wreckage of your ship may be washed back to you on a bleak shore. Let Anders have done what he liked, he and she belonged to one another, were one. That he had hurt her to death and that she had fled from him, and at this moment dreaded nothing in the world as much as seeing him again—all this made no difference.

She stood and looked at the blood which was running out of the old man's body and coloring her stone steps. As if there had been some magic in it, it lifted and steadied her heart within her. She saw, in the red light of it, that whatever unhappiness there had been between her and Anders had come there through her fault. The conviction released all her nature; for that he should be in the wrong, that had been too much for her to bear. The red blood, the great relief of her heart, and the coming daylight which began to fill the air, became all one to her. The darkness would be over. After she had gone from him, Anders had proved that he loved her. And only she and the old man knew.

Like a mænad, her hair streaming down, she began to tug and tear at one of the big flat stones of the fence, to get it loose. When she got it out she stood for a moment, holding it, with all her strength, in both arms, pressed to her bosom, as if it had been her only child, which the old sorcerer had managed to turn into stone.

The Councilor felt his blood running out quickly; if he had a message to give her it would have to be now. Afraid that his lips had given no sound when he had tried to speak to her, he dragged his right hand along the ground until it touched her bare foot. The girl, who had been so sensitive to touch, did not move; she had done with her body.

"My poor girl, my dove," he said, "listen. Everything is good. All, all!"

"Sacred, Fransine," he said, "sacred puppets."

He had to wait for a minute, but he had more to say to her.

He said, very slowly: "There the moon sits up high. You and I shall never die." He could not go on; his head dropped down upon the stone.

If Fransine did not hear him, she understood him through his touch. He meant to tell her that the world was good and beautiful, but indeed she knew better. Just because it suited him that the world should be lovely, he meant to conjure it into being so. Perhaps he would hold forth on the beauty of the landscape. He had done that to her before. Perhaps he would tell her that it was her wedding day, and that heaven and earth were smiling to her. But that was the world in which they meant to hang Anders.

"You!" she cried at him. "You poet!"

She lifted the stone, in both arms, above her head, and flung it down at him.

The blood spouted to all sides. The body, which had a second before possessed balance, a purpose, a conception of the world around it, fell together, and lay on the ground like a bundle of old clothes, at the pleasure of the law of gravitation, as it had fallen.

To the Councilor himself it was as if he had been flung, in a tremendous movement, headlong into an immeasurable abyss. It took a little time; he was thrown down in three or four great leaps from one cataract to the other. And meanwhile, from all sides, like an echo in the engulfing darkness, winding and rolling in long caverns, her last word was repeated again and again.

ISAK DINESEN is the pseudonym of Karen Blixen, born in Denmark in 1885. After her marriage in 1914 to Baron Bror Blixen, she and her husband went to live in British East Africa, where they established a coffee plantation. She was divorced from her husband in 1921 but continued to manage the plantation for another ten years, until the collapse of the coffee market forced her to sell the property and return to Denmark in 1931. There she began to write in English under the *nom de plume* Isak Dinesen. Her first book, and literary success, was *Seven Gothic Tales*. It was followed by *Out of Africa* (also available in Vintage Books in a facsimile edition of the first printing); *The Angelic Avengers* (written under the pseudonym Pierre Andrézel); *Winter's Tales, Last Tales, Anecdotes of Destiny, Shadows on the Grass* and *Ehrengard* (all available in Vintage Books). Isak Dinesen died in 1962.

VINTAGE FICTION, POETRY, AND PLAYS

VINTAGE BIOGRAPHY AND AUTOBIOGRAPHY